a
time
to
die

Other Dover Books by Hilda Lawrence

Blood upon the Snow
Death of a Doll

A Mark East Mystery

HILDA LAWRENCE

DOVER PUBLICATIONS, INC.
Mineola, New York

Bibliographical Note

This Dover edition, first published in 2018, is a newly reset, unabridged republication of the work originally printed by Simon & Schuster, New York, in 1945.

Library of Congress Cataloging-in-Publication Data

Names: Lawrence, Hilda, author.
Title: A time to die / Hilda Lawrence.
Description: Dover edition. | Mineola, New York : Dover Publications, Inc., 2018. | Series: A Mark East mystery
Identifiers: LCCN 2018013127| ISBN 9780486827605 | ISBN 0486827607
Subjects: | GSAFD: Detective and mystery stories.
Classification: LCC PS3523.A9295 T56 2018 | DDC 813/.54—dc23
LC record available at https://lccn.loc.gov/2018013127

Manufactured in the United States by LSC Communications
82760701   2018
www.doverpublications.com

*"For everything there is a season, and
a time for every purpose under heaven;
a time to be born, and
a time to die. . . ."*

Ecclesiastes

CHAPTER ONE

I T was five o'clock in the afternoon and the burning August sun still registered contempt for time. It sat on the top of the mountain with the arrogance of midday and sent wave after wave of killing heat down the pine covered slope to the little town at its feet. Bear River, with four thousand native souls, two hundred transient, turned for relief to the mountain on one side and the river on the other. It failed to find it.

Mark East, sagging under the seasonal load of fishing tackle, tennis rackets, golf clubs, and suitcases, moved slowly under the limp maples of Main Street and asked himself bitterly what he was atoning for. He sidestepped panting matrons with shopping bags and cringed before the onslaughts of baby carriages helpfully pushed by hands that had clutched bottles themselves only two years before; he tangled with directionless dogs and roller-skating girls in shorts who screamed prettily when they ran him down. He hoped Mrs. Perley Wilcox, his prospective hostess, would have a tub full of cold water waiting for him, and a cold glass of something in which the water was negligible. He remembered it was Friday and knew he would wring her fat little neck if she gave him fried fish.

Ten minutes before, and already it seemed like a year, he had been ejected from a Cadillac driven by friends en route to a camp farther north, a cool camp by a rushing stream. He'd been urged to continue with them, and had declined. He didn't like to think of that. Ahead of him stretched a two-week holiday rashly arranged for when the snow was on the ground and he had been full of gratitude toward the people who had helped him on a case;* one week with Perley and Pansy Wilcox and one week with Bessy Petty and Beulah Pond.

He stopped under a dingy awning to shift his luggage and mop his face, and idly scanned the window it pretended to shelter. It was a dusty window, filled with dead and living flies, an undecided fern, and a faded burlap screen on which were mounted about a dozen examples

---

* *Blood upon the Snow*

of the photographer's art. A large sign announced that J. T. Spangler, Prop., specialized in cabinet photos of all occasions and took pleasure in developing, printing, and enlarging own films at reasonable rates, no job too small. Mark saluted this with a grin and went on to a second, smaller sign that further identified Mr. Spangler as the official police photographer. The grin widened happily and then slowly faded when he saw the third sign.

It was a hand-lettered card, tacked crookedly to the top of the screen. It said—THERE IS THE PICTURE OF A MURDERER IN THIS WINDOW. GUESS WHO?

Mark put his head in at the open door and shouted. "Buster!"

A perspiring gnome with a bald head tottered out of the dim interior and stood blinking on the threshold.

"Mr.—Mr. East!" he cried joyfully.

"You ghoul," Mark said. "How long have you been getting away with that sign?"

Mr. Spangler looked hurt. "You oughtn't talk to me like that, Mr. East. Here I been looking forward to the day when you'd come back, and right away you nag."

"Take it out. It's indecent. Why do you want to keep that story alive?"

Mr. Spangler lowered his voice to a confidential whine. "Business," he said. "It's something wonderful. You ought to see the trade that little sign brings in. All the summer people, up in the mountain hotel. They come down here with their films and they see that sign and they can't stand it."

"I don't give a—"

"Wait, wait. The cut-rate drugstore on the corner does the same work better and cheaper, and the customers know it, but they see that little sign and they come in here. They ask me what it means and I tell 'em. I tell 'em how I did the police work on that case and all about the blood and everything, and they're grateful. You see, they read about it in the city papers when it happened and they're grateful to get in touch. So they give me their little jobs to do." He gave Mark a begging look. "It don't hurt anybody and it's two cents every time."

"It hurts more than you think. It reminds too many people of things that ought to be forgotten. Take it out now, or I'll tell the sheriff and he'll come down and do it himself. No kidding, Buster. Crawl in that window and get busy."

Mr. Spangler did as he was told while Mark watched from the sidewalk. He crept into the window on all fours and reluctantly wrenched a blurred snapshot from the top section of the screen. A roving thumbtack caught him in an unexpected quarter, and he sat back on his heels and wagged a sorrowful head. He was suddenly engulfed in misery.

That nice young feller out on the sidewalk with his pockets full of money, what did he know about two cents here and two cents there? What did he know about the cut-rate on the corner? "Take it out or I'll call the cops!" That's what he said, or something like that. Take it out. Like putting your hand in somebody's purse and taking out seventy-five cents, that's what it was like. Around seventy-five cents a week, that's what he stood to lose. His cold beer before he went to bed, that's what. All gone now.

He sighed tremulously and reached for the offending sign. At the same instant the sound of a new distraction came through the open door. He turned with upraised arm to stare into the street, and his tormentor also turned.

The vehicular traffic had wound itself around a battered Ford suddenly stationary in the center of the road. Shouts and horns clamored. A freckled boy scrambled out of the disputed car, wove steadily to Mark's side, and seized his luggage.

"Come on before somebody feels like they have to arrest me," he said. "It's pure luck me seeing you. Come on."

There was no question about the urgency, and the boy was his host's son. Mark threw Mr. Spangler a backward, warning look and followed. The Ford moved off, and the traffic uncoiled.

Mr. Spangler accepted this departure with fortitude. He eased himself out of the window and stood in the doorway while the car clattered up the street.

"Going to have fun, I bet," he said wistfully to nobody. "Going to have a high old time sitting down to home cooked meals and all that." He blinked at the still blazing sky and turned back into the shop. A thin pork chop and two cold boiled potatoes only half filled the cracked plate on his desk. He sat down and took up the chop. "Wherever that fellow goes something always happens," he mumbled. He ate slowly, staring into space, unmindful of passing time.

The sun relinquished the day to twilight. The footsteps on the sidewalk grew less, and an empty sprinkling cart, drawn by two weary horses, crept down the dusty street. Mr. Spangler sat on in his dingy room, his trembling old chin resting on his chest. He snored gently. A cat stalked out of the shadows, found the chop bone on the floor, and slunk away.

Outside a small wind blew down from the mountain and stirred the papers in the gutter. Here and there a solitary figure, drooping with the day's heat, walked slowly nowhere. No one stopped to examine Mr. Spangler's dark window. His little jobs, executed with pleasure, looked out at nothing.

The place of honor in the center of the screen was held by a Polish wedding picture, brightly tinted and curling at the edges. Around it was a border of snapshots. They were the usual snapshots of boys with dogs and men with guns, fishing tackle, and horses; young and old women with picnic baskets, wild flowers, and bright, determined smiles; little girls with dolls and bicycles. There was one of a pretty girl alone, and one of a shadowy, clutching couple. There was a large trout, bedded in grass. There was also the empty space at the top, lately occupied by a murderer, a small, clean, empty space that told no tales. But the hand-lettered card still hung crookedly from its nail. It still said: THERE IS THE PICTURE OF A MURDERER IN THIS WINDOW. GUESS WHO?

After young Floyd Wilcox had stowed Mark in the back seat he drove slowly up Main Street, blowing his horn needlessly and asking questions at the top of his lungs. It was Mr. East this, and Mr. East that; he wanted everybody in town to see who was riding with him.

He needn't have troubled. Bear River had watched Mark's arrival with melancholy pleasure, and even the summer visitors had turned to stare. People always did that, and they never knew why. He wasn't handsome. He was tall enough and broad enough, and his eyes and hair were a warm brown; but children and dogs, after the first appraising second, tried to get into his lap, and all women, whether they liked him or not, wished they'd worn something else. He looked lazy. He wasn't.

"I guess you were talking over old times with Mr. Spangler," Floyd shouted fraternally. "That was some case we had, wasn't it? Mom still has a fit when she realizes the danger I was in." The last statement held a wistful note that seemed to call for confirmation.

"And well she might," Mark said obligingly. "I was pretty worried about you myself."

"I don't think I know the meaning of fear," Floyd conceded. This was accompanied by a grim look that swept the far horizon and took no account of a middle-aged pedestrian in the foreground who thought his last day had come and said so. For a few seconds Floyd looked his age, which was a small thirteen, and exhibited at least one synonym for the emotion he denied.

Mark held his own breath. "Aren't you a little young for a driving license?" he finally insinuated.

Floyd looked over his shoulder and made certain all was well before he answered. "Sure. They won't give me one. But when your Pop's a sheriff and your passenger's a dick they kind of leave you be. . . . Want to know what's going on tonight?"

"Yes and no. What?"

Floyd swung the car around a corner and dropped to a snail's pace. "I got an uncle on this block and he's always watching for me to kill somebody. . . . We're going to the Covered Dish Supper." He saw Mark's eyes close and added hastily, "You'll like it. It's fun."

"What—does it cover?"

"Well, it's for charity. Mom's church needs coal for next winter. So all the ladies cook something and take it along, only they don't have to cover it if they don't want to, and they pay a quarter and eat all they want of everything else. The men and other people that don't cook anything have to pay fifty cents, but they can eat all they want also. I'm paying for you."

"You are not."

"Well, thanks. I guess we'll make a lot of money this year. Me and Pee Wee Peck have the lemonade concession, five cents a glass. Some other kids have the archery concession, five cents for three arrows. There ought to be some fancy shooting."

Mark winced. "What kind of food do we get?"

"I don't know. Whatever did good this year and everybody's got a lot of. Pop's going to drop dead when he sees I found you. He wasn't sure when you'd get here, so he fixed it for Mom and me to go up to the church first. You and him will come later. Mom's taking baked beans. . . . Are you hot, Mr. East? You can put your feet on that sack. It's ice."

Mark sighed and moved closer to the ice. All along the street on either side men in shirt sleeves were mowing lawns and talking over hedges. Smells of frying food drifted out of open windows and mingled with the smells of fresh cut grass, dust, and hot tar. Fried fish, fried potatoes, fried onions, fried—so help him—doughnuts. He could almost see the blue smoke rising from the bubbling fat in the hot, littered little kitchens. He tried to remember what church suppers were like, covered or uncovered. He couldn't, so he mopped his face again and silently offered his soul to any Christian woman who could and would give him a cold salad full of cucumbers.

The car hit a curbstone, bounced, and stopped. He had reached the beginning of his holiday. Perley Wilcox was coming down the garden path to meet him, his thin, tired face wreathed in smiles.

"Well," said Perley, "so the boy found you. He'll make a good sheriff one of these days." He burdened himself with Mark's luggage and staggered into the house. "Cheer up," he said out of the corner of his mouth. "I got something in the icebox, hidden behind the milk."

Floyd and Pansy, after a suitable interval, drove off importantly, hugging two bean pots. The men took over the deserted kitchen.

"Here's to crime," Perley said gently, baring his teeth in his version of a snarl.

It was nearly seven o'clock when, clean, comparatively peaceful, and almost cool, they sauntered up the street toward the open country. Perley said it was ten minutes' brisk walk to the church grounds, out by the cemetery. Mark would remember that old cemetery, wouldn't he? It looked different in the summer, though, almost pretty, you might say. They made it in twenty minutes.

They saw the Covered Dish Supper long before they came to it. Late comers, clinging to plates and baskets draped with fringed napkins, scurried up the hillside, calling out excuses and explanations. They were preceded by whooping children and followed by plodding men. Farm Fords and town cars trailed each other in an orderly line. Perley counted the town cars with evident pleasure.

"Summer people," he said. "Hotel guests and all that. It shows a nice feeling."

It showed, Mark thought, a nice sense of direction about finding all you could eat for fifty cents, with altruism thrown in free.

There was white clover in the churchyard grass, and the grounds were ringed with locust. Paper lanterns hung from the trees although it was still light. Mark drew a deep breath and counted the long tables. There were fifteen of them, and he thought he could hear them groan. He saw platters of baked ham and chicken. He loosened his belt and reached for his pocket.

"Your money's no good here," Perley said.

They found places at Pansy's own table, where they were hovered over by plump, aproned women who rushed back and forth with laden plates and made furtive little dabs at their back hair. Mark ate steadily and contentedly, sizing up his neighbors. The regular parishioners were a well-behaved lot, inclined to spun rayon with large floral patterns; no elbows on the table, no unseemly noise, no grabbing. The summer visitors were a different breed, favoring plain cottons and no manners at all. They screamed up and down the length of the tables and snatched food from each other's plates. It was also easy to spot the coal committee. These sat quietly at the cashier's table and talked in low tones while their roving eyes counted the house.

Mark was watching the coal committee and planning an anonymous donation when he saw something that took the flavor from his food. It was a small thing but he found himself wishing his eyes had been elsewhere. A very small thing, but it struck the first false note.

A little colored boy with clean bare feet, wearing immaculate and perfectly patched overalls, approached the cashier's table and timidly counted out fifty cents. It must have been in pennies because it took a long time. A startled and confused woman received the money and indicated that he might wait.

The boy stood carefully out of the way, digging his bare toes into the grass, his child's eyes proudly taking in the scene around him. Presently he was given a full plate, and he carried this over to a tree and sat down. He rested the plate on his thin knees and began to eat. He didn't have a fork because he didn't need one. He could eat the fried necks and backs with his fingers.

Mark was not the only watcher. A starched and ribboned toddler, overcome with curiosity and envy, staggered over to the boy and steadied herself with a fat hand on his shoulder while she peered down into his face. He drew back hastily, but gently; he needn't have, because almost immediately his youthful admirer was snatched away.

Perley looked up from his plate and followed Mark's eyes.

"I wonder if he paid for that?" he said uneasily.

"Yes. . . . Who is he?"

"He helped the sexton last winter. Shoveled coal, cleaned the walks. I guess he feels an interest. . . . Come on, eat. Short joint? Breast?"

"No thanks."

The light faded slowly and people left the tables and began to walk about. One by one strangers were brought up and introduced. Mark smiled until his face was stiff. So he was the Mr. East who was over in Crestwood last winter when those terrible things happened? Well, think of that. Well, well. He shook hands like a candidate for office and

explained that this was a vacation. Every time he said vacation somebody slapped him on the back and promised to kill six people before
the week was out. Whenever he moved on he was followed by a few
small boys. It was dark when he and Perley finally found a quiet tree
and stretched out on the grass.

They closed their eyes and listened to the muted wailing of harmonicas, the squeals of Drop the Handkerchief, the steady ping of arrows
that found their target in the archery set. Behind them the little white
church stood against a starry sky.

Mark yawned. "Wonderful air. What's the outlook for the coal?"

"Bright. We may even run to a strip of carpet for the middle aisle. . . .
You know what those young devils did?"

"Which ones?"

"Floyd and Pee Wee Peck. He's a summer kid from the hotel,
father's in the oil business. He and Floyd have that lemonade stand,
nickel a drink, but some of these old timers won't spend a nickel for a
drink. They go to the well, like they always did."

"Hard luck."

"Wait. They go to the well but there isn't any bucket. Bucket,
chain, and dipper, all gone. Do you think Floyd thought that one up
himself?" Perley looked hopeful. "I'm afraid it sounds like Pee Wee,
but I kind of wish it was Floyd."

"It's Floyd all over. What's the outlook for the lemonade?"

"Two new batches. . . . Hey—something's going on!"

They sat up. People were converging on the archery set, and a child
was screaming shrilly. Perley struggled to his feet. "I hate that thing,"
he said testily. "Had trouble with it before. Some fresh kid always acts
up for the girls and shoots wild. Come on."

They pushed their way through a crowd of women frantically
counting children, and found Pansy. The illuminating flares beside the
target hissed spitefully.

"Now what?" barked Perley. "Who got it this time?"

"It's the Briggs child." Pansy made soft, clucking sounds. "The one
that just got over the whooping cough. But it's only a scratch on her
arm, Perley, she's just frightened to death, that's all. Poor little thing,
and her first day out too."

The Briggs child, a pale, unpleasant creature, lay languidly in her
mother's arms and permitted the application of iodine. A worried-
looking clergyman had taken charge.

"Mr. Walters," Pansy said, "here's the sheriff now."

The Reverend Mr. Walters corked his little bottle and smiled gently. "I always carry iodine to church affairs," he said. "Who hurt you, Maisie?"

A dozen voices took it up, and the guilty name rolled out like a chant. Nick Sutton, Nick Sutton, Nick Sutton did it. Mark stood back and watched the eager hands that pulled and pushed Nick Sutton forward. He felt as if he were watching a small but hideously perfect race riot, and he expected to see some terrified dolt who would eventually be led away by his embarrassed parents. But it wasn't like that.

Nick Sutton was a frail youth, probably under twenty, obviously better born and bred than the sweating farm boys who were turning him in. He stumbled forward and steadied himself on the arm of a girl. Mark saw that he was lame and that he was trembling with rage, not fear.

"It's only a scratch, Nick," Perley said, "but it could have been worse. How come it happened?"

Sutton glared at the ring of hostile faces. "Somebody pushed my arm, and it wasn't an accident either. Somebody wanted me to miss and gave me a deliberate push. Don't ask me why because I don't know. I guess you'd call it clean country fun."

"He's been drinking," Mrs. Briggs shrilled. "I smelt it on his breath when he put my baby in my arms!"

Sutton shook off the girl's restraining hand. "Drinking," he said bitterly. "Two Martinis three hours ago. If you want to smell liquor around here why don't you go over to where those—never mind." He turned to Perley and shrugged. "Do I get bail?"

Perley grinned. "Come along, son. You and me are going to confiscate this pretty little game and bust it into matchwood." They wrenched the target from its post and moved off, the girl following. The women closed in on the Briggs mother and child, and the men drifted away. Somebody laughed. The fun was all over.

Mark felt a tug at his sleeve. Floyd, reeking of lemons, stood at his side. He had a smaller boy in tow.

"This is Pee Wee," he said. "We want to tell you something. Look." He held out five arrows. "The one with the kind of bend is the one that got Maisie, but there's no blood on it."

"Somebody wiped it clean," sighed Pee Wee.

"But look," Floyd went on. "Count 'em, Mr. East. Five. There ought to be six. Where's the other one?" There was a rim of sugar around Floyd's eager mouth, and his eyes glistened.

"Oh," Mark said heartlessly, "that'll be over in the tall grass. Want me to help you search?"

The boys exchanged looks. "Nope," said Floyd. "You won't find it. Want me to warn Pop?"

Mark jingled the coins in his pocket. "I'll warn him myself, later. I'm going to look him up in a few minutes." He looked at his watch. Nine o'clock. "Who is Nick Sutton, Floyd? Live around here?"

Pee Wee took over importantly. "He lives in New York, like me. He's at the Mountain House too, for the summer. He's in love."

"Well, that seems to cover everything. Now suppose you tell me why you're so upset about the sixth arrow."

Floyd plunged into a long and garbled recital. Nick, who was the best shot in town, paid for six arrows, ten cents, and lots of people hung around to watch him shoot. Maybe his arm did get pushed. It must of. Nick never missed before. Well he got the bull's-eye with the first two, and the third one got Maisie. And did she holler. Everybody hollered. When they hollered like that Nick was scared and he dropped the other three on the ground and picked Maisie up. "I," said Floyd, "would of left her lay."

"I," said Pee Wee, "am the person that remembered to pick up the ones he dropped. It's a good set and people were tramping all over the place like crazy. But there was only two of them. Right away somebody had swiped the other. Quick as a flash, just like that, somebody had swiped it on me."

"Don't that mean anything?" begged Floyd.

"Souvenir hunter," Mark said easily. "Like me. Will you boys sell me the five? It'll be all right with your father, Floyd. He's going to break them up anyway."

They struck a bargain, and the boys returned to their lemonade. In spite of the extra dollar, they didn't look happy. They looked as if he had failed them, and he knew it wasn't because of the money. He fingered the points of the five arrows and began to wonder. Pre-war, and sharp. He moved off to find Perley.

The sheriff was over by the church woodpile, axing the target into next year's kindling. He was morosely watched by Sutton and the girl. She was Roberta Beacham, Perley said

"Miss Beacham's one of our summer visitors," he said. "I've known her a long time. She was standing right by Nick and she didn't see any shoving. It must have come from the other side, only nobody remembers who was there."

Roberta was both pretty and sarcastic. If Nick said somebody shoved him, why then somebody did, she declared. But why all the fuss? Nobody was dead.

"My father gave this contraption to the church for their picnic last year," she said. "Three kids got half-killed then, and nobody cared. Why all the fuss now?"

Perley looked harassed. "That Briggs woman! . . . Give me those arrows," he said to Mark.

"Not now."

Roberta gave Mark a long stare. "What do you want with them?"

"I'm making a collection," he said.

The two nearest lanterns flickered and went out. Perley relighted one with a candle stub from his pocket and doggedly went on with his work. He was making a chore of it. Nick Sutton watched grimly.

"I'm going down town," he said suddenly. "With your permission, Mr. Wilcox."

"You don't need my permission," Perley said mildly. "I just took you away to keep your face from getting scratched."

"I'm going down town," Nick repeated. "And if Mrs. Briggs wants to smell my breath when I come back all she has to do is open any window in her house. On the street side. Coming Roberta?"

"For two lemon sodas," Roberta said calmly. "And a moonlight swim. Wait a minute though. I've got to get something out of the Sunday school room." She talked over her shoulder as she walked away. "The chef up at the hotel deviled about a thousand eggs for us, and I swore I wouldn't forget the hamper. I hid it in a cupboard."

Mark leaned against a tree and looked up at the sky. The pale yellow moon was in complete agreement with the stars. He lit a cigarette, gave one to Nick, and wondered what would happen to him if he drank two lemon sodas. He counted back fifteen years to the last time his night bathing had been performed in anything but a porcelain tub.

"Where do you swim?" he asked.

"Hotel pool."

They smoked quietly and listened to the diminishing sounds. The Covered Dish was calling it a day. The lanterns burned low, and the harmonicas grew silent. One by one the women drifted down the hillside, bundling their crumpled aprons and tablecloths, dragging fretful children, and telling each other that tomorrow would be another scorcher. Their tired voices floated back.

The Reverend Mr. Walters moved from tree to tree with a long pole, extinguishing lights. Two men took the trestle tables apart and carried them to a waiting truck.

"Where the hell's Roberta?" Nick said to nobody.

Mark watched Perley as he reduced the last scrap of target to a handful of splinters and snapped the bow. Funny, he said to himself, how men get a kick out of destruction. Those guys over there are knocking those tables down as if they were alive. Even old Perley swings his ax like a headsman. He shuffled his arrows thoughtfully.

Something blew across his consciousness as lightly as the night wind across the clover, but it wasn't pleasant. He saw the little colored boy paying out his hoard of coin for scraps; he heard the eager voices that turned Nick Sutton in. He told himself to stop that. "I'm tired," he said softly.

"I say," Nick said suddenly, "do you hear anything?"

They listened. Faintly, and yet nearby, someone was calling for help.

The Reverend Mr. Walters heard it too. He put down his pole and hurried toward them. The men at the tables turned and stared before they too moved silently and swiftly across the grass. Perley looked at Mark with a question in his eyes.

"Who is it?" Mark asked. "Where's it coming from?"

"That's coming from the church," Walters said. "But everybody's gone home. I don't understand it. Everybody's gone home."

Perley went first, and Mark followed. "Not this time," he said under his breath. "Not tonight." But when Nick Sutton tried to push ahead he held him back. "Let the old men do it," he said.

A dim light burned in a room to the left of the vestibule. Roberta's voice came out to them, distressed and urgent. They shuffled and crowded through the door, and someone turned on the ceiling lights.

Mark saw the rows of small, varnished chairs, the wall maps of the Holy Land, the colored lithographs of shepherds and sheep, the glass-enclosed bookcase with its neat shelves of shabby books; all the old familiar paraphernalia of a God-fearing childhood, even to the lingering smell of black shoe polish. He saw Roberta Beacham bending over something dark in a far corner. She turned a frightened face.

"It's Miss Rayner," she said. "She seems to be hurt but she won't tell me anything about it. She's—there's blood."

They crowded close. A frail little woman in thin black silk crouched on one of the small chairs, moaning softly. She clung to Roberta's hand. "If you'll just take me back to the hotel," she beseeched. "I'll be all right when I get in my own bed. I don't want all these men around. You shouldn't have called them. Send them away."

"It's only Mr. Walters," Roberta said. "And Mr. Wilcox." Her eyes begged the others to stand back. "I can't get you out to a car all by myself, Miss Rayner. I need somebody to help me. Nick's here too. You don't mind Nick?"

Miss Rayner flinched. "Nicholas? Not Nicholas Sutton? I thought I saw the sheriff arrest him."

Perley coughed genteelly behind his hand.

"There wasn't anything to arrest him for, Miss Rayner. That was just a little bit of foolishness. Now, suppose you tell us what's the trouble. The Reverend here has something for cuts, that is if you cut yourself. You tell us what's wrong, and we'll fix you up and get you back to the hotel in three shakes of a lamb's tail." He put his hands under her elbows and lifted her up. She gave a little scream of pain and fell against him.

"Take her on the other side, Mark," Perley said. "She can't stand. What have you been doing to yourself, Miss Rayner? Did you have a fall?"

"She won't tell you," Roberta said. "She wouldn't tell me. I've been in here for ages, trying to make her talk, but she won't. Miss Rayner, you've got to tell Mr. Wilcox. It might be serious!"

Miss Rayner gave a wry smile. "Such a fuss," she said. She looked doubtfully from face to face. "Well," she admitted, "well, maybe I did have a little fall."

The story came out slowly. Yes, it was a fall, but you might call it more of a stumble. It was a root, or something, that tripped her when she was running. And there was nothing funny about an old lady running, either. It was serious, and she wouldn't say another word until those men left. And if they didn't leave at once and she got blood poisoning it would be their fault.

Her little heart-shaped face crinkled like a crying child's. Why did they look at her like that, as if they didn't believe her? Why couldn't Nicholas Sutton bring his car up the hill? If he could do that, she'd try to walk out to it. She didn't want to be carried by anybody and she didn't want to talk any more. If they'd just get her back to the hotel, the maid on her floor would know what to do. She looked up at Mark. "You may take my arm," she said surprisingly. "I'm inclined to trust strangers."

He shifted his arrows and obliged.

Nick, smiling broadly for the first time, limped off to get his car, and Perley herded the other men through the door. Their laughter, sly and raucous, echoed in the vestibule.

Mr. Walters, his thin face anxious and confused, hovered over the wounded member of his summer flock. "I don't understand your remark about blood poisoning," he said. "I believe Miss Beacham also mentioned blood. I'm—I'm afraid I don't see any."

Miss Rayner ignored him and steadied herself against Mark's arm. She touched the sheaf of arrows. "Only five?" she said. "Couldn't you find the other one?"

"No," Mark said. "Why?"

"Because I couldn't find it either, and I looked everywhere. . . . I think that's what hit me." She enjoyed the tributary gasp. "Now I'll tell you the rest of it," she said.

She'd been watching the boys at the archery set. Very interesting, and very instructive in its way. The country boys, for all their talk about squirrels and foxes, were sadly outshone by the children from the cities. You so often found that, didn't you? With her own eyes she had seen young Peck give an imitation of William Tell, using little Josephine Beacham and a lemon, which everyone knows is smaller than an apple and much more difficult. Then Nicholas Sutton, poor boy, had made that dreadful mistake with the adenoidal child.

"Not adenoids, Miss Rayner," Perley corrected patiently. "That's the aftermath of whooping cough."

"Call it what you like," Miss Rayner said, "but I do think she was a mistake. And if you want to know what happened you mustn't interrupt." She went on to tell how she'd walked away from the crowd because people were being coarse, and the next thing she knew something struck her. With force and accuracy. She gave them a grim, triumphant look.

"You were doubtful about the blood," she said to Mr. Walters. "Well, here it is." She bent over with difficulty and raised her long, full skirt. The floor was wet and red around her feet. "It's my leg. It was an arrow, and it went through—everything. You can see." She showed them a cut in the silk.

"Miss Rayner!" Roberta was aghast. "We've got to get you to a doctor!"

"I made a tourniquet with my handkerchief," said Miss Rayner. "Now I'll wait for that car."

Perley frowned and looked unhappily at Mark. "Where were you?" Mark asked. "How far from the crowd and how long ago?"

Miss Rayner couldn't remember time and distance, and they didn't press her. Her face was like parchment, and her hands were trembling. She'd had her little hour in the limelight and now she was querulous and fretful.

"How can I remember?" she complained. "I don't carry a watch. And if you think I felt like marking the spot with an X then you're very silly. I tell you I was just walking along, and there was nobody near me. Nobody that I could see. I was walking over by that stone wall because it seemed cooler there. And then it happened. And I ran and fell, because I'm too old for that kind of thing. And I used my handkerchief because I do have a little sense, and I sat down and rested. Then I came in here. I knew people would have to come in for their baskets and things, but when I got here they'd all gone. At least I didn't see anyone until Roberta—Roberta—"

Perley cleared his throat. "Now, now. And you looked for the arrow? Before you came in here you looked for the arrow, didn't you?"

"Certainly. But I couldn't find it." Then she said a surprising thing. "I didn't even see it, you know. I mean when it struck me. I heard it swishing through the air, that's all, and it must have been an arrow because one is missing." She paused and frowned. "Do you think it could have had a string on it?"

"A string?" Perley looked bewildered. "Now what would a string—"

"Here's Nick," Roberta said, "and about time, too."

Perley turned thankfully to the door. "Come over here and take an arm," he said. "Now Miss Rayner, I want you to let Nick take my place. He and Mr. Walters will put you in the car and drive you home with Miss Beacham."

"And what are you going to do?" she asked with suspicion.

"Mr. East and I are going to have a look for your weapon."

"You'd better get used to calling it an arrow," she said, "because that's what it was." She left them without further comment.

Perley sighed with relief, made an audible note about remembering to clean up the blood before Sunday or they'd have parent trouble, and put out the lights. He locked the door behind him.

"Where's that wall she was talking about?" Mark asked.

It was the cemetery wall. They walked over to it in the dark, with Perley's flashlight pointing the way. It stretched along the north side of the grounds, a strip of fieldstone about four feet high. It was high enough to hide behind and low enough to shoot over and, as Perley pointed out, it was a lonesome kind of place.

Perley shivered. The moonlight was soft and friendly where they stood, but it struck harshly at the posturing angels on the other side of the wall.

"He'd have to stand on a grave," Perley said.

They went over every inch of the ground and found nothing. A little blood in one spot, that was all, and the tall grass bent.

"'It fell to earth I know not where,'" Perley quoted mildly. "I learned that poem when I was a boy. . . . What do you make of this?"

"Nothing. Local yokel having fun." Mark kicked at an empty gin bottle half hidden in the grass. "This is what Mrs. Briggs smelled so opportunely. I noticed some of the lads making little journeys to a truck parked down the road. Just clean country fun, as Nick says."

"You're always taking cracks at the country."

"The country's always taking cracks at me. I think one of your barber shop boys was trying to give the city dick a thrill. If I ever find out which one I'll beat the pants off him."

They returned over the deserted grounds and walked slowly down the hill.

"I notice you're still hanging on to those arrows," Perley observed.

"I'll give them to you tomorrow. What time is it?"

"Half past ten. Want to go home or do you want to walk down Main Street? It's kind of gay in summer."

"Home. . . . What's that white stuff that grows on your side porch?"

"Clematis."

"We'll sit out there and you can tell me where we'll go fishing tomorrow."

Young Josephine Beacham, who ordinarily answered only to Joey, woke at midnight because she was having a bad dream and was also thirsty. The moonlight poured in at the window and showed her that Cassie's bed was still empty. Cassie was Miss Cassidy, a perfect peach who let you say your prayers in bed in the winter but wouldn't let you sleep without your tops in the summer. She didn't nag about anything but the tops, and she let you wear boys' pants and didn't follow you around like an old sheep.

Joey shook off the bad dream which had to do with being caught without a shirt in the hotel lobby, and padded across to the bathroom.

She drank three glasses of cold water; she had to, because of the pickles. Cassie had been at another table, so she'd had her own way about all the pickles within reach. Eleven kinds.

Cassie was probably over at the Peck cottage, playing poker with the Pecks and Miss Sheffield and Mr. Kirby. Their light was still on. She must have come home with them in their car. She herself had come home in the hotel station wagon with the other kids. She wondered if Cassie was winning any money from Mr. Kirby. He was a dope. She stood at the bathroom window and considered removing her top just the same. Just for a few minutes. She twisted a button thoughtfully. The light in the Peck cottage went out.

Cassie would be home in a minute. Joey padded back to bed, top on. Tomorrow when her father came back from New York she'd ask him about the top. She stretched out on her bed and pretended to be asleep. Roberta would be coming home soon too. She was out with Nick. Nick was a dope. Joey fell asleep in spite of herself and didn't know that no one came home for another hour.

Mark emptied the last bottle of beer and eased it quietly to the porch floor. "Is that your phone?" he asked.

Perley struggled upright in the swing. "Golly, I been snoozing. Yep, that's it. Now who in time is that? It's past one o'clock." He tiptoed across the moon-spattered boards and opened the screen door. "Shut up!" he hissed at the nagging bell. "You'll wake Pansy."

Mark heard his rumbling greeting and listened idly. Somebody's car was gone. Or was it somebody's gas? Or maybe it was somebody parking in somebody's field. And why not? It was a night for it. Anyway, it was a fool thing to be calling about at this hour. Then he sat up, suddenly alert. Perley's voice had changed abruptly. Gas, he was saying; gas gone. No, it wasn't gas. It was Cas. . . . Cassidy. Gone. Cassidy. He got up and went inside. Perley was replacing the receiver.

"Well?"

"Get the car out while I leave a note for Pansy. I'll tell you as we go along."

A few minutes later they were driving through the sleeping streets, out into the country. They could read each other's faces in the white moonlight.

"It's only a disappearance," Perley said. "If it was a kid I'd say get out the hairbrush and wait till morning, but this is sort of different. It's not one of our own people either."

"Who?"

"Miss Cassidy. She's a kind of governess for the little Beacham girl. She didn't come home from the church supper, and they just found it out. It may not be anything, but I will say it looks odd."

"So will I. I wonder what she found to do."

"Don't talk like that. Miss Cassidy's a fine, good woman, in her late thirties. She's well-known and well-liked around here. Been coming up summers for about five years. Wore a small blue hat with little white birds on it. Blue and white dress. White shoes. Star sapphire ring that the Beachams gave her last Christmas. Would you know a star sapphire if you saw one?"

Mark said he would. "Who called you? Beacham?"

No, Beacham wasn't there. He'd made a quick trip to New York and was due back in the morning. Roberta had called. Joey was the little one, around eight or so. Beacham, a widower, was a business partner of Pee Wee Peck's father. He and Peck rented the two best cottages the hotel had. "Now you know as much as I do," he said.

They turned off the road and began to climb the mountain. They could see the hotel lights, far up.

Mark laughed softly. "You know what I'm making out of this, don't you? Widower Beacham and a governess who wears star sapphires. If I were you I'd say sweet nothings to Roberta, who looks pretty young for her age, and wait for that morning train. Maybe the girls are going to have a new mama."

Perley gave him a look of affectionate disgust. "Always dragging in love. Don't you ever look for anything else?"

"Nope. That's all there is, with variations. . . . Anyway, what else can I think under the circumstances? Look at that moon. Smell that hayfield. And then if that doesn't soften you up, take a deep drag of the stuff that's growing along the fence. What is it, by the way?"

"Honeysuckle. Want to stop and make yourself a wreath?"

Mark grinned. "On the level, Perley, doesn't the small blue hat with the little white birds sound bridal? Or semi-bridal? Or if you don't like that, let's say she took a nice, long walk, all by herself."

"She didn't. She's not the type, at one o'clock. And I don't like the elopement angle either. I don't like anything about this. I don't like anything that's happened tonight. I feel like I'm being taken advantage of."

Mark went on easily. "You get it that way sometimes. . . . You know it needn't be an elopement. It can be one of those unrequited affairs calling for drastic action on the lady's part. If it is, everybody's going to have fun and you're going to feel worse than ever."

Perley spoke slowly and with caution. "Does an unrequited affair calling for drastic action boil down to one of your variations?"

"It does. A lopsided one. I've handled two in my day and I don't want another. You clean them up, hand in the facts, and the family tries to kick you downstairs."

"Why?"

"Well now, let's see. You say Miss Cassidy's in her late thirties? And a very good creature? That's the time they do funny things if they haven't had a chance before. They write themselves scandalous letters full of words you'd choke over, fake illness, stage disappearances. Anything to grab off a little attention. But they usually snap out of it. Don't worry."

"I've got to worry! Beacham's prominent. And all that stuff you just said is out. A better women than Miss Cassidy never lived. Beacham told me so himself one time when we went fishing together. He's a very democratic fellow. He told me that when his wife died he didn't know which way to turn. She died when the youngest girl was two weeks old. Miss Cassidy was the nurse and she stayed on. It got to be so he couldn't get along without her. She managed everything. He'd sort of hoped for a boy that time, you know how men are about wanting boys, but he never said a word to anybody. Still, she caught on. She was the one who started calling the baby Joey instead of Josephine. And later on she egged the kid to climb trees and all that, and she bought her some little fishing pants like Beacham's. But she didn't go too far that way. She dressed Joey like a little lady on Sundays. Joey's a picture on Sundays. Why that woman gave that family something to live for! If him and her have run away to get married, why I guess it's all right. But they didn't have to do it that way. They could stand up in anybody's sight!" He cleared his throat furiously. "Why did this have to happen? What did happen?"

Mark was non-committal. "I'd be a fool to guess. . . . This it?"

"Yep." Gravel crunched as they swung between gateposts and passed under a brightly lighted portico before a long, dark veranda. They went on for several yards until they came to an aggressively simple cottage nestled in trees.

"Waiting for us," Perley said. He sounded impressed.

A small group of people moved out of the shadows. Mark knew Roberta and Nick Sutton, but the others were strangers. There were no introductions. They all seemed to know who he was, and he fitted names to people as the talk went on. He stood behind Perley and watched and listened.

Archie Peck took charge. As Beacham's partner he felt a natural responsibility for the Beacham household, and said so, over and over again. He looked as if he had fallen out of bed and dressed in the dark. He was short and fat. His sparse red hair stood on end, and his round, red face glistened with heat. He was a little drunk, but not enough to give Perley ideas. He took Perley's hand and clung to it.

"Wilcox," he said, "this is terrible. You've got to do something before Mike gets here." Mike was Beacham.

"Now, now," said Perley. "Maybe there won't be anything to do. Maybe the lady is taking a walk by herself in the woods." He waited hopefully.

Peck's fat, babyish mouth opened to reply, but his wife closed it promptly with a look.

"Not in those shoes," she said.

Franny Peck was a blonde little creature in something pink that might or might not have been a dress. She shook her curly head and widened her eyes. Mark told himself that she would have dimples when she smiled, and guessed that she would smile as soon as it was humanly possible. But she wouldn't go overboard, he decided. She'd give them something wan and suitable to the occasion.

"Let me tell you what I know," she begged softly. "It isn't very much because I'm not clever at things, but maybe I can make you see why we're a little worried."

"You go right ahead, Mrs. Peck," Perley said heartily. "I expect you can help me a lot."

"Well, I'm going to try." She smiled. It was a grateful one, with two dimples, appropriate and promising. "Cassie," she went on, "that's Miss Cassidy, sat with Arch and me at the supper. Miss Sheffield and Mr. Kirby were at the same table but farther down." She nodded to the other man and woman. "Then after supper we all strolled around. We crawled over that wall like children, absolutely like children, and read the names on the headstones in that quaint old cemetery. Then Cassie said she ought to see what Joey was doing and she went back to the picnic grounds alone. We didn't see her again. Arch had to drive downtown for something, and I drove home with Hank and Cora." She nodded to the other pair again. "We were going to play poker, and we did. Cassie had promised to play too, but when she didn't come we decided she'd gone home to bed. Arch came back, and we played until midnight. That's absolutely all."

The other woman took it up. Mark had seen and heard her at the supper, and marveled. She had reached for food beyond man's grasp and got it every time. She was dressed now as she had been then, in flowered chiffon and flowered hat. From top to bottom she was all awry. He remembered her voice; she'd told the immediate world that she was from Kentucky and had extolled its two prime products at the top of her leather lungs. She bore a striking resemblance to one of these and had recently consoled herself with the other. She was Miss Cora Sheffield, and he envied her breath.

"Never trust a motherly woman," she neighed at Perley. "Cassie said she was going to look up Joey. Joey says she didn't. Make what you can of that. Now when I say I'm going somewhere, I go, like a homing pigeon."

"That's fine," Perley said helplessly. "Now what time would you say it was when you people left the grounds? And why didn't you try to find Miss Cassidy, considering you had a date, so to speak?"

Miss Sheffield brought Mr. Kirby forward with a hearty shove. "Talk," she commanded.

Henry Kirby, Hank, dapper, dyed, and pushing seventy, looked as if he had been riveted together by an expert. He didn't have much to say. Miss Cassidy had driven down to the supper in the hotel station wagon. He thought she'd come home the same way. What was wrong with that? As for the time, he didn't know. It looked like eight-thirty when they left. The sky looked like eight-thirty. He hadn't examined a watch. He didn't like watches. He shrugged his beautiful shoulders as if he were shaking off years.

Perley turned to Roberta. "Can you add anything?" he asked weakly.

Roberta said Joey had returned in the wagon because she thought Cassie had gone with the Pecks. Cassie often let Joey shift for herself because she thought it was good for her. And Joey didn't think there was anything funny or queer about it. Maybe it did sound kind of care-less, nobody taking the trouble to find out where poor Cass was, but she was always so capable. It just seemed natural not to bother. As for herself, she and Nick had been too upset about that arrow business to think of anything else.

"Arrow!" Miss Sheffield showed her fine teeth. "I heard about the brat, but I didn't see it happen. Nickie, I love you! Did you pink the old girl too?"

Nick turned, limped over to the steps, and sat down.

"Mr. Wilcox." Roberta's voice was urgent. "Cassie may be hurt too, like Miss Rayner, I mean. She may be lying somewhere, hurt."

"She was a trained nurse, wasn't she?"

"Yes, but—"

"She'll know what to do then. Where's the little girl, Joey?"

"Joey's with Pee Wee, over in their cottage. Mr. Wilcox, will you let Nick and me go with you? You're going to look for her, aren't you?"

"Now, now," Perley said. "Mr. East is going to help me and you all know who he is. Miss Cassidy's as good as in her bed right now."

She returned his look soberly. "But if she isn't, who's going to tell my father? My father's coming tomorrow morning—this morning. He'll be here for breakfast. Who's going to tell him she's gone?"

No one answered. Mark began to smile in the dark. He wondered whether he dared say what he thought, that Beacham already knew. He was framing the sentence when something stopped him. A shrill whimper broke the silence, a sad little crying that might have come from a very small and not quite human heart. He looked down at a puppy groveling at his feet.

"Cassie's," Roberta said.

Before he could speak there was another sound, this time from a cottage farther on. It was a whimper too, but there was no doubt about its origin.

He took the cringing animal in his arms. "I'll tell your father," he said. "I'll meet the train." He walked over to the other cottage alone.

CHAPTER TWO

MARK and Perley were on the station platform early the next morning. There was the usual crowd of women and children out to meet week-ending husbands and fathers; there was also the usual crowd of hangers-on, augmented by the town sluggards who were willingly breaking the habits of a lifetime because, except for resurrection morn, there'd never be another day like this one. But the normal horseplay was absent. The women stood close together and talked in whispers; even the children were silent. Off to one side, a crate of live chickens grew suddenly clairvoyant and rent the air with piteous appeals.

Miss Cassidy was still missing, and the sun beat down without mercy. A shout went up. "Here she comes!"

A puff of smoke appeared above the pines down the track, and the little branch line train chugged around the bend. Perley nodded to Mark, and they stepped forward. The crowd made respectful way.

When Michael Beacham moved across the platform and sent eager looks in all directions, the first familiar face he saw was Perley's. His own face showed no surprise. He strode forward, white teeth gleaming in a broad smile.

Perley took Beacham's bag and clapped him on the shoulder. "Come on over to the freight shed," Perley said. "I want to talk to you."

"What's this?" Beacham's laugh boomed like a fiesta cannon. "A pinch? Don't shoot, I'll come quietly!"

Once again Mark watched and listened in the background and considered what he saw and heard. He saw a huge man in his middle forties, with shrewd blue eyes and the easy smile of a joiner. He saw that there were no fraternal buttons on Beacham's coat, but he knew Beacham would have them; they'd be tucked away in the box with his pearl studs and worn only to conventions and rotary luncheons. He knew Beacham would give his children too much spending money and confess to crying at sad movies. Elderly widows and victims of infantile paralysis would always send his hand into his pocket, and if what came out was only a small fraction of what they and their kind had innocently put there some time before, nobody cared. Beacham would probably fleece a lamb while it was still damp, if he didn't know the lamb personally.

It was no cooler in the freight shed but it was dim and quiet. A sickly smell of chicken feathers filled the stale air. Perley sat on an upturned crate and indicated two others.

"Sit," he said. "This is Mark East, a friend of mine. He's a private investigator from New York. He's up here for a vacation. Well—." He looked hopefully at Mark, who returned a blank gaze. "Well, it's like this. Pansy says the only thing I can break is china, so I won't try to soften this up. Mr. Beacham, Miss Cassidy has gone off somewhere."

Beacham looked incredulous. "Cassie? What are you talking about? She's got no place to go."

Perley told him. Beacham listened as if he were hearing a lecture in a foreign language, and the story had to be told all over again. When it was finished the second time he made no comment. He slumped on the crate and stared at his shoes.

"We searched all night," Perley said. "Mr. East and I and some of my boys. We had a bright moon. As near as we can find out she never left the church grounds. At least nobody saw her. No reason to doubt the word of any of those people, either. All town people and the Mountain House crowd. All people you know. I figured she might have walked downtown for soda mints or something—that supper was a lulu—but I've got a fellow directing traffic at Main and Mountain Road these days, and he says he didn't see her. She'd have to pass him no matter where she went. . . . Of course he could have skinned off for a beer, but he'll never admit that."

Beacham raised strained eyes. "I don't get it. I don't get it. She's got no place to go. Joey—Joey ought to know." He dragged out the name of his small, freckled daughter with boastful confidence. "They're never far apart, those two. What does Joey say?"

Perley hesitated, and Mark stepped into the break. "Joey," he said, "was avoiding Miss Cassidy last night. No quarrel, just a small matter of dietary indiscretion. I think you ought to see Joey as soon as possible, Mr. Beacham. I talked to her at five o'clock this morning and she told me she was a Spartan boy. But I think the fox is winning."

Beacham looked bewildered. "I will, I will. But I can't get this thing straight! Cassie! It's crazy. It doesn't make sense." The shrewd look returned to his eyes. He looked at Mark. "What do you think?"

"I can't think anything yet. I didn't know Miss Cassidy. I didn't even see her at the church supper, but that's not strange. They tell me she was self-effacing, and, added to that, she was in pretty flamboyant company. It's easy for a woman like that to be—invisible."

"I guess you mean she was with Kirby, Sheffield, and the Pecks," Beacham said quickly. "No, you wouldn't notice her then. . . . She couldn't be lying somewhere—hurt?"

"That's been considered. Wilcox and I covered the roads and the grounds. Also the cemetery. If your family and friends hadn't insisted it was out of character, I'd say she walked out because she wanted to."

"No," Beacham said. "No. She didn't have any place to go. . . . Did she cash any checks, take any luggage?"

"No checks. We woke the bank up to ask. And no luggage, according to your daughter. What about that ring? Was it worth much?"

"What ring? Oh, the sapphire. Sure it is. We wouldn't give her anything but the best. What about it?"

"Good way to raise cash," Mark said mildly.

Beacham flushed. "She wouldn't sell that if she was starving. Even Joey put her nickels in for that. No."

Perley spoke thoughtfully, rubbing his unshaven chin. "I keep thinking about that ring," he said. "Expensive jewelry is always a temptation, even to honest people. I keep wondering if maybe she did stroll downtown, and if maybe somebody got a look at it and—. You know there's that army camp up the line at Baldwin. My man on traffic duty says some of their fellows were skylarking in town last night. Nothing against the army, you understand," he added hastily. "But I was only wondering. Would she talk to strangers?"

"Yes. She was like that. If a boy came along and told her he was homesick. . . . Yes." He turned his head and looked through the open door; the sun-bleached platform lay beyond, the grimy tracks, the row of listless trees, and then the hills going up, up into the hot blue August sky. His look traveled far beyond that. When he turned back his eyes were smoldering.

"You," he said to Mark. "East. I want you to get busy with Wilcox! I can't have this! Name your fee. Anything you want." He dragged out a checkbook.

"On vacation," Mark said, suddenly laconic.

Beacham stared. "What are you holding out for?"

Mark returned the stare. "Nothing. You can't believe that, can you?"

Perley stirred uneasily. "Now, now."

Beacham made an impatient gesture. "I've rubbed you the wrong way, I guess. I didn't take time to size you up, and that's a mistake I don't often make. You're one of those fellows that won't take orders. I'm sorry. But—I'm upset. I don't know what to think or what to do. I don't even know why anything like this should happen to me." He shook his head like a dog coming out of water. "I'll ask you again. Will you find Miss Cassidy for me and bring her back? I want her—want her bad."

"Thank you, but I don't want the case. I'll lend Wilcox a hand, but that's all I can promise."

"Why?"

"Because I'm a softie about missing persons. Nine times out of ten they're missing because they want it that way. They're happy that way. Why should I come along and smoke the poor devils out like rats, all for a few dollars? They hate your guts for it and you can't blame them. And the people who hire you for the job wind up hating you too, because you nearly always turn up something in their own lives that isn't very pretty. Thanks for asking me, but you see how it is."

"I don't like the way you talk. Are you trying to tell me Cassie went away because we—mistreated her?"

"Not at all. Although I haven't been impressed by any signs of genuine concern, except on the part of your two daughters. They were upset all right, and I was and am sorry for them. But your friends only looked worried, and not enough, and even you talk more about what's happened to you than about what's happened to Miss Cassidy."

"You're wrong! I'm half crazy! I haven't had time to think!"

Mark smiled gently. "It'll work itself out," he said. "Just let it ride along. You see I think Miss Cassidy knows what she's doing. Still," and he smiled again, "if anything changes my mind I'll come in with you."

Perley saw the thunder in Beacham's face and spoke hastily. "Why don't we leave it that way? I'll do everything in my power, and Mr. East here will keep his eye on me." He stood up. "We brought your car down with us, it's parked outside. I think those little girls will be glad to see you."

Beacham knew when he was dismissed. He went out to his car and they watched him drive off. He was pale under his tan, but he was also scowling. Perley looked worried.

"If that's an elopement," he observed, "I'm glad I got married the hard way. But did you have to bite him like that, Mark? He's a prominent man, you know."

"He acts prominent. Sure I had to bite. He can't cast me as a bloodhound in his little domestic drama."

"Honest, do you think that's all it is?" Perley's voice held both relief and disbelief. "Tell me why, go on and tell me why."

"Did you see any of his good, kind pals down here this morning? Did any of them even offer to come? If they thought it was a legitimate disappearance they'd have been here at the crack of dawn, breaking the news and holding his hand. They didn't even search. Nope. I think he had some trouble with the lady and she walked out. And now he's trying to impress her by hiring a private detective. Or maybe he tried to hire me because there I was, sitting on a chicken coop. Nope again. You fool around with the usual routine, Perley, and he'll call you up tonight and tell you she's back." Then he added, "If he doesn't, we'll begin to take everybody apart."

"Poor chap," Perley said doubtfully. "He looked terrible."

Mark squinted at the sky. "Does Bittner still run the busses from here to Crestwood?"

"Sure. Other side of the platform, around the corner. Why do you want to know?"

"I thought I'd pay a social call on Bessy and Beulah. Why didn't those two turn up at the Covered Dish last night?"

"Wrong church. They're funny that way. Listen, why don't I ride over that way with you? That is if you don't mind. I thought I might go on up the line to the camp and check on the boys who had leave last night. I got to do something." He slapped his dripping shirt and exhibited a wet hand. "I'm sweating like a pig and I didn't have any breakfast."

"Breakfast," Mark repeated thoughtfully. "That reminds me of something. On just such a morning Lizzie Borden served a breakfast of hot mutton soup."

"Who?"

"Lizzie Borden. Fall River girl. Gave her mother forty whacks."

"Oh, that one. Whatever happened to her?"

"Nothing. That's the point. Nothing. Come on over to the bus."

Perley began to look uneasy again. "I'm like Beacham," he admitted. "I don't like the way you talk. You sure you haven't got something up your sleeve?"

"Not a thing. Look, Perley. How did we clean up that bloody mess last winter?"

"I dunno. Fancy detective work I guess."

"Nothing fancy about it. We didn't know where we were, so we sat tight until we did. Then we talked to everybody who'd stand still long enough to answer. If we heard that somebody broke the habit of a lifetime and went to bed at nine instead of ten, we found out why. And always we talked and listened. Well, we're in the first stage of that now. We'll do nothing. But if Miss Cassidy is still missing after three days and Beacham is honestly worried and comes after us again—why then we'll start 'em rolling. . . . Here we are. Upsy daisy."

They climbed aboard the odorous yellow bus that carried pigs and people with Christian impartiality. It was known as Bittner's Folly, but not to Bittner. There were seven Follies, each with a bright red slogan painted on its battered side: SAME TIME SAME STATION. The slogan was Bittner's challenge to the branch line railroad.

Years before, Bittner had walked in front of an incoming train to show his contempt for the schedule, and lost both legs. In retaliation he collected a fleet of opposition busses and trucks. Bittner's busses went everywhere the trains went, neck to neck, hugging the tracks. They were fleas on the cast-iron hide of rapid transit. Once, an engineer, young and new to the line, tried to shake one off. He stopped his train in the middle of the country, climbed down from his cab, and, strolling to a nearby field, picked himself a buttercup. This was supposed to confound the bus. Bittner's driver got six to his one and beat him to the start.

Bittner undercut the train rates, carried weddings and funerals free, and transported all livestock that would fit in the aisles. He could afford it; he was rich. He lived an abundant life in a fearful wheel chair, in a tidy little house next door to the station in Crestwood. The house was honeycombed with ramps and had an unobstructed view of the branch line railway and the parallel state road. He spent his days sailing up and down the ramps and wielding his powerful binoculars at the windows. People said he could read the date on a nickel in a driver's pocket.

Mark had never met Bittner, but he had often coveted the binoculars. He was thinking of them when he boarded the bus. It was Folly Number Three.

They had hardly found places when a two-coach train on a nearby track gave a warning cough. The bus shuddered and plunged forward.

They were off. Mark clung to a seat that had too recently been occupied by a very young child whose other weakness was chewing gum. There was no conversation.

Five miles later, at Crestwood, he crawled out and waved a limp farewell to Perley. The tiny red brick station was as picturesque as he remembered it, covered now with vines instead of snow. The once bare bushes bloomed and the summer dust lay thick on paths where he had once walked arm in arm with murder. This time there was no icy wind, no wailing in the trees. But he felt that winter wind again, and he shivered and looked down at the gooseflesh on his bare, sunburned arm. "I need sleep, or something," he said. "There's nothing wrong. It's coming back here that does it."

Amos Partridge was on the station platform, struggling with the mailbag and hurling his obligatory imprecations at the departing bus.

Mark waved. "See you later," he shouted, and hoped he sounded cheerful. He started up the lane of little houses.

Bees droned and gardens sent out waves of perfume. He turned gratefully in at Beulah Pond's gate and wasn't surprised when she burst through the door before the gate clicked. The old grapevine still worked; Ella May, the hawk-eyed spouse of the legless Bittner, had seen him come and telephoned ahead.

Bessy Petty beamed over Beulah's thin shoulder. She'd dropped in to pick beetles, she said. They chirped, screamed, scolded, and kissed. In five minutes he was sitting under a peach tree in the back garden, with a Tom Collins in his hand because lemon juice is so good for you early in the day.

"Do you want sunstroke?" shrilled Beulah. "What are you doing without a hat? What are you doing here anyway? We didn't expect you until next week."

He didn't have a hat because he'd left Perley's in a hurry, and he was coming next week as promised. This was a dividend call, in reverse. When they didn't mention Miss Cassidy he knew they hadn't heard, so he told them. They were suitably distressed and delighted.

"That good woman!" Beulah said happily. "But I'm not surprised. Why do people go to church suppers anyway?"

"To get a lot for fifty cents," Bessy said soberly. "Poor Miss Cassidy. She had the look of death in her eye last week in the five-and-ten."

"She had a sty," Beulah said. "Go on, Mark. What do you want to know? You didn't come over here in all this heat to tell us something we'd have found out for ourselves in an hour."

He admitted that. "I'm not working on the case," he said. "I'm not even sure it is a case. I sort of think it's what we call a voluntary disappearance. But I'm curious. What do you know about these people? How long have they been coming to Bear River? Who hates who, who loves, if any and at all? And don't censor anything for me, not that I think you will. I'm interested in Beacham, Cassidy, Peck, Kirby, Sheffield, Sutton, and Rayner."

Beulah launched herself like a ship, but with lemon juice. The Beacham history was clean to the point of sterility. Widower, rich, oil. No women that anybody ever heard of, but that didn't mean anything because he was a New Yorker, and everybody knows what you can get away with in New York. Some people said they wondered about Miss Cassidy, but she, Beulah, didn't. "I can tell," she said richly.

Joey, she said, was nice; Roberta was nice too, but mopish. In love with Nick Sutton. The Beachams and Miss Cassidy had been coming to the Mountain House for five years. Nick Sutton was new this year. He was an orphan; nursemaid dropped him when he was a baby and hurt his spine. His grandfather was with him, an old gentleman who sat in the sun all day and never went anywhere. He had a valet. Rough boys called Nick "The Little Lame Prince." He was forever fighting them, or trying to.

"Miss Cassidy got any relatives?"

"Sure you don't mean survivors?"

He didn't answer.

"I know you, Mark," Beulah said. "I know you've made up your mind that Miss Cassidy is dead, and that's why you didn't want the case. Right?"

"Wrong. My mind is definitely not made up to anything. What about relatives?"

"She hasn't any. I got to know her pretty well, coming up here every summer as she did. She was a good creature."

"I don't think that was a sty," Bessy said unexpectedly.

They ignored her, but she was used to that. Nevertheless the scar on her cheek reddened with embarrassment. She touched it gingerly, remembering too well how she had come by it. They could kill everybody in the state this time, she said to herself, and she wouldn't lift a finger. Not a single one. The gutters could run blood and she wouldn't care. But the old habit of cozy interference was still strong. She stared into the bottom of her empty glass.

"Mr. Spangler has a terrible sign in his window," she said softly.

"Not any more," Mark said. "I made him take it out. Get on with the record, Beulah. Peck, Kirby, Sheffield, Rayner."

There wasn't much to tell about them, Beulah said. They drank a lot but didn't do anything awful. Not Miss Rayner, of course; the others. Miss Sheffield. But it's no sin to knock down the traffic light. Cora Sheffield bred horses in Kentucky, but she wanted Mr. Kirby. She was sixty if she was a day, and he was over seventy, and one night one of the maids saw him without his hair. He'd carried on so she had to take another job in Baldwin, but that didn't stop her talking. Cora Sheffield and Mr. Kirby had been coming to the Mountain House for two summers. The Pecks were old timers like the Beachams. Rich, oil, and nothing you could put your finger on. Miss Rayner was new, like the Suttons.

"Miss Rayner got shot last night," Mark said.

Bessy fell back in her chair. So it was going to be like that again, was it? Well, the gutters could run. But she sat forward again.

"Shot!" Beulah glowed. "Where?"

"She was walking along by the cemetery wall, and an arrow got her in the leg. Roberta Beacham found her in the Sunday school room after everyone had gone home. The doctor says she's all right now. Upset a bit, naturally."

"Naturally. An old woman takes a walk on holy ground and gets an arrow in the leg, when all her heart was set on was a bit of shrapnel. . . . In heaven's name, did you say arrow?"

They listened enthralled while he told about the archery set and the flood of nickels and dimes it had poured into a canvas bag now hanging from a nail in the back of Pansy Wilcox's jelly closet.

"Same as gambling," Beulah said. "Go on."

"The set was a gift of Beacham's to last year's Sunday school picnic, and it owned to a bloody history even before last night. I understand three children had already felt its sting. Then last night a child called Maisie Briggs—"

"Not Maisie!" Bessy was horrified. "She's just had the whooping cough, which spoiled her dreadfully, and now if she's been shot too!"

"A small nip in the arm. Her mother did her best to squeeze it into a big one, but with all her efforts it continued to look like a mosquito bite. A few people got pretty nasty about it. . . . Nick Sutton did it."

Beulah beamed. "So impetuous. Did he shoot Miss Rayner too?"

"He says no. Pee Wee Peck and Floyd say no too. If you want me to go on with this I'll have to have more of that lemon juice. And a sandwich. I didn't have much breakfast."

Beulah immediately took charge. Bessy was sent to the kitchen to make sandwiches of toast and grilled ham, a time-consuming job and one that she invariably did badly. She didn't want to go. She went.

"She always burns the toast and has to do it all over," Beulah said briskly. She refilled Mark's glass from a pitcher. "Talk fast. Later on I'll tell her all I think she should know. Now—"

"Nick bought six arrows. He hit his mark with the first two and got our Maisie with the third. He dropped the other three and ran to pick up Maisie, who was making the most of the situation. Pee Wee and Floyd tell me this. They were standing beside Nick, who is regarded by them as something of a wonder. Of course everybody got scrambled up immediately, and the light wasn't any too good to begin with. I didn't see it happen. I was under a tree with Perley."

"Tck, tck," grieved Beulah.

"Thank you. Well, when Perley and I fought our way through the mob everybody tried to hand Nick over to the law. Funny how easy it is to turn a nice crowd into a rabble. They pushed and shouted and shoved him around. . . . I'd like to know who started that demonstration."

"I don't think anybody deliberately started it," Beulah said. She gave him a pious look. "It's the war. When I see my delphiniums out there and think of all the dreadful things that are happening—." She broke off and swatted a mild-mannered bee with her palm leaf fan. "Now why did I do that?" she asked regretfully. "I like bees. But there, you see what I mean? We simply sock the thing nearest to us because we know somebody's getting socked somewhere else." She covered the bee with a leaf.

Mark looked down the bright little garden to the meadows beyond. "Do you think somebody shot Miss Rayner because the woes of la petite Maisie gave him the idea?" He sounded half asleep.

"Why not? She's very sharp with the servants at the hotel and doesn't tip at all. . . . See here, aren't you forgetting the real trouble? What about Miss Cassidy, poor thing?"

"I know, I know. That fine woman, that good woman, beloved by all. Skip Miss Cassidy for the moment and return to Miss Rayner. How old would you say she is?"

"About sixty-five. But what's her age got to do with this?"

"I'm just wondering why anybody wanted to wing an old woman in the leg. Unsporting, pointless, and no fun. Also there weren't any hotel servants at the supper, so it wasn't a tipless revenge. . . . Now listen Beulah. Here's the setup. Dusk. Paper lanterns. Crowds of people milling about. The only decent light's a flare by the target board. Everybody happy, and the coal rolling in. Nick shoots his third arrow and gets Maisie. Instantly a howl goes up. He says somebody pushed his arm. It could be. In the excitement that follows one of the three remaining arrows disappears. Pee Wee and Floyd look for it but can't find it. Some time later, nobody knows exactly when, the missing arrow turns up in Miss Rayner, boomerang style. That is to say, she heard it, felt it, but didn't see it. She thinks it had a string on it."

Beulah wrinkled her long nose. "I never heard of such a thing."

"Anyway it's missing, vanished. And she has an arrow wound all right. The doctor says so. He measured it with one of the five I salvaged. Well, after that everybody went home or somewhere. At one o'clock Roberta and Nick came back to the Mountain House, full of moonlight and lemon sodas, and found Miss Cassidy's bed empty. And they called Perley, immediately."

"Umm," said Beulah.

"Yes. Perley and I talked to everybody. Nobody knew a thing. Miss Cassidy was last seen at the target, shortly before the Maisie business. Joey says she saw her standing near Nick, but Joey had vinegar on her breath and was keeping out of the way. She didn't speak to Miss Cassidy, and she's too excited now to remember exactly where Miss Cassidy stood. . . . What have we got now, Beulah?"

"One child pinked in the arm and one old woman in the leg. One youngish woman and one arrow missing."

"Is that tragedy or comedy?"

"Which does it feel like, Mark? Never mind about how it looks. How does it feel?"

"Odd. Take these incidents singly and they don't mean much. The good Cassidy may be pulling an act to frighten Beacham to his knees, and the Rayner arrow may be some oaf's idea of a practical joke. Think so?"

"I hate to say it, but I'm afraid it is a joke. I mean the arrow. Some of these boys ought to be in a reform school. But I don't know about Miss Cassidy. She isn't the runaway type."

"I'd like to see that paragon! And I'd like to know, just for fun, who was playing with the sixth arrow. It's a pre-war toy with a beautiful head. I'd like to know where it is now."

"You'll find it after all this has died down, tacked to the wall of some wretched little boy's bedroom. With a notch in it for Miss Rayner. Why don't you worry about poor Miss Cassidy?"

"She's Perley's job," he said. "And don't call her poor Miss Cassidy. I suspect she's very clever, going-to-be-rich-some-day Miss Cassidy. . . . Here comes my food."

Bessy had turned out two sandwiches after four tries, but she reminded them that the failures would do nicely for the birds. Mark ate steadily and gratefully.

"Spend the day with us," Bessy urged. "We can have a lovely time. And I'll call up some dear friends who are expecting brandy on the noon train."

He leaned over and patted the scarred cheek. "No thanks. I've got a message for Amos, and then I'm going back to Pansy's and change my clothes. After that I think I'll pay a visit to the Mountain House."

They let him go, but they followed him to the gate and watched him all the way down the lane.

Amos Partridge, stationmaster, postmaster, and the law of Crestwood gave him hard boiled eggs and beer. He downed them with a prayer while he relayed Perley's message. They might need Amos, Perley had said, if nothing turned up by nightfall. Just for the looks of the thing. Just to please Beacham. It would make Beacham feel good if Amos came over to the Mountain House with a couple of husky men and beat the bushes. Did he have an understudy who could cope with the evening train?

Amos said he had. He'd rented the Lacey cottage to a lovely lady, wife of a colonel. She had a reliable son who liked trains. Only fifteen years old but one of those Groton boys, and you know what they can do.

Amos asked no questions. In fact, he was disturbingly incurious.

"You seem to know all about our little trouble," Mark said. "Who told you?"

"Bittner. Got it from one of his drivers. They never miss a thing."

"Do you know Miss Cassidy?"

"Kind of," said Amos. "I'll know her if I see her again." He shut his mouth with a snap, and Mark knew the Cassidy subject was closed. At least temporarily.

He looked at his watch. "I've got to get back to Bear River. What about a train or a bus? Or do I hitch a ride?"

Amos considered. "There's the Roving Folly, Number Four. She's a small job, but she's all right. She roves around all day for the benefit of tired berry pickers and city hikers that peter out. She went by half an hour ago to look for a pedigree dog that got lost. She'll be back soon. I heard dogs up the line."

They talked about nothing while they waited because Amos maneuvered the conversation, and in ten minutes the Roving Folly drew up with two dogs aboard, unpedigreed and unashamed.

Back in Bear River, Mark entered the empty house and went up to the little room Pansy had given him. It was the only extra room she had; it was under the eaves and stifling. The single window was closed against the dust, and a large fly beat hopelessly against the cheap screen.

He took off his shoes and socks because the strip of matting on the floor looked cool; it was like the top of a working stove. He opened the window, released the fly, and went downstairs to the bathroom. Pansy had put out her best towels, covered with painstaking monograms and bright pink flowers, but someone, probably Floyd, had left the bath mat in a twisted wet heap. The soap was shriveling in a cracked saucer. There were two more flies.

He condemned himself for noticing these things and blamed his bad manners on the heat. He knew that Perley's salary was small and that he also helped Pansy's people, who had farmed determinedly for fifty years without learning anything. He also knew that Floyd's education hung like a shadow over Perley's shoulder and snatched the extra nickels and dimes whenever they made a rare appearance. There was no money for plumbing elegance. Having finished calling himself names, he filled the tub and moaned when he saw that the water was rusty.

He thought of his own apartment in New York, with the Venetian blinds drawn, of clean white rugs and clean walls, of the prodigal shower and the sunken tub, of the fat, fresh cake of good soap. He watched the rusty water run down his arm and thought of a restaurant in a Village backyard where he could have salmon mayonnaise under a tree of heaven, and a tall bottle in a bucket of ice.

"God help me," he groaned, "and send me appendicitis."

He felt no better when he was shaved and dressed, and no cleaner. He tried telling himself that he'd never run out on a case in his life, and then he remembered that it wasn't his case. It was Perley's. He'd only be running out on a vacation. Wonderful. But how could he do it, quickly, decently, and still look Perley in the eye? There was only one way. If he could deliver the evanescent Miss Cassidy, little white birds and sapphire ring intact, then he could bow out with friends and reputation unsullied, to say nothing of his own morale.

That was it. He'd give himself until Monday morning. If she was still missing then, he'd stay. If he found her, he'd go. And if he found her playing house in a nearby cave and she said—"Where am I?"—, she'd remember the location for the rest of her life. The prospect cheered him to the point of song.

He went down to the kitchen and made his own contribution to the family blackboard. He wrote, "GONE UP TO THE HOTEL. TAKING THE CAR. BACK FOR SUPPER." Then he went out to the garage and tried not to notice that its cheap paint was cracking and peeling in the sun.

It was three o'clock. The Mountain House guests had wisely retired for siestas. The page who offered to park the car told him that much. "Everybody goes to bed after lunch," he said. "They don't get up till four o'clock, and then they stay up past midnight. They're rich. Who do you want? I don't mind banging on a couple of doors."

Mark said he wanted one of the cottages and that he could find it himself. He didn't like the way the boy had instantly classed him with those who couldn't afford to sleep in the daytime.

The door to the Beacham cottage stood open. He stepped into the wide living room and called softly. There was no answer. He went out again and looked over at the Pecks'. Archie Peck was sleeping in the porch swing, lying on his fat stomach, his face buried in a pillow. In another hour, according to the page, Archie would wake up by himself and stay up till past midnight. He walked over and twitched Archie's pillow, and the schedule collapsed.

"Hey!" Archie bellowed. "Oh—Mr. East." He sat up and smiled foolishly.

Mark smiled back. "Sorry I had to do that, but I want your permission to break and enter the Beacham cottage. Nobody seems to be home there."

"Mike took the girls for a swim on the other side of the mountain. They were going crazy sitting around. No news?"

"No. All right if I go in?"

"Sure. But I'll go with you if you don't mind. What do you want over there anyway?"

"I thought I'd have a look at Miss Cassidy's things. It's customary. Letters, bankbooks, and so on. We always do that and we don't talk about it afterward. We don't swipe things either. Glad to have you come along."

The screen door opened and Franny Peck came out, completely and exquisitely dressed for the afternoon. Another schedule broken, and for no apparent reason. She wore pale blue and flaunted dimples on every exposed surface.

"Hello, Mr. East," she said. "How nice of you to come." With those few words she managed to suggest a rendezvous, carefully contrived by both of them.

For one long moment he fought panic. Could all this be for him? He backed away hastily and nearly lost his footing.

"Hello," he said coldly. Then he saw that he needn't have worried. In that time she had transferred her attention to her nails and her husband. It was nice to know that little Franny couldn't stay with any emotion longer than a minute, grief and love included.

"I couldn't sleep," she said to Archie. "Isn't everything terrible? I keep hearing things and I'm scared to death." She ruffled her curls. "Is Mike back?"

"No. East says nobody home."

"That's funny. I thought I heard somebody on their porch a while ago. I must have dreamed it. I knew they meant to stay all day, but when I heard somebody on the porch I thought they'd come back."

"You didn't hear anybody," Archie said. "You dreamed it all right."

She put a soft hand on Mark's arm. "You look hot. Why don't you let me mix you a nice drink?"

He declined. He told her what he planned to do and saw her eyes widen thoughtfully. She looked as if she'd like nothing better than a few minutes alone with Miss Cassidy's private papers. Archie also read his wife correctly.

"You stay here, baby," he said. "Have a tall one waiting for me when I get back. I'm just going along with East for the looks of the thing."

The Beacham cottage was a bungalow. Archie led the way through the living room to the bedrooms. They opened on a long hall, and the doors were all closed.

"Why do people close doors in this weather!" he said. "There's nothing to steal in these places." He opened the second door from the end. "Here. This is Cassie's. She and Joey have it together."

They went into a room hung with chintz and furnished with wicker and maple. Archie looked doubtfully at the larger of two chests. "I guess that one's Cassie's. The other one looks like Joey's size." He opened two closets. "Yep, this one's Cassie's too. Go right ahead and don't mind me. I'll sit." He did, and turned on an electric fan.

Mark went to work. He saw at once that he was dealing with a woman who had nothing to hide, or a great deal. The only letters were two from Beacham, without envelopes and undated, and beginning "Dear Cass." One of them complained about the caretaker in the town house and asked her to do something about it. The other told her when to expect him. There were no bankbooks, no picture postcards from friends who were having a wonderful time elsewhere; no bits of broken jewelry or tangled skeins of baby ribbon.

There was a laundry list in the handkerchief drawer, written in a neat, characterless script that was almost like printing. If he hadn't already known it he would have guessed that she had been a nurse. It was the kind of writing you see on charts, hanging from the foot of hospital beds.

He handled the underclothing carefully, conscious of Archie Peck's good-natured leer. He'll try to tell me a story in a minute, he said to himself, and I'll stop him because I've heard it. The white slips were simple, but surprisingly fine, with monograms that Pansy would have disdained: M.C.

"Is her name Mary?" he asked.

"Sure is. Did you detect that or was it on a letter?"

He grinned and didn't answer. A tray of bottles and jars caught and held his attention; creams, hand lotion, rouge, eye shadow. Eye shadow, still sealed and never used. An unopened bottle of perfume, labeled MY SIN. He slipped this into a drawer because he didn't want Archie Peck to see it. It said too much or too little, and he began to worry about his first theory. He knew that women sometimes bought expensive perfume to cheer themselves up, and that often they didn't use it; they kept it, and looked at it, like something hoarded for a rainy day. It was part of a private world that was almost always a happy one. Mary Cassidy was beginning to emerge and take form, and she was upsetting his calculations.

He went back to the lingerie drawer and shamelessly hunted out the nightgowns. There were six plain white ones, matching the tailored slips, but under these he found six others. They were carefully folded in tissue paper and they were what he called fancy. He heard Archie snort with appreciation.

"You could knock me down with a feather," Archie said. "Wait till I tell Franny!"

"You'll tell her nothing," Mark said. "There's nothing funny about this."

"Sorry." Archie looked foolish. "But I didn't know Cassie was like that."

Mark shut the drawer. "She isn't. I think I had her all wrong. But that's not odd because I never saw the woman in my life. Black hair, blue eyes, weight one hundred and ten; that's all anybody could tell me, and it's so little it sounds phoney." He paced the room, kicking at chairs. "I don't know anything about her. I know she plays poker, but I don't know what she reads."

"I wouldn't worry about what she reads," Archie said, his eyes on the closed drawer.

Suddenly Mark wanted to protect the unknown Mary Cassidy from that loose-lipped grin. He didn't ask himself why, or wonder what had changed him. He only knew that he wanted to find her, unhurt, and keep her that way. He wanted her back in that room with its big and little beds, and he wanted her to open the bottle of perfume and use it up.

"Can't you tell me anything about her life?" he asked. "What did she do, aside from looking after Joey?"

"I'm beginning to wonder myself," Archie said. "Those little bits of fluff and lace are giving me ideas."

"Me too, but not the same kind. Those bits of fluff are rather pathetic."

"They are?" Archie looked bewildered. "I don't get it."

"They've never been worn. They've never been laundered. They're still wrapped in the paper from the shop. I have a hunch she bought them because they're something she always wanted and couldn't afford until now. Bought them for the kick she got out of it. . . . She really was nice, wasn't she?" He heard himself talking in the past tense and didn't like it.

"Sure, she was all right." Archie was still confused. "Kind of quiet though. Played a good game of poker but—you know—kind of quiet. . . . Say!" He sat up straight and gave Mark a shrewd look. "You didn't talk like this to Mike this morning! He was as sore as the devil when he came back from meeting you. He said you acted like it was a gag or something. What changed you, pal?"

"I don't know." Mark went over to the closet and gave a quick glance at the rows of neat dresses, the trim little hats on the top shelf, the orderly line of shoes on the floor. He closed the door. "I don't know," he said again. He did know, but he wouldn't admit it. "I think I'll take this on if Beacham still wants me. I didn't actually turn him down this morning, either. I told him I might change my mind. . . . I guess I'm sorry for Joey." Not for anything would he admit, even to himself, that a little heap of hoarded finery had bound him fast.

"Come along," he said. "I'm through here. If Mrs. Peck still wants to give me a drink I'll accept with pleasure."

"Sure." Archie brightened at once. "We've got everything and Franny knows what to do with it." He led the way back to his own cottage. "You name it and Franny'll get it."

"I've had gin and beer," Mark admitted.

"Gin," Archie decided. "Hon!" he yelled as they mounted the porch. "Gin for the Scotland Yard boys!"

They sat around an iron table, under a tree. The Mountain House guests, properly awake at four o'clock, sat under other trees. A few starched children and clean, subdued dogs promenaded with nursemaids.

"They call this place Little Switzerland," Franny said. "And it is, isn't it? They don't take anybody, either. They're very careful."

Mark saw Nick Sutton lead an old man to a cushioned seat on the veranda.

"Grandfather?" he asked.

"Yep. Copper mines."

"Nick's a good catch," Franny said earnestly. "But I'm glad Pee Wee isn't a girl. You have to worry so."

The Beachams came back shortly before five, looking, Mark suspected, worse than they had when they started out. There were rings under Beacham's eyes, and Roberta looked pale and drawn. Even Joey dragged her sandaled feet as she came across the grass and leaned wearily against Franny Peck's chair.

Beacham's eyes asked Mark a question, and his shoulders slumped at the silent answer. He went into his own cottage, followed by Roberta.

"I'll tell him what I've done later," Mark said to Archie. "I'll talk to him alone."

Joey sank down on the grass. Her denim shorts were muddy, and her face was streaked with dust, but there was nobody to tell her to change. Franny Peck wasn't interested.

"Cassie's puppy ate his breakfast like a little pig," Joey said to Mark. "He's too young to understand."

I wonder if you are, he thought. Out loud he said, "Why don't you take a bath, Joey? You look like something the Child Labor Board dragged in."

"Later," she said. "Mike and Roberta look worse than me." She edged closer. "Did Mr. Wilcox work today, Mr. East? Did you work too?" She had tact and good manners, another entry on the right side of Mary Cassidy's ledger.

"Yes," he said. "We're getting on. Where did you go for your picnic?"

She didn't have time to answer. The Beachams' door swung open and slammed shut and Roberta came running across the grass. Her face was twisted into an ugly scowl, and she went straight to Mark. He saw that she was frightened and he stood up quickly.

"Easy. What is it?" He took her arm.

She pulled away. "Of all the cockeyed things," she said. "You've got to do something right away. Of all the crazy, cockeyed things." The tears welled up and ran down her face. "You'd better come inside and see for yourself. Of all the idiotic, cockeyed things—"

"What's up?" He took her arm again and shook her gently. "What are you talking about?"

"Crazy, crazy," she whimpered. She put her hand to her head as if it ached. "Sorry," she said, "but you'd better come and see. Somebody got in the house while we were away and cut Joey's clothes to ribbons!"

"What!" They all stared. Archie Peck laughed and slapped his knee.

"That's a good one," he said.

"It's true, it's true! Somebody went to the chest where we keep her everyday clothes and cut them to bits. Crazy, crazy, crazy."

"Wait." Mark pulled up his chair. "Sit down. You needn't go back there. Joey?"

Joey was staring at her sister.

"My clothes?" she demanded shrilly. "My clothes? Why?"

Mark nodded to Franny Peck, whose eyes were as round a Joey's. "You three stay right where you are," he said. "Come on, Peck." They crossed quickly to the cottage. Chairs creaked on the big veranda, heads turned and eyes followed, but no one asked what had happened. Perhaps no one had heard.

Beacham met them inside. Nothing in the room was disturbed. It was exactly as they had left it, except for the smaller of the two chests. Two drawers had been pulled out.

"Roberta opened those," Beacham said. "She wanted to get some clean things for Joey." He drew a deep, furious breath. "Have a look."

Someone had indeed cut Joey's clothes to ribbons. Not the party clothes, the Sunday clothes, with their rows of lace and ribbon; they still hung primly in the closet, on padded hangers. But the small tailored shirts, the shorts, and the fishing pants had been methodically slashed into strips and squares and maliciously jumbled together. There were scraps of lint and thread on the floor in front of the chest.

Beacham echoed Joey's question. "Why?"

For the second time that day Mark shivered in the heat. "Only one kind of person does that," he said.

Beacham's voice was harsh. "What kind?"

Mark walked to a door on the right side of the room and opened it. It led into another bedroom. "Who sleeps here?" he asked.

"Roberta." Beacham's eyes narrowed. "The one on the left is the bath. Mine's at the end, across the house, and you enter it from the hall. It has a door to the bath too. What are you looking for?"

"An entrance." The bathroom window overlooked the Peck cottage. So, presumably, did the window in Beacham's room. "Got a back door?"

"No. . . . Did some kid crawl in and do this out of pure devilment?"

"No. No kid. . . . Look here, Beacham. I came up to see you this afternoon, thinking I might reconsider your offer. That, of course, was before this happened. Now I'm going to take it whether you want me or not. Take it on my own, for my own satisfaction."

Beacham relaxed. "I won't pretend I'm not glad to hear that. What made you reconsider in the first place?"

"Conscience. And the heat. I wanted to get back to town, but it looked too much like running away. Then, I came in here with Peck a while ago, to check over Miss Cassidy's things. That's routine, doesn't mean a thing. While I was here I changed my mind about the case. No particular reason, just a—feeling. . . . I'm not sure now that she ran away. I'd put her down as a—well, as a possible neurotic. I think I was wrong. I mean that as an apology to you. I'll make another to the lady when I see her."

"Thanks," Beacham said shortly. "What do you want with that stuff?"

Mark was scraping bits of thread and lint from the floor. "I didn't notice this before, probably because I didn't look in this chest. But it must have been here then. The Pecks and I have been outside, and no one came near the house, front or back."

"Hey!" Archie spoke in an awed voice. "Hey, East, remember? Franny said she heard somebody before you came! Remember?"

He did remember. It was the siesta hour, when the rich people slept and the servants had the run of the place. Deserted grounds, trees and tall shrubbery; grass, soft and thick and soundless. A man in a white mess jacket, carrying a letter or a tray of glasses; a woman in a black dress and a white apron, with a bundle of laundry. They could walk in and out, unchallenged.

"Shall I get Franny?" Archie was eager. "We could ask her what kind of a noise she heard. We might even make her remember what time it was. We could try, anyway."

Mark had a clear picture of Franny, dimpling and twisting her curls. "No good," he said. "You told her she was dreaming and you can't talk her out of that now."

"No," Archie agreed.

"Fingerprints on the chest?" Beacham suggested.

"None that we want. Even Pee Wee could tell us that." He lit a cigarette. "I want to stay here, do you mind? You can tell the girls I'm doing it to keep you company. You can move Roberta in here with Joey and I'll take her room. If that's inconvenient I'll get a room in the main house."

Beacham looked terrified. "Do you think the girls—"

"No. But we won't find the answer to this down in Bear River. It's here, right here." He hesitated. "At least I think it is," he added slowly. "What do you say? All right?"

"You'll stay, of course, in this cottage. I'll send down for your things. What can I do for you? Do you need anything?"

"Nothing, thanks. But keep this business about the clothes quiet. It was meant to be a sensation, so we'll ignore it and see what happens. And"—he made his voice casual—"and if you get any ransom notes, don't be a fool. Hand them over right away."

He saw Beacham's face fall into new lines and heard Archie whistle. "Don't worry," he said, "and keep away from the other guests. I've got

to return Wilcox's car and I'll have dinner down there with him. He'll
bring me back. . . . He may have turned up something at the camp."

He didn't believe that but it eased the tension, and that was what he
wanted. Beacham walked out with him to the car when he left.

Perley was waiting for him and they sat long over supper.

"That trip to the camp was wasted time," Perley said. "I nearly got
sunstroke, and that's all. Ten boys had leave last night and I talked to
each one, separate. I couldn't find a lie in the lot. They went to the
movies and had some beers. They didn't see anybody to talk to except
a couple of girls. I beat the girls' names out of them, but that's no help
either. I've known every last one of those girls since the day they were
born and I don't mind telling you I'm kind of surprised. But I guess
that's the war."

"Stop picking on the poor war," Pansy said. "If you ask me, it's lack
of family prayers. And I'll thank you to change the subject. Remember
Floyd."

Floyd gave Mark a worldly smile and did the changing himself.
"What's your theory about Joey's clothes, Mr. East?"

Mark had been keeping that for Perley. "Where did you pick that
up?" he demanded. "That's supposed to be very hush-hush."

"Pee Wee telephoned."

"Clothes?" Pansy brightened. "What's wrong with clothes?"

Mark told them. Perley spread his hands in a hopeless gesture. "In all
my life," he said, "I never heard of such a thing. I don't mind telling
you I don't know where to begin."

"You can forget about the old quarry for one thing, Pop," Floyd
said. "There's no bodies or nothing there. Me and some fellows
dragged all one side today. We're going to do the other tomorrow."

"On Sunday!" His mother gave him a look, and he quailed.

Mark repacked his bag and sat on the porch with Perley until
Roberta drove down for him. She'd telephoned to ask if she might.
Perley, with his shoes off, had urged him to accept. "I need sleep," he
moaned. "She's young and she wants to help."

They made quiet plans for the next day. "You can't do much on
Sunday," Perley said. "Nothing ever happens on Sunday. We'll just sit
around and maybe interview a few folks." He yawned. "You'll like our
Sundays here."

"Will I?" Mark looked dubious.

CHAPTER THREE

A CHURCH bell rang faintly in the valley and echoed in the hills. The guests of the Mountain House heard it, and paid tribute to the day by moving more slowly than usual and wearing a few more clothes. Card games came quietly to life in corners of the big veranda and on cottage porches. Sunday papers rustled and the smell of roasting beef drifted out from the service quarters at the rear. A few cars rolled sedately up to the portico, accepted groups of elderly women with prayer books and fans, and moved off down the mountain. Over in the parking lot by the gates a fat bay horse, hitched to a buggy, switched his shining tail and stamped his hoofs with controlled regularity. The sun was like brass.

Mark sat at an iron table before the Beacham cottage, ostentatiously reading *The New York Times*. The Beachams and the Pecks were golfing three miles away. He'd insisted on that. Anything was better than the sight of the Beachams moving from chair to chair, from room to room, not talking, not looking at each other. They'd accepted his suggestion with relief. It was what they always did on Sunday morning. Even Franny, who'd started the day with a drooping mouth, had changed her clothes in ten minutes.

Cora Sheffield and Henry Kirby had gone off in Kirby's boyish roadster immediately after breakfast. There was, Cora had told the listening world, a little antique dump over near Baldwin where they had a cherry wood commode that might have come out of her own grandmother's attic. It hadn't, of course, but it looked like it.

"And damn if I don't tell everybody it did!" she screamed as they drove off.

Mark wondered whether the sun would do anything to Kirby's little black mustache.

Nick Sutton came down the veranda steps with his grandfather. The old man was very old; he leaned heavily on the boy and looked as if he couldn't stand alone. He was tall, and he had one of those faces sometimes seen in old Italian paintings of a saint confronted with a devil. He could be either. He ought to be in Maine, Mark told himself irritably, or in Canada; this heat will kill him.

He watched while Nick put the old man in a comfortable chair under the trees and took a seat beside him. Nick looks like the devil too, he thought. What good does his money do him? He wondered if the boy's back was painful and decided that it was; the thin face was white and unhappy.

He was returning to his paper when Miss Rayner appeared at the top of the veranda steps and created a mild flurry. A dozen people ran forward to take her arm, but she waved them airily aside. She was in beaming possession of a walking stick, man size, and Mark smiled for the first time in many hours. Miss Rayner was a proper sight in her small violet toque, her violet silk, and her fine white kid gloves.

She hobbled from step to step, drew a deep and satisfied breath, and moved over to the Suttons' chairs. There was one chair vacant, and she eased herself into it gently.

"I've fooled that doctor," she said to the Suttons. "I'm always doing that. He lent me this stick and said I wouldn't be able to use it for a week." She saw Mark and waved. "Come on over here," she called. "I can't remember if I thanked you nicely or not."

He took his chair and paper with him. Nick nodded curtly and said nothing.

"Do you know Mr. Sutton?" Miss Rayner asked. "Mr. Sutton senior? Of course you know this dear boy. This is Mr. East. . . . Mr. East, is there anything about me in that paper?" She smiled archly. "Because if there is I shall be very angry."

"No," he said soberly. "There isn't anything about Miss Cassidy either. I think Mr. Beacham got hold of the right people."

Old Sutton, who had briefly nodded before, now gave Mark his full attention. "You're working for Beacham, aren't you?" he asked in a high, querulous voice.

Mark said he was. He waited for the old man to go on, but nothing more was said. The sunken eyes gleamed under their heavy white brows; they could have been amused or malevolent. Nick moved closer to his grandfather and took his hand.

"Want to go in?" he asked.

"I've just come out. Leave me alone." He sank down in his chair and gave his attention to the cloudless sky. He couldn't have made a more definite exit if he had slammed a door behind him.

Mark turned to Miss Rayner, who was making small, chirping sounds. She was digging about in the bottom of her violet silk bag; calling cards, handkerchief, and small purse lay in her lap. The handkerchief was scented with violet.

"Aren't you going to be late for church?" he asked.

"I would be if I were going," she smiled. "But I'm not. I did think of it, but it's too hot, and I don't feel equal to the ups and downs. And the building is smothered in ivy. Smothered, and I don't like it." She lowered her voice. "Have you ever heard that ivy dust is poison?"

"I've heard it," he said, startled. "But I've never seen a case."

"Then let's hope you never do," she said. She stirred the bottom of her bag in a frenzy. "Too annoying. I'm looking for a piece of sugar. I saved it from my breakfast tray and put it in here before I dressed. And now—oh, here it is!" She held a lump of sugar up to his astonished gaze. "For my horse. I should say, my rented horse. There he is, over there." She nodded in the direction of the glistening bay. "He's very clever and takes it from my hand with very little fuss. I drive almost every day and Mr. Sutton often goes with me. You're coming today, aren't you?" The smile she gave old Sutton was almost arch.

But he didn't answer. He looked as if he hadn't heard. He was still staring upward, and his thin neck turned inside his too large collar as his eyes followed something in the sky. His mouth was wet and open.

The others looked up.

Two dark shapes wheeled and circled against the brilliant blue, swooping and dropping and rising again. They were full of grace, and even from a distance they were powerful.

"Chicken hawks?" Mark asked idly.

"No," Miss Rayner said. "I'm afraid not."

Nick Sutton limped out into a clearing and studied the sky, his hands shielding his eyes from the sun. He came back and sat down without a word.

"Hawks?" asked Miss Rayner.

"Yes."

"Where are they?" she insisted.

"Where? I don't know. It's hard to tell that. . . . You can't tell exactly where an airplane is, can you?"

"I suppose not." She put the clutter of things back into her bag and drew the string tight. "Come along, Mr. Sutton. It isn't good for you to sit like this. You need a bit of shaking up. You and I will have a nice drive together and be back in plenty of time for lunch. I do believe it's beef."

Old Sutton shifted in his chair. He drew a clean handkerchief from his sleeve and touched it to his lips. "Not today, thank you. I'll stay home today. It's too hot, it's too hot out here. I think I ought to go indoors and lie down." His thin, fretful voice appealed to his grandson. "Why don't you go with her? You ought to go. I tell you I want you to go. But first you must take me in and call George. George will put me to bed and then you can leave me."

"I don't want to leave you, grandfather. I'll stay here."

"No. You must drive. She'll take you down that lane behind the pool. It's cool there. All trees, all trees and a little brook." In his babbling eagerness he ran the words together. "You go like a good boy, Nickie, and I'll wait for you to come back." A trickle of saliva slid from one corner of his mouth.

Mark forced himself to study the old face and wondered, as he always did, why inevitable things like age and death were too often shocking and ugly. This was the wrong companion for a boy like Nick. Nick ought to be off somewhere with someone like Roberta, someone who was young and emotionally sound. But Roberta was with her father, and the other guests were too old or too wise. Even Miss Rayner was faintly ridiculous, but at least she could get him away for an hour or two.

"You cut along and take your drive," he said. "I'll look after your grandfather."

"My grandfather has an attendant," Nick said stiffly. Then he gave Mark an odd look of speculation. "Do you really mean that? Will you stay here and keep an eye on him? I don't think he ought to go in yet, and George is taking a nap. He was up all night." He brushed the old man's lips with his own handkerchief and talked over his head as if he weren't there. "Last night wasn't so good," he said.

"Sure I'll stay," Mark said. "Get along and enjoy yourself." There wouldn't be much joy in a buggy ride with a frail spinster, he thought grimly, but they had one thing in common. They both limped.

The old man sat up suddenly and struck at Nick's hand. "No!" he shouted.

The veranda card players turned in amazement and then looked quickly away.

"It's no use," Nick said. "He's made up his mind and we can't do anything about it." He hoisted the old man to his feet.

Miss Rayner watched with a frown. "Are you coming back?" she asked.

"Wait for me." He patted his grandfather's shoulder and gave him a broad wink. "Come along. We'll look for George. George will make you a nice drink, the way you like it, and then you can sleep." The old man dropped one eyelid in agreement and let himself be led away.

Miss Rayner settled her toque and openly returned a dime to her bag. "If you'll help me unhitch I won't have to tip the boy. I don't like those boys. I think they laugh at me when my back's turned. . . . Is there anything about me that looks—odd?"

Mark smiled at her serious face with its network of fine wrinkles. "You look as dashing as all get out," he said. "I'm mad about your hat."

"Now you're teasing," she said. "Don't. I'm almost too familiar with my own appearance." She got to her feet, gripping the stick with open pleasure. "Don't help me. If I favor this leg it'll never get well, and I need it."

They walked over to the parking lot. He wanted to say something about old man Sutton but decided against it. Too gossipy. He compromised.

"Miss Rayner, have you given any more thought to that arrow business?"

"I've thought of little else," she said soberly. "But it seems unimportant in the light of other things. I wonder how long it will be before she—."

"Before what?"

"Before she comes back. But let's not talk about that. Here we are." She closed the subject with a snap.

He kept a straight face while she removed a glove and gave the horse his sugar; she was like a child offering a penny to an organ-grinder's monkey, willing but dubious. When that was done she sighed with relief and scrubbed her hand fastidiously with a piece of cloth evidently hoarded for that purpose in the bottom of the violet bag. "I think we should be kind to animals," she said.

"We certainly should," he agreed. He unhitched the horse with grave solicitude. She said it was a lovely day for a drive even though it was the hottest day they'd had. He said yes, it was pretty hot, and he hoped to go back to New York soon. He said that New York was the greatest summer resort in the country. She agreed, smiling.

"I know," she said. "It's my home too. Why in the world don't we stay where we belong! Vacations!"

Nick came up and they drove off, with Miss Rayner tenderly slapping the reins on the fat bay's back. He watched them turn into the wood road. He looked at the sky again, but the hawks had gone.

He picked up his newspaper and went back to the cottage porch. Twelve o'clock. The Beachams and the Pecks would soon be home, tired enough, he hoped, for the regulation siesta after lunch. He didn't care what the Pecks did as long as they kept out of his way. Franny Peck's conversation might go down in a night club, with something to celebrate in champagne.

He put his feet on the railing and reviewed the recent past. He knew very little more than he'd known the night before. Roberta had kept her mouth shut on the drive home. He'd been able to extract one piece of information; she was eighteen years old and she didn't have her own latch key.

He'd also collected one new character, old man Sutton. Old Sutton had certainly not shot Miss Rayner in the leg and neither had he lured Miss Cassidy from the church supper. He hadn't even gone to the supper. Also, he had probably forgotten that there were two sexes. His grandson and his valet, who made a special drink, filled his life.

Twelve-fifteen. Perley would be checking telegrams at the Western Union office, every telegram that had come to Bear River in the last two months, every telegram that had gone out from Bear River. And after that he would check long distance calls with the telephone company. Amos Partridge and two other deputies were even now beating the bush on the other side of the mountain.

He craned his neck as a car drew up to the big veranda. Cora Sheffield and Kirby were returning from their treasure hunt, and it took three service boys to grapple with the lone fruit of their quest. Cora saw him and screamed a summons. He went over and stood by while she pulled off bits of burlap to show the grain. Kirby excused himself and strode manfully up the steps and out of sight.

"He's melting," she said fondly, "and the poor fool thinks I don't know it. Rouge and mascara. I don't have to use anything. I was born with this complexion."

He murmured something suitable and she laughed at him. She sounded like an exhilarated crow.

"Well you don't look as if you'd found Cassie," she said.

"Give me time," he begged. "Or give me an idea, if you can."

"Something funny's going on," she said, dropping her voice to a hoarse whisper. "Hank and I saw a lot of men with poles and rakes, crawling under bushes and things. On the other side of the mountain. We drove around there looking for cider."

"Cider?" he echoed incredulously.

"What do you care?" she roared. "We found something! One of the drawers in that commode is packed full. Boys!" She loped up the steps after the sweating attendants. "If you drop that I'll have your hides!"

He went back to the cottage porch and sighed. The church-goers returned, limp from the struggle of righteousness over heat. A family of new arrivals made a royal descent from their own car and immediately demanded the service they felt entitled to at twenty dollars a day per head. The Beachams and the Pecks came back, the Pecks glowing and full of chatter, the Beachams weary and hollow-eyed.

Somebody in this outfit has got to get some sleep, Mark said to himself.

"Good game?" he asked Beacham.

"Fair."

The Pecks went to their own cottage, and Roberta and her father went indoors to change. Joey lagged behind, kicking at the rockers and scowling at the sky. He gave her a fraternal boost to the railing. She was wearing a bedraggled white linen frock and a hair ribbon, and she looked bitterly unhappy.

"My other laundry comes back tomorrow," she said suddenly, "so that old louse can't stop me wearing pants anyway."

He weighed his words carefully before he answered. "Are you pretty sure it was an old louse?"

"Of course. This place is full of old louse—leese—"

"Louses," he amended gravely.

"Louses that don't know anything," she finished.

"I wonder if we're thinking of the same one?" he asked idly. "I've got my eye on several."

"Old Mr. Sutton's one. He's always calling me little boy."

"Well now, Joey, that may be all right. You know he's very old and probably he doesn't see very well."

"He sees all right. He sees me coming, doesn't he? He sees me coming from way off and he says little boy, sit on my lap, I like little boys."

"He gets mixed up. He thinks you're Nick. . . . What do you do then?"

"I don't do anything. I say good morning and I walk away."

"That's right."

She hugged a post with one thin arm and studied his face. "You look like you're thinking. Are you?"

"Sort of."

"I thought so," she said with satisfaction. "Are you going to work for my father after lunch?" she added delicately.

"Yes. I worked this morning too, even though it didn't look that way. And after lunch I'm going down to Bear River and talk to Sheriff Wilcox."

"That's good," she said.

"And you," he went on, "you are going to take a long nap. Without argument."

She shook her head. "Not today. I can't. I got to go to Sunday school at three o'clock. We got to beat Pee Wee's class."

He made a rapid survey of his own past and came up with a vague recollection. "It's the attendance record you beat, isn't it?" he asked cautiously.

"Sure." A fugitive gleam came and went in her eyes. "They got a blue silk banner on a gold stick, and if everybody in your class comes every Sunday for a month they let you have it. But you have to give it up if somebody else gets perfect attendance. Pee Wee's class has got it now but we got a chance to get it ourselves today. All us girls swore on the Bible we'd come. I got to."

"I can see that," he agreed. "You know, I had you all wrong. You didn't strike me as the Sunday school type."

"I'm not," she admitted. "I don't go when I'm home, but here it's different. . . . Here they sing swell songs."

That was as good a reason as any, he thought. Swell songs had played victorious parts before. And it was a better reason than the one that used to woo him from the quiet Sunday streets. He remembered his own double life, when he was a family Episcopalian in the morning and a lone Presbyterian in the afternoon; Presbyterian because they gave the biggest box of candy at Christmas.

Joey touched his arm. "Do you know the one called 'Jesus Loves the Little Children of the World'?"

"I'm afraid I missed that one," he regretted. "But it sounds like good stuff."

She jumped down. "Here comes our lunch," she said. "Mike thinks we ought to eat in our own rooms—for a while." She ran in ahead of him.

He was sorry to see her go. Now that he had her confidence, she was ready for questioning. She could fill in the background that he needed, and he knew he could trust her. He glared at the two stewards who were trundling dinner carts across the grass. One of them recoiled, but that was because he was a reformed pickpocket.

When Mark joined the others at the living room table, Joey was already planning her afternoon wardrobe.

A blue hair ribbon, she told her father; and if Roberta was out when it was time for her to go, would he tie it? He would. And the white dotted swiss with the Irish lace insershom; and the Milan straw with the field flowers on it. She rattled off these items of her Sunday wardrobe with an ease that went oddly with her scratches and mosquito bites. "Irish lace insershom is perfectly beautiful," she said firmly.

Mark listened with amazement and a grin that he didn't know was fatuous. Tough Joey must have been a surprisingly attentive audience on her shopping trips; or else, and he thought this more likely, she was being faithful to someone she loved. He patted her grubby little hand and was mildly shocked to find his thoughts dwelling on paternity.

Beacham spoke in an undertone. "Anything yet?"

"A little," he answered.

He turned to Roberta. She was pushing the food about on her plate, and she looked too old and too tired for her eighteen years.

"You missed something," he said lightly. "Nick went off driving with Miss Rayner."

A faint smile softened her mouth. "Finally got him, did she? There ought to be a law! What happened? Grandpa have a stroke?"

"Roberta!" Beacham's voice was sharp. "I don't like that kind of talk."

"Sorry," she said, "but you know what I mean. Grandpa and Rayner have been holding hands in that buggy ever since—"

"Roberta!"

"Oh, all right." She pushed her plate away. "What's the dessert?" She reached over to the carts and uncovered dishes until she found it. "Strawberry shortcake and whipped cream, for heaven's sake! Whipped cream! There's not a woman in this hotel who can afford to eat that. I guess the chef wants it all for himself. Or maybe we're being fattened for the slaughter." She stood up. "I'd like to be excused, please," she said thickly, and stalked out.

Mark felt a pang of pity. Something wrong there; too nervy and too tense. But she was still close enough to childhood to blush at her own gaucherie, and he liked that.

Joey watched her sister's departure with wide eyes. "A little bit of church wouldn't hurt that young lady," she observed. "Well, I'm not afraid of getting fat." She took her own portion of shortcake and Roberta's too, and licked off the cream like a kitten. Nobody told her not to.

After lunch Archie Peck sauntered over and offered to drive Mark down to town. "Franny's locked herself in her bedroom," he said. "She says she has a headache, but I know better. She's got something up her sleeve. She's fixing her face and she'll come wheedling out of there around four o'clock, looking ten years younger and begging for something." He stared at the sky. "Sundays are terrible. I never know what to do. I don't suppose you could fix it up with Wilcox to let me help? I found a Peon once, down in Mex; they'd given him up for dead and he was, too."

"I think Wilcox has all the help he needs," Mark said carefully. "But thanks."

Archie didn't seem surprised. "I didn't think you'd take me up on it. Just thought I'd offer anyway. I always liked old Cass. . . . What are you guys doing, by the way? That happened Friday, and here it is Sunday."

Mark told him they were doing all right. "We have to scrape the surface first, you know. Like raking a lawn before you plant the seed." He thought that would please Archie, and it did.

"Sure, sure," Archie said, openly delighted because he understood another man's shop talk. He stored the words away for future boasting. "Then you get down to bed rock and blow her up."

"Something like that," Mark answered. "I think I'll take you up on that drive. When are you leaving?"

"Right now. Come along. I had to go down anyway." He saluted Beacham and trotted off to the lot. "I picked up a bit of information from Hank and Cora," he confided. "They found a place where they got some good stuff." It was easy to see he wasn't talking about antiques. "They won't tell me where, but I'll track it down if it kills me. Don't tell Franny."

Two boys rushed to open the car doors. Archie was evidently a good tipper.

"What about a lift for Joey and Pee Wee?" Mark asked.

"Too early for them. They'll go down in the wagon." He beamed. "Old Pee Wee's in a bad spot. One of the kids in his class showed signs of mumps last night. His folks fed him a test pickle and it don't look so good. . . . Fine thing, Sunday school."

They wound down the mountain under a blazing sky. Bear River was deserted. The neat porches were empty, the shutters drawn together against the heat. The solitary traffic cop at Mountain Road and Main Street sat on a camp stool under a green umbrella and nodded.

"Fine time to rob a bank if a bank was open," Archie said. He stopped the car at Perley's gate. "Want me to pick you up later?" He sounded wistful.

"No thanks. Wilcox will drive me back."

He watched Archie drive slowly away, watched him drive even more slowly when a pretty girl in summer finery came out of one of the houses and walked jauntily toward Main Street. Archie, with his big diamond ring and his twelve dollar shirts, might whistle, but that's all he would do. Mark walked up the path.

Perley was in the converted woodshed that he called his den. It opened off the kitchen; it was cool and slightly damp, and reminiscent of kindling. Pansy was stacking Sunday school papers on the kitchen table and worrying about her hair. It was as straight as a poker, she said to Mark. The heat did that. That was the kind of hair she had, and why did it have to happen to her? Her sister's hair was lovely. But then her sister didn't have any children either, so you see things always even up. She straightened her hat, ran a nervous hand over her back buttons, and told Floyd she was ready and to come on.

"I give out the library books before class," she explained to Mark; "that's why I have to get there early. They get in fights over who's to get what. But I say it's all right to fight over a book. A good book."

She gave Perley a hasty kiss, told him not to worry but do his best, told Mark she missed him around the house but understood, and trotted out into the sunshine, followed by Floyd.

Perley settled back. "Now," he said with authority, "we'll get some work done. You'll want to hear about the telegrams. I read through about seventy, sent and received by the hotel people. Five or six by town people. Unless somebody used a code they're harmless."

"No code," Mark said absently. "At least I don't see why there should be. Get on with it. What kind were they?"

"Ordinary summer stuff the operator tells me. Outgoing: ladies who forgot their good white slip telling somebody to rush same; men who forgot to tell the office where they put the keys to the place, telling them where; girls like Roberta Beacham running out of nail polish. Incoming: answers to above and some requests to meet trains. Funny thing though. Miss Sheffield sent sixty words, day rate, to Louisville when her pet horse had a colt. And a lady here in town did the same thing when her daughter had a baby in Chicago. Put 'em side by side and you couldn't tell the difference. . . . They'll make you copies if you want 'em."

"No. What about long distance calls?"

"Business only. Men at the hotel ringing up their offices and brokers. Couple of girls here in town calling fellows at camps. What made you think of that angle, Mark?"

"I thought she might have had a wire or a call. Something urgent and personal that she kept to herself."

"Well, she didn't. Her name didn't turn up once. . . . You find out anything?"

"Everybody asks me that. I don't know. We've had a few exhibitions of temper and nerves, but that may be the weather. What about Amos?"

"Still at it. Not even a cigarette butt with rouge on it, he says. He was a little worried about Miss Sheffield and Mr. Kirby though. They were sneaking in and out the back roads all morning with a big bundle roped on their car. But he didn't think the outline was human."

"It was a cherry wood commode with a drawer full of illegal whiskey. . . . Perley, I wonder if I'm wrong to concentrate on the hotel?"

"No, you're right. You got to be right. Nobody in Bear River would harm Miss Cassidy. Not for any reason. You take that ring of hers now. I've heard people say somebody might have been tempted by that, tried to get it, and hit too hard. I don't believe it. You want to know why? No body. You can't hide a body in this weather. And there's other ladies with ten times that much jewelry. You take that little Mrs. Peck. She can sparkle like a frosty morning when she wants to. I've seen her driving around by herself, day and night, looking like a show window. And those little white beads Miss Sheffield wears around her neck. Pansy says they're pearls. No, it wasn't any robbery."

"What was it then?"

"Could she have walked off by herself and had a heart attack?"

"You've already answered that. We'd have found her. Try another."

"The only other I can think of is yours. The one you had first, about her going away on purpose, to scare somebody. I never did believe that. And we know she didn't take any clothes. That's all the angles except—"

"Except what?"

"Somebody killed her."

"The body, Perley, the body! And—why?"

"Why? Why? I don't know!" Perley cleared his throat, and Mark recognized the resulting mild rasp as the Wilcox snarl. "And I don't know why anybody'd shoot an old lady with an arrow and cut up a nice little girl's clothes, either!"

"That's the fascinating part," Mark said. "That part about the clothes. That's the part that gets me. Lovely hot afternoon, everybody out or asleep. Somebody breaks in with a pair of shears or a razor and wreck's a kid's wardrobe. Sparing, oddly enough, a choice item with field flowers on it and Irish lace insershom."

"Insertion," corrected Perley. "Insertion is dress trimming." He added hastily, "I happen to know that because Pansy keeps her sewing machine in the kitchen."

"Thank you," Mark said. "That's the kind of thing that broadens a man. . . . Got anything cold to drink?"

"Iced tea with lots of ice. Can you swallow that?"

"Yes."

Perley brought the tea and they drank in silence. Once Mark said, "I think I'll stop by Sunday school and pick up Joey. I can ride home with her in the wagon. Don't talk to me. I want to think." He closed his eyes and thought about Joey. He wondered if the blue silk banner, complete with gold stick, had changed hands.

Sunday school was nearly over. The occupants of the varnished chairs, set in circles, had recited a text in unison and rendered two songs. They had listened to a little talk by Mr. Walters. He'd looked over the shining heads out into the blue and green world beyond the windows and told them to fear not. They didn't know what he was talking about.

They had also listened to their individual lessons and been encouraged to ask questions. Some of the children did, but not Joey. Her eyes were on the banner, still standing proudly in Pee Wee's circle, and her mind was on the library book she was sitting on. It was *The Little Colonel's Knight Comes Riding*.

Somebody struck a bell and the end drew near. Two of the big boys collected the warm pennies and nickels. Everybody sang, "Dropping,

dropping, dropping, dropping, hear the pennies fall." Then Pansy Wilcox stood up, drew a deep breath, and read the attendance record of her class. The class stood up too. It was Joey's.

Joey had trouble keeping her hat on at this point; she felt impelled to twist her head around for gloating purposes, and the anchoring elastic under her chin had been chewed into a useless string. She righted the hat with a blow that made the field flowers quiver, and shot a triumphant look at Pee Wee. In Pee Wee's circle the mumps had left a gap like a lost tooth.

"And now," continued Pansy, "Joey Beacham will fetch the banner, please."

The word fetch, implying alacrity, was wasted. Joey had world enough and time, and while she didn't actually sit down and think which way to walk, that was the impression she managed to give. She approached the banner like a pilgrim advancing on a shrine, pausing for a prayer at each step. Her moving, silent lips formed the words, "Beatcha, beatcha." The pale young divinity student who shepherded Pee Wee's class found himself unable to meet that fixed stare and finally seized the banner himself and handed it over. Relief, like a soft wind, swept through the stuffy room. There hadn't been a fight.

Mark walked up the hill to the church and crossed the clover grass. The big birds had returned and were wheeling in the sky. When he came up to the church itself he moved quietly from window to window until he found one that gave him the picture he wanted. He looked in, unobserved.

The sing-song drone of prayers rose and fell like a swarm of bees. Joey, he was happy to note, was on her knees with the rest of the children, her head bowed over the seat she had recently vacated. Pansy sat with bowed head propped on a hand that was in turn propped on a hymn book. He saw the banner in its new position and rejoiced. His eyes returned to Joey, and he stifled a whistle.

What he had taken for devotion was exactly that, with a difference. She was not praying, she was chewing her hat elastic; her eyes were not closed, they were wide open, devouring the pages of a book iniquitously cradled in her arms. He stared intently and soon she began to twitch. Finally she turned around. He beckoned. She sent an appraising look over the still bowed heads and shoulders of her neighbors and fluttered across the room and out the door like thistledown. He didn't know she could do it.

"You weren't getting a thing out of that," he said mildly. "Aren't you ashamed?"

"No," she said. "The important part's over. The end doesn't count."

"That's what I thought," he said, easing his conscience. "Like grabbing your hat and beating it before the last curtain. It was too hot in there, anyway. Let's walk under the trees and talk."

"I don't care if I do," she said graciously. "Will you carry my hat? It itches."

He hung the hat over his arm, and they walked under the locusts. He planned to lead her gradually into a mood for confidences. He didn't like to do it, but it was his only hope. He asked her about the library book, and she was relieved because he didn't scold.

The library book was wonderful. It was going to have love in it, but what could you expect? The Little Colonel was getting old and this boy she was going to be in love with was an old friend from when they were kids. So it would be all right. She didn't mind at all. She'd followed the Little Colonel from childhood to girlhood, and now it was womanhood. The childhood was swell.

"I used to practice talking like her," she confided. "When nobody was around. Southern. You know, 'suh.' That's sir. She had a colored mammy and I wanted a colored mammy, but Mike said if I did I couldn't have Cassie too."

It was going to be easy, he told himself with relief.

"So?" he asked.

"So I kept Cassie." Her thin, scratched little legs missed a step, but only one. They walked on.

"Do you mind if I talk to you a little about Cassie?" he asked.

She didn't answer at once. Then, "She didn't run away!"

"I'm pretty sure of that myself." He took out a package of cigarettes. "Do you mind if I smoke?"

"Nope. . . . Then why did you tell Mike she did?"

"That's what I thought at first, but I've changed my mind. I think she was nice. That's why I want to talk to you about her. Everything you can tell me will help to bring her back again."

"She didn't run away. . . . Go ahead and ask me something."

"Did Cassie get many letters?"

"No, I guess she didn't. I mean I never saw her get any except from Mike. When he went away he wrote to Cassie the same as he wrote to Roberta and me."

"That's fine, Joey. That's just what I wanted to know. Now what about parties and things like that? Did she go out much? When you were in New York, for instance, did she go out calling in the evenings? To see friends?"

"She didn't like having friends. She said so. She said she'd seen enough people to last her the rest of her life." She chewed soberly on a thumbnail. "Sometimes she'd go out to hear music, but that's all."

"And when you came up here in the summers, didn't she go calling then? She might have liked the kind of friend she could make in Bear River, you know. I've seen some nice people down there."

"No. She didn't go anywhere. Except to the Pecks. We know the Pecks very well. They live near us in New York. No." Her eyes clouded. "No, she never went away before without telling me."

He insisted, gently. "Not even on a little vacation, by herself?"

"Not by herself. We always had vacations together. We went everywhere together. Except a couple of times, but they don't count. Sometimes when we were away she had to go back to New York. That was Mike's fault." She managed a wan grin. "Mike is a worrier. A couple of weeks ago he had to go to New York on business and he had a fight with the caretaker in our house there. So he wrote Cassie to come down and fire him and get another one. He was scared to do it himself. . . . Men!"

"We're terrible," he agreed. He swung the hat casually. "Did Cassie go?"

"Sure. When Mike hollered she always went. We took her to the station and she stayed two days. She got a good caretaker too, named Albert. And while she was there Mike made her balance his checkbook, She laughed like anything about that."

Mark laughed too, and they walked on. She accepted his sudden silence without comment. He looked down at the small, frowning face and saw that she was thinking. He hoped it was about the Little Colonel.

He wondered what had happened to that summons to Cassie. He remembered the letter about the caretaker, but it was nothing more than a complaint. It said nothing about a trip to town. There must have been a second letter. Destroyed? But why?

A faint and straggling Amen floated out of the windows behind them, hung briefly in the air, and drifted away.

Joey turned. "It's over," she said.

"Yes, it's over," he answered absently.

Almost at once she began to jump up and down. "Look, Mr. East, look! Boy oh boy, I bet they're mad as hops!"

He turned obediently. Floyd and Pee Wee, led by Mr. Walters, were heading for the well on the far side of the grounds. They carried a bucket, a chain, and a dipper. The chain dragged across the grass as slowly as their feet.

"Mr. Walters gave them a good talking to before Sunday school," Joey said with relish. "He said he hadn't realized what they'd done. Some old louse told him. But he took the money they made. Almost six dollars."

When Floyd and Pee Wee saw they had an audience, they immediately fell into a lockstep. They capered and grimaced and indicated by signs that their disgrace was only temporary. They beckoned generously, if furtively.

"Let's go over and see what happens," begged Joey. "Maybe somebody'll fall in. Or maybe they'll lose the bucket."

He took her hand and they moved out from under the trees into the glaring sun. The smell of the locust followed them.

After a few yards, Mark stopped. "Wait," he said. He put his hand on her shoulder. They stood where they were, watching.

Mr. Walters lifted the heavy wooden cover from the well. He held it high for an instant and dropped it with a clatter. They heard it strike the stone curbing. They also heard him shout.

Joey looked up into Mark's face. "W-what are they doing?" she quavered.

He put her quickly behind him. "W-what are they doing?" she repeated.

Mr. Walters and the boys were running away, back to the church, back to the security of living people, running away from the uncovered well. A shrill, exultant cry tore the air and two dark shapes rose from a tree and circled.

"Come along, kid," Mark said. He picked her up and walked away as fast as he dared. "They lost the bucket after all. They're coming back to get a pole or something. They're clumsy."

She buried her face in his neck. "You don't have to tell me," she wailed. "I know. . . . Cassie's in there."

Ten minutes later Archie Peck, idling along the church road, met a stream of frightened children; some were laughing shrilly, some were crying, and they flowed down the hill toward town as if a piper were playing.

He swung his car around and sped up the hill to the church grounds. Mark and Joey stood in the vestibule with two hysterical townswomen and the rest of the hotel children. The children had always been told to wait until the wagon called for them. Today the wagon was late and there was no place to send them. They huddled in a corner.

"Peck!" Mark took his arm. "Get these kids back to the hotel. You know what's happened?"

Archie didn't know. Mark drew him aside and told him.

Archie's fat cheeks quivered. "Where's Pee Wee?"

"He and Floyd ran down to get Wilcox. Don't worry about them. They're—perfect. You get these other kids home as fast as you can and bring Beacham back. Right away. Wilcox will round up his own men." He hesitated before adding, "Better play dumb up there. Let Wilcox do his own talking."

He herded the children out to the car and packed them in. He put Joey on the seat beside Archie. "Cheer up," he said heartily, dealing out indiscriminate pats and feeling like a helpless fool. Archie drove off.

The two townswomen, relieved of their responsibility, scuttled down the hill. He closed the door to the empty Sunday school room before he went out to the well.

The cover had been replaced. Pansy was there, and Mr. Walters. The man stood bareheaded, his hat on the grass beside him. He was fumbling through the pages of a pocket Bible and his hands shook. For the first time in his life the words he knew by heart refused to come to his lips. Pansy took the book from his lax fingers, found the place he wanted, and silently handed it back. Mr. Walters stared at the page and began to read, softly, under his breath. Prayers for the dead and comfort for the living. He read desperately, as if for his own sake.

"Go home, Pansy," Mark whispered. "You can't do anything here."

She looked up at the wheeling birds and placed her small hands firmly on the wooden cover. "Those buzzards," she said painfully. "They're awful strong."

"I'm strong too," he said. "Go home and wait for us. We'll be back."

She gave him a long look and turned to go away. He went with her as far as the church porch, where she collected her fan and Sunday school paper, and watched her start down the hill. He knew he would remember for a long time how her hands had looked in their carefully mended cotton gloves. There were two cars coming up in a cloud of dust. Perley. There was a third car, still far away, like a toy. He stood and waited.

Perley, Amos Partridge, Dr. Cummings, and two deputies got out of the first two cars. They carried grappling hooks and chains. Amos had providentially turned up at Perley's house with his negative report just as Floyd and Pee Wee had hurled themselves panting up the path. Mark indicated the third car. "We'll wait," he said.

A few minutes later Beacham and Peck drew up. "Follow me," Mark said, and he led them back to the well. Mr. Walters had kept his vigil; they sent him away, although he protested. When he was safely out of sight the deputies kicked the useless well chain aside and laid out their own equipment. Dr. Cummings stepped forward as Perley raised the wooden cover.

Mary Cassidy had never reached the water. She hung, head down, on a long hook set in the side wall and used as a step by the man who periodically climbed down to fish out dead leaves. The hook had caught her leather belt and held her. She weighed only a hundred and ten pounds.

When they brought her up, the hat with the little white birds was still securely fastened to her black hair. There was an arrow in her throat.

Mark took Beacham's arm and led him away.

CHAPTER FOUR

M ARK, Perley, and Beacham sat around the big table in the living room of the Beacham cottage. There was only one lamp burning because of the heat and the moths, but a few moths found their way in none the less. They were alive when they crept under the lampshade and dead when they dropped to the table.

Amos Partridge sat in the shadows beyond the ring of light, turning his battered panama over and over in his hands. He looked beyond the table, out into the summer night where a yellow moon hung over the trees.

There were no sounds out there. Even the crickets were hushed. It was eleven o'clock. A light wind, sweet with pine, came through the open windows and shook the curtains gently. They felt it move across the room. Then it was gone.

Amos shivered. "Well?" he asked. "Well, what now?"

Beacham, haggard in the lamplight, turned to Perley. "Why can't I have her? Why can't I take her to New York tonight?"

"Because," Perley said wearily, "because there aren't any trains this late. That's one reason."

"I can drive to Albany and get a train there! I can drive all the way if it comes to that! Give me the name of the man to see and I'll fix him. She's got to be buried. She—she's waited—she's waited—"

Perley sent Mark a pleading look. "You try," he said hopelessly.

Mark spoke flatly. "You can't have her now because it's against the law. Cummings has to do an autopsy. He can't do it until tomorrow. After that, I don't know. But I can tell you plainly that there's no man to see and nobody to fix. You're not bargaining for an oil concession this time. . . . People feel sorry for you now, Beacham, but if you keep this up they'll begin to feel something else."

Beacham muttered, "I can't help it."

"Yes you can," Mark said. "The kids are behaving better than you are." He was thinking of a closed door down the hall, a door from which no sound had come for more than an hour. "Wilcox and I need your help, and all you give us is a bad imitation of Franny Peck."

64

Franny had been put to bed with sleeping pills, cold compresses, and stern hands. The hands were Cora Sheffield's, and they could slap. Out of all the eager, tearful women who had beat a path to the cottage with offers of help, only Cora had kept her head. She'd met them at the entrance gate when they came, trailing red lace in the dust and swearing under her breath; she'd led Beacham away for a stiff drink in her own room and was now sitting in the dark, behind that closed door, her malevolent eyes moving from the beds to the windows. She'd boasted that she could hear a pine needle fall. She was waiting for that now, or something else.

Beacham struck the table with his fist. "What do you want me to do? What do you expect me to say? Put yourselves in my position if you can. I wasn't even here when this thing happened. Cassie looked to me for protection, the way my girls do, and I wasn't here to give it. Can't you see how I feel about that? I owe—I owe her something. If I could give her a quick and decent burial I'd—I'd feel better."

"I know," Mark said. "But you'll have to wait. I'm sorry. And don't blame yourself too much. I don't think you could have—prevented this."

"Maybe not," Beacham said savagely. "But it seems to me that you could have. You and Wilcox. The whole thing reeks of negligence! Maybe not in your case because you came here in a private capacity, but Wilcox is a sheriff. How do you think it's going to sound when I tell the newspaper boys that the sheriff was sitting under a tree when a woman was murdered a few yards away? And that it took him two days to find her? And by heaven, he didn't even find her then! That took two kids and a country preacher!"

"You won't say anything to the newspapers. You've already called them off. They'll print only what they have to, all personal angles out. Even the tabloids. You're pretty influential, aren't you?"

"I had to do something," Beacham mumbled. "I don't want Joey and Roberta reading a lot of—a lot of—"

"I don't blame you. I'd feel the same way. . . . But why are you so certain she was killed on the church grounds? Wilcox and I aren't. It's true that we found some blood over by the cemetery wall, but we thought that was Miss Rayner's. We still think so, but unfortunately it's too late for analysis now."

"Why didn't you have it analyzed at once? Isn't that negligence?"

"No reason for it. We didn't even know she'd disappeared. We didn't know that until hours later and even then there was no thought of murder. She was just gone, that's all, and we figured she was old enough to know what she was doing. And what's more, there never has been any reason for believing she was killed where she was found. That could have happened anywhere, in town, in Crestwood or Baldwin, even here in the Mountain House. It was beginning to grow dark when she was last seen. And it was hot. It was a nice night for a drive. She could have gone for a drive with an old friend. See?"

"I don't believe it!"

"I'm not sold on it myself, but it could have happened that way. He could have driven her back later, sitting stiffly beside him in the front seat, maybe with her head on his shoulder. After midnight, when the citizens were safe in bed."

Beacham winced.

"Don't like the picture, do you? Well, we'll paint another one, with a background of white church, paper lanterns, kids, and music. And a detective and a sheriff under a locust tree. You know what those grounds are like at night? Dark with trees. There were crowds of people moving about, too; happy people, having fun. There was plenty of noise over by the archery set, and beyond that a bunch of children were playing Drop the Handkerchief. Squealing and falling down—you know the way they do. It was a perfect and normal set-ting. So—what's wrong with an invitation to a little walk? Down by the well where it's cool and quiet and where it's also dark? Your Cassie wouldn't think about the dark because she knew every step of the way. . . . That arrow—in strong hands it couldn't miss and there wouldn't be a sound."

Beacham put his hands on the table. "What do you want to know? What do you think I can tell you?"

"You heard us interview the people here tonight. Every one of them saw Miss Cassidy at the supper and talked to her. They all told us the same thing—nothing. Some of them are casual hotel acquaintances, some are old friends of yours, like the Pecks. I'd like to know if any one of the latter was also an old friend of Miss Cassidy's. You know what I mean."

"No!"

"Is any one of them a good liar?"

"No."

"All right. Tomorrow Wilcox and Partridge are going to talk to every man, woman, and child who was at the church that night. I expect we'll hear the same thing from them, nothing. But with a little luck we may turn up one slight discrepancy. That's all we need. One small piece of unnecessary information, dragged in and emphasized. The guilty guy always does that. He thinks it makes him sound natural."

Beacham was a listener now, not a heckler, and Perley's confidence returned. He took over with a no nonsense look.

"Do you think Mr. Peck was telling the truth about what he did around that time? I mean, is he the kind of man who'd leave his wife and friends and go off by himself to get——?" He paused delicately.

"I can vouch for Peck," Amos said unexpectedly. "As near as we can figure the time, he was doing just what he said he was. He came over to Crestwood looking for a bottle. I told him where to get it."

"He's a fool!" Beacham's anger returned. "He should have stayed with those women. He knows as well as I do that Kirby's worse than useless."

"Useless in the face of what?" Mark asked.

"Anything. Everything. Emergencies." Beacham's fist struck the table again. "Talk, talk, talk. We're not getting anywhere! If I ran my business like this I'd be ruined. Why in God's name didn't you people look in the well when you searched the grounds that night? There it was, out in plain sight, screaming at you!"

"It was not in plain sight," Mark corrected. "Even in daylight you had to know where to look. I knew there was a well somewhere on the place, but I didn't see it. And I admit I didn't give it a thought. That was wrong, I know now, but I had a good reason for thinking that way. I was sure nobody had gone near it after dark."

He told about the lemonade stand. "It was seven o'clock when those kids decided that well water was unfair competition. They drew up the bucket and chain, confiscated the dipper, and hid the entire lot in the church cellar. Floyd says a few thirsty farmers tramped around the place in a frenzy, but in no time at all the lemonade stand had all the business. The well was shunned like a plague."

"You see?" Perley took it up. "When the word got around, folks didn't bother to go there. That made it— safe."

"Can't you narrow it down?" Beacham asked.

"There were two hundred people there by actual count," Mark said. "And they all knew what the boys had done. All except Mr. Walters." He sent Perley a thoughtful look and made a small, arresting gesture. Perley, his mouth open to speak, sat back and said nothing. Amos, deep in the shadows, rocked in his chair like an old woman. The silence continued, and Beacham looked from one face to the other.

"Is—is it the same arrow that struck Miss Rayner?" he asked finally.

Mark answered. "It must be. There were only six and this one rounds out the set. It's a good set, or was. You bought it, didn't you?"

"Yes. . . . Fingerprints! You're testing for prints, aren't you?"

"We will, but there won't be any. I saw that myself. Not even Miss Rayner's. She says she didn't touch it and didn't even see it. She heard it and she certainly felt it. She seems to think it was on a string."

The color came back to Beacham's face. "Does she expect anybody to believe that?"

"Why not? I think it sounds swell." Mark looked at his watch and yawned. "Now I think we'll call it a night, but before the sheriff and Mr. Partridge leave I want to give you all a time-table. It's the best I could do and I think it's fairly accurate." He consulted a notebook. "At eight, or thereabouts, Miss Cassidy left the supper table and told the Pecks, Miss Sheffield, and Mr. Kirby that she was going to look for Joey. Joey saw her over at the archery game. So did Roberta, Nick Sutton, Miss Rayner, Mrs. Briggs, and a town couple named Moresby, relatives of Mrs. Wilcox. Mr. Moresby remembers distinctly because Mrs. Moresby called his attention to Miss Cassidy's ring and regretted the day she gave up a good teaching job to get married. Small talk. . . . That was the last time Miss Cassidy was admittedly seen.

"The Peck party left the table when Miss Cassidy did. They crawled over the cemetery wall and read names on tombstones while it was still light enough to see. Then they went home, all except Peck, and Partridge clears him. That was approximately eight-thirty. Somewhere around eight-forty-five Nick Sutton got Maisie Briggs. A few minutes before nine the sixth arrow was missed. At nine-fifteen, which is as close as I can get it, Miss Rayner was struck. She dragged herself to the church, where she hoped to find help without adding to the general confusion. By that time the Briggs fiasco had frayed a few nerves, and people began to leave. Roberta went back to the Sunday school room to collect a hamper and found Miss Rayner. Roberta and Nick alibi each other, and the same thing holds for the Peck crowd.

"Now we come to the first hurdle. Why was Miss Rayner shot? Did somebody steal the arrow with that in mind? Or was he crouching in the dark, playfully waiting for the first person who came along? You don't have to raise your hand, Amos. Speak up."

"Whoever done it didn't know he was going to do it," Amos said flatly. "He swiped the arrow when Nick dropped it because he's the kind of fellow who swipes on sight. It was Maisie Briggs that started him off. He got the idea about shooting when he saw Maisie laying there. He got the idea from seeing blood."

"But in spite of her mother's efforts, Maisie wasn't a bleeder."

"He got the idea from Maisie anyway. Then, when he saw Miss Rayner snooping around with that look on her face, he followed her in the dark and stabbed her for the hell of it. Rayner bled good, didn't she?"

"Very good."

"Well, you see? That set him off. He sees Miss Cassidy, walking along by herself to the church. There's a whatnot in the basement. So he waits till she comes to a good dark place, and there you are. No noise. Soft grass to fall on. Maybe she didn't even fall. He carries her over to the well, or maybe drags her. Nice and dark all the way. He drops her down." He looked at Beacham and then at Mark. "I'd like to call your attention to one peculiar thing," he said formally. "Both of the ladies in the case was unmarried. It might mean something." He stood up. "Goodnight. I've had a hard day." He gave Beacham a cold, accusing stare.

He left with Perley, studiously ignoring Beacham's outstretched hand.

"Is he crazy?" Beacham asked.

"No," Mark said. "Better send Miss Sheffield away now. I'll take over in there."

"I feel as if I ought to do that," Beacham said, "but I'm all in."

"It's all right. But get the lady out before I stroll through."

Cora Sheffield came out when Beacham knocked, blinked at the light, said nobody owed her any thanks, and swore she'd do as much for a horse.

When she left, Mark stretched out on the bed in Roberta's room. He was determined to stay awake, but in spite of himself his eyes closed, and he slept for half an hour. He woke at three o'clock when something struck the window screen a soft blow. When he went out to investigate his knees were shaking, and he shivered in the chill night air. It was the hour when the cold crept down from the dark, shrouded peaks. The moon was high and white. Cassie's puppy came out of his small kennel, stared fixedly at a patch of shadow, and whined. Mark picked it up and returned it to the kennel although he didn't want to. He walked over to the patch of shadow, but there was nothing hidden there. Nothing that he could see. He told himself that a bat had flown against the screen.

He had turned to re-enter the cottage when a light flashed in one of the hotel windows. It stayed on for the count of ten, long enough for him to check the location. A small window, under the roof, second from the front end.

The puppy whined again and he took it indoors with him. It was what he'd wanted to do all along. He looked in at the three occupied beds before he pulled a chair up to his own window. He sat there until dawn, with the puppy in his lap. Then he went to bed.

It was nine when he woke. Someone had taken the alarm clock from the room and drawn the shades. It was a thoughtful gesture but one that he didn't appreciate. He'd planned to breakfast with Perley at eight.

Beacham was in the bathtub; he called apologies through the door and told Mark to bathe at the hotel. Cora Sheffield, he said, would be happy to provide facilities. Mark declined, shrugged into fresh clothing, put his razor in his pocket, and went out to get Beacham's car, also provided.

Joey was under the trees with the puppy. She had darkened his room, she said proudly, and hidden the old alarm clock. A person had to have sleep. He thanked her and inquired after Roberta. Roberta was over at the hotel with Nick.

"Nick came over to get her," she said. "Old man Sutton had a fit or something last night. But he won't die. He never does."

"Old man Sutton doesn't have a room up under the roof, does he?"

"Under the roof!" She sat back on her heels, scandalized. "I should say not! He's got three rooms on the second floor, the biggest in the whole place. One for him to sleep in, one for him to sit in, and one for Nick. And a bath." She was being very chatty and slightly arrogant, and he knew why. The Spartan boy again. "Only servants sleep under the roof," she said loftily. "You ought to know that."

"Well I didn't know, and I thank you. I'm going down to town. Want anything?"

"No, thank you. I've got everything. . . . You're coming back, aren't you?"

"On the wings of a dove." He went over to the parking lot, found Beacham's car, and drove off.

That would be George's room under the roof, he decided. George, called suddenly in the middle of the night, would turn on his light just long enough to find his clothes before he hurried down to his employer. Sutton's rooms were probably on the other side.

The sun boiled down, and the wind that made him shiver in the night now burned like a blast from an oven. Dust filled his eyes and mouth.

It was washday in Bear River and every backyard boasted of some woman's industry. There was something decent and cheering in the flapping lines of sheets and shirts. Something enviable too. He watched with pleasure as a woman eased a laden basket through her kitchen door and let the screen close gently against her comfortable bottom. She set her basket on the brick walk and soaked it with a garden hose. The water gushed and foamed through the wicker sides. He restrained an impulse to throw himself at her feet and drove on.

Pansy was up to her elbows in suds when he walked into her kitchen, howling for a bath. She was full of apologies. It might be hot and then again it mightn't. If he didn't mind waiting she could put some kettles on. He didn't care if it was hot or cold. He only wanted to be wet, immediately and all over.

She was full of questions as she laid out the lumpy bath towels and straightened the damp mat. How were they taking it up there? Perley hadn't had time to tell her a thing. He'd gone out at sunup. How were those poor children and their father?

"But there," she said, whisking at a dead fly, "you don't have to tell me that. I know. They're broken-hearted, I know."

He said she was probably right. "Could you give me some breakfast, Pansy? In about fifteen minutes? I'm starving."

Breakfast! She was out of the room before she had finished the word. He heard her talking to herself all the way downstairs. Breakfast! Sending a man out in all this heat without a couple of eggs. Even death was no excuse for that. Even murder. What's the use of having a million dollars if you haven't got a heart to go with it!

He ran the water into the tub and forgot to look at the rust. Pansy's emphasis on hearts had started him thinking. There was no doubt about Joey's; it was broken all right. But he wouldn't bet on the state of Beacham's and Roberta's. When Cassie was first reported missing Beacham had been genuinely upset, but there was no indication that he thought it was a tragedy. He'd acted like a man whose wife had justifiably threatened to leave him if he didn't stop what he was doing, and he hadn't stopped and she'd gone. Now that he knew she was dead he was sullen and quarrelsome, but there was no apparent damage to his heart. That might be his own particular style of grieving. Everybody had one.

He considered Roberta. She'd run a fine emotional gamut in the last few days. She'd been tender with Miss Rayner over the arrow business and decidedly snappish over the drive with Nick; she'd been angry and almost hysterical about the destruction of Joey's clothes. Cassie's disappearance had frightened her, but it was a childish fright, and she had shown less poise than Joey. Then she had suddenly changed.

He remembered how she had looked when he described Cassie's dead body. She'd insisted on details and listened with a calm and almost clinical detachment. Then she had gone to bed, brushing Cora Sheffield aside, and she had slept. Joey hadn't slept, he knew that, but Roberta had. And now she was off with Nick, pampering old man Sutton and ignoring her own family. Eighteen years old, the never-give-yourself-away generation.

He reached for the soap, lost it, and grinned because that reminded him of something. Lost. That's what they used to call his generation. Lost. Running away like rapids, somebody had said. All right, he told himself, run. He pulled out the plug and reached for a towel. He knew what he was going to do next. He was going over to Crestwood and talk to Bessy and Beulah. Their generation was called the Age of Innocence and what they didn't know you could put in your eye.

He ate his breakfast to the gurgling accompaniment of two rinsings and a bluing and went on his way.

Beulah was cutting sweetpeas, not because she wanted them, but because there were too many. Bessy sat under the peach tree, knitting a pink afghan for somebody's baby, she didn't know whose.

"We always have a great many in the fall," she said. "And now here you are, bringing death again."

He declined refreshment on the grounds of three prevailing fried eggs and at once asked Beulah to name her favorite suspect. He knew she had one and he also knew he could eliminate her choice with perfect safety. She never failed him that way. He expected her to say George, who was Sutton's valet, simply because George was the one person he hadn't interviewed, but she fooled him.

"Franny Peck," she said promptly.

He laughed because she was leering. "Why?" he managed to ask.

"I feel it. You know how I am when I feel things, Mark. She was walking around in that cemetery until dark, wasn't she? Is that normal?"

"Beulah! She was with her husband and two other people."

"In cahoots."

"And they left the place before anything happened. That's practically proved. I don't know why I bother with you." He waited for her to toss her head and she did. "Have you got a down on Franny?"

"I don't like kitten women. . . . What do you make of Cora Sheffield?"

"That's no kitten woman. I like Cora."

"All right, but watch her. She's man crazy, and Beacham's a handsome devil with a lot of money. Why couldn't she throw Miss Cassidy down a well to clear the deck?"

"Just to save my sanity, I'll admit it's temperamentally possible. But we're pretty sure Cora left the party at eight-thirty, while all six arrows were hitting legitimate targets. And, for the record, Miss Cassidy didn't die because she was thrown down the well. She never reached the water. She bled to death."

"We know," Bessy said. "Ella May told us. Head down and with her hat on." She carefully folded the afghan. "I wonder what she thought about?"

He watched her plump hands patting the pink wool into shape, and felt a little sick. He'd been thinking of Cassie as he'd first seen her, still and dead, even mercifully dead; and now, because of Bessy's words, he saw another picture. He tried to blot it out, but it stayed. He closed his eyes to the bright sunlight. What had she been thinking about? What were the thoughts that flooded her tortured mind before they slowly ebbed? He hoped it hadn't been long.

"I—," his voice wavered and he cleared his throat furiously, "I wonder if a woman could have done that? I've been thinking it had to be a man."

Beulah was watching him. "Don't worry," she said quietly. "You'll find out. Go on home, Bessy. You bore me stiff."

Bessy rose obediently and trotted off. "I have something to do anyway," she said, "so I don't consider this a dismissal."

"She's not all there," Beulah said. "Of course she's my oldest and dearest friend, but sometimes I think the wrong people get killed. . . . Mark, can't you find out who that poor soul was talking to between those times? I mean between the time she was seen at the target and the time you think it happened?"

"We don't know when it happened. I've interviewed the hotel people who were there, and they say they didn't see her after the Briggs affair. Perley's talking to the others now. We may even find that she left the grounds and was killed miles away. Brought back later. Amos is looking into that. Some farmer may have seen something, or some kid parked by the road, but I'm not counting on it. The mind that planned this won't give itself away. It's vicious and depraved and it wears a false face. We'll trap him, and rip it off."

She didn't say anything and he went on. "Beulah, do something for me, will you?"

"Money?"

"No! Take me down to Bittner's. I want to talk to him and I don't think he'll let me in without a convoy."

She looked startled. "Why Bittner? He hasn't been out of a wheel chair for years."

"He has a pair of binoculars and he uses them day and night."

"Oh." She stood up and shook out her skirts. "Leave it to me to get you in. Come on."

Mark was right about his welcome. Ella May stood firmly between her spouse and intrusion.

"He says you can't come in," she said with enjoyment. "He says he wants to wake up alive tomorrow. He says whenever you come around here somebody gets killed. He says this time it ain't going to be him. He says," she curled her thin lips, "he says you said Folly Number Three had a bad smell. The driver heard you, so don't deny it. He says if you want to know something that really smells—"

"Ella May!" Beulah seized her neighbor by one sharp elbow and lowered her voice. "Did you hear what the doctor found?" She paused, and let this sink in. The light changed in Ella May's small eyes.

"What?" she whispered. Mark edged closer to the door.

"Oh, go on back to the kitchen," Ella May said. "The old fool won't bite you!"

He left them with their heads together. The doctor's report hadn't come in, but Beulah had a fine, confusing vocabulary.

Bittner sat at his kitchen window, his binoculars trained on two small boys sitting in a ditch beside the road. They were sitting because they were tired, but Bittner had another interpretation. He looked like an overturned beetle.

"This is what I get for leaving the front of the house," he said when Mark entered. "Is my wife lying in a pool of blood by the door?" His pale eyes raked his caller from head to foot. "Sit down. I was only fooling. Sit closer. You're too far away."

Mark moved his chair forward an inch and opened fire with the first thing that came into his head. "Did you see Peck anywhere around here last night?"

Bittner's eyes lighted up like Ella May's. "Who says he was here?"

"He does, but I need proof. If you won't tell me I'll take you to court."

Bittner had been to court many times and each time it had cost him money. "Of course I'll tell you. You're a very spirited young fellow and I like that. . . . When does he say he was around?"

Mark told him.

"Well, he was. He went into Partridge's, but he only stayed a few minutes. You didn't ask me this but I'll tell you anyway—he was alone, too. When he came and when he left. All alone."

"Thanks." He gave Bittner a gratified look. "Did you happen to see anybody else?"

"Plenty of people. Trains full, busses full, some on foot. I didn't see the Cassidy woman, if that's what you're driving at. I didn't see her and I don't know her."

Mark asked his next question carefully. "If you had known her, Mr. Bittner, and she had been on one of the busses or one of the trains, would you have seen her?"

Bittner patted the binoculars. "Government's been trying to get these away from me. Wants to buy them. Yes, I'd have seen her."

Mark started to describe her clothing, and Bittner stopped him with a fat white hand. "Save your breath, my dear boy. Ella May told me what she was wearing. And I tell you she didn't pass this way up to midnight. The last bus went through then and I went to bed. And you can forget about the trains. Last train from Bear River went through at eight, and she was alive then. Ella May says so. . . . Here, take these glasses and tell me what those boys are doing out there."

Mark took them. "Sitting," he said. He handled the binoculars lovingly. "Do you ever rent these to responsible people?"

"I don't know any." Bittner gave one wheel of his chair a quick spin which brought his bloated face too close. "Do you know anything that hasn't been—brought out?"

Mark tried not to recoil. "No," he said evenly.

"Too bad. I hoped, I hoped there might be a little something. You know what I mean. A little something that the papers wouldn't print. I thought you'd tell me."

"I haven't anything to tell." Then to his horror he heard himself adding, "I mean I haven't anything yet."

Bittner sighed, and drummed on the arm of his chair.

"I'm a shut-in," he said huskily. "I have to depend on my wife for everything. It's hard. I haven't talked to a man for years, except drivers.

I'd give almost anything for a good man-to-man talk." He gave his guest an oblique look.

"There's Partridge next door," Mark said. He tried not to look at those fat, drumming fingers. He wanted to crack down on them with a board.

Bittner ignored Partridge. He put out a hand and touched Mark's knee. "You'll come in and tell me things from time to time, won't you? You can trust me. No matter what you hear, you can trust me. You don't know how hard it is, depending on a woman. They don't—hear things."

Mark moved easily out of reach. "I hear a good bit," he said diffidently. He knew then that he was going to bargain with this monstrosity, but on his own terms. Bittner's house stood on the direct traffic route to Baldwin. Every conveyance to and from Bear River to Baldwin passed the windows. And Baldwin was important. That was where the branch line trains and the busses met the Montreal-New York Express.

If he couldn't get the binoculars for himself he could at least inveigle Bittner into using them for him. And he'd wash out his mouth with soap when he got home. He walked over to the window.

"That wasn't a very cordial message you sent to the door when I came," he said.

Bittner showed his bad teeth. "I told Ella May that to make her happy. She's jealous." He gurgled. "I was going to call you back if you went away. . . . What are you looking at? Here, give me back those glasses!"

Mark handed them over. "I wasn't looking at anything. I was thinking. You know, maybe you can do me a favor. A big one. And in return I promise to keep you posted on—things."

The chair rolled over to the window with inhuman eagerness. "What can I do? A poor old fellow like me. What can I do?"

"You can watch the road traffic as you never watched it before. Watch it as if your own life depended on it." He thought this was a good touch, and it was. It had results beyond his wildest hopes. Bittner backed away.

"Not my life," he boasted without confidence.

"Yours, mine, everybody's." He didn't believe this, but if a little exaggeration could put a yard or so between him and his new friend then more of the same would be even better. "We're all targets now," he added.

"Get re-enforcements! That's what you need. Re-enforcements!"

"Now now. We're not ready for that yet. For a day or so I think we can handle this ourselves." He gently stressed the word we.

Bittner's vanity fought its way to the surface and announced its return with a smirk. "Maybe," he said. "Maybe we can. But you'll have to confide in me. You mustn't hold anything back."

"I won't. Now this is what I want you to do. You know all the regulars who travel back and forth by bus, don't you?"

"Do I! I even know the ones who walk on the dark side of the road and think nobody sees 'em. I could tell you things if you were a true friend."

"Don't," Mark said hastily. "I mean not now. You can save all the little tidbits for the next time I call." On the phone, he said under his breath. "This is what I want you to check on." He pointed north, toward Baldwin. "Every traveler from Crestwood or Bear River to Baldwin must pass along this road. Right?"

"Right. Everybody knows that. But there's nothing in Baldwin. I don't know why people go."

"Sure you do. The train terminal. The big works. The link with the outside world. All the Mountain House guests, no matter where they came from, had to go to Baldwin first, then transfer to the branch line. They'll do the same thing when they leave. I want you to keep a list of all Mountain House people who travel to Baldwin, from today on. That goes for employees too."

"Why? I want to know why."

"Listen. Suppose somebody up at the hotel wanted to get to Montreal or New York without calling attention to that fact. Suppose he wanted to go in a hurry, without luggage. How could he do it? Well, he could stroll into the station at Bear River, no hat, everyday clothes, pockets full of money, and hop the branch line train or a bus. He could tell everybody in sight that he was going up the line to look at a likely hound or a promising stream. He might even carry fishing tackle. Catch on?"

Bittner's eyes paid tribute. "You could be my own brother," he said. "Think somebody's going to run away?"

"If and when I begin to get warm, I think somebody may try it. And Baldwin is the only way out. The only quick way. So you see why I want the road covered. When somebody takes a sudden and casual jaunt north, I want to know about it. I can't do anything at my end, short of forbidding people to leave the grounds, and I've no authority for that. And I don't want to ask the Bear River ticket agent to keep tabs. He has too much to do already and he'd probably go hog wild and turn in some honest farm hand out to get drunk. Also, he may not be discreet. You," he paused, "are."

Bittner acknowledged this with a lowering of eyelids. They were lashless.

"Hmm," he said. "Automobiles too?"

"Those too. It's a thin possibility, not many people have the gas, but I want it covered. You know all the ordinary riders, the regulars. Don't bother with them. Forget all about the women who go to mama's every Thursday afternoon and the men who ride up to Lodge meetings every week. I want the unusual passenger, the one who's going to Baldwin for the first, or even the second, time. What's the time-table on the Express?"

Bittner spat the words like venom. "Summer schedule: Montreal to New York. Stops at Baldwin at ten a.m. and seven p.m. New York to Montreal stops at six a.m. and nine p.m. Fixed it that way for the swells at the army camp. Generals. They ask the generals what time they want the trains to run and then they run 'em that way."

"But you're up and around at those hours, aren't you? You'll be able to watch the road?"

A warm glow suffused Bittner's features and he lowered his head like a coy child. "I may not be up but I'm always around. I don't go to bed. I do this." He brought one hand down on a lever and the chair instantly flattened into a bed. "Like it?"

"It's—amazing."

Bittner struck the lever again, petulantly. "It is. You've no idea. . . . Now what do I do when I want to get in touch with you?"

"Call me at the Mountain House. If I'm not there call Wilcox. Keep after us." He looked at his watch. "All this has been very interesting and I'm sure I'm going to be grateful. But I've got to get hold of Wilcox."

Bittner's chair flew over to block the door, nicking the table en route. "No," he said. "No!" He backed hastily away from Mark's look. "But you haven't told me when you're coming back!"

"I can't be definite. I'll give you a ring." He edged by the chair. Bittner's hand shot out and held him fast. "You didn't say anything about the autopsy," he whispered. "You didn't tell me what they—found."

"I haven't heard myself. So long, I'll see you later." He got the door open, closed it behind him, and ran out into the sun.

Beulah was talking to Ella May on the front porch. "Come on," he said, "I'm late. Thank you, Mrs. Bittner." He took Beulah's gaunt arm and held it tightly as they walked up the lane. "You're a beautiful woman, Beulah," he said.

"What's the matter with you?"

"Nothing . . . What did you tell Mrs. B.?"

"I made up an autopsy report. She loves them."

He didn't answer at once because he couldn't. "So does he," he said finally.

"I know. He gives little boys ten cents for dead cats and dogs and then he cuts them up. To see what they died of, he says. . . . Mark, are you sick?"

"Not yet," he said.

He refused lunch and drove back to Bear River, and even though he looked straight ahead when he swung out of Crestwood he could feel the augmented eyes of his late host following him.

At the Bear River railway station he introduced himself to the sweating little man behind the ticket window. He needn't have troubled. The man was Maisie Briggs's father, and he said he'd had Mr. East on his mind for several days.

"I was coming up to call," he said. "This very evening I was coming up to call on business. My sister's boy was going to drive me." He removed his sleeve garters, rolled down his cuffs and buttoned them, and immediately became a man who says "See here!" instead of "Where to?"

Mark's modest hunt for information went into temporary eclipse before Mr. Briggs's chirping onslaught.

"I want to engage your services," Mr. Briggs said. "I don't care about the money and I'm willing to pay ten dollars. I want you to find out who shot my daughter."

Mark replied soberly. "But there's no mystery about that, Mr. Briggs. It was an accident, and young Sutton apologized."

"I know he did and I don't hold anything against the boy. But it was no accident. He says somebody pushed his arm and I believe him. Somebody pushed that innocent lad's arm with the devilish intention of causing confusion, under the cover of which he could appropriate an arrow for his further nefarious purposes. Using my Maisie for bait!" The first part of his speech tripped off his tongue with the fluency that comes from paper work and rehearsal, but the last line catapulted from his heart. He removed his green eyeshade and gave Mark an unimpeded glare. "Using my Maisie for bait!"

Mark was plainly impressed. "That's an idea, Mr. Briggs. Thank you for calling my attention to it."

"Happy to oblige. You find out who was standing next to Nick Sutton that night and you'll apprehend the monster. For monster he is. Concealing that arrow on his person and mingling with innocent women and children, waiting for a chance to strike. Do you want the ten now?"

"No, no. I don't want it at all. Mr. Beacham is retaining me, and that covers everything. Thanks, though." He gave little Mr. Briggs a friendly smile. "You know you may have something there. I don't suppose you were anywhere near Sutton yourself?"

"Me?" Briggs returned the smile with wan gravity. "You forget I'm a railroad man. Fridays I'm here until eleven. It takes me that long to clear things up. Last Friday I left this office tired but content. I dragged myself through the sleeping streets, turned a corner, and met tragedy. There was my house, lit from top to bottom. A 'death,' I said to myself. I had to sit on the curbing."

Mark waited a suitable interval. "No strangers hanging around the station?"

"No strangers," Mr. Briggs insisted. Of course, he said, there was always a crowd for the Mountain House on Fridays. New people. But he never paid them any mind. The Mountain House auto collected them as soon as they got off the train. When and if it was on time. He never saw them himself except sometimes when they bought a return ticket. Half the time the Mountain House porter did that. A helpless, wasteful lot.

The conversation had made a full swing and come back to the place where Mark had hoped to start it. He held it there.

"Miss Cassidy always bought her own tickets, didn't she?"

"When she traveled, she did. Capable lady, she was, like one of ourselves, with her own way to make, not born with a spoon in her mouth."

"I'm glad to hear that," Mark said. "You're helping me enormously. When's the last time she took a train out, do you remember? I'm just checking, you know. Routine."

"Being a devotee of crime literature," Mr. Briggs said modestly, "I understand perfectly." He covered the lower part of his face with an inky hand and stared upward. "Let me s-e-e-e. I got it! Two weeks ago or a little more. I can't come closer than that. No record. Say two weeks."

"New York?"

Admiration glowed in Mr. Briggs's eyes. "You've hit it. Took the nine a.m. branch line to Baldwin, connecting with the ten a.m. Express." He visibly swallowed the questions he wanted to ask.

"That's an awkward business, going north for a southbound train. Can't you get it any other way?"

"No sir, you cannot. Unless you drive to Albany, and nobody ever does. These summer folks seem to enjoy the inconvenience. Peculiar. Even Miss Cassidy now, she was laughing about it. She was saying that every time she took a train in or out of this place she felt like a chicken with its head cut off. . . . Almost was, too, or so I hear." He looked expectant.

Mark drove steadily on. "Was she alone when she left the last time?"

"Oh no. The Beacham young ladies came down with her. And Mrs. Archie Peck. The young Beachams went back to the hotel, but Mrs. Peck rode as far as Baldwin to get some special brand of cigarette. I happened to overhear. She came back on a bus." He could have been saying she came back a Lady Godiva.

An elbow was unmistakably planted in Mark's back. He looked over his shoulder and saw a straggling line of hot and hostile people. "Thanks," he said hastily, and stepped aside. "I'll see you again."

Mr. Briggs retrieved his eyeshade and sleeve garters and began saying, "Where to?"

Mark walked out to the car. The sun nearly knocked him down. He sat forward on the blistering leather seat and drove to Perley's.

Pansy had gone to bed with a well-earned headache, and Perley was drinking iced tea in the damp little shed. He was a picture of dejection at ease, but he brightened when he saw Mark's face. Mark looked worse than he felt.

"Cheer up," Perley said, rattling the pitcher invitingly. "It's one of those days. You walk your legs off and nothing happens. But you better not let Beacham see you looking like this. He'll get discouraged. What's the matter? Lose your last friend?"

"No. I made one. I'll tell you about it when I get my old fire back."

"Sandwich?"

"Not with my stomach in its present condition. I've been calling on Bittner."

"What's Bittner got to do with your stomach?"

"You're a good fellow, Perley."

"Don't talk to me like I was a dog. Why did you go to see Bittner? He hasn't been out of the house for ten years."

"I thought we could use him. Also, I wanted to borrow his binoculars." He told how he'd been wakened the night before. "It might have been a bat and it might have been a falling twig. But it certainly was something. I went out to look but there was nothing in sight. Then I saw a light go on in one of the hotel windows. Up under the roof. Sutton had an attack during the night, so I suppose it was the valet's room. But I longed for those binoculars. I still do."

"Wouldn't let you have them?"

"No. But I rechecked Peck's alibi and asked if he'd seen anybody else. He hadn't. Then I dangled what I'm afraid is my immortal soul before his eyes and got him to promise to watch the traffic to Baldwin."

"I don't get it," Perley confessed. "What's Baldwin got to do with this?"

"Maybe nothing, but it's the only way to get out of here except by car. Forget it. I'll tell you later if and when it looks good . . . Bittner's safe, isn't he? I mean he won't talk about what he's doing?"

"Not him. He only talks about what other people are doing."

Mark sighed. "I noticed that. I saw Briggs too."

"Briggs! Now there's a fellow with a real element of surprise in him. Crazy about girls. Women and so on. That little shrimp. You wouldn't believe the complaints I've had. Once a week all summer long I have to go down to the station and shake my fist at him. Next time, I told him, I'll go direct to the Missus."

Mark recalled Mrs. Briggs and shuddered. "Don't," he begged.

"Scaring girls. Jumping out of bushes. No trouble with him in the winter because there's no place to hide. What did you want Briggs for?"

He told him what Joey had said. Beacham had sent for Cassie to come to New York about two weeks ago, to fire a caretaker, but there was no letter about it among her things. "A letter about the caretaker, yes, but nothing about coming to New York. She may have destroyed it, or it may never have existed. It could be a tale invented for young ears. Briggs says she took the train, all right. At least she took a train to Baldwin, ostensibly to catch the New York Express. Franny Peck went along as far as Baldwin to get her favorite cigarettes. Does that ring any bells?"

"No. I had bad luck too. I can't understand it. I must have talked to forty people this morning and nobody knows anything. Nobody saw anything either. Miss Cassidy could just as well have stayed home for all the attention she attracted."

Mark's feet, resting on a soapbox, hit the floor. "Say that again!"

Perley did. "Who claims to have seen her, except her own crowd? Even Pansy can't remember when you pin her down, and I pinned her. Nobody even remembers seeing those people reading tombstones in the cemetery. I'd have thought Miss Sheffield would have been something outstanding in a graveyard, but no. Blank, blank, blank."

Mark returned his feet to the box. "For a minute I thought you had something there. But it won't hold water. The man who drove the hotel bus saw her and talked to her. And Pansy's own cousins, the Moresbys. Don't forget them. They could have imagined everything but the sapphire ring. Mr. Moresby saw that, and Mrs. Moresby will never let him forget it. No, she was there."

"I know she was." Perley's mild face wore a sudden look of distress. "I hate autopsies!"

Mark said nothing. He was comparing Perley with Bittner.

"I went over to Cummings's office," Perley went on. "He was just finishing up. . . . She had her dinner all right."

"Go on, Perley."

"The arrow was the only damage. She died between one and two hours after she ate, and that's all I know."

Mark looked thoughtful. "Between eight and ten. Did he say how long it took?"

Perley poured himself another drink and spilled half of it. "Matter of fifteen minutes all told."

So it had been long. "Perley, I wonder if Miss Rayner was shot because she was in the way?"

"Why not?" Perley brightened. "That sounds better somehow. I mean it's better than having her shot out of pure spite. What time did we make that?"

"Nine-fifteen, but it's only a guess. It would fit, though. Miss Cassidy could have been lying a yard or so away. Rayner could have been walking straight at them. It fits, all right."

"How'd he know Miss Rayner wouldn't holler and bring a crowd?"

"Took a chance. Even if she had—hollered—and brought a crowd he was safe. He'd only have to mingle with the others and be as surprised as hell when Miss Cassidy was discovered."

"But," said Perley, leaning forward, "don't forget he had only one arrow. And he didn't knock Miss Cassidy insensible first because Cummings says there isn't another mark on her. What did he do? Stab her, then remove the arrow when he saw Miss Rayner coming? That would explain why the old lady thought she heard it. He was probably lying in the long grass, and what she heard was the swish of his arm. He had to work fast. You saw how Miss Cassidy's throat was torn. He—he put it back."

"A signature, huh? Why?"

"I don't know. Mark, I'm so nervous about this thing that if I wasn't a grown man with a family I'd cry."

"Go to bed early tonight. You need sleep. That's what I'm going to get—if I can." He yawned. "After I have a little talk with my employer. I want to know why he hasn't told me himself about Cassie's trip to New York. Something may have happened there, something that ties in with this."

Perley looked uncomfortable. "Cummings says Beacham was hanging around his office all morning, waiting for the report. He had to be very harsh with him. Made Mrs. Cummings nervous the way he talked about death. He thinks it's undignified. . . . That could be natural distress, couldn't it?"

"Sure it could."

"And Beacham was over here too, about an hour ago. He wanted to know when he could have the body. I told him in a day or so. Said I couldn't promise. He's half crazy to get her buried. Well, sort of buried. It's going to be cremation."

CHAPTER FIVE

THE following morning Mark sat on the porch of the Beacham cottage, studying birds. He'd even borrowed a bird book from Pee Wee, going into the Peck cottage to help Pee Wee find it. He'd managed to get his hands into every drawer in the living room and himself into several cupboards before Franny Peck complained and Pee Wee found the book where it had been all the time, under a chair cushion. Pee Wee couldn't imagine how it had got there.

The birds were plentiful and cooperative and the book was open on his lap, right side up. He flipped the pages over at precise intervals and followed each chirping flight with an unblinking stare. At the end of an hour he could still recognize a Central Park sparrow and a Public Library pigeon on their home grounds.

His mind was not on birds. He was waiting for the morning to get under way, for the golfers, the riders, the fishermen to scatter themselves to the four corners of the mountain. He wanted to see them leave with his own eyes. Also, he was remembering his session with Beacham the night before.

He'd come back from Bear River at seven and found Beacham alone. Roberta had gone off with Nick again, and Joey was dining with Pee Wee. Beacham had been haggard and peevish.

He'd told Mark in an oddly thin voice that he wasn't satisfied with the way things had gone and were going, and that Wilcox was a fool. He'd refused to release Cassie's body. It was enough to make the poor girl come back and haunt the place. And what had Mark done? Why didn't he have a report of some sort by this time? As far as he, Beacham, could see, Mark was running around the countryside, paying visits to old friends.

"I want results," he'd said. "That's what I'm paying for. I can't sleep for thinking."

"I haven't done much sleeping myself," Mark had said. "These interesting circles under my eyes are not make-up. Also, I've done some deep thinking on my own."

"What's the result?"

"A little something, very nebulous at present. . . . Why didn't you tell me about Miss Cassidy's trip to New York a short while ago?"

He remembered how the dull red had crept up and spread under Beacham's tan. "You didn't ask me anything like that. And she came back, didn't she?"

"Yes, she did that. Were you in New York at the same time?"

"Of course I was. She came down because I asked her to. It was personal business."

"I'll have to know more than that, Mr. Beacham," he'd said. "I can't afford to overlook anything. That trip may have started something that had to—end. What was the business?"

Beacham had looked uneasy and faintly chagrined. "Domestic stuff. I wanted her to fire the caretaker and get a new man in. I don't like to do those things myself. I—I lose my temper."

"I understand she was gone two days. Did the job take that long?"

"No. She had some things of her own to do. Shopping, I suppose. I didn't ask. I didn't see much of her." He'd suddenly looked defiant. "The house is closed. I stayed at one hotel and she at another, if that's what you mean."

"Nothing to add to that? Nothing else you can tell me?"

"Nothing. I can't think of a thing. . . . Why can't I go back to New York? Anything's better than sitting around here, waiting! I asked Wilcox and he says no. Is that final?"

"Yes, it is. You'll have to stay. . . . Why do you want cremation?"

Beacham had taken a long time to reply. "She wanted it herself. She asked me to promise. Don't get any ideas about that, East. I mean about poison. You can tell your country doctor to do his damnedest. He won't find any, or if he does, I didn't give it."

Then Beacham had left, with an abrupt good night, and Mark had sat on alone, waiting for Joey and Roberta. He'd felt an almost ridiculous relief when Franny Peck brought Joey home at ten and Roberta came stalking in shortly after midnight. He'd tried to talk to Roberta, using what he hoped was his most disarming smile, but she'd walked into the cottage with a curt nod.

He'd looked after her with appreciation. Viewed from the front she was decidedly haughty, with an I-sit-at-the-head-of-the-table-now look, but from the back she was a kid with drooping shoulders, expensive clothes, and a burden.

He'd gone to bed himself after that, but it was no more than a gesture. He was fully dressed and alert to every falling twig and rustle outside the windows. And he'd fortified himself with a companion. Cassie's puppy, at the foot of the bed, chased dream rabbits all night long.

And now he was camouflaged behind a juvenile bird book, seeing the ugly wound in Cassie's white throat, while the normal life of a summer resort ebbed and flowed about him. It was ten o'clock. Joey and Pee Wee had gone to a distant brook, at his suggestion, with high hopes, bent pins, and a can of earthworms. Roberta, in yellow linen and too much lipstick, slammed the screen door behind her and gave him a look of unconvincing surprise.

"I thought you'd gone," she said pointedly. "Aren't you working with Mr. Wilcox today?"

"Later," he said amiably. "And what are you doing?"

"Cards with Mr. Sutton and Nick. Can you suggest anything else?"

"Yes. A little conversation with me. You can be an angel of the tenements later on if you still feel like it."

She colored, but she didn't walk off. "I don't know anything," she said. "Mike keeps pumping me too, but I don't know anything. I'd tell you if I did." She made a clumsy, childish attempt to change the subject. "Did you have any breakfast?"

"I did. I went over to the main dining room." He closed his book quietly. "Roberta, you suspect somebody, don't you? And it's making you unhappy. Well, let me tell you something; the chances are that you're a million miles away from the truth, but I think you ought to let me in on it just the same. Tell me what's on your mind and you'll sleep better."

To make it easier for her to answer, he turned away and watched a group of riders canter briskly through the gates.

"I don't suspect anyone," she said slowly. "I don't know anyone who'd do a thing like that. Nobody here would. I think you ought to work in Bear River."

"I'm doing that too, but I've got to know more about Cassie herself. You can see that, can't you? She must have made friends with some one here; there must be at least one person she knew fairly well and liked. Sutton? Sheffield? Rayner?"

Roberta frowned. "She talked to Mr. Sutton sometimes. That's all. And once she went buggy riding with Miss Rayner. Everybody has to do that at least once, I guess." A grim little smile twisted her mouth. "It's terrible, crawling along like a snail. But Cassie got even. She took Miss Rayner out for a long drive in Mike's car. Miss Rayner looked

like the wrath of God when she got back. I think she's afraid of cars. I
bet she wrecked one once. But Cassie was a whizz at driving. Tore up
and down the back roads like mad. I guess Rayner was scared to
death." She hesitated.

"Nothing else?" Mark asked.

"No, that's all I know."

"Thanks." He changed the subject suddenly. "Isn't it early in the day
for cards?"

"Mr. Sutton isn't well. When he gets like this the only thing to do
is play cards. It quiets him."

"Joey said he was ill. What's wrong?"

"I guess it's age. He imagines things. He doesn't like to be left alone.
But George has to get some rest, and that's why Nick and I stay with
him."

"He ought to have a nurse, somebody to stay with him while
George sleeps. You and Nick ought to be having fun."

"We don't mind. And you can't have fun when everybody stares at
you and whispers when you go by. . . . Is that all?" She turned and
waved too gaily in the direction of the big veranda, and nodded and
smiled. He followed her look and saw no answering wave. A sad little
act, he thought, because she wants to get away and doesn't know how
to do it politely.

"Run along, Roberta," he said, "and stop eating your heart out."

She gave him a confused stare. "You don't really mind? They're
waiting for me."

He watched her scurry across the grass and disappear into the hotel.
Then he took out his notebook and marked a clean page with a series
of private hieroglyphics. Translated, they said: *Search Peck cottage? Can
do. Search Kirby's and Sheffield's rooms? Doubtful. Shine up to Miss Rayner?
Sure. Buy George a drink if possible. Get Nick Sutton alone. Get home
addresses of all concerned and check. Tell Beacham nothing.*

He rolled the pencil between his fingers and added another note. *Is
Roberta grieving for Cassidy or for the murderer?*

The door slammed behind him, and he pocketed the book.
Beacham, fresh and clear eyed, came out and sat on the railing. He
carried golf clubs. It was too evident that no nightmares had straddled
his chest.

"Want to come along?" he asked Mark. "Just for a couple of hours?
Do you good."

"No thanks. I may not look like it, but I'm working."

Beacham raised an eyebrow. "Do you think your man is going to walk across the lawn and give himself up?"

"Something like that. They often do. They get worried when you leave them alone. Then they try to pump you. In the process of pumping they give themselves away." He reached into his pocket and pulled out a pair of handcuffs. They glittered in the sun like surgical instruments. "Pretty, huh?" He held them high and swung them back and forth. "I got these from Wilcox. He seems to think I'll need them before he does. Well, you never know."

Beacham stared. He bent forward and touched the shining metal as if it were hot. "I've never seen any before," he said slowly. "Do they—snap?"

Mark demonstrated. The strong clean click carried like a shot in the still air. Beacham drew back and laughed. "Ouch!" he said. He looked thoughtfully over Mark's head into the dim room he had lately left. "When I said I hadn't seen any I didn't mean exactly that. I meant I'd never been so close before. Sometimes, in the Grand Central Station, I'd run into a couple of fellows fastened to a detective. Waiting for the train to Ossining. They always looked defiant. Do they ever put up a fight?"

"You'll see. Maybe I'll let you help when the time comes. After all, you have a personal interest. But don't waste any pity on the man who's going to wear them. The guy who snaps them on often feels worse. Wilcox won't use them if he can help it. He says he'd rather shoot a man down than tie his hands. I feel a little the same way myself. So—." He took out a handkerchief and carefully wrapped the cuffs before he dropped them back in his pocket. "There's Peck."

Archie Peck and Franny came up the steps, dragging golf equipment and arguing about the heat.

"Isn't this weather absolutely insane?" Franny wrinkled her smooth white forehead. "We'll all have sunstroke." She swung a wide, ribboned hat. "All except me. But Arch insists. He thinks Mike ought to take his mind off things. Don't you, Arch?"

Archie mopped his face. "He needs to take his fat off. Come on, horsethief." He lunged playfully at his business partner. "Two hours of honest work in the open air won't kill you."

Franny dimpled at Mark and shrugged eyebrows and shoulders. Her eyes told him that they were only rough boys and she didn't like that kind. "Did you find any nice birds, Mr. East? I think you're cute, wanting to look at birds when everybody else is scared to death."

"Jail birds," roared Archie.

"But I do think so," Franny insisted. "It shows he has poise, I think. It's much better to relax in the daytime when it's hot and do your real work at night, isn't it, Mr. East?"

"Much," Mark said.

"What do you do at night?" Franny went on. "Do you drive around in dark lanes looking for things? Or do you just walk around here, like a watchman? I saw you the other night. You were standing still, sort of listening. I felt so safe. . . . I wish you'd let me help you. Archie always sleeps, but I don't."

Archie gave Mark a friendly leer and clapped a ringed hand to his forehead. "Come on, baby," he said to his wife. "You'll sleep tonight."

Beacham left the railing and joined them. "Will you be here when we get back?" he asked.

"I don't know," Mark answered.

"I see. Well, use my car if you need it. We're taking Peck's. And ask them to send your lunch over here if you'd rather not go to the dining room. We're eating at an inn over on the other side." He moved off with reluctance. Mark wondered why. He'd been eager enough to go before.

He watched them leave. A few minutes later one of the yard boys brought two horses around to the parking lot and went into the hotel. He knew the big black was Cora's; the fat roan was one the children led around and overfed. Cora and Kirby? He couldn't see Kirby on any horse, even the roan, but maybe love would give him a leg up.

He took the handcuffs from his pocket, examined them carefully for Beacham's prints, saw there were none, and snapped one bracelet over his own wrist. Then, with the other swinging loose, he sauntered over to the lot. A page boy came around the corner of the main building with an armful of camp chairs, and opened his mouth to greet the paying guest. No sound emerged. As Mark moved on he heard the chairs crash to the ground.

He was opposite the veranda steps when Cora and Kirby came out. In riding clothes she was human and presentable, but Kirby looked as if he had been lifted bodily from a shop window and wished someone would put him back at once. Cora saw the dangling handcuff first.

"Yoicks!" she screamed. "Did you lose him?"

He waved his manacled arm in a wide arc, and the sun struck it like a snake and sent out waves of light. A dead hush fell on the crowded veranda; the creaking rockers stilled, cards destined to slap the table remained in mid-air. Two pages, summoned by the chair dropper, crept around the corner of the building and stood with bulging eyes.

Mark dropped his arm. "Rehearsal," he whispered to Cora. "That's all, but don't give me away."

She put her leathery cheek close to his. "I know what you're doing, you devil," she hissed. "You're scaring somebody into a trap. It's just what I'd do myself."

"Don't tell me I could be your brother," he begged.

"That's not the way my mind works," she brayed. "Come on and help me get Hank on his rocking horse. Its name is Happy Days, and I'm not lying."

Kirby, who had been frozen to a pillar, now came forward dragging his beautiful boots.

"It's very warm for August," he said tremulously. "It's too warm, really. I'm not sure that it's healthy."

His lady answered promptly. "If you ride with me every day for the rest of the summer, you won't need a girdle next winter. Don't deny it. I know."

Mark followed them over to the lot. He, in turn, was followed by the scrape of chairs. He could almost hear heads turning. Cora slapped the big black with affection and flung herself into the saddle.

"Give Hank a boost, will you?" she said. "I'd do it myself, but the last time I tossed him clear over."

He did as he was asked, pitying the cringing Kirby from the bottom of his heart. Cora nodded her thanks. "I dare you to wear that thing in to lunch," she said out of the corner of her mouth.

He watched them through the gates, the black mare prancing, the fat roan rolling an amazed eye over his shoulder. Then he walked the gantlet past the veranda. He went directly to the Peck cottage, as if he had business there. The door was unlocked, but he locked it behind him. If anyone came back before he was ready, he was returning the bird book and looking for another instructive volume.

The cottage was a duplicate of the Beachams'. Each Peck had a separate bedroom, he was pleased to note. A proper arrangement for sleeper and non-sleeper. It also had the air of a suite on a luxury liner. Half-eaten boxes of candy, with their covers off, littered the tables; fading roses dropped their petals on the floor. There was even a basket of fruit. It all looked like two days out.

He removed the handcuffs and started to work. He had no qualms of conscience when he turned over the contents of Franny Peck's bureau and closet. Her things were designed for both eye and hand. He fished among the rainbow colors with something like distaste. Franny shunned linen and cotton and her monograms were large and unreadable. He wished Pansy could see them; he was afraid Pansy would be envious even while she blushed.

Franny's letters were easy to locate. They were tied in big bundles, with blue baby ribbon, and they were from people who signed themselves Boy and Fitzy and Sheik. After reading two or three he decided he was either too young or too old. Franny's life, if her room was any indication, was an open book, to be read in bed and afterwards hidden under the mattress. He closed her door behind him with relief, but he kept her in his mind.

Archie's room was surprisingly neat. It was heavy with the scent of a Russian toilet water, and the top of his bureau was covered with an orderly litter of hair tonics, shaving lotions, and elaborate brushes of all kinds. The drawers themselves were stocked with English socks, ties, and shirts. His handkerchiefs were French, his silk underwear Italian. It was easy to picture Archie on a grand tour.

There were stacks of comics and Real Life Art Studies on the table, flanked by a file of geological magazines. There was one telegram, two weeks old, weighed down by an overflowing ash tray. It was from Beacham, and it said, simply, that Venezuela was willing. There were no letters, business or personal, and Mark thought he knew why. Archie, with his fat baby face and international wardrobe, had probably came galloping up from the wrong side of the tracks, and he would have learned early how to keep his business securely thatched under his sparse red hair. As for his personal life, maybe nobody loved him. He compared Archie's English flannels with his own seersucker pants and wished the same for himself.

It was nearly twelve when he closed the Pecks' door and wandered out into the sun. He was both disturbed and satisfied, and he had no reason to be either. He knew instinctively that he and Perley were right. The answer was somewhere within sight and hearing, somewhere inside the clipped hedges and neat white fences. He wondered what would happen if he stood where he was, full in the blazing sunlight, and shouted—"Come out, I've got you covered!" What faces would appear at what windows? Whose chair would whine on the veranda boards as it hastily backed away from a card table? What door would slam, which feet would pound the stairs? He grinned and shrugged. None. Nobody's. The voice that hailed Mary Cassidy in the lantern-lighted dusk was not the kind to tremble at high noon; and the hands that dragged her body across the clover grass would be firm and steady on—on what? A golf club? A fishing rod? A bridle rein? The wheel of a car? A warning chill crept along his scalp. He was right. He knew it.

He took out the handcuffs and the notebook. Time for a little clerical work before lunch and, thanks to Cora's suggestion, a little harmless theatricalism. He climbed the veranda steps, swinging the cuffs like a censer, and walked firmly inside to the desk. The clerk gave him a look of combined respect and agony.

"Please," he begged. "Please, Mr. East. Our guests!"

He had expected that. He put the cuffs on the desk and opened the notebook. "I want the home addresses of these people," he said genially. "Confidential, of course, although I don't see why it should be. You have them on the public register, haven't you?"

"Oh yes, sir! Yes indeed! We comply with all the regulations!" The clerk swung the register around. "If you don't mind," he said weakly, "if you don't mind, I'd rather you hunted them out yourself. I don't want to—I don't feel exactly right about—I don't want to have anything to do with it!"

Mark carried the book over to a table as if it were an encyclopedia, and sat down. He turned the pages in a scholarly manner. A general influx began. The veranda door opened and shut with remarkable regularity and conspicuous lack of noise; he heard the stealthy tread of feet walking softly in a prudent circle and at a safe distance. He was a cannibal island, surrounded by uncertain missionaries.

He flipped the pages and copied what he found into his notebook. Cora Sheffield, The Cloisters, Lexington, Kentucky. He snorted in spite of himself. The Cloisters. Wouldn't she. And underscored at that. On the same page, which was dated July first, he found the precise signature of Henry R. Kirby. The Yale Club, New York City. Wouldn't he, too. He wondered if she'd picked him up on the train or if it was a case of long-standing pursuit. He decided on the train. Hank was certainly not the man to put himself in the way of a horse.

On another page he learned that Miss Rayner had registered from New York City. East Twelfth Street, May first. An early bird.

On June first Mr. and Mrs. Archie Peck and Archie Peck, Jr. had also registered from New York. He recognized the address; it was a big and opulent apartment building consisting of duplex and triplex apartments. At the corner of Fifth and one of the lower Sixties. On the same date the Beachams and Miss Cassidy had arrived. The Beachams lived in a private house around the corner from the Pecks. He copied all of this into his notebook.

It took him some time to locate the Suttons, but they eventually appeared on the page allotted to April fifteenth. They were the only arrivals on that day, and the preceding pages showed few names. The Suttons had practically had the place to themselves. The sprawling signatures were in one hand, a young one, obviously Nick's. He raised his pencil to copy the address and instantly paid it the tribute of a sharp and quickly strangled whistle. The Suttons' address was the same as the Pecks'. Macklin Sutton, Nicholas Sutton, George Parmelee.

He thought he had all he needed for the moment, but to be doubly sure he checked the names of the few other guests who had gone to the church supper. He ruled out the children; there were nine of them, all very young. The adults were the Carberrys, the Huntingtons, and the Slaters, and they were two-weekers. He knew them by sight, and Perley had talked to them. They came from Boston and Albany and had apparently saved all year for a vacation at the Mountain House. Their contact with the Beachams was confined to respectful greetings from the men and eager little bows from the women, followed by wordless and admiring estimates of Roberta's clothes. They didn't fit in anywhere, and he filed them away in the back of his mind, convinced that they would stay there until the station wagon drove them down to the homeward train.

Joey and Pee Wee clattered through the door with a dripping can of sad, small fish for the hotel cats. They were entirely satisfied with their morning's work. Joey leaned confidingly against his knee and spilled water on his clean white shoes. She smelled of sun, mud, fish, and licorice.

"Go wash," he said firmly.

She was agreeable even to that. "We had a beautiful time. Will you eat lunch with Pee Wee and me?"

"No," he said, "but thank you just the same. You'd better eat with Roberta."

"That's what she says. Well——." She swaggered off, followed by Pee Wee. They left a trail of mud and water behind them.

He returned the register to the desk and considered an early lunch. He had no illusions about avoiding a crowd that way; he was a marked man and he knew it, so he patted his bulging pocket and strolled into the empty dining room.

The room immediately filled. People who ordinarily lunched at one and one-thirty now poured through the doors like transcontinental bus riders at a fifteen minute stop. He was halfway through a cup of jellied consommé when the captain pulled out the other chair at his table, and he looked up to see Miss Rayner primly seating herself.

"You don't object, do you?" There was a wink in her voice.

He struggled to his feet, said he was delighted, and wondered why all the old girls were inhabited by pleasant devils and the young ones were inhibited.

Miss Rayner ordered her lunch in a tone that attached suspicion to every dish, and sat back. "I heard about your performance this morning," she said. "I daresay you enjoyed it almost as much as I'm enjoying this." She lowered her voice like a conspirator. "Wouldn't you like to place the cuffs between us and shake your fist at me? It would give an air to our table."

He complied. "I was going to do that anyway."

"Wonderful," she sighed. "This is the nicest summer I've ever had. What'll we talk about?"

"How's your leg?"

For a moment she looked peevish. "I'm not at all pleased with it. It isn't mending as it should, but then I suppose I shouldn't complain. After all, it's only a leg. How are your—duties progressing?"

"So-so. Want to help me?"

"I! You're letting your good manners run away with you." She was trying to sound diffident but her snapping eyes gave her away. "I could probably trip somebody up with my stick."

"You can tell me what you know about some of these people. You've been here since May first."

"But how—? Oh, the register! Dear me, things are so simple when you know how they're done." She pushed her soup cup away with a look of horror and demanded an extra salad as recompense. "Salad is so healthy. Why don't you ask Mr. Sutton what you want to know? He's very approachable on his good days, and he's been here since April. But of course you know that."

"Yes, I know it. But I imagine you've seen more. How did you happen to come here in the first place? You're the sort of person I'd expect to find at the seashore."

"And that's exactly where you will find me after the war. Bournemouth, if they don't raise the rates too much. I like winkles and cress for tea."

"I don't. But you haven't answered me."

"You make it sound important, and it isn't. I drove through here several years ago and I liked it. I thought it would be restful." She looked suddenly ruffled. "But it hasn't been at all. It was very pleasant early in the summer, until the hordes descended. I can't imagine where these people come from."

"I can probably tell you," he grinned. "New York, Boston, Albany, and points south. Had you known any of the New Yorkers before?"

"I don't play poker," she said tartly. "Neither do I drink, smoke, fish, golf, or ride. Or spoon. I don't know what they call that now, but it was spoon when I didn't do it."

He laughed. "I don't believe that."

"Don't you?" She was plainly delighted. If she'd carried a compact she'd have taken it out. "What exactly do you want to know? I don't promise to answer but I'm willing to listen."

"Did Miss Cassidy spoon?"

Miss Rayner stared down at her plate. Finally she said: "I think we ought to let her rest. . . . I never saw it if she did, but I think it's probable. She was very pretty in an undistinguished sort of way and she carried her age well."

Never too old to be a cat, he marveled. "Did everybody like her?"

Miss Rayner drew herself up. "You must remember she was a paid employee, Mr. East. Although a superior type. I believe some people thought the Beachams made too much of her, but I could understand. We exchanged very few words. She didn't mingle."

"But you went out with her, didn't you? Driving, and so on?"

"The usual hotel courtesies. I took her, she took me. Once, I believe." She held her fork suspended and stared over his shoulder.

"Don't look now," he suggested softly. "What's creeping up behind me, Miss Rayner?"

"Nicholas Sutton," she said in a low voice. "But he's not creeping. He's with Roberta Beacham, and they're sitting down with Josephine and young Peck. They look—very odd."

"They've been keeping the old gentleman's mind off his troubles, whatever they are," he said easily. "It could be fatiguing." He turned around and waved. "They ought to get out more."

"Do you know what time they get in at night?" she asked crossly.

"Sure," he said. "I sleep in Roberta's bed." Let that one travel from stable to attic, he said to himself, and if it gives Roberta a jolt, so much the better. "What's old Sutton's trouble? Joey says he has fits."

"Josephine says a great deal and very little of it is reliable. But it's not the child's fault; it's lack of supervision. Mr. Sutton does not have fits. I'd hardly trust myself in a buggy with a man who was so inclined. No, Mr. Sutton is getting on in years and he's being very ungraceful about it. He gives in."

"You don't give in, do you?" he said admiringly.

She looked startled. "I?" Then she laughed. "How old do you think I am, Mr. East?"

He knew at once that he'd said the wrong thing. "Forty-five," he answered, crossing his ankles because his fingers were visible.

She flushed. "You're very close," she admitted. She laughed again, and leaned forward. "I hear you were reading a bird book this morning. Were you preparing yourself to recognize a buzzard next time?"

"There won't be a next time," he managed to answer. "Say, I believe you knew what they were all the time!"

"I did. I lived in the country when I was a child. Whenever we saw the buzzards we knew something had died, off in a field somewhere. We went out to find it."

"Why didn't you tell me? Why didn't you say something then?"

"Why should I? This is farm country. It could easily have been a dead sheep. . . . Don't look so distressed, Mr. East. You know you couldn't have done anything. It was much too late."

He drew designs on the tablecloth with a spoon. Old Sutton knew what those birds were. They had frightened him half to death. He saw old Sutton's face again, the drooling mouth, the terrified, upturned eyes. No country background, no long remembered sheep rotting in a field, had given him that look. He must have known, or guessed. He looked up and saw her watching him.

"I told you not to worry. You couldn't have done anything," she said.

The waiter brought their coffee. She pushed hers away. "Not fit to drink," she said. "Will you help me to my feet, Mr. East? That man jolts me." She unhooked her stick from the back of her chair and accepted his assistance. "Keep in touch with me," she said softly. "Sometimes I see things. And you must admit I have what might be called a personal interest."

He suppressed a grin. If she'd been Joey, she'd have literally shaken a leg to prove her point. Being herself, she wagged a finger. He walked with her as far as the elevator and returned to his coffee, which was surprisingly fit. Then he joined what he called the nursery table.

"What's on for this afternoon?" he asked largely. Naps, he was told. The schedule was falling into line. And tennis at four. Did he want to play? Or was he going to be busy? Nick asked that one.

He said he was going to be busy. He was taking Beacham's car down to Bear River. He took the notebook from his pocket and read it with a portentous frown. Pee Wee watched with large eyes and Joey with bursting pride. "I may go to New York for a day or two," he said. "Probably tomorrow."

"Hot tip?" breathed Pee Wee.

He nodded. The older pair looked indifferent but Joey beamed. "That's good," she said. "Pee Wee says you ought to comb out New York. He says it all the time. He thinks you'll find something there. So do I."

He bowed to Pee Wee and Joey. "With such encouragement I can move mountains." He turned to Nick. "How's your grandfather?"

"Better. That's why we're having tennis. One of the maids will stay with him." He elaborated. "George has the afternoon off. Miss Sheffield said she'd keep an eye on things too. And Mr. Kirby."

He left them then, with a hurried excuse, and went out to the lobby. If George had the afternoon off it wasn't likely that he'd spend it on the premises; he'd probably make for the nearest movie. Neither, he suddenly thought, was George likely to stroll through the lobby en route to his pleasure. With this in mind, he found himself a chair under the trees. It was a few steps from the entrance gates and the service yard was nicely visible. He killed time without effort while he watched the carrying out of swill buckets, the back door feeding of seven cats and four dogs, and the surreptitious retrieval of two heads of lettuce from a garbage pail. He told himself firmly that somebody kept rabbits, but at the same time he drew a heavy mental line through future salad courses.

A fat woman in one of the second floor suites opened a window screen and put a pink silk girdle to sun on the sill. She saw him and hastily withdrew it and herself. He wanted to tell her to put it back like a good girl, but refrained.

He wondered whether Sutton's room was next to the pink girdle and decided that it was. He could see thermos jugs and medicine bottles on the inner sill. Soon old man Sutton would be in the hands of a maid, nameless, and under the promised eye of Cora, with Kirby as alternate. He tried to picture Cora at the bedside, willing and bored. Would she try to read to him? He was tempted to tell her about the copy of *Black Beauty* in Joey's room.

A farm wagon jolted up the road and stopped outside the gates. A plump and pretty girl climbed down and adjusted her skirt and stockings. The wagon lumbered through and around to the kitchen door, but the girl entered on foot, as became her Sunday best. Her dress was bright blue and her new permanent was embellished with two pink velvet gardenias. She followed the wagon on high white heels that teetered on the gravel. When she came within a few yards of the kitchen door she stopped and leaned provocatively against the fence. This pose, he soon discovered, was not for him although he was the only male in sight. The door opened and a stocky youth with hair like a beaver's emerged in the glory of white pants and blue jacket. The girl moved languidly forward and they clinched. The youth whispered something and she screamed, "You George!"

Mark got up and strolled over. She was ruffling George's hair when he came up to them.

"Mr. Parmelee?"

George turned a perspiring face. His collar was already beginning to wilt. "That's me. . . . Oh!" His recognition was instantaneous and confused. He gave his girl a mannerly shove. "Nothing wrong upstairs, is there? I just came from there a few minutes ago."

"That's what I wanted to ask you." Mark held out his hand. "I've been worried about the old fellow and thought I'd inquire."

George took the hand and looked relieved. "Age and heat," he said professionally. "He'll be O.K."

Mark nodded gravely. "That's fine." He let his eyes rest appreciatively on the vision in blue. "I hope I'm not intruding." It sounded like the proper thing to say.

"Oh," said George. "My lady friend, Miss Homesdale. Mabel, this here is Mr. East that you've heard about."

"I'll say," declared Miss Homesdale. "I'm really pleased."

She was too pretty even in her ridiculous make-up. She looked like the kind of girl the neighbors make prophecies about. But she also looked capable; of what, Mark wasn't sure. Probably everything. He shook hands again, vigorously. "Were you going off somewhere?"

"Well," George said doubtfully, "we kind of thought of going to the movies. We can get a lift in the wagon." He jerked his thumb in the direction of the unloading farm cart. "It's her Dad's. It's her day too," he added, as if that explained all.

Mark expressed his pleasure. "This is what I call a coincidence," he declared. "I was just going to drive myself down in Mr. Beacham's car.

I had," he lowered his voice, "I had beer in mind. Do you ever—I mean, if you care to, I'd be delighted."

Miss Homesdale was also delighted and George said that whatever suited Mabel suited him. They scrambled into Beacham's car like two children taking over a merry-go-round.

After she had settled her gardenias, Mabel became confidential. George, she said—and please call her Mabel because she never stood on ceremony—George wasn't in the army because he had lungs, although you wouldn't think it to look at him. That's why he was working for Mr. Sutton, because it was mountains. If things turned out the way they should, and she gave the pine covered hills an admonishing look, if things turned out, they'd marry in the fall. Mr. Sutton could live or die, it wouldn't change their plans. George was through with all that. And no more city for him. Over her dead body no more city.

Mark turned into the road that ran between two fields of shimmering corn. "City?"

"George is a New York boy," Mabel said, "but he isn't a bit like that. He loves the country, he really does, and my Dad can use him any time. On the farm. Plenty for everybody, my Dad says, and I've always got my job if I want to keep it."

"Congratulations," Mark said heartily. "George is a lucky man." He was amazed at the way the proper phrases came rolling off his tongue. "What is your job, Mabel?"

There was a moment of silence. He hardly noticed it because his mind was on the winding road.

"She does upstairs work," George said briefly. "I don't like it."

"It's all right," Mabel said. "It pays a lot and it's close to home. Couple of miles the other side of Baldwin. Sanitarium."

"What kind?"

"T.B. Gets me down sometimes when I think of George, but he's doing fine. The ones we've got out there are real sick. Some of them are—well, they're real sick. But it pays a lot, like I said. Still, it isn't like when I was at the Mountain House. That was a scream."

"Mountain House?" Then he remembered. "Don't tell me you're the girl who saw Kirby with his hair down!"

"Off!" roared George. "The door was open but she knocked just the same because that's what she's supposed to do, but he didn't hear her. Looking at hisself in the glass. So in she goes and there he was. Teeth too, wasn't it, Mabe?"

"Teeth can happen to anybody," defended Mabel. "I've known young girls even. But the hair really got me. Lovely chestnut, sitting on the bureau like it was alive. What person wouldn't scream?"

"He didn't have to get you fired," said George.

"Yes he did! He had to because it made him feel terrible every time he looked at me. And he gave me a nice tip, too. How do you think I got those silver foxes? Trap 'em?"

By the time they entered Bear River, Mark had more than he'd hoped for. People calling themselves Foote, on the third, Pittsburgh, weren't married. People named Haskell, on the second, had their own sheets, pink silk. Miss Sheffield was nice and the language she used was her own business. She gave you the candy Mr. Kirby gave her. Miss Roberta Beacham was stuck up. Mrs. Peck was not, but she wasn't as young as she looked. She, Mabel, had cleaned up the cottage a couple of times, and you could start a store with all the bottles and jars she had. For her face.

At this moment George indicated a tavern next door to the picture palace. He indicated it by remarking that there was a cool looking place. They parked the car and went in. Mabel ordered a Martini.

"Because I've never had one and Nick Sutton drinks them all the time," she said. She stared raptly into space. "Nicholas Sutton," she repeated.

"She looks like she's going to pick the petals off a daisy," George said fondly.

She said it wasn't like that at all. She was just sorry for him. He was afraid of his grandfather, and one night she'd heard him crying when she went in with fresh towels. Well, not exactly crying, but his eyes looked funny and red. Still, that could have been Martinis, couldn't it? They could easily go to a person's eyes. She took another sip of hers, and shuddered. George sat back with his beer and let her talk.

Miss Cassidy? Well, nobody saw much of Miss Cassidy, and that was the truth. She'd have paid more attention herself if she'd known what was going to happen. "She liked her own company, Miss Cassidy did, and never went on picnics and such with the others. Sometimes she did take Mr. Beacham's car out. Said she was enjoying the country roads. Imagine! She was kind of interested in the place where I'm working now. I guess she came across it when she was driving along. Anyway, she asked me about it, and I told her it was high class. Real interested, she was. On account of being a nurse once. I think she said she was

going to look it over. Not my idea of fun!" She gave Mark a provoca-
tive grin.

He gave her a cautious one in return. "Busman's holiday. Who was
her bosom pal?"

Mabel screamed lightly. "You got her wrong. She kind of made up
to old man Sutton, but that was because she wanted to get Roberta
married off to Nick. Then she'd have Beacham all to herself. Joey
didn't count, too little. But who wants a grown stepdaughter?"

"Who indeed?" agreed Mark. "You had charge of the second floor,
didn't you?"

"Front half, both sides. Suttons, Sheffield, Kirby, and Haskells with
the pink sheets. All suites."

"Where's Miss Rayner?"

"Fourth. All small rooms, singles. Mostly week-enders. You work
like a dog on the fourth and the tips are terrible. They always start the
new girls there but if you're smart, like me, you complain. Then you
get moved." She emptied her glass and shuddered again, happily.

"Have another," Mark insinuated.

George came out of his reverie. "No," he said. He studied an ornate
wristwatch. "We just got time to catch the beginning. Come on,
Mabe, if you think you can stand up. And thank you very much, sir.
We'll do the same for you next time."

He helped his lady friend to her feet and roared approval when she
rolled her eyes and staggered gracefully. He tried it himself and was
approved in return. It struck them both as a nice way to show appreciation, so they kept it up until they reached the sidewalk; once there,
they straightened up and moved sedately out of sight.

Mark paid for the drinks and sauntered out into the sun. It was three-
thirty. Perley's? Not yet. Crestwood? Too hot. He moved on down
Main Street with half-closed eyes and walked into a hunch that soon
developed into more than that.

CHAPTER SIX

M AIN Street sweltered. Creeping pedestrians hugged the narrow line of shade cast by hot brick walls. The usual custom of greeting friends, locally known as "passing the time of day," was suspended. Two dogs, father and son, snarled at each other when they came face to face, and halfway down the block a man with an ice-cream cart sank to the curbstone and devoured his livelihood.

The drugstore on the corner sent out a wave of warm soapsuds, malted milk, and peanut brittle. A printed sign in the window pleaded for ice. Mark walked on, grinding the dust between his teeth. A few yards ahead a familiar awning hung like a rag from its rusty pole; it was a far cry from fiesta bunting, but it quickened his steps. Mr. Spangler's shop might smell like a cellar abandoned to mice, but it probably was cool.

He gave a hasty glance at the unwashed window, blinked, and moved closer. His scowl changed to a look of thoughtful wonder as he studied the burlap screen. He went inside.

Over in a dim corner Mr. Spangler sat at an old-fashioned desk, his bald head cradled in a nest of cracked plates, newspapers, and broken cardboard boxes. His rhythmic snoring rose and fell.

Mark walked quietly to the window, removed the screen and stood it on a table. Then he sat down and carefully examined every inch of it, telling himself he was a superstitious fool and only half believing it.

He saw the empty space, the dark brown patch that had lately held the picture of a known murderer. He saw the Polish wedding group, like an ode on a Grecian urn, the stiff necked bridegroom with his fadeless boutonnière, the rosy-tinted bride, forever fair. He passed on grimly to the other smiling faces; the boys and girls with dogs and bicycles, the beaming men with rod and creel, the women primly posed against a wall. The cemetery wall. He saw them all with frightening clarity, and his eyes went back to the hand-lettered sign that had no business to be there: THERE IS THE PICTURE OF A MURDERER IN THIS WINDOW. GUESS WHO?

He groped in his pocket for the notebook and the handcuffs fell to the floor with a challenging ring. Mr. Spangler gave a guttural cry and woke up.

"Come over here," Mark said. "I'm not asking you why you didn't take that sign out when I told you to. God moves in a mysterious way."

"Amen," said Mr. Spangler in confusion. "What's the matter with you, Mr. East?"

"Do you know all these people?" Mark pointed to the screen.

"I do that. . . . I'm certainly glad you dropped in, Mr. East. I want to thank you for throwing that business my way. The doctor had me over to the undertaking parlor last night, taking pictures. I did some beautiful work, side views and front looking down. He should of asked me out to the well too, but nobody thinks of the old man these days. Except you."

"I didn't throw any business your way. Somebody else did that. Sit down." He turned a page in his book. "Check me on these pictures; the light's bad on some of them. Now, Miss Sheffield and Mr. Kirby with the horses. Right? Miss Rayner and the buggy. Old Sutton and Miss Rayner again, also with buggy."

"It does me good to watch those two," Mr. Spangler sighed. "It makes you think."

"Never mind that. Nick Sutton alone. Roberta Beacham and her father. Roberta alone. That one is Roberta, isn't it?"

"She gives me a feeling of spring. Yes, that's her. Little sister took it, so it ain't so good."

"Franny Peck and stranger."

"Whoa!" Mr. Spangler chuckled. "That's no stranger. That's Mr. Peck after two days' camping."

Mark looked closer. "You're right. Here he is again, with Pee Wee. And that's Pansy Wilcox with two ladies going to or coming from a picnic that included bathing. Who are the two?"

"Mrs. Briggs and a cousin of Pansy's. Name of Moresby."

"I've talked to both of them, but I didn't recognize them. Happiness is a great disguise. . . . And the Reverend Walters, all alone and looking wistful. Is he married, by the way?"

"Not yet, but I've heard some talk that—"

"Never mind." He hesitated over a shadowy print of two figures in a clinch. There was something familiar about it. "Who?" he asked.

"You wouldn't be likely to know her, Mr. East. No, you wouldn't know her. But he's the feller that looks after old Mr. Sutton."

"George Parmelee. I thought I knew that pose. And the lady, I hope, is Miss Homesdale?"

"That's her, but I don't see how you knew. She got him cornered like that and had her cousin take it on the sly. Had the brass to tell me so herself. Ain't girls the limit?"

Mark closed his book thoughtfully. He leaned forward and examined one of the prints again. "You wouldn't know who took the one of Pansy, Mrs. Briggs, and Mrs. Moresby, would you? He got his own shadow in."

"Briggs."

"Careless. . . . And just for the record, what about the wedding picture? That's the only nice one in the lot."

Mr. Spangler glowed. "Name of Bielowsky. Poles. They moved to Connecticut a couple of years ago. That picture's seven years old, would you believe it? Fresh as the day I took it. They got seven children now."

So much for the Grecian urn, Mark said to himself. Bold lover never, never canst thou kiss, though winning near the goal—. Still, it had been a pretty thought when he and Keats had it.

What about Miss Cassidy?" he asked. "Was she camera shy?"

Mr. Spangler rubbed his trembling chin. "Now that's a funny thing, Mr. East. I had a very nice picture of that poor woman, happy as a lark, right beside the Polish wedding. All smiles, she was. But I had to take it out. Right where the trout is now she was."

"Why did you have to take it out? Come on, Buster, why?"

"Well, she came in here herself, a matter of two, three weeks ago. 'I'll give you five dollars if you'll take that picture out of the window,' she said. So I did. It was a young-looking picture too. She looked very young in it. Odd, I call it."

"So do I. When a woman in her late thirties gets a young-looking picture of herself, she buys a dozen and papers the walls. When did you say this happened?"

"Day before she went to New York. Told me she was going. In an awful rush she was. Gave me five dollars and said, 'Tear it up,' and off she went."

"Anybody else ever make any comment on that picture, Buster? Anybody except Miss Cassidy ever show any interest?"

"Now imagine you asking that! Why sure! Same day, as it happens. That afternoon, when I was substituting the trout, in comes the whole kit and boodle. Old customers, new customers, everybody. I had a wonderful business. Well, they all admired the trout, one of Mr. A. Peck's, and I told them about Miss Cassidy. Showed them the picture, too. Hadn't got around to tearing it up. And you know what? They couldn't understand Miss Cassidy any more than I could. Such a young-looking picture to get upset about. Peculiar, they said."

"Peculiar I say too." Mark looked wary. "On the level, Buster, did you finally destroy it? Or did you let it ride, like the sign in the window?"

"Mr. East! You're nagging me again. I certainly did destroy it. Right before I went to bed I did. I've always been a man of my word, and if I'm a little slow about some things it's only because I'm—"

Mark stemmed the flow. "How about a beer?"

Mr. Spangler moved like palsied lightning. The shop door was locked and they were out on the street in less than a minute. Over his beer, Mr. Spangler grew contrite.

"Honest I meant to take that sign out," he said. "I did, honest. I took the murderer out, didn't I? But I must have forgot the sign. I'll fix it when I go back, honest I will."

Mark ordered more beer. "No," he said. "Let it stay. If anybody comes in and asks you about it, you say it's a new guessing game. And write down the names of the people who ask, will you?"

The old head wobbled in agreement.

It was six o'clock when Mark drove back to the Mountain House. Cora Sheffield hailed him from the veranda, but he didn't stop. He went directly to his room in the cottage and worked on his notebook. Beacham came in and said they were all dining with the Pecks. Would he join them? He said no, and asked to have his dinner sent in. When it came, he asked the man to serve it on the porch. He sat there until dark and then went for a walk along the road to town. As he walked he made his plans. In the morning he would arrange with Perley for a trip to New York. The evening train. He thought he could safely stay away for two nights and one day.

The moon was a great spotlight turning the dusty world to silver. The mountain behind him was a giant child's cutout, pasted against the sky. On either side of him the corn rustled. He turned back, almost persuading himself that someone had called his name. But he knew no one had. He knew, or thought he knew, exactly where everybody was.

When he went to bed he took Cassie's dog with him again. Roberta objected. It was her bed, she reminded him. She didn't want dogs on it. He returned it to the kennel and then, when everybody was asleep, he went out and brought it back. Not even a twig fell during the night.

It was nearly ten o'clock when he went over to the hotel for his breakfast. The lawns were deserted, and there were only a few people on the veranda, all strangers. When he returned, the veranda was full and quietly expectant and the chairs under the trees were all occupied. The Mountain House had a grapevine that the New York underworld might covet.

Even old Sutton was in his favorite chair, taking small, experimental whiffs of the hot, resinous air.

It looked like a reunion of some far-flung clan grouped about a patriarch. The Pecks were there, the Beachams, Miss Rayner, Cora, and Kirby. Even George hovered in the background with a palm leaf fan and a bottle of smelling salts. He gave Mark a shy grin.

When Mark walked over to join them, Joey, in clean denim shorts and a striped jersey, gave up her chair and sat on the grass. He counted them all again. Only Pee Wee was missing.

Cora and Kirby were in riding clothes, and Miss Rayner wore her small driving hat, an old-fashioned golf cap tied on with a veil. Over in the lot Cora's black mare pawed the ground and tossed a handsome head. Even Happy Days and Miss Rayner's fat bay flicked their tails and acted far less than their years. At each fresh whinny Kirby craned a desperate neck in their direction, like a tired cobra forever hearing music. Each time he turned back, he had shrunk a little more.

"Look at him," Cora said to old Sutton. "He won't believe I do this for his liver. You're not afraid of horses, are you, Mr. Sutton?"

"No, no," murmured Sutton. He squared his shoulders. "I was quite a rider in my youth, and Miss Rayner has kindly introduced me to the buggy in my old age. It has—advantages."

Roberta avoided Mark's eye by assiduously hunting four leaf clovers.

Nick spoke suddenly. "I'd like to ride today. Kirby, do you think they can let me have a horse?"

"No." His grandfather answered for Hank. "We'll think of something better for you." His sunken eyes held a derisive look. "Perhaps your other good friends will include you in a less strenuous program. Ask the Pecks and the Beachams what they're going to do."

It was a normal question as far as words went, but there was poison running through the old voice. It spread and grew and met another stream, a strong, new current that was almost visible. Some other silent,

busy mind was distilling an ugly brew. It turned the hot August morning into a catafalque. It changed the happy laughter on the veranda into
a grinning effigy and mocked the homely sounds of garden hose and
slamming doors. It stripped away the false security and pointed to the
skeleton of something else.

Here it is, Mark said to himself. It's making signs to me, it's trying
to tell me. It's coming at me, and I can't see it.

"Ask the Pecks and the Beachams what they are going to do," the
old man repeated. No one spoke.

Is he trying to put me wise? Mark wondered. Or is he trying to shunt
me on to the wrong track? Useless to ask, even privately; useless to do
anything but watch. He sat back in his chair and tried to look as if he
hadn't heard. The others followed his example.

Franny Peck leaned over and rubbed her husband's arm. Archie colored foolishly and said nothing. Beacham continued to stare at the sky.
Kirby sent another frightened look in the direction of the horses. Cora
Sheffield intercepted the look and leered. Miss Rayner opened her bag
and extracted a lump of sugar. Nick Sutton tried to catch Roberta's eye
and failed. It all took only a few seconds, and still no one said a word.
Not even old man Sutton. He sat with his eyes closed.

Joey looked uneasily from face to face, saw and felt the tension without understanding it, and began to show off. She seized a hapless
grasshopper by the hind legs, forced its head down on the back of her
hand, and gave vent to a shrill incantation. "Spit tobacco, spit tobacco,
spit, spit, spit!"

At the same instant, George dropped his small bottle and it crashed
against the arm of Nick's chair.

Beacham turned a furious face. "Stop that!" he shouted.

George retrieved the broken bottle and slipped it into his pocket
with a muttered apology. Old man Sutton sniffed the air like a lean and
hungry fox, and sank deeper into his pillows. Joey stared at her father,
aghast.

"Sorry," Beacham said to George. "I meant Joey. I don't like to
see kids torturing animals. Turn that thing loose, Joey. At once!
Now!"

"But he'll spit tobacco, Mike! Look! He spit some already!" She held
up her hand and displayed a small brown stain. Something clean crept
back into the atmosphere and stayed for an instant. "I'm not hurting
him."

"Let it go!"

She did, reluctantly, and her lower lip trembled. Cora Sheffield rose briskly. "Come on, kid, and help me. We've got to get Hank on Happy Days. You might climb up and show him how it's done. Come on, Hank."

"Come on, Hank," Joey repeated. She strode off manfully in their wake, not once looking at her father. His eyes followed her, and Mark thought he looked anxious.

"Are you driving now, Miss Rayner?" Roberta asked.

Miss Rayner gave a tight little smile. "Presently, presently."

The eyes of the group under the trees turned to the parking lot as a drowning man turns to a thrown rope. They assumed new postures and exchanged gay, eager looks. They pantomimed their pleasure in such simple fun. Even old Sutton twisted his thin neck in Cora's direction.

Cora mounted and sat like a valkyrie looking down from an inviolate height. Joey scrambled on and off Happy Days three times, and her demonstrating voice floated back.

"Playing to the gallery," muttered Roberta.

Franny Peck laughed and snapped open the lorgnette she affected with her tailored clothes. "Cute," she said brightly to everybody. "She's cute."

Hank made it after the third try while Joey stood back and rubbed her hands together like a money lender. Then Cora gave Joey an unmistakable signal and Joey promptly gave Happy Days a sound smack on the rump. Happy Days turned an astonished head, and at the same instant a scrap of something white blew crazily across the lot and completed the damage. Happy Days reared like a stallion and tore down the road in a cloud of dust, followed by Cora.

Miss Rayner covered her eyes, and Mark went after Joey.

"What's the idea?" he demanded. "Were you trying to kill Kirby?"

"Miss Sheffield told me to," Joey protested. But she was frightened.

Mark dug into his childhood for a suitable retort. "If she told you to stick your head in the fire I suppose you'd do it," he retorted. "You ought to be whacked yourself. Don't you ever do a thing like that again. It's dangerous."

Joey tried to explain. "It wasn't me hitting so much. Happy Days is kind of used to that. He shied at that piece of paper or something. Those yard boys, they're no good. I bet they left the top of the incinerator off again. What's the use of cleaning up every morning if you're going to leave the top off? Time and time again they've been told about that." She went about, bent over double, gathering scraps.

"You talk like a stockholder. And leave that stuff alone. It's filthy."

But she liked her role of scavenger. "You leave the top off and it blows all over. Look." She held out bits of newspaper and a torn envelope, placating. "If that blowed by your face you'd jump too."

He took the envelope. Was this going to be one of those things? His hand shook. But it was addressed to the management and came from a provision house. He handed it back. "All right, all right, get rid of it. I suppose you want to burn it up yourself."

She scampered around to the back premises and he returned to the chairs under the trees. He was greeted with animation.

"Well?" prompted Miss Rayner. "What was behind that performance?"

"Miss Sheffield's idea of a joke." He sat down. "I miss Pee Wee. Where is he?"

Archie answered. "He's being punished. He shaved himself this morning—with my razor." He laughed heartily. "Great kid. I hate to see him grow up."

"It wasn't the shaving so much," Franny said with a hurt look. "But he talked back. To me. I can't have that. . . . Cigarette, Mr. East?"

"No, thanks."

The silence fell again and he gave them a long, lazy look. Time to break it up, he told himself; time to send them about their business, whatever it was. "Don't hang around here because of me," he said. "I haven't anything up my sleeve or in my pocket, and I don't know any more than I did yesterday." Then he added, "I think I'll go down to New York tonight." There was no reaction. The faces turned to his were bland and incurious

"So soon?" Franny said. "I thought you were staying two weeks? Poor Mr. Wilcox!"

"Don't underestimate poor Mr. Wilcox," he said. "And I am staying two weeks. This is just a business trip. I'll be back before you have time to miss me."

"You won't find anything in New York," Beacham said. "You'll be wasting time and money." He stirred restlessly. "Do you mind if I go along?"

"I'm afraid that won't do," Mark said regretfully. "Perhaps later. I'll see Wilcox before I leave and try to arrange it for you. He may clear the way for you when I come back."

"I wouldn't mind a little fling myself," Archie said. "How long you going to be gone?"

"Not long. I can do what I have to do in a few hours. Back again Friday morning if I'm lucky."

Old Sutton leaned forward and placed a gnarled hand on Mark's knee.

"Now, now," said George. "We don't want to work ourselves up. What say we go inside for a little lie down?"

"No!" The old man straightened up defiantly. "This is one of my good days and I know what I'm doing. I know what I'm saying, too." He gave Mark an artful look. "Friday," he said. "So you're coming back on Friday. That will be seven days after she first disappeared. Are you planning a pretty bit of timing for us, Mr. East? I seem to recall," he turned to Roberta, "I seem to recall something about that. Didn't you tell me, my dear, that Mr. East is a seven-day man? That he always winds up a murder in seven days, by the clock?"

Roberta flushed. "I don't know. Maybe I did. I—somebody told me that!"

"If you're thinking about the Crestwood business last winter," Mark said amiably, "you're right. That took all of seven days, but there were complications."

"Heavens," said Franny. "Is this one easy? How dreadful to think of it as easy! It seems terribly confused to me. Doesn't it, Arch?"

Archie made a sound in his throat. He took out a package of cigarettes, looked at it, and put it back in his pocket. "Yeah. Yeah, it's confusing all right. Say, do you think you're going to bring Cassie's murderer back from New York?"

"Not exactly," Mark said. "I expect to—." He stopped short. He'd lost them; they were no longer listening. Only a second before they had been watching him as people at a zoo watch the lion keeper unlock a cage, but now they were looking in another direction. Even old Sutton was half out of his chair, staring straight ahead.

He turned in astonishment. They were looking at Joey. She was coming toward them, running, her face twisted with either rage or pain, her hands clenched.

"Look!" She screamed and flung herself into Roberta's arms. She thrust a handful of scorched and tattered rags in Roberta's face. "Look! Who did that? I told you I was saving them! Who did that?"

Roberta stared dumbly. Mark took a shred of cloth from the clenched fist. He'd seen it, or its counterpart, before, cut to ribbons and hidden in a bureau drawer.

"My scraps! Somebody tried to burn them in the incinerator! I had them locked up! I was saving them!"

"Hush!" Roberta shook her. "I don't know how it happened. I didn't do it. Hush!"

Old Sutton sank back in his chair and covered his eyes with both hands. George moved closer.

Miss Rayner turned to Mark. "That child is going to make herself sick. What is she talking about? Who burned her scraps? This is too absurd."

Mark explained, carefully and lightly. Apparently the story was new to Miss Rayner, the Suttons, and George. They found it amusing, but agreed that the result could be annoying. All except old man Sutton. He put a trembling hand on Joey's shoulder, but she shrank back and began to cry again, hopelessly.

Beacham turned to Roberta. "This is getting beyond me. Did you put that stuff out to be collected with the trash? You knew she wanted it. . . . For God's sake, Joey, shut up!"

"I didn't," Roberta said evenly. "I wouldn't touch it with a ten-foot pole. She was probably making doll clothes and left it lying about. Ask the maid who does our place. She probably found it on the floor and threw it out."

Franny patted Joey's hand. "That's right, isn't it, honey? You see it was only an accident. That's what happened, isn't it?"

"No," Joey said, but there was uncertainty in her voice. "I don't make doll clothes. But—"

"Go on, honey. But what?"

"Well I did give some pieces to Pee Wee. He wanted them to show to the boys in his school. But I didn't give him much. We—we were saving the rest to make a little quilt for Cassie's dog."

"Josephine." Miss Rayner took the situation firmly in hand. "Perhaps your quilting pieces are still where you put them, all safe and sound. These may be the ones you gave young Archie. Why don't you look?"

Joey was off like a shot.

Miss Rayner looked at Franny. "Very odd," she said. "The whole affair is very odd."

Franny picked up a strip of singed blue cotton and examined it with distaste. "I remember these shorts. Cute. You know I really think these are the pieces Pee Wee had. I don't dare tell Joey but I do believe I threw them in the waste basket myself. It didn't occur to me that anybody'd actually want the rags. I thought it was just some of Pee Wee's foolishness. Don't give me away to Joey, for heaven's sake." Her eyes beseeched Roberta. "She'll hate me, poor child."

Mark had gathered the remaining scraps into a neat bundle. "Give," he said to Franny. "Joey is part and parcel of a crime wave and all of this stuff rates high. Remember your own childhood. I'll see that she gets it back."

Franny dropped the bedraggled scrap into his hand with a pretty grimace. "All this fuss about a lot of horrid old rags. Serve you both right if you catch a germ."

Miss Rayner stood up and shook out her skirts. "I said I was going to drive and I shall," she said. "Will you join me, Nicholas?"

Nick looked at his grandfather. The old man's hands were gripping his chair and his eyes were closed. George shook his head.

"Not today," Nick said. "I think I'll go in." He stalked off, holding himself erect, as if squared shoulders could conceal a dragging foot.

"Roberta?" Miss Rayner sounded plaintive.

"No thanks." She ran across the lawn after Nick, not in a straight line, but weaving. She looked as if she didn't know where she was going.

Joey came out of the cottage with a beaming face. "All there," she announced. "In my secret hiding place." She leaned against Miss Rayner. "Thank you for reminding me to look. I guess Pee Wee and I lost some, and what I found is it. I feel better now."

"I've got the others, Joey," Mark said. "I'll keep them for you."

Her smile grew. "There's fire burns on them, and tomato stains. If I wanted to I could tell the kids at school that it was blood." She saw Mark looking at her. "But I don't want to," she added.

"Drive, Josephine?" Miss Rayner asked desperately. "We might pick poor Mr. Kirby out of a ditch and bring him home. You owe him that much."

Joey's eyes brightened. "Maybe his leg's broke," she said.

"Or his neck," Miss Rayner said primly. Hand in hand they went over to the lot where the fat bay dozed between the shafts. Joey obligingly accommodated her pace to Miss Rayner's; instead of skipping, she treaded air vertically. Even from the rear they suggested the better type of ambulance chaser.

Archie took out his cigarettes again and stared at them as if he'd never seen them before. "Funny," he said.

"What is?" Mark asked.

"I don't know." He lit a cigarette and drew a deep breath.

"It's the heat," Franny said. "It makes you nervous. I've never known such an August. I really don't know why we stay. Why do we, Arch? We were going home soon anyway, so why don't we go now?"

Archie didn't answer at once. Then, "Hey," he said in a low voice. He was staring at old Sutton. "Hey, you George!"

George, who had been watching Joey and Miss Rayner, turned quickly and bent over his charge. "Now we got 'em again," he said resignedly. "What do you suppose started that?" He patted the old man's shoulder. "Now, now," he said.

Old man Sutton was crying. He had covered his face with thin, mottled hands, and the easy tears of age trickled through his fingers. His head moved from side to side in a despairing plea. "No, no," he begged. "I don't want to see, I don't want to see. Oh Lord, be merciful."

"Now you come along inside," George soothed. "Nobody has to see nothing they don't want to. It's a free country. . . . Gimme a hand, Mr. East."

They got the old man to his feet. Beacham and Franny turned their eyes away.

"Don't look, Arch," Franny murmured. "Don't look at him, Arch. He's awful."

"You want the wheel chair, pal?" asked George. "Or are you gonna strut right past them pussies on the porch like a big shot? Come on, pal, show 'em you can take it."

The old man clung to George's arm, weeping silently. "I'm too old," he sobbed. "I can't do anything. There isn't anything I can do."

"You don't have to do nothing, pal. You just come along with George." He took his own handkerchief, as Nick had done, and wiped away the tears.

Mark tried to remember what Buster Spangler had said about George's background. Club? That was it. He'd worked in an athletic club, but the steam room was too much for his lungs. That explained the pal talk. He could see George slapping fat bare backs and urging unco-operative drunks to relax, pal. And now the strong, freckled hands were guiding a sick old man, gently and firmly. He felt a warm affection for George.

"Nick?" George was saying. "Why you know where Nick is. He went inside with the pretty girl." He put his arm around the old man's waist. "We'll go in too, and have a little snifter. Lotsa ice, lotsa you-know-what. Come on, give us a smile. . . . There, that's better." He sent Mark a triumphant look that said he could handle them, he could. They started across the grass, an ill-assorted pair. The old man broke into a shambling run, body forward, neck outthrust, eyes turned frantically to the sky. Mercifully, they passed out of sight.

Beacham frowned. "What brought that on, I wonder?" he said to Mark. "He was sane enough to take a crack at you a few minutes ago."

Mark reached over and took one of Archie's cigarettes. "I don't know. Does he worry much about Nick?"

"No more than you'd expect. Nick's all he has. . . . He ought to be in a nursing home."

Franny shook her head in pity. "Awful, simply awful. What was he looking for, craning his neck like that? You'd think he was watching bombs."

Mark looked long at the cloudless sky; the others, watching him, did the same. A few birds wheeled in the blue, but they were small ones.

"He was looking for scavengers," he said. "I think he was rolling time back."

Archie mopped his face. "Whew!" he said. "I feel as if I'd been through something. Am I nuts, or is everything kind of funny around here this morning?"

"You're not nuts." Mark said.

Franny moved over to the arm of Archie's chair. "It's Joey. I'm getting a little tired of all the fuss Joey's making about those clothes. I think she's getting too much attention, and that's so bad for her. And you needn't look at me like that, Mike. I told Cassie she was making a mistake, dressing Joey like that. She went too far, she really did. It isn't—ladylike."

"It suits me," Beacham said shortly.

"You men! You let that child twist you around her fingers. Look at Mr. East. You'd think he had diamonds or something, the way he hangs on to those rags!"

"I'm a sad case of arrested development," Mark said. "How well do you know the Suttons, Mrs. Peck?"

"Not at all well. Just hello, and things like that. Just Nick."

"You live in the same house in New York, don't you?"

Franny looked blank. Archie tweaked her ear and gave Mark a broad grin. "New York! They die in the walls like rats, and you don't know they're there until the cops come. How many people do you know in your own building, East?"

"All right, I don't know any. But I wondered if the Suttons came here at your suggestion?"

Franny answered eagerly. "I couldn't say, really I couldn't. I may have said something about this place to Nick. I used to talk to him in the elevators. But I didn't know Mr. Sutton at all. Did I, Arch?"

"If you say you didn't, you didn't. I guess Roberta talked the place up, eh Mike? Nick and Roberta used to go to the same parties, you know, nice little parties with a bunch of chaperons. Say," his voice rose, "are you trying to make something out of this?"

"Not a thing. The old man worries me, that's all. I thought that if you were friends you might persuade him to try a sanitarium. George and Nick mean well, but—"

Franny gave him a look of horror. "Oh no, I couldn't. I couldn't do that to anybody. He makes me sort of sick, I can't even bear to look at him, but I wouldn't ever—I wouldn't—. Archie, why don't we go home? Why don't we?"

Archie patted her hand. "We'll go when I get ready," he said calmly. "I like it here."

Mark got up briskly and turned to Beacham. "I'm going to pack. It won't take me five minutes. Will you drive me down to Bear River? I want to talk to Wilcox before I go."

"What's the rush? What about lunch? And you can't get a train now. Not until early evening."

"I'll pick up some food somewhere, and I've got some odds and ends to clear up before I go. I think I'll ask Wilcox to release Miss Cassidy's body. That's what you want, isn't it?"

"Yes, but why? You won't let me leave, and I can't bury her here."

"I'll fix it so that you can take her to New York when I get back. Maybe the Pecks can go along with you. Make a nice little party of it." He strode off, whistling.

Franny looked at Beacham. "Mike, what's he going to do in New York? You ought to make him tell you. You're paying him, aren't you? Well, you ought to make him tell you."

Beacham shrugged. "I can't," he said. He went over to the lot without another word and backed his car out. In less than ten minutes Mark joined him and they drove off.

"Can I talk to Wilcox?" Beacham asked.

"No. I'll do that. He'll make all the preliminary arrangements and notify you. Nothing for you to do but sit tight."

After a pause Beacham said, "Are you on to something?"

"I think so."

"But why New York? I don't want to make you sore, East, but I think you're off the track. I can't—tie it in."

"Why not?"

"Because she had no life there, outside of my own family. She lived with us for nearly nine years, and we always knew where she was and what she was doing. Don't go, East." He looked frightened. "Suppose something happens here while you're away?"

"I'm taking care of that. You want Miss Cassidy's murderer caught, don't you?"

"Yes, of course! But I think this trip is a waste of time."

"Do you? I don't."

"Then why won't you tell me what you're doing? It'll be safe with me. I'm paying you to investigate, and that ought to prove I mean business."

"No. But I'll tell you this, and it isn't much. I think she was killed by someone she knew—or by someone who knew her." He let this sink in. "Someone who knew her," he repeated. "Someone who walked up to her in the dark and said, 'Hello, Miss Cassidy.' Or maybe it was, 'Hello, Mary.'"

Beacham was silent. "That could be anybody," he said finally.

"Yes, it could. But why did it happen when it did? She'd been coming up here every summer for five years and she got along all right with the regulars, the staff, and the townspeople. This year she came on June first, with the same people she came with before. Then why, late in August, does someone decide she must die? Why August, instead of June or July? A newcomer? It looks like that, doesn't it? A recent arrival at the hotel or a visitor in town. But I don't believe it."

"Why not?"

"Because Wilcox and I have checked all the new ones. And a more harmless lot I never saw. Thrifty souls who pinch pennies all winter to pay for a few days at a summer resort; boys and girls who work in the cities, coming back for a week or two to sponge off relatives. Most of them never heard of her and none of them remember seeing her. And Miss Cassidy wasn't the type to invite murder from a stranger. She didn't attract attention or give people ideas. I've asked questions until I'm hoarse and all I get is that she was 'a good creature.' That's been the invariable answer. Nobody says she was pretty, or clever, or fun. All of the usual post-mortems are missing. Nobody says she was nice to old people, or had lovely eyes, or quotes her opinion on anything."

"What do you think, then?"

"I think that all at once she was dangerous to somebody. All at once. There's nothing here to show me why. Her routine hadn't varied, she'd had no unusual mail. So—a little light on the past is indicated. Hence—New York."

Beacham stared at the road ahead.

"And even you've been uncommunicative," Mark went on. "You and your friends. I've had to dig for the little bit I've got and I've even been reduced to hunches. Will you answer some questions now?"

"Sorry. I've trained myself to keep my mouth shut. Go ahead."

"How much did you know about the Suttons before you came up here?"

"I didn't know them at all, except by name."

"Have you ever heard Nick's mother mentioned, by anyone? Did you ever hear her maiden name?"

Beacham gave him a sharp look. "No to both."

"Do you know how Nick's father and mother died?"

Beacham rumbled an oath, threw back his head, and roared with laughter. "Are you crazy?" he demanded. "What the hell has that got to do with this?"

"That's a fine, hearty laugh. Don't you want to answer?"

"I can't! I don't know! Ask old Sutton or Nick himself."

Mark watched the road for a full minute before he went on. "Your own wife died in a hospital, didn't she?"

Beacham took a long time to reply. "Yes. The Reid Memorial. You've been building up to that one, haven't you?"

"I have," Mark admitted. "And now that you're on, I'll ask them straight. Did you ever consider marrying Miss Cassidy, or propose it to her?" He waited for an explosion that didn't come.

"No," Beacham answered calmly. "Never. And she didn't expect it, either. But I meant to keep her with us as long as she lived, or wanted to stay. She's in my will." He gave Mark a shrewd look. "I'm telling you this because you'll probably find it out for yourself and decide it means something. It doesn't. Franny Peck is in my will too, for no reason except that she was kind to me when Arch and I were getting started. . . . You're curious about Arch, aren't you?"

"Mildly."

"He's invaluable to me. He handles his end of the business and gets results. I don't ask him what he does or how he does it. He doesn't ask me what I do. We run with a different crowd socially, but we always get together for a few months each year, usually in the summer. If I were you I'd cross him off."

"Thanks. Maybe I will." Mark knew from Beacham's tone and the set of his jaw that further talk would be useless. Beacham accelerated the speed and they entered Bear River in a cloud of dust. The traffic cop at Mountain and Main waved his arms with frantic delight and blew his whistle. When he saw Mark he shrugged and went back to the shade of his umbrella.

Beacham dropped Mark at Perley's. He shook hands cordially and drove away, but not, Mark noted, back to the hotel. He turned off into Main Street.

Pansy provided lunch and tactfully withdrew. Mark talked and Perley listened. He listened unhappily, with a beaten look; he didn't want to be left alone, not on this case, he didn't. And he preferred to sleep in his own bed.

"Why do I have to stay up there?" he complained. "Why can't Beacham take care of his own family? What's the point? You say yourself that you don't think this one's a double header."

"I want you there for the looks of it, Perley. That's all. While I'm in New York I want to think of you, rocking on the front porch and fondling your gun. You'll be a sensation. And—this part's on the level—you'll probably make somebody very uneasy."

"How will I know if I'm making somebody uneasy? It don't always show."

"Keep your eye on the person who makes the most fuss over you. That'll be the one to watch. And tell Beacham I want you to sleep in Roberta's room."

"No!"

"She isn't in it. She bunks with Joey now. If Beacham objects, or takes it with bad grace, you'll have to put up with the front porch. But stick to that cottage."

"Suppose somebody breaks in the hotel?"

"You stay where you are whatever happens. Don't leave the cottage. Even if the hotel burns to the ground, you stay where you are. We're not falling for any booby traps. And besides, you'll have Amos in the hotel."

Perley rested his chin in his hands. "Will I?" he asked with what he hoped was sarcasm. "Are you arranging that too?"

"No. You are. Tell him to go up there around midnight and sit in the lobby. You can fix it with the night clerk. He needn't stay on after dawn. The staff is up and around then."

"Is that all?" Perley snarled softly.

"I think that's all, except for my New York phone number." He crossed to the blackboard and wrote it down. Then he returned. "There's always somebody at the switchboard. Call me up if you feel like it. But I'll be back on the early train Friday."

"And I'll be there to meet you! You want to know something? You've been making plans for me and Amos ever since you came in here but you haven't said a word about what you're going to do yourself. Is it" —he looked wistful—"is it too big for me to know?"

"Certainly not!" Mark hesitated. "You know that sign in Buster Spangler's window?"

"Know it! I laugh myself sick every time I go by. 'Guess who'! He's a card."

"So am I. I'm going to dig up the background of everybody whose picture is on that screen."

Perley gave a low moan. "Why don't you try a little gypsy tearoom?"

Mark got up. "That'll do. Come on, I want you to drive me over to Crestwood. I don't want to see Bittner, but I must. Also Beulah."

Perley led the way out of the garage. "You're not going to turn Beulah loose in the Mountain House, are you?" He sounded anxious. "I got trouble enough."

"No." Mark produced the little bundle of half-burned rags. "Some of Joey's. I want Beulah to keep them for me."

"Going to braid yourself a nice rug this winter?"

"No, I'm going to weave a nice rope for somebody's neck, and soon. Sutton gives me seven days. Get the car out."

Perley complied. He also put a new dent in the fender. "You make me nervous. It's the way you talk. Get in. . . . What do you want with Bittner?"

"I'm going to give him the new rules in the cops and robbers derby. He was supposed to call me if he saw an unusual traveler on the road to Baldwin. I'm going to tell him to call you. If he does, use your own good judgment. Ignore the lovers in the bushes and unfrock all masked riders."

"Or, in plain English, stop anybody whose picture is in Buster's window." Perley was momentarily delighted with his riposte and then he wilted. "Now you listen to me. I can't arrest people for traveling to Baldwin. I'll get in trouble."

"Who said anything about arrest? Simply get up there as fast as you can and attach yourself to the doubtful party. Buy him or her a beer, stick like a brother, be a nuisance. If he tries to take a train, tell him he can't. Be very sorry and very firm. Coax him back and call me. I wish you wouldn't look as if I'd asked you for money. These are only precautions. I don't expect anything to happen."

"Then why—"

"I want to keep Bittner on our side, that's all."

The car turned into Main Street and headed out of town.

"I don't see Floyd these days," Mark went on. "What's up?"

"You know Floyd. He's got a theory. He says Miss Cassidy had long hair and that something demonstrandum there ought to be hairpins lying around. So he took Pansy's special little rake and started to comb out the church grass. Walters said that seeing as he was on his knees anyway he might as well dig out the burdock too. He's digging out the burdock."

Mark left Perley in the car when he went into Beulah's. He handed her the small bundle of rags and told her where they had come from.

"Hide them for me," he said.

She gave him a long look, full of solicitude. "Are you working too hard, Mark?"

"Do as I say," he said sharply. "Hide them and forget where they are. Until I ask for them later."

"Aren't you going to tell me why?"

"No." His voice was undecided. "No," he said again, firmly. "One dead woman is enough."

She didn't follow him to the door when he left, and Perley saw that his contentment had vanished when he climbed into the car.

"Where now?" Perley asked.

"Bittner's," Mark said, "and then Baldwin."

"You got a couple of hours before the train leaves."

"I need a couple."

He refused Bittner's smiling invitation to enter and talked to him through the window instead. All I need is a guitar, he said to himself, and all he needs is a rose.

Bittner accepted the change in plan with a pout, but he agreed to it. "You'll come to see me when you get back, won't you?" He hung over the sill. "There may be some little thing that I'd rather not tell Wilcox. He's so narrow."

"Sure. Sure I'll come." He got away with difficulty. Bittner had long arms. We also need an iron grille, he amended silently.

On the way to Baldwin he told Perley what he had promised Beacham. "He'll be after you. Tell him he can have the body on Friday. That's on the level. You make the arrangements with Cummings and the undertaker, and take Beacham along with you. Be sure he sees that you're cooperating. I'll take over when I get in Friday morning."

"Tell me what you know," Perley begged. "I don't care how wild it sounds. I'll feel better if I know what to expect."

Mark laid an arm across Perley's shoulder. "I don't know for sure," he said. "I'll tell you when I do."

He left the car at Baldwin, and Perley drove away alone, looking back over his shoulder like an old dog excluded from the day's hunt. He felt that way, too. Go on home, Rover, he said to himself. Go on home, sir! But in a way he was glad to have it so. Maybe these rabbits were too fast. Maybe—he shivered when he remembered how Mark had protected him once before—maybe he was being protected again. After all, he had Pansy and Floyd and the old people to look after. Go on home, he said again, but with a grin. He told himself that if he had a tail he'd wag it.

Mark walked the sun-baked, treeless streets of Baldwin until train time. It was an ugly, sprawling town, surrounded by lumber mills and shoe factories. The army camp was two miles out. He looked in vain for familiar faces, for anything that even remotely touched the residents of the Mountain House.

The business district was two blocks long and it accommodated two old-fashioned saloons and five self-styled Clubs. The latter were garish, noisy, and new, and they looked as if they could and would comply with any unreasonable request. The food stores featured flies, sleeping cats, and wilting vegetables. The Emporium, Ladies' Wear, offered a window filled with shoddy finery, and Sam's Gents' Furnishings did the same. Even the drug store had a spurious look, not unusual in a mill town.

He looked at the depressing rows of small brown and gray frame houses, each with a grassless patch of littered yard. He wondered about Mabel's tuberculars, hoarding their hours into days and nights on the outskirts of this dismal stretch of earth. He also wondered whether

Mary Cassidy had gone to see the place and, if so, why she had bothered.

A few minutes before his train left, he bought an evening paper and crossed the dingy platform to get his ticket. A girl was coming out of the express office, followed by crowing laughter. She looked familiar and he stopped, although he was short on time and the train was pulling in. It was Mabel.

"Hello," he said, slapping his money on the counter. "New York."

Her face flushed. "Why, hello," she said. "Who'd ever expect to see you here." She was plainly embarrassed and tried to ignore the two pimpled youths who trailed her out of the drab little building with audible comments on her weight.

So they still do that, Mark said to himself with faint distaste, recalling other freight sheds, dim and dusty, other girls in thin, tight dresses and boys with fumbling hands and furtive eyes. He could remember other scales, always in the darkest corner, and the slow, deliberate gestures as the weights were pushed along the rod, back and forth, back and forth. He scooped up his change and crossed to the train.

Mabel followed him, nervously. "I went in there for a package," she said, "but it didn't come. . . . Are you going away for good?"

"No," he smiled. "I'll see you in a few days." He swung aboard, and because he was ashamed of his reaction to her cheap little maneuvers he turned back and waved. That soothed his conscience. He told himself he had no right to condemn Mabel, or to compare her with the carefully sheltered Roberta. Mabel and Roberta had learned their lessons in different books. But just the same, he'd tell George to beat her, regularly.

The ugly town slipped away, and gave place to fields and farms and pine-covered hills. Beyond that far line of trees was Crestwood, with its fragrant gardens. More farms, watered by lazy brooks, more hills and fields, then Bear River. He couldn't see it, but he knew it was there, shrouded in green. The mountain was tipped with gold from the mellowing sun. He went into the club car and drank Martinis, still thinking of Mabel.

CHAPTER SEVEN

IT was one o'clock in the morning when Mark took a cab to his apartment. The streets were noisy and crowded and the air was exactly as he knew it would be, stifling, odorous, and unquestionably poisonous. He filled his lungs happily and felt suddenly fit. At two o'clock he was in his own bed, lulled to sleep by the benevolent murmur of an electric fan.

Up at the Mountain House Perley Wilcox was wide awake. He had started the evening at ten o'clock, on the Beachams' front porch; at eleven he had made a faltering entrance into Roberta's room. They had made things very easy for him. No questions and many expressions of gratitude. He had met gratitude on all sides; he'd been feted like a visiting angel sent to save all skins and souls. At first he'd tried to keep a list of those who offered the most insistent courtesies, but he'd had to give that up. He didn't even know who some of the people were.

The Pecks he knew; they were the gin, with an invitation to poker. And the Suttons had sent George over to ask if he wanted some light reading. Miss Cora Sheffield had appropriated the top step, when he was on the bottom, and hitched her chiffons to her knees because it was hot and he was an old married man who didn't count; she sang "My Old Kentucky Home." Mr. Kirby had offered to lend a sword stick which he said was Sicilian. He flashed it in the moonlight.

By this time an uneasy suspicion had entered Perley's mind. He began to be afraid that they were glad to be rid of Mark and were secretly delighted with the substitute. Then he began to worry about the hours ahead.

This impression grew when Amos arrived, deliberately dressed in his most disreputable clothes, and was welcomed like an ambassador by the night clerk. A comfortable chair was set aside in the lobby for Mr. Partridge, with a reading lamp and the latest magazines. Cigars were brought out. Extra cushions were heaped in a veranda swing in case Mr. Partridge wanted the air. Perley, momentarily strayed from his own beat, watched all this and felt his heart sink. When Miss Rayner laid a delicate hand on Amos's oil-stained sleeve and offered to sit up with him, and two perfect strangers tried to give him a flask, Perley went back to the Beacham cottage and locked himself in the bathroom. The flask from the strangers was too much. He didn't know it then, but they were more frightened than he was. They were people calling themselves Foote on the third, not married.

He brushed his teeth for the second time that night and in a voice calculated to reach beyond closed doors announced that he was going to bed. The girls had already gone; it was eleven-thirty and Beacham was at the Peck cottage. He locked the door to his room, was immediately ashamed of himself, and unlocked it. Then he selected the chair most likely to keep him awake and sat by the window overlooking the porch.

The night was serene and cloudless. Once every half hour Amos walked by on his perarranged rounds. They reported to each other in low voices; Perley felt silly and childish, as if he were playing Home Sheep Run with the kids in the next block. It wouldn't have surprised him to hear Pansy's voice, indulgent and chiding, calling from an inner room, "Perley! Stop that nonsense and come to bed!"

To remind himself that this was no game, he laid his revolver on the window sill and kept his eye on it. He wondered what Mark was doing.

Beacham came home at one, just as Amos stopped to make his self-conscious report that all was well. He heard Beacham lock himself in his room.

"I don't think you ought to leave that there," Amos said, indicating the revolver. "It's a temptation."

"I've got my eye on it," Perley said. "Everybody accounted for at your end?"

Miss Sheffield had gone out, Amos said, but according to the clerk she always did. She was a night walker. Everybody else was in bed or said that was where they were going. The clerk had given him a nice lunch, chicken sandwiches and iced coffee.

"Get along!" Perley dismissed him with a low growl. "Want to wake everybody up?"

He leaned back in his stiff chair and tried to stretch his legs, but it couldn't be done. Roberta's four-poster was a pale, inviting oasis in the dark room. He turned firmly away from it and changed to a wicker chair, padded with cushions. It was safe, he thought; the way he felt he wouldn't sleep for a year. He relaxed with a sigh and stretched with pleasure. One-fifteen. Time was moving right along. Wouldn't be long until dawn.

For a while he listened to the night wind in the trees, to the soft, light patter of new green needles dropping to the thick brown carpet of other years. Like rain, he thought; like little April rain. His head lowered until it reached his chest.

Amos scratched urgently on the window screen. Perley woke with a start. Somewhere close by an owl hooted with faint derision.

"Did you hear that?" Amos whispered.

"Owl." Perley raised the screen and looked out. "What's the matter with you?"

"That ain't no owl. It's been moving from place to place, too fast." Amos looked over his shoulder. "First it was over by the parking lot, then it was under the hotel porch, and now it's—it's out there." He pointed to a thicket of trees straight ahead. "You got a flashlight?"

"No. You're working yourself up. It's an owl all right. Wait a minute and he'll sound off again."

They waited but there was nothing more to hear, nothing but the timeless wind in the treetops and the small, disturbing rustle of a summer night.

"It always gets cold," Amos whispered. "I don't know why, but it always gets cold."

Perley coughed quietly behind his hand. It was cold; he could feel it in his mind. "I can't go out there," he said. "Mark said no matter what I wasn't to go out. . . . What do you think?"

"I think some devilment's up. Somebody trying to act funny. I'll show 'em. Lend me your gun."

Perley put his hands on the window ledge. "I don't think I ought to," he said. "You may get tempted to use it and hurt somebody. Still—"

Amos saw him recoil and watched his hands grope frantically along the sill. He saw him stoop to the floor.

"Gone?" Amos asked in a thin, high voice.

"Gone." Perley switched on a lamp. "Come on inside."

They looked inside and out, hopelessly. When they saw that further search was useless they went out to the porch. The stars were paling and the wind had gone. Far down the road an owl called faintly. It sounded as if it were mocking.

The phone rang beside Mark's bed at six-thirty. It was the house operator.

"Wake up," she said. "And no fooling. I did what you told me to. I've got the president of the Turf Club on the line and is he burned up. He says it better be important."

"It is. Put him through." He waited until a surly voice said, "What's the idea?"

Mark told him. He said he wanted to know, as soon as possible, everything on and off the record about Miss Cora Sheffield of The Cloisters, Lexington, Kentucky. He said it was urgent.

"Never heard of her," the president said.

Mark continued. "Police business," he said.

The other voice changed. "She didn't do it," the president said softly.

"Do what?"

"Whatever it is. Cora's been accused of every sin in the decalogue and to my personal knowledge she hasn't committed one. Well, maybe one, but who cares? Who are you?"

Mark explained.

"Murder! That's wonderful!" The president abandoned his r's and rushed in with a replacement of h's. "Murder! Come to breakfast. I've got a ham that melts in your mouth."

"There's nothing I'd like better," Mark said, struggling to keep his own consonants in line, "but I've got a full day ahead. I take it," he added, "that you don't mind swearing to Miss Sheffield's innocence?"

The presidential oaths rang pontifically.

"Thank you. Now what about a friend of hers named Kirby? Henry Kirby."

This brought a purely gratuitous repetition of the same language, but against, not for. It subsided gradually. "Hank is no friend," the president finally admitted. "He's a fifth or sixth cousin of Cora's and nothing like that ever happened to the family before. Namby-pamby, mush and water, milk-drinking, backsliding nincompoop. She'll have to marry him one of these days out of plain shame and embarrassment. You can't let a man like that run loose. But," he added regretfully, "he's no killer."

Mark thanked him and hung up. The house operator rang him again and warned him not to go back to bed. "You told me to do that," she reminded him. "Now go in the bathroom and turn on the water so I can hear it."

He did. He bathed, shaved, dressed, and went out to breakfast. The sky was lowering, and a sticky fog blew in from the river. He thought of Perley on his mountain top, but without envy. After breakfast he went to the Yale Club.

The mannerly custodian had spent fifteen years behind that desk and they had given him the shell of a turtle. He stood firm against persuasion and threats. He snobbishly admitted that Mr. Kirby was a very well-known gentleman, related to the equally well-known Miss Sheffield, and that all mail and communications would be forwarded. Mark gave up.

He checked Cora and Kirby in his book and took a cab to Beacham's house. This was a four-story brownstone, with basement, and it was boarded up. He rang the front bell and pounded on the basement door. After a few minutes the door opened. An elderly man of clerical aspect looked him over. Cassie's new caretaker. "Haven't you made a mistake, sir?" he asked politely. "The family's away." It was a tribute to Mark's gray flannels.

"No," Mark said. He gave the man his card. "I've come down from Mr. Beacham's cottage in the mountains. I'm investigating Miss Cassidy's death."

The man opened the door wider. "Come in," he said. "I read about that in the papers. And Mr. Beacham was kind enough to inform me also." He led the way down a dark passage lined with closed doors, to a small sitting room opening off the kitchen. It was immaculately clean and looked out on a neat flagstoned yard. "I can offer you coffee, sir."

Mark took it gratefully. It was easier to talk when you could swallow between questions. "What is your name?" he asked.

"Albert Shaw." The man looked surprised. He hesitated before he went on. "I hope I'm not making a mistake, sir. I asked you in because I trusted your identification of yourself. Mr. Beacham was very emphatic about reporters."

"I'm myself, all right," Mark assured him. "Now, how well did you know Miss Cassidy?"

"I didn't know Miss Cassidy," Shaw answered. He looked at Mark's card again. "No, Mr. East, I didn't rightly know her. I saw the lady when she came to the agency where I am registered, and we talked for a bit, but I'm afraid I can't tell you anything of value." He looked apologetic. He was a prim little man with an unworldly air, not the caretaker type as it is usually cast. He should have been an old retainer, kept on out of affection and allowed to carry in the extra hot water for tea.

"How did she impress you?" Mark asked.

The answer was given with a deprecating look that acknowledged its meagerness. "Not as a lady who would die a violent death. She was—colorless, you might say. Very kind in her manner and soft in her speech, but when she left a room you didn't remember she'd been in it."

Mark took a leisurely swallow. "Did you know the man who preceded you?"

"No, sir. I don't even know his name. Mr. Beacham told me—I met Mr. Beacham only once, when I first came—Mr. Beacham told me he drank. And not his own liquor, either. Mr. Beacham's." He smiled gently.

"Did he come from your agency?"

"No, sir. I understand he was someone Miss Cassidy was sorry for, someone not registered anywhere. That's not always wise, feeling sorry for people to the extent of taking them into your own home."

Mark put his cup on the small, clean table. "If you were in my place, would you try to find this other man? Do you think he might know something?"

"I couldn't say. I wish I could help you, but I'm afraid there's nothing I can say. You see, I don't really know any of the—parties. Unless—" He paused, and his mild blue eyes looked thoughtful. "There are tradesmen in the neighborhood; I've only been here a short time but I've got to know some of them very well, due to Mr. Beacham allowing me to charge my food on his bills. So I was thinking, maybe they could tell me something about that other chap. I don't know of any other way to locate him. Unless Mr. Beacham knows."

"Mr. Beacham doesn't. Miss Cassidy took care of all domestic arrangements." He saw the man's waiting look. "Why sure. You talk to the butcher and the baker. You can write me whatever you find out. I'm leaving late tonight, going back to the country. Here." He took his card and wrote the Mountain House address on it. "But you don't need that, do you? You have it already."

"Yes, sir." He looked as if he were turning something over in his mind. "Those shopkeepers, they may not want to talk to me if they think there's anything—odd. You know how people are when it's a question of law. Even respectable people. They don't want to be involved. They—they'd rather lie than tell something that might save a chap."

"I know," Mark said, "but do what you can."

"Oh I will, I will! But—"

"But what? Go on, Mr. Shaw."

At the unexpected title the old man's head went up and a faint pink crept into his thin cheeks. "I was thinking," he said firmly, "that if you would write my name on your card, sir, if you'd write something like 'Introducing Mr. Albert Shaw,' why then they'd pay me some attention. I wouldn't abuse it, sir. You could count on me for that. And I'd only use it if I had to."

Mark took out his pen once more. It can't do any harm, he thought. "Don't get me in trouble, now," he said. He wrote the introduction as it had been dictated, and got up to go.

Shaw preceded him to the door and bowed him out. He held the card like a citation.

"So long," Mark said, raising his hand. Mr. Shaw returned the salute gravely.

There was a fine mist falling, but he walked the few yards to Fifth Avenue and entered the classic Greek lobby of the Peck-Sutton apartment house. Here he was greeted with suspicion and what amounted to silence. He was not asked to sit down; rather, he was herded into a dark corner behind a palm.

The manager coldly admitted that the Pecks resided there. They had done so for five years, he said, but he didn't know them. Oh yes, he knew them by sight, but that was all. Mr. Peck paid his rent promptly, gave no noisy parties, and after all—. He shrugged.

Mark tried him on the Suttons. Yes, he knew the Suttons. Mr. Sutton was a gentleman of the old school. The boy was away all winter, at one of our finest universities. So naturally—. He shrugged again.

"Pay their bills promptly too, and don't give noisy parties?"

The manager colored. "We have never had the police before. It has never been necessary. I am afraid I can't give you any further information. Good morning."

"I'm not the police," Mark said. "I'm a private detective in the employ of Mr. Michael Beacham, and I'm investigating a murder."

"Murder!" The manager stepped back. Even his voice was pale. "Whose murder?"

"Miss Mary Cassidy's. It was in the New York papers. You can read, can't you?"

"I don't believe I—I don't recall it. Miss—Miss Cassidy?"

"Yes. A member of what you would undoubtedly call the Beacham menage. She was stabbed in the throat and thrown down a well. Did you know her?"

"I? No!"

"You know the Beachams?"

"By reputation only. I think I've seen them. I don't know. . . . Are the, are the Pecks and Suttons—involved?"

"Not yet," Mark said cheerfully. "But unfortunately for them they were with Miss Cassidy a few minutes before she disappeared. Do you get the point now?"

The man was trembling, but not, apparently, from guilty knowledge; it looked like a personal panic.

"How long have you been in charge here?" Mark asked.

"Eight months!" He was so eager that his words overlapped. A faint but unmistakable accent broke through the veneer of crisp, hotel English. He tried, unhappily, to bite it back, to cover it with gestures, but it was out of the bag like a cat. "Eight months! It is only eight months and already I am doing well! If something should happen to a good tenant, I mean if I should say something that is not my affair at all, and they become angry and leave—!" He mopped his brow. "But I tell you I know nothing!"

"I get it. You're afraid you'll lose your job. I know how you feel and I'm sorry, but think this over. Don't hold anything back. It will mean worse trouble in the end. If you change your mind, or remember anything, anything about Miss Cassidy's relations with your tenants, drop me a line." He wrote the Mountain House address on another card and handed it over. Johnny Appleseed, he said to himself; maybe one of these will grow something too. "Any objection to my presence in that restaurant over there?" He indicated a black and white marble crypt with Pompeian red table cloths.

"No, no!" The manager stood back. "It—it is public."

Mark went in and took a table far from the door. It was only eleven but he thought he could handle a cold melon and some more coffee. He changed his mind quickly when he saw a neat replica of the Parthenon in the opposite corner, stacked with bottles and glasses. When a youthful waiter came to take his order he had already planned his approach.

"Don't tell me it's too early for a Martini," he said; "one, very, very dry. Nick Sutton says they're the best in New York."

"Yessir! That Nick, he knows!" The boy hurried away.

Now, thought Mark, if the boss doesn't get to him before I do, I may find out something. Maybe. When the drink came he told the boy to wait while he sampled it cautiously. His face mirrored a spurious joy. "That Nick, he knows," he agreed.

"Yessir. You a friend of Nick's?"

"Known him ever since he was born. Sad story."

The boy's face was honestly blank. So he didn't know that one.

"We're spending the summer in the same place," Mark went on. "Grandpa's a lively old duck, isn't he?"

The boy agreed heartily. The gentleman had said it! What a guy!

When the gentleman craftily pressed for details it developed that this enthusiasm was only an ambitious young waiter's attempt to please a customer.

"I don't hardly know the old guy," the boy admitted. "I seen him going out and coming in, that's all. He don't talk to nobody. Never buys a drink, neither. George takes care of that upstairs."

"George!" Mark beamed. "Don't tell me this isn't a small world! I was drinking with George and his girl just before I came down here. It looks to me like New York has seen the last of our Georgie. He's in love. He says he's going to settle in the country, on a farm."

The boy collapsed over the back of an empty chair. "Not Georgie! Not Georgie in no country! He'll die. Wait'll I tell the girls!"

"What girls?"

"Sisters. He's got five, up in Eighty-sixth. Nice folks. I was up there a couple nights ago, and they didn't say nothing about George getting married and living in the country. Maybe he never told 'em. Maybe it ain't serious."

"I think it's serious, all right. He thinks it will be good for his lungs. They were pretty bad, weren't they?"

"Yeah, I guess so." The boy was suddenly sober. "He coughed a lot. It hurt you to hear him. It was the girls that made him take that Sutton job in the country. He was only here two weeks before they went away, but in one day he owned the place. Ain't he coming back, honest?"

"That's what he says. He's having a good time up there. You know the Pecks have a place right next to the—"

Then it came, a sibilant whistle from the direction of the bar. They both looked over and saw the barman's beckoning finger. He was replacing the receiver on one of two phones in a corner of the Parthenon.

House phone, Mark said to himself, with the manager on the other end.

"Excuse me, sir," the boy said. "If you want another one before I get back, lean on the bell." He hurried away. Mark knew he wouldn't come back.

He didn't want another one, so he left a dollar bill on the table and went out. Buster's little screen had so far yielded nothing, not even a hint. Cora and Kirby were still doubtful and, short of a trip to Lexington, he could do no more at the moment. Nothing on the Suttons, nothing on the Pecks, nothing on George. He wasn't disturbed about George and old man Sutton. They hadn't gone to the supper and they'd been seen on and off all evening, on the lawn, on the veranda, in their own rooms. Suppose the answer was in Bear River after all? He recalled the beaming picture of Mrs. Briggs, Mrs. Moresby, who was Pansy's cousin, and Pansy herself. Mabel Homesdale. The Reverend Mr. Walters. Even, he reminded himself, the rabbity Mr. Briggs, who had cast his shadow at the feet of the ladies. He hailed a cab and drove down to East Twelfth Street.

Miss Rayner lived in a remodeled brick house and the doorbell placed her on the third floor. He pressed the bell marked "Superintendent" and a colored man in a denim apron put his head through the area railings.

"Suh?"

Just like the Little Colonel, Mark noted. "I'm looking for Miss Rayner," he said, "but she doesn't answer her bell. Is she out, do you know?"

"She been out since way back," the Negro grinned. "She go to the country for the summer."

"Oh." Mark sat down on the bottom step. "That's too bad. Some friends of hers asked me to look her up when I was in town. I thought I'd take her out to lunch."

The Negro's grin widened. "Too bad ain't half. She like nothing better than free meals. Miss Rayner a very close lady with her money and don't I know it."

"Like that, huh?" He made a sympathetic sound. "Maybe I'm lucky after all. What's she like? Pretty?"

"Pretty? Before God, man, she close to one hundred years ole! You ain't miss nothing."

"Cigarette?" It was accepted graciously. "Her friends told me she was very popular. Always gadding about."

"They lie. That ole woman don't go nowhere except it free. Except them little trips she take, couple times year. She go way a couple days now and then. Change of air, she say. Don't do her no good nohow. She come back looking worse."

"When's she coming home, do you know?"

"She write me a penny postcard last week and say to clean her place good on account of she come back soon. My wife going to clean tomorrow."

"I don't suppose you'd let me in her apartment, would you, just to write a little note?"

The man's eyes narrowed. "I couldn't do that, suh," he said politely. "Much as I like to oblige a gentleman I couldn't do that. That against house rules."

Mark smiled. "Well, we won't break them. I'll try to call again. Here." He gave the man a bill. It was worth it to know that loyalty flourished like the green bay tree in basements. "Buy yourself a beer."

He walked to the Lafayette and got himself some lunch; then, fortified by snails in black butter, he went into a phone booth. The Reid Memorial Hospital was mellifluently co-operative. It begged him to wait one minute. He expected to wait ten, all fruitless, and was surprised to find himself wrong. A crisp voice, male, replaced the soft voice, female, and told him that certainly Miss Cassidy had nursed Mrs. Beacham in her last illness. Was there anything else?

He admitted that there was. His own wife needed a nurse, and she'd heard of Miss Cassidy's unusual competence and would have no other. But Miss Cassidy wasn't in the phone book. Could they tell him where she could be located?

The voice hesitated and finally confessed that Miss Cassidy was dead.

Mark was shocked. Could they tell him where she had trained? Perhaps he could find someone similar. "You know how women are at times like these." He heard himself panting and knew it wasn't all acting, either.

The voice gave him the name of a sprawling city hospital, famous for its color, drama, and capability. He thanked the voice profusely and hung up. Another cab, and he was on his way to the last urban lead. If this was a blank he'd go back uptown and try George's five sisters.

The mist had turned to rain when he drew up before the great stone barracks that housed at least one example of all the world's misery and pain. He'd been there many times before, in the early morning, late at night, in summer and winter. He knew which corridor led to the morgue, which to the dipsomaniacs. He knew the sad floor that often rang with empty, frightened cries, and he could still see the blank eyes that reflected nothing, not even life.

After a wait, he was led to a small, clean office, so dark that the lamps were lighted. It was proudly decorated with chintz, books, and potted ivy. It belonged to Miss McKenna, the head of the nursing staff.

She was a stocky woman with graying red hair and too many lines on her calm, white face. Lying to Miss McKenna would be a waste of breath. He told her at once who he was and why he was there.

"I'm playing a hunch, Miss McKenna," he said. "I think the answer to this is in Miss Cassidy's past. I haven't been able to find anything. Can you help me?"

Miss McKenna looked out of the single, open window that faced a gray stone wall. Not even a clock ticked in the room. Outside, the rain wept quietly and remorsefully, like an old, old woman in a graveyard.

Finally she said, "There isn't anything I wouldn't do to help you." She touched her eyes with a folded handkerchief, unashamed. "Mary Cassidy and I were girls together. We started our training the same day. I've been good for nothing ever since I read about her in the papers."

"Has anyone been here to inquire?"

"Not a soul. Not a single soul. She seems to have gone as if she had never existed. . . . But I remember."

"You tell me then. I don't know anything. I never even saw her alive. What was she like? Who were her people? What was her private life?"

She told him, sitting up straight in her chair, her clean, strong hands folded in her lap.

Mary Cassidy had come to America when she was twelve. Her people in Donegal had died, and the priest had arranged her passage. She'd lived in New York with an aunt who had seven of her own, and had gone to work in a tea packing factory. But she'd studied at night; she'd seen enough of poverty and illiteracy, and she was determined to make something of herself. So determined that she was afraid to buy clothes, even when she had the money; so afraid of being hungry again that she'd hoard broken crackers from the nurses' dining room, and wrinkled apples that nobody else would eat. "Not miserly," Miss McKenna said. "Just frightened. I'm glad she had plenty in her life before she left it."

"She had more than plenty," Mark said. He thought of telling her about the unopened perfume, the frail nightgowns still in the tissue paper from the shop, but that seemed cruel and he put the thought away.

"Of course she was a good nurse?" he asked.

"One of the best. She had a kind of passion for service. I guess because she was getting more than she'd ever hoped for and wanted to pass it along. I've known her to follow up discharged cases, on her hours off, just to make sure things were all right."

So she followed up discharged cases. That could be it. He forced himself to move slowly. "Did she ever have any trouble that way? Did any of those discharged cases harbor a grudge?"

"No. No, I don't think so. I'm sure she'd have told me. But—but—"

"Go on," he said quietly. "You know yourself how important little things are. Tell me anything that comes into your head."

"I was just wondering." Miss McKenna looked embarrassed. "You know when she went into private nursing she ran into queer things. She used to stop in here and tell me about them, and we'd have a good laugh. She used to say she wished she was back on the wards."

"What kind of queer things?"

"Oh, men making passes," Miss McKenna blushed, "things like that. They seem to think it's expected of them. But we know how to handle such. One thing she always did say though. Mr. Beacham was a perfect gentleman. She was devoted to that family."

"That's one of the things I was wondering about. Nothing but good to say about the Beachams?"

"Absolutely." Miss McKenna was definite. "At one time there was a little trouble about the oldest girl, about three years ago. She was getting out of hand, you know, impertinent and giving orders like Mary was an ordinary servant. But Mary never mentioned it to Mr. Beacham. He found out for himself, and I understand he threatened to thrash Roberta, big as she was, unless she mended her manners. She mended 'em!"

Mark looked thoughtful. "It's a funny thing," he said, "but I haven't been able to get a decent description of Miss Cassidy. I saw her body of course, but you know what death does to a face. Nobody has a picture. There was one in a small photography shop in the country, but she went in there a few weeks before she died and had it destroyed. I wonder if you—"

Miss McKenna jumped in her chair. "The Lord love you, but you've put me in mind of something I'd almost forgotten. Pictures! Mary was in town not long ago and came down here to see me, but I was out."

She got up and briskly crossed to the phone. "Miriam? Send Angela Scotti down to me at once. I don't care what she's doing, send her." She came back.

"Imagine me forgetting that! And I really was upset at the time. I hated to miss her calls. You see, I was out, and Angela talked to her. She told Angela she didn't have much time and couldn't wait for me, but she wondered if I'd mind if she took an old photograph of herself out of my album. Angela said I wouldn't, but it did strike her as an odd thing to ask. There was only the one picture of her in the whole book, the one we had taken on the roof the day before we graduated."

"Did she tell Angela what she was doing in town?"

"Yes. She said she'd come down on business for Mr. Beacham. Angela said she was very pale and nervous, so she brought her a cup of tea and left her. For a little rest, you know." Miss McKenna patted her hair distractedly. "I'm provoked with myself because I didn't think of that before. I should have remembered. I'm getting old."

He started to say something gallant, but the door opened and a thin, dark girl came in. Angela Scotti was already enjoying the break in her routine.

"Angela, this is Mr. East," Miss McKenna said crisply. "Tell him all you know about Miss Cassidy's visit. He's working on the case for the Beachams."

Angela's wide dark eyes grew wider. She was only a probationer and she pictured herself at the supper table that night. I'll panic them, she gloated. I'll show them. Even that fresh interne. "Yes, Miss McKenna," she said.

She told the same story about the picture and the cup of tea, but her version was punctuated with gasps. Afterwards, she told the supper table that she felt the same way she did when the orderly put a skeleton in her bed. It was the way Mr. East looked at you, she said. Kind of like Cary Grant, but hard.

"Did Miss Cassidy give any reason for wanting the picture?" Mark asked.

"Yes, she did, but it wasn't very sensible. She said she didn't believe in leaving the past lying around. She smiled when she said it, sort of funny. I'd only seen her once before, that was right after Christmas, and she'd changed a lot." Angela waved her hands. "Nervous, and if you ask me she should have had a sedative. But all she would take was tea."

"You went out and left her alone in here, didn't you?"

"Yes, sir. She'd found the picture in Miss McKenna's album, and I'd brought her the tea, and she said she'd like to rest a few minutes. But when I came back about twenty minutes later to get the cup she was gone."

"Did anybody else see her?"

"No, sir. I asked everybody because there she was with a beautiful ring on and a twenty-dollar handbag and I told the other girls that it just showed you what you could do with nursing if you behaved yourself." She gave Miss McKenna a virtuous look. Then she added, "That drawer was open, though."

Mark jumped. "What did you say?"

"That drawer." She pointed to a row of steel filing cabinets along one wall. "Fourth from the left, third from the top. It was open and I closed it."

Miss McKenna gave Mark a look that compared the student nurses of the past with those of the present and left no doubt about the rating. She drew down her mouth.

"Those are private records, Angela. Nobody touches them but me. The drawer could not have been open."

"But it was, Miss McKenna. I saw it right away. And I knew you'd have a fit—I knew you wouldn't like it, so I closed it. I didn't look inside, either."

Angela looked as if she might cry in a minute.

"Cheer up," Mark said. "No harm done. On the contrary, you've been a great help. Miss McKenna, do you mind if I take a look? At the outside only."

"Certainly not." She spied Angela, avidly watching and quietly moving in. "That will do, Angela. You may go now, and thank you."

Angela backed to the door, but not because of manners, and closed it slowly behind her.

Miss McKenna looked at Mark. "I'm beginning to be worried," she said. He was over at the files, reading the date cards on each drawer. "Yes, I'm beginning to be worried. I'm afraid this means something."

"Yes," he said. "I mean, I hope so. Fourth from the left, third from the top." He didn't touch the drawer; he looked at it with prayer in his eyes. "You're going to tell me what these files hold, aren't you?"

"Of course. They're duplicate histories of our—I guess you'd call them our sensational cases. The originals are in a safe in the psychopathic wing. I have these in here because it isn't always easy to get at the safe. The room is often locked. Sometimes we need a record in a hurry. There's a trick lock to these, too. That's what I'm wondering about. Only myself and a few doctors know how to work it."

"Did Mary Cassidy know how?" he asked softly.

"Yes." She looked startled. "Of course Mary knew. That was her work. Mr. East, did Mary open that drawer?"

"I'm sure she did. I think that's one of the things she came for. If you'd been here she'd have asked you to do it." He tapped the file gently. "What do you call a sensational case, and under what circumstance is the record referred to?"

"Nervous diseases," she said. "Or, in plain English, insanity. Sometimes we get several people from the same family, over a period of years. You do, in a place like this. And when that happens, the relatives don't always tell us the truth. You know how people are about mental derangements. Well, that's where this file comes in. If we're suspicious, we check. And we constantly add new details as we come across them, in newspapers and so on. When I read in the paper that so and so has done such and such, I very often hold my breath and wait for the smash-up. It almost always comes, too."

"All charity cases?"

"My land, no! You'd be surprised! Mr. East, those files are confidential."

"I know it. Now I want you to listen to me carefully. Mary Cassidy was a friend of yours. Not long before she was killed she went to a photographer's shop and destroyed the only picture of herself that was available in that part of the country. The following day she came down to New York and looked you up. She came on legitimate business, but I think she'd have found another way to get here if the business hadn't turned up. And what did she do? She came in here and destroyed another picture. You say that was the only one you had?"

"Yes. I think it was the only one in the whole hospital. I'm sure of it. I'm—I'm all that's left of the old crowd."

"Fine. Then she got young Angela out of the room and opened a confidential file. Miss McKenna, doesn't that begin to add up?"

"If I'd only been here," Miss McKenna said unhappily. "I'd have helped her."

"You can still do that," he said. "You can open that file for me."

"You'll have to sell me on that, Mr. East. I want to do it, but I have a professional conscience. You'll have to tell me why."

"I will, and you can make the decision yourself. I'll not try to force you. I think Mary Cassidy ran into somebody, recognized somebody, whose name is in there. Somebody who is now at large and shouldn't be. I think she was afraid the recognition was mutual, but she wasn't sure. That's why she destroyed the pictures. She was playing desperately for time, time to check with your files, time to decide what to do, time to—save herself."

Miss McKenna bent over and read the date on the index card. "Nineteen-thirty. We had a lot of them that year. It was the year we graduated, too." She turned her back squarely and he heard the whir of a well-oiled mechanism. The drawer slid out. "Go ahead," she said. "There are about sixty cases in there, as complete as we could make them. Don't ask me for further details. You're on your own now."

She went over to the window while he carried the manila folders to the table, and stood there, staring at the gray wall and the rain. One by one she heard him slap the folders down as he discarded them. She didn't turn around. He's looking at the names first, she said to herself; then if he doesn't recognize any he'll go back and read the descriptions. Do people alter much in fourteen years, she wondered?

After a while she heard him say, "Miss McKenna?" She turned around then. "Yes, Mr. East?" He was slumped in his chair.

"None of these names mean anything to me and I know that one of them should. What's wrong? Does anybody ever get in here under an alias?"

"Never! Not that they don't try it. At least the family tries, but they don't get away with it. Never. . . . Wait a minute." She looked suddenly shy. "I've just thought of something. Don't think I'm trying to run your business, but why couldn't your man be using an assumed name, out in the world, I mean? People do."

He gave her an awed look, and it made her blush. "Am I dumb or just nervous?"

"Nervous," she said briskly. "You watch yourself or we'll be filing you in there. I'm going to get you a drink and I'll ask you to hold your breath when you pass the receptionist on your way out. And after you've had it, you go back over those folders and check by age and nationality."

She poured him a mild whisky and soda and turned on more lights. It was growing dark outside. He wondered if they were having a storm on the mountain.

"The dead ones are marked dead," she said. "And you'll find the addresses of those who are still living. Some have been transferred to institutions or are cared for by relatives. We don't like that but we can't help it. They're all dangerous, but I guess you know that."

She went back to her place by the window. She heard the slow, deliberate turning of pages, an occasional grunt, a low whistle. She knew it was ugly reading. Even when you were hospital trained, it was ugly. She tried to remember whether Mary Cassidy had been involved in any particular case.

"Her name, Mary's name, will be listed on the cases she worked with," she said over her shoulder.

"I know," he said. "I've found one."

A half hour passed before she heard the sound she was waiting for. It was a deep growl. "Have you got it?" she asked quietly, still watching the rain.

"Yes and no. She had twelve of these cases. Seven died here in the hospital. Three, all men, were transferred to private sanitariums and according to the final notations they're still there. And presumably living under constant guard. Another man went to a state institution and was eventually turned over to relatives. The last one, a woman, was removed from the city by a brother. Went west, no town given. How reliable is the sanitarium information?"

"Not very." She came over and stood beside him. "The relatives don't always tell us when they make changes. And they're always making them. The patient complains, says he's mistreated and unhappy, so of course they move him. But with charity cases we always know where they go. It's the ones with money that cause all the trouble. They move from place to place, and the family keeps quiet about it. . . . Mary felt very strongly about some of her cases. About releasing them, I mean. She advised against it. It isn't hopeless, is it?"

"No. I've narrowed it down to three. The names don't mean a thing, of course; you were right about the alias. But," he frowned, "none of the descriptions fits anyone I've seen. Still, it's got to be one of them. There's a very nice—I guess you'd call it a complex—a very nice complex that figures in all three I've selected, and it fits Mary Cassidy's case like a glove. Want to know something? I don't think I'm looking for one of your ex-inmates." He tapped the folders. "I think I'm looking for one of his relatives. A relative who's as nuts as he ever was but never got caught. A relative who saw Mary Cassidy years ago and resented her, blamed her for the damning charts she kept, for the necessary part she played."

"You could be right," Miss McKenna said thoughtfully. "Once a relative tried to knife the nurse on duty. He was sane, though. It was grief that made him do that. But what you say is certainly possible. . . . Mary felt that way too."

He took out his pen and book. "I'm going to make some notes. That's all right with you, isn't it?"

She hesitated. "All right," she said reluctantly. "I know you could get a court order and take the whole file away with you if you wanted to. But I feel as if—you know I'm doing this on my own responsibility. I ought to talk to the director first, but he'd hem and haw and keep you waiting for days. You can't afford to wait, can you?"

"No," he said seriously. "I want to be back there by morning."

She turned away when he began to write. She didn't want to see which folders he was using. He was humming as he pushed the pen rapidly across the paper, writing down the sad little secrets and mannerisms that would tell him how to recognize a murderer.

"This is dreadful," she whispered to the rain.

She didn't know she'd spoken out loud until he said, "No, it isn't. It's right."

Finally he looked up. "I put the three questionable folders back with the others. What you don't know won't hurt you. . . . You had a good psychiatrist on those cases."

"We always do," she said proudly.

"And thanks to him and to you I know the kind of person I'm looking for." He picked up his hat. "I've got to leave you now and I can't thank you enough. But perhaps you don't want thanks. It isn't often that an old friend has such a privilege."

He left her with that and was glad to see the quick tears spring to her eyes. She'd be all right after she had a good cry. He remembered to hold his breath when he passed the receptionist.

He took a cab to his apartment. It was still raining and the fog was thick, and though it was only four-thirty the lamps were on along the Avenue.

His heart was both heavy and light. Mary Cassidy had recognized a face, and the recognition had come slowly. Prosperity and poverty, as well as time, could bring changes. Or perhaps it wasn't a face; perhaps it was a trick of speech or gesture, carefully guarded against for years and then forgotten in an off moment. But Mary Cassidy had seen it, and it had confused and frightened her. She'd begun to wonder if the recognition had been on both sides.

She knew she had changed with the years herself; she was well-fed and well-clothed, and she had taken on the easy manners of her new environment. But she couldn't be sure that this was enough. That was why she had destroyed her photographs. The snapshot in Buster's window may have held a fugitive reflection of the girl she used to be. The camera sometimes caught that. And the one in Miss McKenna's album, that one would be fatal. Her name was on it and she was wearing her uniform. Suppose somebody came to call on Miss McKenna, a friendly call beginning with—"I've often thought of you and wondered if you still were here." Reminiscences might follow. It would be natural to ask for the album. It was reasonable to think that some of the patients and their relatives would know about it. It would be easy to say—"Whatever became of that little nurse, Miss Cassidy?"

He looked out of the cab window. Almost there. . . . Mary Cassidy had known the black potentialities of the person she was dealing with. She also knew she'd be going back home with the Beachams at the end of the month. Had she planned to keep quiet until then? Or were the danger signals so disturbing that she planned to warn the authorities at once? Was her Nemesis an old patient who was unlawfully at large or was it a relative, as he thought? A mad relative with a sane face and a grudge that gnawed like a cancer.

He paid his cab and ran across the wet sidewalk to the lobby. The switchboard girl hailed him before he reached the elevator.

"Whoa!" she said. "Why don't you tell me where you're going? I've been trying to find you all day. Long distance has been talking my ear off!"

He held his breath. "Who?"

"Bear River called you four times, Sheriff Wilcox. You're to—now wait, baby, wait, let mama do it!"

CHAPTER EIGHT

H E recognized the Bear River operator at once. She was Maudie, Wilcox's sister. She knew him too, as well she might; she'd figured in his calculations the winter before.

"Mr. East?" she said. "Thank goodness! Perley's out on the road somewhere and he told me to put you through to Miss Pond as soon as you called. Miss Pond's at the Mountain House. Hold on."

"What happened?"

"That's not for me to say, Mr. East. Miss Pond will tell you. Here we go. . . . Mountain House? New York calling Miss Pond."

He waited. He was taking the call on the lobby phone because he was unwilling to lose even a few minutes. "Hello," he shouted, "hello!"

Beulah's voice, clear and cross, answered. "It's about time," she said, "and you needn't yell. Now let me do the talking. Last night Perley put his gun on the window sill in Beacham's cottage, and somebody took it. He was asleep, but only for a little while. He couldn't help it, and it could happen to anybody. Even Amos admits that, so don't be too hard on the poor man. He and Amos searched all night but they couldn't find it."

"I told him not to leave that cottage! It was a plant. Somebody wanted him out of the way. What happened?"

"Wait. Nothing happened, that is, nothing too awful. So they searched and they didn't find it. They didn't see anybody or hear anything. It began to look like a practical joke and that's what they thought it was, until this morning. This morning Joey couldn't find Cassie's puppy. She and Pee Wee tore the mountain apart and along about noon they found the poor little thing. Dead. Shot through the heart, just like it was human. And what do you suppose was lying beside it?"

"Perley's gun," Mark said wearily. "And no fingerprints."

"Nothing. No footprints either, and it was sandy there. Everybody's in a panic. It was such a small, mean thing to do. Just a fat little puppy that never hurt anybody. Perley says what's the next move?"

"There isn't one. Sit tight. I'll be in on the train that gets to Baldwin at six a.m. What are you doing at the hotel?"

"Perley called me up. When I heard about the little dog I thought it was a part of the Cassidy cycle, so I came. I've got a room in the main building. I don't like anything about this, Mark, but I'm not worrying about myself. I have a gun of my own, as you may remember, and there's a modest legend about my shooting."

"Where's Bessy?"

"That brandy came. The Caldwell girls—wouldn't you know it? She's with them. What do you want me to do tonight?"

"If you're honestly not afraid, I wish you'd move into Roberta's room. And stay awake! The return of Perley's gun looks as if our pal wants us to think he's satisfied. But I don't know. Tell Perley and Amos to patrol the grounds and hotel. And if either of them takes a nap, it'll be his last. Try to make it look like ordinary routine. Watch out for panic and step on it. I guess that's all."

"Mark? I don't want to say too much because there's a steady procession walking by this booth, and how do I know somebody can't read lips, but—did you get anything?"

He thought quickly She was constant, faithful, and reliable, but she had one secret vice. She thought she was a lone wolf. If he gave her a hint she'd run away with it. She'd start asking what she believed were veiled questions, beginning with the chef and working up to old Sutton, and that would be too bad because she wouldn't live to tell him who answered.

"No," he said. "That is to say, practically no."

"You're lying," she said without rancor.

"Good-by," he said. "Have Perley meet me in Baldwin." He hung up before she could invite herself.

He felt a little better when he went upstairs to his apartment. There was a lot to be said in favor of Beulah in the Mountain House. Nobody there knew her too well. She was mildly rich, which would circumvent the snobs, and so respectable in appearance that she was sometimes painful to look at. And she wouldn't miss a thing. He was even willing to bet that some unmerciful instinct would lead her directly to Franny Peck's love letters. He felt a twinge of pity for Franny.

He changed his clothes and went out again, this time on a shopping tour that took him through five upper bracket delicatessens and two gilded black markets. He finally found what he wanted and paid for it with tears in his eyes. He also visited a music store. Then, after a late supper, he took his train. At midnight he was rolling north with high hopes built on two inconspicuous parcels done up in brown paper. He took out his notes and read them.

He had the names of three people who had been certified as incurably insane in nineteen-thirty, and the names meant nothing These three were presumably alive, as their records did not say otherwise. Two were men; one would be eighty-five, if living, and the other fifty-one. The third was a woman whose birth certificate had not been available Her age, as given by her brother, had been twenty-two at the time of her admission. She'd be thirty-six now.

The older man had been removed by his daughter to a private sanitarium outside Philadelphia. Five years later the hospital had made a routine check; he had been moved again, and there his history ended.

The younger man had been transferred to a state institution, and after two years of exemplary behavior had been allowed to go home to his family. Also, the institution admitted, his bed had been needed for a new patient. His home was in New York City. The final notation on the record said that the family had left town, address unknown.

The woman, while incurable, was passably dangerous only to herself. Her brother had convinced the authorities that he was able to care for her. He had taken her to a small town in the west. Neither town nor state was identified.

But here the obscurity ended and the psychiatrist entered. Nothing had escaped this man's eyes, nothing had been too trivial for listing in black and white. It was almost as if he had known how desperately his diagnosis would be needed some day. He had shrewdly and sympathetically analyzed each case, and his findings had been taken down by Mary Cassidy.

In each of the three cases there was one arresting similarity, the emotional conflict between patient and next of kin. In each one, a fanatical love or hate had met with indifference or antipathy.

Mark remembered how those stories had looked, written down in Mary Cassidy's neat, characterless script. He remembered the heavy underscoring. The man who had dictated those reports had wanted to call attention to the danger signals, and Mary Cassidy had drawn those heavy lines because she had been told to. And she'd never forgotten.

The older man had hated his daughter, and she, in turn, had worshiped him. The younger man had hated his mother, who came to see him every day and who sat beside his bed and wept and prayed audibly.

The woman, who was a young girl then, had groveled when her brother came into the ward. Once, when he was leaving and she was begging him to stay, she put her hand in one of his pockets and drew out two theater ticket stubs. She had nearly killed him then, and after that he'd been told to stay away. But he'd returned the next week with his own doctor, and they'd taken her home. Mary Cassidy had seen all of that and much more. And she'd worried.

Mark closed the notebook with a feeling of dismay.

It was already Friday, the day old Sutton had called the deadline. Mary Cassidy had disappeared the Friday before, and he, the seven-day wonder, was expected to deliver by midnight. He loosened his tie and rearranged the deadline. She'd been found on Sunday. He'd do his adding from that. And if he didn't have a definite lead by Sunday midnight he'd take young Nick into protective custody. That would start something.

His mind returned to the unfinished business in Bear River. There were other backgrounds to check; the Reverend Mr. Walters, the Moresbys, the Briggs pair. And Mabel Homesdale. Something might be dragged up from the bottom of Mabel's cluttered little head. Mabel may have collected more than rumpled linen and silver foxes when she sauntered in and out of the Mountain House rooms. And Mabel's sanitarium. Had Mary Cassidy gone there?

Perley could handle all of that. He knew these people. They'd talk to him. And if there were any strait-jackets in the family closets he'd know who wore them and when. The Reverend Mr. Walters might give a little trouble, but the whole thing would keep Perley busy, if not happy.

He knew he had to go easy with Perley. Perley was a holy terror with chicken thieves and illegal hunters, but the possibilities of this case would reduce him to a useless jelly. In his frightened innocence he would be a danger to himself. No, better keep the facts under cover and let Perley hound the probably harmless natives with a few mildly upsetting questions. It would be enough if he could put the fear of God into Miss Homesdale.

Between cat naps and long drinks of judiciously flavored water he managed to get through the night.

Perley was waiting on the platform at Baldwin. It was only six o'clock, but a burning red sun battled with low hanging clouds, and the wooden platform dripped with moisture. Perley's clothes clung to his thin frame and he hadn't shaved.

"Am I glad to see you!" he groaned. "Get in the car." He looked ready to cry. "What did you find out?"

"Tell you later. Why haven't we done something about Mabel's sanitarium?"

"Because the man we want don't spend his life in bed, that's why! They're all half-dead out there. What are you getting at?"

"I want to see the place. Now."

To Perley's frenzied expostulations and demands to know more, he simply replied that the idea had come to him on the train. "It's the only stone we haven't turned over, that's all. It'll take you a little out of your way of course, but if you don't want to drive me——"

Perley swung the car around. "Consumptives," he muttered. "Can't even walk." Then, "Maybe Miss Cassidy was a consumptive nurse? That it?"

"You're getting warm."

They drove through the tall iron gates and up to the front door. Mark asked to see the head resident. The doctor was out of town, he was told; would Matron do? He said she would, and she came almost at once. She made no attempt to conceal her curiosity and annoyance.

Mark asked if she had heard about the Cassidy murder in Bear River. She said she had, and waited for him to go on. Had Miss Cassidy ever visited the sanitarium? She couldn't say. Strangers sometimes came and walked about the grounds, but only relatives were allowed inside. She emphasized that. Only relatives, she repeated, at proper visiting hours. She looked at her watch, pointedly, and transferred her gaze to Perley's unshaven chin. Mark decided that he didn't like her.

"Police business," he said crisply. "Sheriff Wilcox and I would like to look the place over. Routine only. We'll be quiet."

With elaborate courtesy she turned them over to an orderly and left them.

There was nothing much to see and too much to hear. For ten long minutes they tiptoed up and down aseptic corridors, trying not to see the trays of white enamel basins, trying not to hear the intermittent silence that was louder than the faint, recurring sounds. They were glad to reach the stifling air outside.

The orderly waited patiently.

"What's that?" Mark pointed to a row of bungalows in the rear, half hidden in shrubbery.

"Special care," grinned the orderly. "Special money."

They strolled over. "Only one occupied now," the orderly went on. "Number four. You can't go in. Treatment going on."

Mark looked in the window of number four. He saw white figures bending over a bed and heard a strangling cry. Perley plucked at his sleeve. "Come on," he whispered. "Haven't you got any heart?"

They returned to the car and drove toward home.

"Satisfied, I hope," Perley said bitterly. "I feel sick myself. What do you want me to do next? Rob a grave?"

Mark didn't answer at once. Then, "No. The next job is right up your alley. I want the private histories of the Walters, Briggs, Moresby, and Homesdale families. Very hush-hush. You're looking for somebody who went away from home for a long visit, about thirteen or fourteen years ago."

"Am I? How long did they stay away?"

"A year. Maybe more, maybe less. I'll give you an example. If somebody tells you papa's youngest sister went to California in twenty-nine and stayed longer than she meant to, you make a note of it."

"You're on the wrong track again, Mark. Nobody's been to California. Only to Virginia, and he died."

"Unless you saw the body, don't believe he's dead. Now concentrate. We want somebody, man or woman, who had a little private trouble and went away to get rid of it. Somebody, let's say, who had to take the cure on the q.t., or do a stretch in jail, or get out of marrying the girl. See?"

Perley nodded. "Yep. I see. Somebody who'd feel disgraced if the truth got out. Nope. Not here. I've known these folks from the cradle up."

"How about Walters? He's new."

"Walters!"

"Why not? Where did he come from before he came here?"

"Rhode Island. And if you think I'm going to talk like that to a man of God, you're crazy. And don't go quoting me the names of preachers who got hung!"

"I'll ask Amos to do it."

Perley looked offended. "All right. But how'm I going to go about it? With Walters, I mean. Walk right up to him after church on Sunday and say—'Thanks for the lovely sermon and were any of your folks ever drunkards, jailbirds, or you-know-what?'"

"Call up his Rhode Island church, confidentially. If he turns out innocent, it'll only make him glamorous. If he's guilty, everybody will

love you for finding it out. And go after Mabel Homesdale, hard. She
was around the hotel early in the summer, and although she wasn't at
the church supper she might have been on the outskirts, in the dark."
This was missionary work, pure and simple. He felt that George's
future would be happier if Miss Homesdale's present took a slight beating. "Ask her what she's been doing every night since Friday."

"You must have had yourself a time in New York," Perley said
admiringly. "Can't you tell me a little more? I've been real patient
so far."

"No." Perley accepted this with so much humility that Mark weak-
ened. "I mean I can't tell you much. I'm sure the motive is buried in
the past, and I'm pretty sure Miss Cassidy's past is above reproach. That
points to somebody around here who can't show as clean a slate. I think
Miss Cassidy caught on and was killed before she had a chance to
spread the news."

"She wasn't a gossipy woman, Mark."

"She didn't have to be. The other person just wasn't taking chances.
Suppose, for the sake of argument, that the present Mrs. Briggs, when
young and unmarried, went down to New York to have her appendix
out. And suppose she turned up in the hospital where Miss Cassidy was
a nurse. And suppose Miss Cassidy knew an appendix when she didn't
see one. We pause here for the passing of time. Then, years later, in the
sleepy little town of Bear River, the now affluent Miss Cassidy runs
into Mrs. Briggs for the second time and recognizes her under the lay-
ers of fat. And Mrs. Briggs knows Miss Cassidy, too. You see, Perley?
It's all a lie, of course, but you get the idea?"

"You turn my stomach. . . . All right, I'll start insulting people this
morning. Mark, who took my gun and shot that little dog?"

"Someone who hates Miss Cassidy even though she's dead, and
wants to wipe out everything she loved. Your gun was a piece of ego-
istic melodrama. I hope and think we'll have more of it. No killing, just
a bit of showing off. And one more dumb move like that and we've
got him. . . . You went to sleep, didn't you?"

Perley admitted to a short nap, but he still couldn't figure how the
gun was taken. Amos had been awake and prowling, and he'd seen nothing and nobody. "There was an owl following him around though."

"A what?"

"Owl." He gave a graphic account. "Amos said it was human and
durn if it didn't sound like it. And"—he gave Mark an anxious look,
eager to be believed—"and all the rest of the night I could feel some-

body watching in the dark outside. Standing there, and watching in the dark."

Mark nodded. "Possible," he admitted. He frowned. "Anything happen last night?"

"Not a thing, except that everybody in the hotel was scared to death. But that didn't last long. It was worse yesterday morning. Some folks were all for leaving, but I said they couldn't. That was right, wasn't it? We can't have people walking out to the four winds, can we?"

"We cannot. Who wanted to go?"

"Mr. Kirby, some folks from Pittsburgh named Foote, and Miss Rayner. They claimed they were all going next week anyhow and tried to give me an argument. So I telephoned Miss Pond. I told her about the dog and all that, and she said leave it to her. So I did. She came right up and took a room, and in five minutes you wouldn't have known the place. She carried on about the lovely air, in which you could have fried eggs, and taught everybody a game of solitaire that she said was called Idiot's Delight. They stayed."

Mark swore softly. "Idiot's Delight! Did anybody refuse to play?"

"No. Why? You don't look good."

"I don't feel good. What's the latest on Beacham and Miss Cassidy's body?"

"All settled. Undertaker'll put it on the seven p.m. from Baldwin tonight. Beacham's going down with it. He's already made arrangements over the phone for cremation tomorrow. Then he says he's coming back to pack up his family. You ought to hear him on death, but I guess you will."

"Got a new name for it?"

"I wouldn't say that. But he tells everybody how undignified it is and it beats me why he don't drop dead from blasphemy. The Reverend Walters came up last night to talk to him, out of pure Christian kindness, and they tell me it was terrible. Miss Sheffield heard 'em. Do you know what that woman did?"

"What?"

"She gave Mr. Walters twenty-five dollars to have the well cleaned out, right in front of everybody. I kind of didn't like that. Wouldn't you say it showed a lack of feeling?"

"No. Not from Cora. . . . Did Bittner call up?"

"Not him. You still want that road watched?"

"I certainly do! I wish I knew how much gas all these people have. Can you find out?"

"I don't have to find out," Perley answered dryly. "I know. Nobody has any but Beacham."

Mark gave him a warning look. "All right, but don't let your enthusiasm for a pinch run away with you. I don't want Beacham questioned about a thing like that. Oil's his business and I suppose he's entitled to a little graft. If you want to be mean about it, wait until Sunday."

"Sunday? Why Sunday?"

"Anniversary. If I haven't got our ugly friend by Sunday midnight I'm going to lock up the first person who smiles at me."

Perley thought that over and gave it up. They rode along in silence. He took several sidelong looks at his companion and decided that the conversation was over.

They entered Bear River. The town was still asleep except for a straggling line of mill workers heading for the bus to Baldwin. There were men and women in the line and they looked tired, dirty, and unnecessarily evil in the murky light.

Mark watched the shambling gaits, the stooping shoulders, the vacant faces. I wish it was one of them, he said to himself. Then he said, "Stop at your house, will you, Perley? I want a bath and some sleep before I face the Mountain House. Nobody'll be up there for hours."

Perley beamed. Hospitality was one thing he understood and enjoyed. "Pansy'll give you a good breakfast. She'll be glad to see you. And while you're there, I'll tackle her on Hazel. That's Mrs. Moresby. Her own cousin. It'll be a waste of time and it'll make Pansy mad, but you asked for it." His laughter was almost normal. "Hazel taught school down state for a while; she was away two years. But that was less than five years ago and she boarded with relatives. Still, it's going to make Pansy mad. And Hazel's folks have been dead a long time. She's an orphan."

"Too many whole and half orphans in this case. What did the folks die of?"

"Dunno. I'll ask Pansy."

They parked at the front gate and went in the back way. Pansy was in the kitchen with her hair hanging in two neat braids.

"Have you no shame?" she hissed at Perley. She grappled with the braids. "I'm a living sight. How are you, Mr. East? You look done in. Isn't New York terrible? I'm glad you went yourself instead of sending Perley. Is it too hot for pancakes or would you rather have an omelet? Get along, an omelet's no trouble." She trotted to the icebox and brought out a bowl of eggs. "From Mama's. Last night's. You didn't get eggs like this in New York. Perley and I went there on our honeymoon and I wouldn't touch an egg the whole time because I couldn't be sure."

Mark turned his back to Perley. "What year was your honeymoon, Pansy?"

"Let's see. Floyd's thirteen. That makes it nineteen-thirty."

"I can account," Perley said, "for every minute. Get on with your cooking, Pansy." Then, casually, "By the way, Mark thinks Hazel Moresby is a lovely girl."

"And so she is," Pansy agreed, cracking eggs. "But discontented."

"What did her parents die of?"

"Die of?" She gave her husband a startled look. "Pneumonia. Everybody died of it then. What's the matter with you?"

"Nothing," Perley said. "Mark was only wondering. Did they have a nurse?"

"No they didn't! Poor people couldn't get nurses then. It was a long time ago. I think you've got a touch of the heat or else you're making fun of my family "

She cooked and served breakfast with a hurt expression that was very becoming. Several times she opened her mouth to say something and each time she closed it with a snap. Finally she said, "I'm not going to have my son follow in his father's footsteps. It's very coarsening, and I've already done something about it. The minute I heard about that little dog I sent Floyd out to Mama's to stay. If somebody's going around shooting animals then I say let it be some other mother's son." She made a dignified exit, marred only by two swinging pigtails.

"Let her go," Perley said. "I'll fix it later."

It was nearly noon when Mark walked across the Mountain House lawn. Perley had driven him as far as the gates and then returned to town.

The Mountain House was waiting for him and he wondered whose heart, if any, had beat a little faster when he'd failed to arrive at the expected hour. Once again the rocking chairs on the crowded veranda grew silent and the voices subsided. He sent a triumphant smile along the line of rigid figures and was rewarded with a single burst of sudden, shrill laughter.

Cracking up? he wondered. Probably not. Some woman always laughed like that in the face of tragedy. Take a street accident, a bad one; some woman on the curb always laughed like that before she screamed.

But the watchful crowd of unmoving figures disturbed him. Not one of them was on his list of suspects; still the old, uneasy feeling returned and he wondered again whether Mary Cassidy had left the church grounds and gone for a walk in town. And met someone.

Out of the corner of his eye he saw two people hastily leave their chairs and go indoors. He recognized them as the self-styled Footes. Poor devils, he thought; they're finding out the hard way that their particular pleasure is the world's most overrated pastime. He'd give them a kind word later on, and maybe he'd drive them to the train himself.

A page came running from the hotel to take his bag, but he sent him away and moved on. His own little crowd was out under the trees, grouped around old man Sutton and the attentive George. With the exception of Joey and Pee Wee, no one was missing, and there was an addition, obviously unwelcome, in the gaunt shape of Beulah. She sat erect, with a piece of snarled knitting in her hands, looking as if she held the keys to life and death. The ability to look like that at the drop of a hat was one of her less endearing accomplishments. He wondered why she hadn't been killed for it. Sometimes he'd been tempted himself.

There was an empty chair which George eagerly pushed forward. They greeted him with smiles and nods, all as false as penny masks. He had another thought, one that appalled him. They all looked guilty enough to be innocent.

"New York was hot, too," he said with complete safety. "But I like it. I don't know why I ever left it in the first place."

"Miss Cassidy is probably wondering the same thing," Beulah said piously.

He would certainly kill her, he promised himself. The look he gave her said as much. That self-conscious, silly quip had hardly left her mouth when he saw and felt the tension change to patronizing amusement. And he didn't want it that way. Suddenly, he was furious; with Beulah because she'd struck the wrong note, with the Beachams and the Pecks because they were too well-dressed, with Cora and Kirby because they acted as if they were slumming, with the two Suttons because they looked at him as if he ought to be under a glass bell, and with Miss Rayner because she was trying not to laugh. The only person he liked was George, and that was because George gave him a covert wink. He decided to fire one small shot, and if it went around the world that would be fine.

"I talked to a friend of yours, George," he said. "A kid in the bar at your place. About eighteen, with his hair in his eyes."

"Mike!" exploded George.

Beacham turned an offended face and raised his eyebrows.

"Mike," George said again, turning a rich red. "I mean Mike is his name. It's my friend's name, Mike, this fellow in the bar." He made a final, desperate attempt to straighten out the social order. "Mike is a common name," he said earnestly, and returned to his role of valet with relief.

Nick bent over his grandfather. "Mr. East is trying to tell us that he stopped at our house and asked questions," he said distinctly.

The old man, who was himself again, broke into a laugh that sounded like the rattle of dry bones. "I wonder why Ernescu didn't throw you out?"

"If that's the manager, he tried to." Mark smiled. "But he changed his mind." He went on, "What's the program for today? Riding, driving, golf?"

Beacham cleared his throat. "The sky looks threatening. And frankly, most of us don't feel up to the usual routine. We didn't get much sleep last night. You've been informed of the—gun affair?"

He's frightened, Mark thought. He doesn't talk like that ordinarily. These big shots always get pompous when they feel the ground giving way.

"Yes, I heard about it," he said. "It's nothing to worry about. I'm sorry for Joey, though. She was fond of that pup."

"Nothing to worry about!" Beacham's voice rose. "It was an exhibition of rank carelessness! You don't see me leaving guns on window sills! If you go away again, East, I shall insist on more competent guards."

"I'm not going away again," Mark said, "until I go for good. And Wilcox and Partridge weren't careless. Ten guards armed to the teeth couldn't have saved that puppy."

Miss Rayner nodded. "I know," she said. "I found that so interesting. So very interesting that I gave myself the little chore of watching the fire escape. Last night." She sent a faint smile around the circle; it deepened when it came to Beulah. "You had the same idea, didn't you,

Miss Pond? That was you I saw climbing in and out of a third floor window?"

Beulah looked affronted "I didn't see you," she said sharply.

"Naturally, my dear. I didn't want to be seen."

"At your age," Beulah said, "and with your leg."

Mark took the conversation into his own hands. "Where's young Joey?" he asked Beacham.

"I don't know. I never know where she is any more. Where is she, Roberta?"

"She and Pee Wee went off together. They didn't say where they were going, and I didn't ask."

Franny sighed. "Those two! Always whispering! I don't like secrets. I don't think they're nice."

Cora Sheffield guffawed. "Whahoo!"

This time Franny reddened. Archie gave Cora a thoughtful look, but he didn't say anything. It was a long, appraising look that went from her grizzled blonde hair to her sturdy white oxfords. When he turned to Mark his eyes were blank. "What do you say to the Peck family going down with Beacham tonight?" he said quietly. "We can get ready. Franny's shot to pieces."

Mark knew what his answer would be but he waited before he gave it. Franny did look shot to pieces, and the change had been almost instantaneous. The skin of that carefully treasured face had wrinkled like a bowl of thick cream.

"I'm sorry," he said. "But I turned up a few things in New York that make that impossible. Much better for all of us if we stay here together." He repeated, "All of us."

"You ought to tell us what you know," Archie said. "You ought to warn us what to look for. Give us some kind of an idea. You could tell Mike, you ought to tell him. You act as if you expected something else to happen and if that's true, why then we've got the right to know what it is. You can't expose us to—to danger. I'm going to get me a lawyer!"

"Don't force Wilcox to hold you all as material witnesses," Mark advised. "That will be worse than sitting under a tree all day. Mr. Beacham, will you come inside? I want to talk to you privately."

Beacham got up and walked to the cottage without replying. Once indoors, he turned on Mark furiously.

"I told you to cross Peck off your list!" he said. "What are you trying to do, pin something on him? You'll turn him into a nervous wreck and then he'll be no use to me! We've got a deal coming up soon. I need him."

"I wasn't thinking about Peck, or anybody in particular. I wish I were, but I haven't reached that stage. Do you want to hear what I found out?"

"Go on. You'll only tell me about half, or a third. I know you fellows. But go on."

"I'll give you more than half. I know what Miss Cassidy went down to New York for. The caretaker business was only a small part of it. Actually she went down to check the records in her old hospital." He told as much as he dared. "She went because she recognized somebody, suddenly. An old patient, or a member of the patient's family. I don't think physical resemblance had anything to do with it, I think it was a mannerism, or a trick of speech, that suddenly cropped out. You can hide those things for years, you know, and then—bang. Out in the open. I copied a lot of stuff from the records she was interested in. I've even memorized it."

Beacham was unimpressed and showed it. "Patients! Relatives! You're crazy!"

"Not me. That's somebody else. She wasn't always a baby nurse, you know. At one time she had a ward full of lunatics. Beginning to get the drift?"

Beacham stopped his pacing. "She didn't tell me that," he said slowly. "She didn't say a word about that. . . . I don't believe you."

"I have the information in my pocket."

"Names?" There was something in Beacham's voice that might have been reluctance.

"Yes." Mark reached in his pocket for the notebook, changed horses in midstream, and brought out a cigarette instead. Not even Miss McKenna knew those three disputed and apparently useless names, and he suddenly realized that they must stay as they were, unknown and hidden from general knowledge. True, Beacham might recognize one of them; he might be able to tear away the fog with a single word, uncover, in one minute, an original identity now lost in a shuffle of remarriage or adoption. And then again, he might not. He might know at once who had stalked Mary Cassidy with a toy in his hand, and say nothing. The killer might mean more to him than Mary Cassidy ever had. What did old Albert Shaw say about people keeping their mouths shut where crime was concerned? "Even respectable people, even when it would save a chap." Shaw knew.

And Mark knew too. Instead of drawing in a net he might be sending out an alarm. "Yes," he repeated, "I have some names, but they're not worth much. They don't mean a thing."

Beacham was over at the window, pleating the curtain with his strong, brown fingers. He looked as if he were deep in his own thoughts. He made no comment.

The names ran smoothly through Mark's mind. He knew them as well as his own. Peter Martin Delaney, eighty-five, and his doting and hated daughter; Norbert James Kelso, Jr., fifty-one, the poor, unlucky devil who was returned to an unhappy home because he'd behaved himself for two years and somebody else needed his bed; Louise Murdoch, thirty-six, who didn't want her brother to know other women. No, the names didn't mean a thing but there were other words that did; other words, underlined by Mary Cassidy with heavy, black strokes.

Beacham turned from the window. "You said something else, about mannerisms, wasn't it?"

"Yes. You can't change those permanently. Somebody let the bars down at least once, and Miss Cassidy got wise. It can happen again. That's what I'm watching for."

"Have you seen anything that—fits?"

"One of the angles fits three of you."

"Of us!" Beacham stared, first at Mark and then out of the window. He turned back. "Of us here—of us out there?"

"Yes. But one angle can easily be coincidence. If I get another, or two more, then I'll know."

Beacham crossed to the table and took a cigarette. There was no apprehension in his manner, only annoyance and disbelief. "Will this new development keep me from going to New York tonight?" he asked. Then he added, "I still think you're crazy."

"We'll see who's crazy in about forty-eight hours," Mark said. "No, you can go to New York all right. You're returning immediately, aren't you?"

"Yes. And please understand that I'm not going because I want to. I'm only doing it because I promised Cassie. She talked to me about death once and made me swear to do as she asked. Cremation. No service. I'll get it over as soon as possible and come back on the next train." He struggled with match and cigarette. "I hate the whole business," he said. "All the mechanized foolery that goes with putting a body away. Hauling it on and off trains, in and out of hearses, creeping through the city streets in broad daylight. The blackest heathen has more sense."

Is this the line he gave Walters? Mark wondered. "What would you do?" he asked.

"Bury her where she was found, beside the well. Bury her at once, in the place where she died."

"That's very pretty," Mark said, "and I hate to be sordid, but you can't bury people near wells."

"You know what I mean. I mean here, in that graveyard." He began to pace again. "People act like fools at times like this. I had to clamp down on a couple of women canvassing for flowers. Strangers, going around with a list and asking hotel guests to contribute to a wreath!" He ground out his cigarette on the floor. "And there'll be no viewing of the body, either. The undertaker seems to think he's hit an all time high with this job and he wants to show off. I fixed that too. Stood over him while he sealed the top on. . . . I need a drink."

Mark thought before he spoke. "Not even Joey?"

"Certainly not Joey! She's—she's never seen anything like that. I don't want her to. Scare her to death."

"I think she can take it, and it might make her feel better later on. She has a lot of sense."

"No. Nobody."

Mark waited. Then, "Not even Albert Shaw?"

Beacham stood still in the middle of the floor. "And who is Albert Shaw?"

"Never heard of him?"

"No. Why should I?"

"He's your caretaker."

"Oh good God, East, I don't think I ever heard his name before! Cassie told me she got a good man, and that's all."

"Shaw says you talked to him the day he was hired."

"Maybe I did! I can't remember things like that. I talked to half a dozen people she was considering. She wanted me to. I don't remember any of them."

"You remembered Shaw enough to write to him when she died. At least he says you did. Did you address the letter to Caretaker?"

"I must have. I didn't know his name. Are you trying to make something out of that?"

Mark looked amiable. "No. But it was a lot of trouble to take for a stranger, wasn't it? Or maybe he wasn't a stranger—to Miss Cassidy."

Beacham glared. "He can be her long lost grandfather for all I know. She told me he needed help, and I told her to go ahead and give him the job. That's all. And I didn't write him because I thought he'd be personally interested, although he probably was. I wrote because I wanted him to keep away from reporters. I told him I'd fire him if he talked to anybody. . . . How did you get to see him, if I may ask?"

"I rang the bell and told him who I was. He believed me. And don't worry about reporters. They'll not fool him. He's an unusual type. I think he's come down in the world."

"Only two ways to go," Beacham said. "That—or up. . . . Have we finished with—Mr. Shaw? Then I'm going to phone over for some ice. Have a drink?"

Mark said he would. He watched while Beacham crossed to the phone that connected the cottage with the hotel. It rang before he reached it. "Hello," he said. "Oh—it's for you, East. Crestwood."

Mark took the receiver. "Hello," he said. "Wait a minute, will you?" He turned to Beacham. "Do you mind if I take this alone?"

"Want me out of the way?" Beacham laughed. "Help yourself. I'll go over to Peck's and drink his. Come along when you're through." He walked out, whistling.

"Bittner?" Mark said into the phone.

It was. "Where have you been for the last fifteen minutes?" Bittner asked.

"Right here, in Beacham's cottage. Have you got something?"

Bittner strangled with laughter. "When did you see that Beacham girl last? I mean the one with the—you know, the older one."

"I practically just left her. Get on with it!"

"Well, she called me up about ten minutes ago and engaged a bus for tomorrow afternoon. Sounded like she was crying too, or maybe somebody had insulted her. She sounded like she'd been running. Or crying. Or something. She wants a bus for three o'clock tomorrow because she's taking a party over to Baldwin."

"What for?"

"Band concert at the camp. How do you like that, my boy? Didn't I tell you to trust me? There you were, sitting on a stove, and you didn't even know there was a fire in it. I have to tell you everything. Aren't you going to thank me? You ought to come over here and thank me in person."

"Sure, sure. Thanks. Wait a minute while I do some thinking." That little devil, he said to himself. She went to the phone the minute I left. Why? Why all of a sudden? She had the whole morning. A harmless excursion designed for frazzled nerves? An elopement? There I go, he said, falling back on love again. "Bittner? What time does that concert come off?"

"It begins around four and ends around five. They have one every month. Are you going? You won't like it. You won't have any fun. If you come over here, we can play my victrola." Bittner began to wheedle. "I have some perfectly beautiful records."

"I'll come sometime and bring my own. Listen. Put your best driver on, will you? Tell him to memorize the faces of his passengers and make sure he brings back the same people he took. Can you do that without making him suspicious? "

"I'll tell him the hotel asked me to. I'll say the hotel thinks somebody may run away without paying his bill. How do you like that?"

"Bittner, I didn't know you could do it!" The words weren't out of his mouth before he knew they were a mistake.

"You underestimate me," wailed Bittner.

"No I don't. And here's another thing. When you see Beacham on the branch line tonight, don't tell me. He's going to New York and I know all about it."

"With the body? With the woman's body? You haven't told me about the body! You said you'd come over and tell—"

"Excuse me," Mark lied in a hoarse whisper. "Beacham just came in." He hung up.

He didn't go to the Pecks' at once. He went over to the hotel and called Perley's house. He told Pansy that he wanted Perley at the Mountain House after dinner. Then he called a colleague in New York and spoke to him in French, completely confounding the elderly woman who ran the hotel switchboard. He said "Oui, oui" a couple of times to give her a fair start, and watched her eyes glaze as she dropped out of the running. He knew she was regretting the copy of Mary J. Holmes propped inside her *Beginner's French*.

When he had finished his conversation he wondered grimly what Beacham would say if he knew that he was going to pay for two detectives to watch himself.

Joey and Pee Wee walked hand in hand down a lane that twisted and turned between the rolling hills and fields. Here and there along the sagging fences were lush clumps of tiger lilies. When Joey and Pee Wee saw one of these they silently broke away from each other and demolished the lot. There was little or no talk between them; they walked and worked slowly, their eyes forward, right and left. They'd have looked the same if they'd been foraging for food.

Once they found a small patch of wild asters and beyond that a straggling line of black-eyed Susans. These joined the lilies until their arms were full. When Joey could carry no more, she sat by the road and wiped her hot face with a grimy hand.

"You got enough?" she asked Pee Wee.

"My arms are busted." He placed his sheaf on the grass beside hers. "They look good, don't they?"

"They'll be all right if they don't die." Her voice was worried. "Do you think it's going to be all right? Do you think Mike—"

"I'll talk to Mike," Pee Wee said. They both cast uneasy looks at the pile of flaming orange. "I'm thinking though," Pee Wee admitted. "It's all kind of bright."

"What's the matter with that?"

"All that color. We ought to have some white."

"Where's any white? I've been looking my eyes out. There isn't any white except wild carrot and that's a plain weed."

Pee Wee considered. "It's a weed if you call it wild carrot, but if you call it Queen Anne's lace—"

"Pee Wee!" They scrambled up the bank into the field. The Queen Anne's lace was waist high. "Only the ones with the little red spot in the middle," warned Joey. "They're the hardest to find and they look fancier."

It was after one o'clock when their arms, which were unrelated in size to their eyes and hearts, could hold no more. They turned back the way they had come, and the sun was in their faces. Pee Wee scowled at his scout watch.

"We're going to be late for lunch if we don't run," he said, "and if we run we'll get sunstroke."

"I know how to get something to eat," Joey said. "Even when the dining room's closed. I know how. You go to the kitchen door and there's a man there who's second cook and he gives you something. Better than the regular lunch, too. You can get five desserts."

"A lift would be nice though," Pee Wee said. He shaded his eyes and looked ahead. "Don't some of our people ride down this way? People like Miss Sheffield and Mr. Kirby?"

"Sure. But Mr. Kirby's mad at me. And nobody rides at lunch time."

"Unless they're late, like us. You don't have to gallop like somebody was chasing you, Joey. If we're going to catch it, we're going to catch it. I wish I didn't keep seeing those big pitchers of cold milk on the tables." He spat hopelessly.

"I'd hook a ride with anybody," Joey said recklessly. "Even though I'm not supposed to. Even with somebody I didn't know, I would."

They trudged on a few more yards. Little flurries of dust rose from their dragging feet. Suddenly Pee Wee stopped.

"I hear something," he said. "But it's coming from the wrong direction. It's coming this way and it's a car."

"Maybe we can hire it to turn around! Mike would pay!"

They crawled up the bank because Cassie had told them they must always do that, and waited for their invisible hope to materialize. They didn't wait long.

Around the bend came an ancient Ford with its top up. It moved uncertainly from one side of the road to the other.

"Ole man Walters," Joey said out of the side of her mouth. "Wouldn't you think he'd learn to drive."

"Shall we ask him to take us back?" Pee Wee whispered. "He'd kind of have to. Don't he always say we're his flock?"

"Sure. Let me do it. He likes me." She slid down the bank. "Hey, Mr. Walters!"

The Ford jolted to a standstill.

"Well, well," said the Reverend Mr. Walters. "Of all people!" He climbed down stiffly and brushed the dust from his hands. "Do your families know you're wandering far afield?"

Joey beamed. "No sir," she said.

On his way to the Peck cottage for the promised drink, Mark stopped to talk to Beulah. She was still under the trees but she was alone.

"Where did they all go after I left?" he asked bluntly.

She told him. "The Pecks went back to their cottage, the Suttons and George went into the hotel, Sheffield and Kirby to the stables. Beacham went over to the Peck cottage a few minutes ago, but I guess you know that. Miss Rayner is on the veranda, talking to the woman who has the suite next to the Suttons. Roberta went into the hotel when the Suttons did. With Nick.

"What did Roberta talk about before she went?"

"Nothing. She didn't open her mouth until Franny Peck told her that frowning would ruin her forehead. Then she whispered something to Nick and they left. No manners. Why?"

"I've been talking to Bittner. He says Roberta rented a bus for a trip to Baldwin tomorrow. Band concert at the camp. She's taking a party. I wonder where she got that idea?"

"Out of the nowhere, baby dear. I wouldn't worry about it. Do you think I'll be invited?"

"It won't do you any good if you are. You can't go. Beulah, are you free and willing to stay on here until Sunday night?"

"You couldn't drive me away. You're closing in, Mark; I've seen the signs before and I know. But don't tell me anything. I'm afraid of this one, and the less information I have in advance the better I'll behave. I hope." She yanked at her unbecoming frilled collar. She looked like the wrong kind of dog dressed up for a trick. "I've got the chokes today. Everything's in my throat."

He knew how she felt. It was always like that towards the end. Empty and hopeless days would go by, and then, suddenly, the old chills and fever would set in. That meant that you had to walk softly, because something was waiting for you around the corner. But not, he told himself, with an arrow this time. He had all six.

"Beulah," he said, "I'm thinking about those rags of Joey's. Are they safe?"

"They'll have to tear the house down to find them."

"Good. We're late for lunch and that's bad. Where's Joey? Hasn't she shown up yet?"

"No." She looked at the watch that was fastened to her dress with a gold *fleur-de-lis* pin. "They've been gone since ten."

"I don't like that." He looked down the hot, empty road that led to town. "Which way did they go?"

"Not that way."

"I don't like it," he repeated. "I wish I knew what to do." His eyes came back to her face and he glared. "You know where they went! You've known all the time! Why didn't you tell me? You don't know what we're up against!"

"Don't lose your temper. It's all right. I couldn't tell you before because it was a secret Beacham wouldn't appreciate. But I told them to go ahead. If Beacham acts up, I'll take care of him. They went after flowers for Miss Cassidy's coffin. They didn't have any money, so they planned to pick whatever they could find. I told them that would be nicer than anything they could buy. Poor little things. I hate Beacham."

"Where did they go?" He wanted to shake her. "Where did they go? Is it isolated?"

"Of course it's isolated. They went down the lane that leads to the pool and changed over to a hunting trail. About two miles down. That's where you find the fields and deep woods, and that's where you find the best wild—" She stopped. He was on his feet, running to the parking lot. She followed.

"Mark!"

"I'm taking Beacham's car. Don't say anything to anybody and don't look like that. You're attracting attention."

"Mark, if those—if something's happened and you didn't warn—"

The wheels of a heavy cart and the rattle of harness cut across her voice. They both turned. The lumber wagon, back from a morning in the woods, rumbled out of the lane with its burden of brush and twigs. Beside the driver two animated bouquets quivered in the sun.

"Hey!" yelled Joey.

Mark released his breath in a bubbling hiss. "Excuse it, please," he said to Beulah. "Everything's in my throat too."

He lifted the children to the ground. "Don't do that again without telling me," he said. "Don't move off this place without telling me! If you do, so help me, I'll beat the living daylights—don't do it!"

Joey's eyes widened. "What are you mad about?"

"You."

"But Miss Pond knew. We told her and made her swear not to tell. She swore."

"Miss Pond's swearing cuts no ice with me." He ducked the swaying lilies and the Queen Anne's lace that they thrust under his nose. "Yes, they're beautiful. Go put them in a bucket of water, and if you fall in yourself I won't be sorry. You don't know how lucky you were to—to get that ride."

"Double lucky," Pee Wee said jauntily. "We could of ridden in two different things but we liked the lumberman best."

"You don't say? What was your other offer?"

"Mr. Walters. He had his Ford, but he was heading the other way."

"He said he didn't mind turning around though," Joey said. "He's all right. You got to give him his due, he was willing to turn around. He even knew a short cut, he said. And we got in and were all ready to start when our own lumberman came along. And he was going in the right direction. So we got out."

Mark took the flowers from both pairs of hands. "Do something about your faces and general appearance, will you? Then have your lunch. I'll take charge of these. And if you have any trouble about putting them where they belong, I'll take charge of that too."

"That's just what Mr. Walters said," crowed Joey. "He said he could arrange it."

"I hope you thanked him properly. How was he?"

"He said he wasn't very well. His hands shook. I asked him why, and he said his heart was heavy. Do your hands shake when your heart is—"

He pushed them into the cottage and slammed the door. Then he went to get his lunch.

Beacham didn't see the flowers until several hours later. They stood in twin buckets on the cottage porch. Pee Wee and Joey had been argued into naps, but Mark was lounging in the swing. Beacham crossed the lawn and mounted the steps.

"What's this?" he asked. He kicked at the buckets. "And this?" Beside each bucket was a small roll of absorbent cotton, a sheet of brown paper, and a ball of twine.

"That?" Mark got up and walked over. "That's the result of a morning's hot work in the fields, four miles there and back." He didn't mention the lift. "The stems are to be wrapped in wet cotton first and paper second. Then they'll keep fresh, we hope, and look pretty when they reach their destination."

"What are you talking about? What destination?"

Mark told him. "New York. Baggage car. Just like a song."

"Whose idea was that?" Beacham bent down, and one dripping bunch had already left the bucket when Mark's voice stopped it in mid-air.

"I wouldn't do that," he said pleasantly. "The idea was Joey's. She and Pee Wee wore themselves out getting that stuff. She was afraid to tell you so I said I would."

"Afraid? Afraid of her own father?"

"Why not? You expressed yourself pretty strongly. But she feels just as strongly the other way. Do you mind telling me something? Was there anything in those funeral instructions about omitting flowers, or is that your own idea?"

"It's mine." Beacham's defiance was loud but unconvincing.

"Then if I were you I'd forget it. I'd let these tributes go with Cassie all the way. You might even help tie them up." He waited.

Beacham gave in gracefully. "I guess you're right," he said with engaging frankness. "But not this junk. If Joey wants flowers I'll get her something decent in town. I'll get orchids. I can't be seen with these things. I'd look like a fool."

"Think so? That's a matter of taste. I know that if I were standing on a city street, or in a railroad station or anywhere else, and saw a coffin covered with two bunches of wild flowers with their stems wrapped up in wet brown paper, I'd say to myself—there goes somebody who rated."

Beacham returned the flowers to the bucket. "Right," he said thoughtfully. He started to go indoors.

"Wait," Mark said. "You're leaving New York tomorrow night, arriving here Sunday morning?"

"Yes, that's what I said. Why?"

"I thought you might be interested in my plans for the time you're away. Wilcox will be here with me both nights. And I want you to tell Joey to stay on the premises. Orders. I've already told her, but I want it to come from you too. Make it clear. I simply can't take the responsibility while you're gone."

Beacham looked alarmed. "But what in the world could happen to Joey? Everybody loves that kid!"

"That's what they said about Miss Cassidy. Everybody loved her. . . . Joey makes friends too easily, that's all."

The long afternoon droned its way to six o'clock. Mark drove Beacham down to Bear River and saw him take the branch train to Baldwin. Beacham had done a complete about face; he wore dark clothes and black tie and gloves, and his expression was correct.

Mark stood on the platform and watched while Mary Cassidy, sealed first in mahogany and silver and then in pine, was gently lifted into the baggage car. The tiger lilies and the Queen Anne's lace dripped disconsolately over the plain wooden box. But they were holding up, he noted with satisfaction; they were doing a good job. He'd tell Joey.

CHAPTER NINE

SATURDAY morning followed a night of such manifest calm that neither Mark nor Perley had been able to sleep a wink. The Mountain House guests had conducted themselves like orphans on the night before Christmas. No opportunity for courtesy had been neglected, and the offers of flasks, bottles, poker games, sandwiches, coffee, and a nice walk in the moonlight (Cora Sheffield), had been made in person. A steady procession of white-flanneled and finger-waved Magi had trooped one by one to the Beacham cottage, bearing gifts and looking nervous. They'd trooped back, still bearing them and looking worse.

"No favors," Mark had warned Perley.

"I know," Perley had agreed. "It's just like the night Amos and I were here. And you know what happened then."

"Sure. But nobody's going to stay me with apples and then swipe a gun."

One offer had been accepted. When Mark admitted that he hadn't been read aloud to since Peter Rabbit, which was too young for him now, he was immediately promoted to and entertained by a battered copy of *The Peterkin Papers*. Outside the circle of lamplight, Perley had armed himself with a diffident expression that didn't match the hand inconspicuously cupped behind his ear.

At ten, Joey had gone to bed. Roberta had followed at eleven. The Pecks' light was on until two and Franny Peck's laughter came through the night. Cora Sheffield and Kirby had joined the poker game.

And now it was Saturday morning, clear and hot.

Mark and Perley breakfasted early and returned to the cottage. On a card table set up on the porch, they laid out their papers and notebooks and checked and rechecked.

"Give me all of that stuff you gave me last night," Mark said.

"Again?"

"Yes. I want it in the book, not in my head. Down in black and white. Get on with it. Walters."

"Don't you ever do anything like that to me again! Walters! His Rhode Island church was ready to throw me to the lions. They finally put me on to a banker who passes the plate on Sundays. That's one place where I'll never be able to borrow money. Well, Walters never married, never had any female relations except his mother and grandmother, who brought him up and died when he was sixteen. He was a poor boy, educated by church people, and has led a clean life."

Mark wrote it down in his own style of pot hook. "Maybe his mother and grandmother were too good? Maybe he didn't want to be a preacher? Maybe he took up preaching only because he thought he had to? Maybe—"

"None of that, now! Forget him. He's never been away from whatever church he was appointed to. Never took a vacation. Never been what you'd call sick."

"Ever been to New York?"

"Once." Perley looked startled. "But that was strictly business. He had a small church in Brooklyn one summer when he was young. Substituting for the regular pastor."

"All right. But only for the moment. Let's freshen up with Mabel."

"There's nothing on Mabel that a good walloping won't cure. I gave it to her, verbally or orally. Which is it, verbally or orally?"

"This is no time for self-improvement. What did you find out?"

"She's never been anywhere except on all-day picnics. I asked her what she'd done with her evenings since last Friday. She told me." Perley wiped his brow. "Her father went to school with me, too," he said faintly.

Mark averted his face. "Go on. Mrs. Briggs."

Perley straightened up with relief. "Now there's a woman! She tried to talk my head off, but I didn't let her. When I got through she was eating out of my hand. It seems that Mrs. Briggs did go away from home when she was a girl. She went into domestic service in Boston and didn't want anybody to know. She gave out that she was studying stenography. Stayed away two years, came back for a visit with a lot of fancy clothes, and caught Briggs. She had tears in her eyes when she told me. I think she's all right."

"Do you? That's fine. How about Briggs himself? Aside from his summer bush-jumping."

"He's been going to New York for twenty years or more, ever since he started with the railroad. He says he went because he could ride on passes. Never stayed more than one night and slept in a Y. The sweat was running down him like a river when I finished. He says he never even went to a burlesque show. I didn't ask him that. He told me; he kept telling me every five minutes. . . . It must have been a hot one."

Mark was silent.

Perley waited. "Moresby's next," he said finally. "Don't you want Moresby? I had trouble there, being as she's in the family."

"O.K. Moresby."

"Nothing on her. Nothing on him. She went to summer school at Columbia University in New York City. One summer only. Roomed with two girls, and they were never out of each other's sight the whole time. Scared of everything, she said. Moresby is a local boy too. Never went anywhere. He owns that feed store in town. . . . What are you looking at?"

Mark was watching the hotel. A group of golfers had collected on the steps and they were parting to let George and old man Sutton through. The old man was moving briskly, for him. He brushed George's hand aside and walked down the steps alone. Nick followed with pillows and Roberta followed Nick. Behind them, absently and firmly loitering, came Beulah.

"I'm not looking at anything," Mark said. "I'm thinking. Why wouldn't some of these people hold out on you?"

"No sir! They told me the truth. I knew I wouldn't find anything. I only did it to please you."

"That was the wrong approach," Mark said absently. "You had yourself sold on innocence before you started."

Perley drooped.

"Never mind," Mark said. "Did Pansy actually send Floyd out to her mother's?"

"She did! I'm real provoked about that. Never said a word to me, just went ahead and did it. She says somebody else is going to get killed before this is over, and it won't be a Wilcox. She'll turn that boy soft!"

"I doubt it. Now listen. I've got a nice little job for you this afternoon. I want you to go home and get yourself up as a patron of the arts."

Perley's thin eyebrows went up in horror. "That concert! You want me to go to that concert! I can't do it! I never have!" He keened softly into his cupped hands and then suddenly raised his head. A new thought had struck him visibly, and it looked strong enough to close the argument. "I haven't been invited," he said triumphantly.

"You mean Miss Beacham hasn't asked you for a bus ride. That's not necessary. The music is free. You'll drive yourself over and sit as close to the Mountain House contingent as possible. That's all you have to do, sit and watch. And don't get too wrapped up in *Poet and Peasant* or gems from *The Prince of Pilsen*. . . . I want a beer."

"No!"

"To everything? Listen Perley, this is a must." Mark was firm. "I'm staying here because I've got some ransacking to do. This is my first real chance to get into Beacham's room, and a few others. You watch those people and phone me the instant anybody leaves the party. Bittner's man will partially check, but I can't rely or confide too much there."

"Who's going?" Perley was licked.

"The hostess, the three Pecks, Nick, Cora, Kirby, and probably Joey. I haven't made up my mind about Joey. She talks too much. The Haskells are going too. I don't know why they were asked, unless Roberta wants to fill up the seats. Mrs. H. can easily use two. Old Sutton and Miss Rayner declined with thanks, the first because he hates music, the second because she doesn't like to be jounced. George stays home with the old man. I have been pointedly overlooked, and if you hear something cracking it's not my heart but my patience."

"Wasn't Miss Pond invited?" Perley was scandalized.

"No. I don't know what happened there. At the moment Beulah rates with Roberta like a leper." He looked annoyed. "But she won't be wasted. She's been dogging Miss Rayner's footsteps at my suggestion and has almost managed to get herself a bid to go buggy riding. She loves a gentle horse, she said. I heard her."

"I think you're going to search Miss Rayner's room," Perley said with frank disapproval. "I don't like that. I don't think it's nice."

Mark drummed the table. "Why not? She was one of our casualties." He looked absently over Perley's head and his eyes traveled over the bright green grass and down the dusty road.

Perley knew it was time to stop talking for a while. He took out his old pipe and smoked quietly, waiting for the sign to begin again. It came when Mark lighted a cigarette and swore at the match. "Mark?" He had to say it a second time. "Mark, what are you thinking about?"

"Tomorrow," Mark said.

"Then you have got hold of something. You don't have to tell me what it is. I'm not asking any questions. I'm willing to take your orders when the time comes."

Mark returned his gaze to the distance. "Thanks."

"You haven't been fooling me any with your smooth talk," Perley said contentedly. "No siree. But why are you letting Beacham run around New York alone?"

"He's not alone. He won't be, even for a minute. There'll be guests at Cassie's funeral in spite of his convictions, and they'll wear striped pants and look like morticians." He made a sound in his throat, a sudden, ugly sound that Perley had never heard before. "I'm not satisfied! I don't like what I'm thinking!"

"No?" Perley dismissed this with quiet assurance. "You're all right."

"No I'm not. I came back from New York with three cases that could fit the situation here and I haven't been able to discard one of them. All three still hold water. Look." He flipped the pages of his notebook. "Read those three names and tell me if they mean anything to you. Then forget them."

Perley read with a finger on the page. "No," he said regretfully. "I never heard of any of them. They're forgotten already." He returned the book.

"You see? Time's going by and every minute counts. As far as I can see, the trail's getting cold, but at the same time I can feel somebody breathing a nasty hot breath down my back. I'm being laughed at."

"You know that isn't so. About the trail getting cold, I mean. Trouble with you is, you don't like the way it's leading."

Mark gave him a long, sour look. "You're getting too clever," he said. "How would you like to make the pinch yourself? It's your job anyway. I'll run the last act through to the curtain and you can step in and say, 'Boo!'"

Perley looked unhappy. He didn't know it, but his lips were desperately framing his tag line. "When are you planning to—start?"

"Tomorrow night I'm giving a little evening party. Here. About nine o'clock. Or rather, Beacham's giving it. Beacham's paying for a lot of things he didn't order. We'll have refreshments, and the guests will be chosen from all of the so-called walks of life. Their emotions will be so divided that they won't be able to eat, and that will knock the experiment into a very expensive cocked hat."

"Do you know what you're talking about? I don't."

"It's simple. I'm asking a few friends in for conversation and light viands, with a background of soft music played on Roberta's portable victrola. I'm calling it a farewell party on account of my imminent retirement in the role of a failure. They'll come on the run."

"I wouldn't."

"These will. I'm inviting them this afternoon, by phone and note, politely, like a little gentleman. Like this. 'I want to show my appreciation before I leave because you've been so sweet to me.' Slightly modified in the case of Mrs. Briggs. Perley, did you ever eat a truffle?"

"I hope not. What is it?"

"To the uninitiated, something that got in by mistake. But a lot of people like them and would pay a fat sum to get hold of a tin. And—catch number one—some people don't like them at all. The latter take one nibble, break out in a rash and swell up something lovely. Catch number two—one of Mary Cassidy's heavy black underscorings warned about truffles. In the personal peculiarity department."

Perley's eyes showed his distrust of the whole thing. "A person that's made sick by food don't eat it," he said flatly. "He says no, thank you, I like it fine, but it don't like me."

"If our pal says that, then I'm temporarily stopped. But I don't think he will. The very sight of that practically extinct food will put him on his guard, and a man on his guard makes small, crazy mistakes. He overdoes. This one will know I'm at least partially wise, and he may eat to spite me. Then he'll step out of the room and put his finger down his throat. Behind a locked door. That's when I follow and kick the door down."

"Suppose it's a lady?"

"I still kick the door down."

"And I still think it won't work. Maybe five or six of those people won't like the stuff. Maybe they never saw it before and won't take a chance. It's no sign people are mental when they don't eat things. I'm that way myself about fresh pineapple. Hives."

"Serve fresh pineapple at home?"

"Sure. I just give it the go-by."

"Pretty common this time of year, isn't it? Only costs about thirty-five cents. But if you knew it was imported from France and was almost non-existent, to say nothing of costing a pretty pile, what would you think if Pansy suddenly popped one on the table, right under your nose?"

Perley sighed. "I guess I get the point. These truffles are hard to come by?"

"I haven't tasted one since the war started, but I've got a precious tin locked in my suitcase."

"That lets out the Briggses, the Moresbys, Mabel, and Walters. They're poor people and they've never had a chance to find out if they'd swell up or not."

"Truffles used to be fairly inexpensive," Mark said calmly, "and fairly plentiful."

Perley fought on. "I don't care. It still seems like an awful round-about way to break a roomful of people down to one person."

"It's only one way. If the sight of my little plateful doesn't smoke that one out, I'll know he's either dead, under lock and key, or sinning elsewhere. And I'll cross him off. Then I'll begin on the music. Another one of our hopefuls has a habit of foaming quietly at the mouth when he hears *The Beautiful Blue Danube*."

"You're making that up!"

"No I'm not. I've got it in black and white."

"Then I'm not going to be hungry," Perley said. "I'm going to wait outside."

For the first time that day Mark grinned with pleasure. "You might watch for *The Beautiful Blue Danube* this afternoon at the concert."

Perley looked ready to faint.

"I'm kidding," Mark said hastily. "I got Beulah to call up the camp and request a few omissions. We can't have it happen there."

Perley's color returned to normal but he was far from happy. He wailed: "I used to read in the papers how the police would find a girl's body in an alley, identify her from the stuff she carried in her purse, talk to her landlady, get the boy friend's address, go to his house, tell his mother it wasn't nothing but a parking violation, rap on his bedroom door, walk in, and pull him and the bloody knife out from under the blankets. Don't they do that any more?"

Joey came pounding across the lawn from the hotel, waving an envelope. Mark stopped laughing and waved in return. She panted up the steps and gave him a letter.

"Miss Rayner says you might as well save tipping the boy, so I brought it myself. I think so too. The mail just came."

"Thank you, Miss Beacham. May I?" He slit the envelope.

"It's beautiful writing, isn't it?" she said.

"It is indeed." He read silently. "Just a note from a friend of mine. Hey!" he added, as she poised for flight. "You running away again?"

"That yellow cat had kittens. Pee Wee's with her now. She doesn't mind." She was off at once.

Mark turned to Perley. "The letter's from Albert Shaw. He's been looking up the caretaker Cassie fired, and he ran him down, too. The name is Higgins, and he is and has been in jail ever since he lost his job. Automobile thief on the side. That's that. I never did warm up to that angle."

Perley got up and stretched.

"Going to look at the cat that doesn't mind?" Mark asked.

"I'm going home to dress for the concert. I need sleep but I guess I'll get that there." He walked like a beast of burden.

Mark sat on the porch until lunch. He checked and rechecked his book, added Perley's data, and reread the meager and picturesque information he had copied from Miss McKenna's files. He computed ages and dates, made a composite picture in his mind of all the things he had to go on; the result was dim. Aside from the emotional set-up and the identifying flaws, there was too little of the private life that preceded the collapse. Love and hate were there in emphasis and detail, but only as they existed between two people; the older man and his daughter, the younger man and his mother, the girl and her brother. There had to be other people in those lives. Who were they? Did the older man have a living wife as well as a daughter, a quiet woman who moved from hotel to hotel, inwardly seething, inhibited, grudge-bearing? Or could he, for instance, have had another child? And if so, would that child recognize the too familiar signs when they began to creep into its own life?

And the younger man. Had he brothers or sisters? Nothing was said about that. Only his mother had come to the hospital, weeping and praying. Suppose he had brothers and sisters with good memories, who lay awake at night, staring at the ceiling, waiting for the telltale twitch of arms and legs, the curious lightness of the body, the driving urge to laugh out loud and then to cry? And his mother. There was no reason for believing her dead. She could be alive and strong, and she could have other children between the ages of nineteen and fifty.

He went over the notes again, carefully and hopefully, and wrote down the names of his possibilities. There were too many. The circle grew wider instead of smaller. Soon the circumference would be out of sight.

He turned to the last case. The girl. The girl who went away with her brother. Did she ever marry? Maybe. Out west, in a new town, and the brother would help her to put it over. He'd probably stop at nothing to get rid of her. He could ask her to marry; bribe her, prey on her raddled emotions, tell her his happiness was at stake. He could make her promises that he never meant to fulfil; and they'd bury her past like the dark secret it was. Did he fit in, the brother?

He saw Roberta heading toward the cottage and closed the book. She came up the steps, swinging a tennis racquet.

"Good morning," he said grimly. She'd managed to keep out of his way until then.

She sat on the railing. "I owe you an apology or something, don't I? About my party this afternoon."

"I'm not really angry," he said. "Just hurt."

She looked confused. "I never know when you're serious. But honestly I didn't leave you out on purpose. After I invited the people I wanted, I counted the seats. And there simply wasn't any more room. Do you see?"

"Too clearly. But don't disturb yourself. I couldn't go. Too busy."

"You look busy." This was delivered with a crushing air. When she saw he was unscathed, she tried again. "We're going home next week. I expect we'll see the last of you, and all this, when we get on the train."

"I've never heard a more hopeful speech. . . . Roberta, when are you going to talk to me?"

"What am I doing now?"

"Putting on an act and it's a waste of time. You're an amateur. How old are you?"

"Well! Eighteen, and you know it."

"How old is Nick?"

"Nineteen. Anything else?"

"Yes. Joey and Pee Wee."

"He's eleven and she'll be nine next week. Wednesday. This is positively fascinating, but I've got to get ready for lunch." She stalked across the porch and opened the screen door. There she hesitated, and turned. "Why do you want to know all that?"

He stretched lazily. "I'm giving a party myself tomorrow night, and I wondered if you and Nick were old enough to be invited. I think you are."

The door slammed. He sat back and waited for her return. In five minutes she reappeared and walked by with a cool nod.

"Have them send me over some lunch, will you?" he called after her. "Sandwiches and coffee will do."

While he waited, he planned the hours ahead as well as he could. Arrangements with the chef about party food. Invitations. Arguments with the chef about how to serve the truffles strictly undisguised. He winced when he thought of that touch. Was he as crazy as his quarry, baiting his trap with a victrola record and an underground fungus brought to light by the snout of a rooting pig? Perley's face had said so, and he didn't know about the pig's part.

The lunch gong rang, and he watched the strollers converge on the hotel. Without exception, each head turned in his direction. He put his feet up on the railing; a disarming gesture, he hoped. The door behind him slammed again and Joey came out, wiping her wet hands on her shirt.

"How did you get in there?" he asked sharply.

"Through the bathroom window. That's nothing, we always do it."

"Who is we?"

"Everybody. It's kind of low and it's wider than it looks like, and it saves time if you're in the back." She saw that he was frowning and made a hurried and indignant defense. "I've washed!"

"I can see that. Run along."

"Aren't you eating any lunch?"

"They're sending it over. Run along and get yours and don't dawdle after you've finished. Come straight back here."

There was an edge to his voice that she'd never heard before; he didn't smile at her either. She backed slowly down the steps, her eyes on his face, and missed the bottom one. She thought he might laugh at that, so she laughed first, to encourage him. But he didn't notice. He's working, she told herself as she trotted over to the hotel; he's working out the answer to his job.

She was right. He was. He was remembering what she'd said about the window. She'd said: "Everybody does." He walked around to the side of the cottage and checked for himself, wondering why he hadn't done that before. There was a rise outside the bathroom and the distance from the ground to the window was only two feet. There was also a large, overturned flower pot for the use of juvenile entrants. He measured the removable screen, and the result was an ugly surprise. If he had to get in that way, he could; and with very little inconvenience. And visibility from the Pecks' could be nicely avoided by a crouching approach along a low growing hedge.

He went back to the porch and found his lunch on the card table. He pushed it aside, changed his mind, and ate absently.

Who had come through that window the day Joey's clothes were destroyed? Somebody, anybody, who weighed less than one hundred and sixty well-distributed pounds. Anybody who moved quietly and knew his way about. And why was it necessary to play that childish trick?

He didn't have to ask himself that; he'd known the answer all along. It wasn't a trick and it wasn't childish. The destruction of Joey's clothes was a part of the destruction of Mary Cassidy.

But who? Someone who had hated Mary Cassidy, who had killed her in cold blood and was still unsatiated. Someone who had hated her in the past and transferred that hate to the present; who'd hated her for what she'd made of her life, for what she'd given and received.

He said the last words over again, for what she'd given and received. And what had she given? New life and confidence to a family of strangers, people to whom she was neither related nor obligated. New life, confidence, and a small girl who was both son and daughter. Joey. Was that it? Was Joey the key? She was Cassie's own job, her own creation. And even a puppy had died because Cassie loved it.

Or was Joey herself, without Cassie, something enviable, challenging, and intolerable? But he couldn't find a reason for that. If that were true, then Joey would have met Cassie's fate, and Cassie would be alive.

No, the motive was Cassie. The puppy had been hers and hers only, and the clothes had been one of her successes. Cassie was behind it all. Someone still hated the half-starved little girl from Donegal who had tried to better herself, and succeeded; who had known how to make people happy; who, in a few hours, would be a handful of gray ashes.

He heard a voice say: "They told me, Heraclitus, they told me you were dead," and he was astonished and embarrassed when he realized the voice was his own. He looked around hastily but there was no one in sight. Just the same, he said to himself, I think I'll read that one to Joey some day.

He left the cottage and went over to the hotel. Cora screamed from the veranda and he screamed in return, but he didn't stop. He went around to the service entrance because his business was with the chef. He found that worthy, a huge Swede, not in the kitchen where he belonged but in a string hammock under the trees. Their conversation gave them both pleasure. Axel, it seemed, liked parties. Private parties. He frankly admitted that they were all profit, to him. Sandwiches, yes. Five kinds. Lemonade? It was poison, certainly, but he'd brew it. Coffee by all means. Small cakes, naturally. A large platter of choice strawberries arranged around a mound of powdered sugar? Very pretty.

"What can you do with a tin of truffles?" Mark asked.

The chef's eye glistened. "You have not!"

"I have so! But see here, this is important. No disguise, no fancy business, nothing squeezed out of a tube. I want them recognizable, on sight. What's wrong with a background of little squares of hot buttered toast?"

Nothing, the chef admitted, except lack of inspiration. But if that was what Mr. East wanted, he could have it. They parted with mutual respect.

Mark returned to the front of the building and entered the lobby. He wrote his invitations and put them in the mail boxes, covertly watched by the nervous clerk. Then he frustrated the telephone operator by making several calls to Bear River, and speaking English. His town guests accepted with a mixture of reluctance and curiosity. He thought several of them sounded as if they were consenting to an evening in the Black Hole of Calcutta. Mrs. Moresby, he imagined, was making a more scholarly comparison, due to her summer course at Columbia.

He went back to the cottage, found Joey on the steps and his lunch tray removed.

"Roberta says I can't go to the concert," she said.

"And so you can't. You wouldn't like it."

"I would! I will! I'm crazy about music! Pee Wee's going! What's the matter with everybody all of a sudden? All of a sudden I can't do this and I can't do that! I'm almost nine!"

"I know. But wouldn't you rather stay home with me and play Russian Bank?"

"No."

He didn't know how to insist; he didn't want to frighten her. "Have you ever heard one of those army camp bands?" He pulled down the corners of his mouth.

"Yes I have, and you needn't make faces. I'm crazy about them."

He looked at her thoughtfully. It was broad daylight; they'd be back by six o'clock at the latest. There would be a crowd, a normal, friendly crowd. "Wait here," he said, and he went inside and called Perley on the cottage extension. When he came back he was smiling. "You can go," he said, "but only if you follow instructions. In the bus going down, you and Pee Wee will sit together. The driver will let you both off at the railway station, and you'll transfer to Mr. Wilcox's car. He'll be waiting. And if anybody wants to know why, you tell him you love Mr. Wilcox the same as you love music. And you'd better love him too, because you're going to stick to him like a brother. He'll bring you home."

She accepted the terms joyfully and with only one question. "Why?"

"Rough element at these affairs."

She agreed, and made a dash for the door.

"What are you going to wear?" he asked. Her eyes were already dreaming over hooks and hangers.

She paused. "This is like a party. Or Sunday. I got a pale blue handkerchief linen with Valenciennes," she said glibly. "Real Valenciennes."

He let her go, and sat on the steps to watch the other preparations. Roberta came, silent and preoccupied, and he heard her moving about in the room she shared with Joey. Miss Rayner's horse and buggy were brought to the parking lot, and Miss Rayner, in black silk, took a seat under the trees. Folly Number Seven, the newest and cleanest, roared up the hill like a Juggernaut and came to a snorting stop before the veranda. Cora and Kirby joined Miss Rayner, and Cora's intermittent hoots mingled with the Folly's fretful coughs. The Haskells, fat, overdressed, and flattered, rocked sedately on the veranda. Nick came out, examined the waiting guests with a cool stare, and walked over to the cottages. He was limping more than usual and his face was drawn and tired.

"Coming for the girls?" Mark asked. "They've been long enough. I'll call them."

"Don't bother," Nick said flatly. "I'm on my way to the Pecks'. I'll stop here on the way back."

Mark watched as he moved on, dragging his foot. He was turning one phrase over and over in his mind. Dropped by a nurse, dropped by a nurse.

The three Pecks came out, surpassing the Haskells in raiment, and stopped to talk about the weather. It was a lovely day, and the sky was a lovely blue, and later on there might be a breeze.

Franny was eloquent. "I was talking to Mr. Haskell at lunch," she said. "He thinks we'll have a storm. A perfectly dreadful one. But he doesn't think we'll get wet. He thinks it will hold off until late tonight, or maybe tomorrow. He's really wonderful. He went to sea when he was a lad."

Joey can talk better than that, Mark thought with satisfaction. She could talk better than that the day she was born. "We need the rain for the crops," he said solemnly.

Roberta and Joey came out. He looked the latter over with pleasure; pretty as a picture, and not the candy box type.

"Remember," he warned softly.

Franny heard him, puckered her mouth, and dimpled. "Remember what?" she asked.

"To come back," he grinned. He waved them on.

They swooped on the Folly with loud laughter, and piled in. The Haskells hurried down the veranda steps like two Wagnerian characters late on cue. The Folly roared off.

Mark saw Beulah join Miss Rayner under the trees. She said something, and pointed to the sky. Miss Rayner followed her look, rose, and shook out her skirts. Then the two of them walked arm in arm over to the fat bay, who watched their approach over a shoulder that looked as if it would shrug if it could.

He sat on, smoking cigarettes. The concert party, together with the siesta hour, had cleared the lawns and the veranda. He gave everybody a chance to settle down before he strolled into the lobby.

"I'm running up to see George Parmelee," he said to the clerk. That gave him a wide range; George could be almost anywhere.

The second floor halls were quiet and deserted. He knew the rooms he wanted and wasted no time. There was, he noted, nothing about summer hotel locks that a backward child couldn't master in a minute.

His first stop was Cora Sheffield's suite, and it was as trim as a thoroughbred's stable. The one visible concession to lure was a bottle of Blue Grass perfume tied with a yellow satin ribbon. The ribbon said "THIRD PRIZE," in gold letters. He read the label on the bottle. Six ounces. About right for a likely colt.

He opened the bedroom closets and fell back before their contents. The first was devoted to tweeds, and the devotion ran close to infatuation. He was in that room on serious business, and his mind was filled with a black foreboding, but he took time out to finger the material lovingly and visualize it in pants. It was all too good for Cora.

The second closet held the chiffons and all that went with them. They were far from clean, and the trailing, bedraggled hems showed signs of heavy travel through dew, dust, and a brier patch. They also looked as if they'd been bought blindfolded in a sub-basement. He went from the closets to the bureau and chest.

In that quarter, Cora was unexpectedly like Mary Cassidy, tailored and immaculate. But there was no secret cache of silk and fine lace.

Cora wore her weakness openly, on the outside, every evening from six o'clock on. As for her toilet articles, she had a hairbrush and a comb.

In the small sitting room he found a desk, disarmingly open and discouragingly neat. With one exception, her mail was a small stack of feed bills, paid, and a dozen painfully correct letters from her stable man. The exception was a personal note: "I'm sorry, dear. Hank."

He went over both rooms again, turning the rugs and lifting the mattress. He didn't know what he was looking for and he found nothing. If Cora was a killer she had a foolproof front. There were no drugs in her bathroom; she disdained even aspirin. She had a ten cent cake of soap, two toothbrushes, a can of tooth powder, and a case of whisky. He moved on.

Hank Kirby was irreproachably bedded two doors down the hall on the other side. It was a smaller suite, with only one closet in the bedroom. His clothes were magnificent, but few. The bureau and chest of drawers yielded nothing. A clothes brush, used, a whisk-broom, used, and a pair of military brushes, pathetically unused, stood on top of the bureau. There was one tin of aggressively masculine talcum in the bathroom. The sitting room was as bare as a cell and not much larger. Hank had no bills of any kind, and no correspondence, but a box of fine stationery stood open on the otherwise empty desk. Dedicated, no doubt, to the simple ballads that fluttered two doors up the hall and across.

He stood in the center of the bedroom and scanned every visible inch. Something was missing. It had to be there. He went over to the bed and lifted the valance, revealing a large, square leather box. He dragged it out and opened it. It held bottles, jars, boxes, tubes, and tins; tiny brushes, cakes of dye, mascara pencils. There were three wigs, perfectly groomed. One of them was a shade more perfect than the other, having a high gloss and a discreet wave. For the opera?

He started to light a cigarette and remembered that Hank didn't smoke. He left the room with relief.

The elevator shaft was next door, and he saw that the cage was standing empty at the first floor. He didn't want it anyway; all he wanted was not to meet it in transit. The main stairway wound up beside the shaft. He took the steps two at a time.

Miss Rayner lived on the fourth, at the rear end of the hall. Above the fourth was the servants' floor. She couldn't have had a less desirable location. There was probably a sound monetary reason behind her reluctance to tip.

It was a tiny, single room, with running water concealed behind a stained and faded screen. The bed was narrow and hard, no valance there, and the floor beneath was clean and bare. A spotless dustcloth, hanging from a corner of the screen, indicated that she took care of the room herself. A flimsy, built-in wardrobe showed rows of pleasant, old-fashioned dresses, small hats, slippers with low heels and pointed toes; the plain pine bureau held bottles of violet, verbena, and rose geranium toilet water, and a toilet set of well-worn and carefully polished silver. Miss Rayner's efficient little hands had almost buffed the fat cupids and their *repoussé* garlands out of existence. There was also a hotel plate filled with lumps of sugar, each one wrapped in a square of clean cheesecloth.

He opened the drawers and surveyed their contents with one quick look. Underwear, plain. There was a small trunk behind the door, and he stood before it while he belabored his conscience. It was one thing to unearth Hank Kirby's beauty secrets and Cora's feed bills, even to read Franny Peck's love letters, but Miss Rayner's little round-topped trunk had a sacred look. And it was uncomfortably like the picture of Pandora's box.

He raised the lid and stepped back to make way for the scrabbling troop of human ills he half expected to see come swarming over the sides. Nothing happened. There was not even a creak. The trunk was an old lady's storeroom, filled with prudent preparations for a change in weather. There were galoshes, rubber sandals and rubbers, bed socks, extra blankets, and an old plaid cape with a hood. In a small top compartment that had a Turner landscape pasted on its lid, he found extra handkerchiefs and heavy stockings, brochures in praise of English watering places, and a yellowing envelope containing something that felt like cardboard. He opened this with commendable shame.

The cardboard was a photograph of a baby with its curling hair severely and wetly combed into a Thames Tunnel. It was not a pretty baby, but someone had thought so once. A line of faded ink on the back said—"My darling, age 6 mos."

He put it away in its envelope, returned it to the compartment, and closed the trunk. Then he went to the single, small window and stood looking down into the back yard four floors below. The chef had returned to his hammock, and a few cats grubbed around a garbage can. A man wearing a bloody apron came out of the poultry shed with a basket of dead chickens. Their limp heads hung over the sides. It wasn't a pretty view.

Perley sat between Joey and Pee Wee, replete with frozen custard, peanuts, and potato chips. The streak of custard on his neat serge sleeve had been applied by Pee Wee in an excess of emotion brought on by the overture to Wilhelm Tell. Pee Wee had accepted the overture as a personal tribute, fostered by some aesthete who had seen his own performance with the lemon. The band had burst into the first notes as he walked down the makeshift aisle to take his seat.

There was shade for the band but none for the audience. Perley tipped his stiff straw hat over his eyes. In spite of his fears he was having a good time. He liked children and didn't care what they did to his clothes, and he liked the kind of music he was hearing. *The Stars and Stripes Forever* was a fine piece. You couldn't have too much of that kind of thing these days. The *Tell* piece was good too, but he thought he must have heard it somewhere before. So far there had been no gems from *The Prince of Pilsen* but they'd had gems from *The Student Prince*. One of the latter gems had words, and was sung by a quartet of manly looking young fellows. He wished Pansy could see them. They could sing fine, too. "The golden ha-a-aze of student da-a-ays," he hummed under his breath. And there they were, happy as larks, with no time to finish their own educations, and a bad time ahead.

He craned his neck unobtrusively and counted the familiar hats three rows ahead. Still all there.

The band gave itself an intermission and a major made an inaudible speech.

"It isn't over, is it?" whispered Joey. "They're going to play again, aren't they?"

"Yes indeed," Perley whispered back. "Two or three pieces, I expect. Then they'll finish with *The Star-Spangled Banner.*"

He hoped they rolled the drums good and loud in that one. So many bands didn't. A good, long, loud roll. Gave you the chills and made you want to poke somebody. A half-forgotten memory stirred at the back of his mind and nagged him into reminiscence, and after several tries he finally traced it to a movie he'd once seen.

"What are you thinking about, Mr. Wilcox?" Joey asked solicitously.

"Nothing much," he told her.

Yes, that was it, he said to himself. A movie. They'd rolled the drums in it. A beautiful roll. He could hear and see it all as plain as day. One of those movies about aristocrats in the French Revolution.

They'd rolled the drums when a high class fellow walked up the steps to that big knife and got his head chopped off in a basket.

Mark went into Beacham's room and made what he knew would be a fruitless search. He felt that it was a waste of time, but he was afraid not to cover everything. He found a few Pullman stubs in the bottom of a drawer and took them.

He had gone over Roberta's original room the first night he slept in it, and he knew nothing had been changed since then. She had moved all her things into the room formerly shared by Joey and Cassie. He went there, as a matter of routine. Roberta's clothes were in Cassie's closet and bureau, and Cassie's were gone.

He covered the entire cottage before he found them. They were crammed into a chest in the bathroom and stowed away on the top shelf of the hall closet. Roberta's work?

Roberta had a large correspondence tied in bundles like Franny's, but there was no further resemblance. The letters were from girls, ecstatic when not despairing, hopeful when not crushed to earth. They hated or loved their parents' idea of a vacation and had met absolutely nobody, or somebody. There was an album of snapshots on the table, and he went through this slowly and carefully. Names and dates were written in white ink under each picture. There were none of Cassie. Not even an empty, telltale space. He turned the pages a second time to make sure.

He went back to the porch and stared thoughtfully at the hotel. Old Sutton was still in his suite; at least he hadn't appeared for his afternoon air. George, if he wasn't with the old man, was up under the roof in his own cubicle. He probably shared it with a chauffeur or a waiter. No chance to get in there; too risky at all hours. Employees were always sneaking up for a smoke.

He looked at his watch. Four-thirty. He took a shower, put on fresh clothes, and went out to the trees to wait.

At six o'clock the Folly roared up the hill, and behind it came Wilcox and the children. Roberta's guests dragged themselves into the hotel like a defeated army. Perley, frankly happy and with a child clinging to each hand, crossed to Mark's chair.

"Very enjoyable," he commented. "I'm glad I went." He lowered his voice. "But we're right where we started from. Nothing done, nothing said. Nothing at all."

"Beat it," Mark said to Pee Wee and Joey. "And wash whatever that is off your face," he told Joey. "Otherwise you look so good that I may ask you to dine with me tonight."

Perley settled in a chair. "Nobody made a move after we got there. Not even to go to the water cooler. I got the feeling they knew they were expected to do something, and didn't do it on purpose. Except the Haskells. They were bowing right and left like it was a sociable. They had a real good time. Nobody even said anything when I took the children in my car. I thought there'd be an argument. Would you say that was good or bad?"

"Neither. Everybody's nervous. If you walked behind that crowd and clapped your hands together, you'd have to pick the whole lot of them up."

"Oh!" Perley struck his forehead. "I nearly forgot. Briggs hollered at me as I came by and said the telegraph office had a wire for you. Asked me to bring it along. Here."

Mark took it. It was the reply to his telephoned instructions to New York. It said, briefly, that the watch–dogs had found nothing to bark at.

"You'll be relieved to know that Beacham's been behaving himself," he said. "Let's hope he keeps it up." He eyed Perley's best serge, not overlooking the custard. "Are you prepared to spend the night here?"

"As much as I'll ever be. Pansy keeps asking when I'm coming home."

"Tomorrow. After the party."

Perley fanned himself with his hat. "Pansy heard about the party. She says you showed good sense when you didn't invite her. She says she wouldn't come if you got down on your knees and crawled. She remembers the one you gave last year."

"Does she know the Moresbys are coming?"

"She does. Hazel called her up. Pansy made out like she was going herself, to calm Hazel down. She's no fool, Pansy."

"No."

"What are you sitting out here for? What kind of afternoon did you have?"

"I'm waiting for dinner because I didn't have much lunch and I had a beautiful afternoon, thanks."

"Okay, okay," said Perley. They sat on without talking.

Old man Sutton and George appeared at the top of the veranda steps. The old man lowered his head between his shoulders like a charging bull and glared in all directions; when he saw Mark and Perley under the trees, he spoke to George in a rapid undertone, and they both turned and went back into the lobby.

Perley coughed gently. "Any luck in that direction?"

"Couldn't get in. There was too much risk."

A few minutes later Nick and Roberta came out and crossed to the parking lot. Mark raised an arm. "Nick!" he called. The boy turned. "Come here a minute, will you?" Then, "Did you people get your invitations to my party?"

"We did. Thank you."

"Coming?"

Nick laughed. "What do you think?" He was still laughing when he joined Roberta.

Mark watched them climb into the car and drive off.

"No," he said in answer to Perley's look. "They won't run away. They'd like to, but they can't." He twisted and turned in his chair, stared at the sky, and got up to walk to the cottage; halfway there he turned back and resumed his seat. Perley lit his pipe and smoked stolidly.

When the dinner gong rang Mark was on his feet before the reverberations had died away. "Joey!" he shouted. Heads turned in his direction and he looked sheepish. "Joey," he called again in a reasonable octave. She came running. "I'm hungry," he said. "Let's eat now. You stay here," he said to Perley. "Right where you are. You can take my place inside when I've finished."

Dinner was long, poorly cooked, and badly served; the upper class jitters had spread to the kitchen. Joey, however, found nothing to complain of. Old Sutton was apparently dining in his room. He didn't appear. The Pecks came in with Cora and Kirby and the Haskells, the latter looking as if they'd made the social register. Miss Rayner, walking primly to her own table, stopped to talk, and Mark thought there was more than civility behind her bright smile. He learned almost at once that he was right.

"Such a nice drive," she said. "But I'm afraid Miss Pond has a headache. She's having a tray upstairs, so wise. I gave her some aspirins. She came all the way up to my little room to ask for them."

"Did she?" Mark said vacantly.

"Yes." Miss Rayner's smile deepened. "And she wasn't my only caller, either. The other one was less considerate. He came while I was out." She patted Joey's beribboned topknot, and moved on.

"What does she mean?" Joey asked.

"I'd give a lot to know," he said truthfully. "Stop that!" She was reaching for a bowl of pickles.

Twice during dinner he was called to the phone. The first time it was Bittner. His chartered driver had turned in receipts and report. He had known all of the passengers, had carried them before. Nobody had tried to beat the hotel bill, and nobody had talked secrets. All of the talking had been good and loud, so a person could hear.

Bittner cleared his throat pitifully after making this statement; when he continued, he sounded as if he were fighting back tears. "I'm so out of things. I might as well be dead and nobody would care. . . . Would they?"

"Is that all?" Mark asked.

"That's all I can think of. I may call you later tonight. Saturday's a big night. You ought to see the—"

"I have. Listen. Don't call me for a light blue roadster carrying Nick Sutton and Roberta Beacham. I know all about it. They're simply taking a little air."

"Oh, Oh, all right." He coughed again. "Ella May says you're inviting people to eat tomorrow night. I couldn't come anyway but I hope you enjoy yourself."

Mark hung up. When he got back to the table Joey had ordered ice cream with chocolate sauce for both of them. "Business?" she asked soberly.

"No. Bittner just wanted to thank Roberta for hiring his bus. I took the message for her." He hesitated. "Do you know where Roberta and Nick went?"

"They went to eat Chinese food. She's going to ask him to marry her."

"What!"

"She says she has to ask him. It's a secret, but I'll tell you how it turns out. She's old enough, isn't she?"

"Yes, she's old enough."

The second call came while he was having coffee and Joey was finishing his dessert. This time it was Beacham. Mark was not surprised.

Beacham was full of hearty apologies. "I'm calling from my office," he said. "I dropped in here to look things over and found a few snarls. Right now it looks as if I won't be able to make the train tonight. You don't need me, do you?"

"You can answer that as well as I can," Mark said.

"No trouble up there?"

"All serene."

"That's good." Beacham dropped his voice to a confidential tone. "Know something, East? I think it's going to stay that way. I've been running things over in my mind and I'm pretty sure the whole affair was an accident, a dreadful accident. I honestly think we're on the wrong track when we try to bring in any other element. Why don't we let Wilcox handle it his way? It's his territory, after all."

"Accident?" Mark repeated softly. "Did you say accident?"

"Yes. Give Wilcox time and he'll clean it up. I'm convinced that he, or one of his men, will eventually tie it to some crazy kid who was cutting up and lost his head."

"Lost whose head?" Mark queried gently.

"You know what I mean. You know how dark it was. I mean somebody killed Cassie by accident and hid her body in the nearest place. Panic. Sheer panic."

"Sure I know what you mean. Sheer panic. I call it that too. So I'm fired?"

"Don't put it that way. I have every confidence in you but I think this is out of your class and mine."

"All right. I'll resign tomorrow night and turn the case over to Wilcox. How's that?"

"It's all right only if you agree with me. I'm thinking of your own good. We'll talk it over when I get back."

"Fine. I'll be looking forward to that. Do you want to speak to Joey now?"

"I haven't time. Tell her everything was—was done properly. Tell her I'll be in on the evening train tomorrow. If she wants to, she can meet me in Baldwin. Somebody can bring her." That was all.

Mark wondered about the layout of Beacham's office. He knew one thing definitely; if there were two doors, there was a nondescript man outside each one. He returned to his table, finished his coffee, and escorted Joey out to the lawn. He signaled to Perley, who settled his hat under his arm and tiptoed up the hotel steps like a shy sacrifice.

It was growing dark outside. The air was cooler but there were no stars, and the trees were silent. Mark sat on the cottage porch and Joey took the steps.

"Your father can't make the early train," he said. "He'll be along later. Do you want to meet him?"

"Yes," she said quietly. He told her what Beacham had said about the funeral and she listened without comment. After a while she came up on the porch and leaned against him, resting her sharp little chin on his shoulder. He absently pulled her into his lap.

"Why don't you go to bed?" he said. "Big day today."

She didn't answer. "Joey," he said softly, "what did your mother look like? Like you or like Roberta?"

She waited before she spoke. "I don't know that."

"No pictures?"

"No sir." She closed the subject. "I think I will go to bed," she said.

"No reading out loud?"

"No sir."

This was unnaturally formal and indicated stress. He let her go and he knew better than to offer his assistance.

The Pecks came by, proudly flanked by the Haskells. They called jovial and noisy greetings. Thanks for the party invitation. They'd be there with bells on.

"The bells of hell go tingalingaling, but not for you and me," sang Archie.

The Haskells looked wistful, even in the twilight. They hadn't been invited. Mark addressed them mentally. Wait until Monday, he said silently, and you'll be glad.

Perley came over for instructions. He was bristling with information of his own at the same time. "You know what they call a cabbage in there?" he asked. "Shoo! Like you say to a fly, shoo! Fellow waiting on my table told me that. It's French. Shoo! Pansy's going to call me a liar when I tell her."

Mark stood at the railing that overlooked the Peck cottage. He watched the lights go on in the living room.

"You're not paying me any mind," Perley said. "I was telling you what they call a cabbage—"

"I know what they call it. . . . Take the hotel until midnight, then I'll relieve you. Go up to the second floor and stick to the side of the hall that leads to the fire escape."

CHAPTER TEN

A
T 5:00 a.m. Mark came back to the cottage and told Perley to get some sleep. He took the porch hammock himself and slept until Joey called him. She told him it was nine o'clock and said she couldn't keep on chasing people away. Everybody was hungry, she said, and Roberta had ordered breakfast sent over.

He struggled up. "Where's the sun?"

"There isn't any today. It's a terrible looking day."

The sky was low and dark and the tree tops met each other with sibilant whispers, recoiled, and met again.

He bathed hastily and joined the others at the living room table. Joey had already bolted her food and was trying to see how far she could tilt her chair without falling over backward.

"Don't do that," Roberta said. Her voice was mild and preoccupied. Mark gave her a covert look. The old sharpness wasn't there and she looked as if she'd had twelve hours sleep. He knew she hadn't. He tried to read in her eyes what had happened the night before, but they were as bland as a child's.

Joey straightened up and made her napkin into a cocked hat which she tried on. Perley sat stiffly at the end of the table, conducting himself according to the code he had heard Pansy lay down for Floyd; left hand in lap, right hand grimly but daintily wielding his fork. His elbows were so far removed from the table that they might have been underslung wings, and he chewed his food as if it were a deadly secret.

Joey slid down from her chair and asked to be excused. Mark paid no attention until he heard the lock turn in her door.

"What's the idea, locking herself in?" he asked Roberta.

"She's going to try on clothes and look at herself in the mirror. Deciding what she's going to wear."

"Wear when?"

"This afternoon. Sunday school."

"Well she can save herself the trouble. She's not going. Run along and tell her I said so, will you?"

He heard Roberta knock, heard the door open and the low murmur of voices. Joey came out instantly and frantically. She had tied herself into a pongee bathrobe, wrong side out.

"You're not going," Mark said before she could open her mouth. He fell back before the avalanche.

She had to go, she told him furiously. He couldn't make her stay home. He hadn't the right of bossing over her. She had to go. It was her birthday next Wednesday. He knew that. She had to.

"What has next Wednesday got to do with today?" he managed to ask. "I thought you were still steamed up over keeping that banner."

Well, the banner too. But Wednesday was why she had to go. Didn't he have any sense at all? Didn't he know anything? If Mike was here he'd say she could. He knew. He understood.

His own nerves were raw and he counted ten twice before he was sure his voice would have the right quality. "Tell me all about it," he said. "Maybe, just maybe, I'll understand too."

She told him earnestly, looking from him to Perley. It was, she said, all because of Baby Moses. He asked her to say it again, to make sure he'd heard it right. She did. It was all because of Baby Moses and the Guardian Angel. The Angel was no good and they had six of them left, but there was only one Baby Moses.

He threw Perley a frantic look and got no help. Roberta carefully looked away.

"Can you enlarge on that?" he asked faintly. "I mean, tell me a little bit more?"

Certainly she could, she said, grinding an elbow into his knee. As the words rushed out, he sifted the wheat from the chaff. There was, it seemed, a pleasant custom attending birthdays. Children due to celebrate were cordially invited to drop their age, in pennies, into a goldfish bowl. Publicly.

A jack-knife convulsion brought the pennies out of the bathrobe pocket. He could see, couldn't he? Nine of them. Nine. She would walk up the aisle to the little table and drop them in the bowl. Right in front of everybody and all the kids would count out loud. And after that they let you pick out a picture for a present. A colored picture, pasted on cardboard so you could have it framed. But there was another kid who had a birthday on Tuesday and he was bragging around to everybody that he was going to pick the Baby Moses. He bragged all over town that he was going to get it. And there was only one. She stopped for breath, and Mark intervened.

"What, exactly, is there about this Baby Moses?"

Joey's eyes glistened. He was beautiful. He was lying in a little yellow basket with green cattails all around. The basket was floating on blue water, and a lady with big brown eyes and a long white veil was peeping at him. And there was only one Moses and she had to have him.

"But the Guardian Angel?"

"That's two kids picking flowers on the edge of a precipice and if they walked another step they'd fall over and get killed."

"But the Guardian Angel—"

"It's floating over their heads, low down and almost touching them with its feet. And they don't even know it. There's a pretty good yellow butterfly in it, but it's no comparison to Baby Moses. They've got six Angels left and only one Moses. That goes to show you, doesn't it?"

Perley sent Mark a pleading look, and Joey intercepted it. "They let you pick out a song too," she added plaintively. "Any song you want."

Mark played his only card, hopelessly. "Can't we postpone the whole thing until next Sunday?"

She wailed. "I won't be here! I'll be gone! Next Sunday I'll be gone! This is my very last day!"

It ended as he had known it would. He gave in. He told her they'd ride down together in the station wagon and he'd pick her up after the performance. Performance didn't sound like the right word, but he had to talk fast to avoid a deluge. "And don't tell me what you're going to wear. I want to be bowled over."

Then almost at once he realized he had been too quick, too eager to please. He couldn't go. He couldn't leave the grounds. He didn't dare.

"Joey," he began. He stopped, and started again. "Listen, Joey, I—"

Perley took over with a pair of paternal arms. "Now, now," he said. He stood Joey between his knees and briskly turned the bathrobe right side out, retying it properly. "I guess we can go all right. I've got to drive home for some clean clothes and I can put this young lady in Pansy's care. That station wagon isn't going down today. I heard the fellow say so. He's a sugar baby, he is, afraid of the rain. Well, we'll just turn things over to Pansy. And then when you've got your nice picture, I'll come by and drive you home again." He leaned back, satisfied with himself, until he saw that he'd left the spoon in his coffee cup. He removed it hastily, with a sidelong look at Roberta.

But Roberta wasn't looking at him; she was facing the door, expectantly. Nick came up the steps with tennis rackets and swimming bag.

"Coming," Roberta called out. She took her own things from a chair and went out. "We've got to have exercise," she said over her shoulder. "I don't know when we'll be back." The door slammed, defiantly.

"That's mighty foolish," Perley said. "If they stay out long they're liable to be struck by lightning. I've seen it happen. They'll stand under a tree to get out of the rain and fry to a crisp."

Mark gave him a wondering look. "What's the matter with you all of a sudden? You sound like Bittner."

"I'm nervous. It just came over me. I'm nervous as a cat."

"Well, get over it," Mark warned in a low voice. "Little pitchers."

Perley looked at Joey on the floor; she was counting her pennies and practicing the routine with the goldfish bowl. He got down beside her, wincing as his knees cracked in protest.

"If you'd have told me," he said to her, "I'd have got you some new ones from the bank. But we can fix these up. Gimme, I'll show you." He buffed a penny briskly on the grass rug and proudly displayed the resulting shine. "Learned that thirty years ago."

Joey fell to, wordless and enthralled. Mark left them, and went out to the porch. Beulah was coming across the grass.

"What kind of a night?" he asked.

"Frightful. People tramping up and down the halls all night long." She came up to the porch and sat down. "Frightful."

"I know. I was there most of the time."

"I don't think anybody slept," she went on. "And old Sutton gave poor George a terrible time. My room is over his, and I could hear George arguing. 'Come back, pal, it's too late,' he kept saying. 'You can't go anywhere now.' Things like that. It sounded awful in the middle of the night. Does it mean anything?"

Mark shrugged. "Who knows?" He waited a minute. "The Pecks had a party. Know anything about that?"

"I heard about it from the maid on the Haskells' floor. She said the Haskells couldn't get up this morning. Nobody got up, as far as I could see. Miss Rayner, the Pecks, the Haskells, Sheffield, Kirby, all missing at breakfast. What happened here?"

"Nothing special."

Perley came out, rubbing his knees. "Joey's trying on clothes. She says do I think she'll look good in all white. I told her yes." He examined the sky. "I don't like the way that looks," he said. "So low you'd think you could touch it. She's going to be a bad one when she comes. She'll take a while to get going. First you get the wind, slow and steady rising. Then the dark. I've seen it dark as night at five in the afternoon."

"Yes," Beulah said. "I know." She shivered, and scowled at the whispering trees. "They sound human."

Perley went on as if he were talking to himself. "Then you get the lightning and the thunder. Bad, real bad. I've seen the lightning blast a tree into the shape of a cross and overturn a gravestone."

"Are you enjoying yourself?" Mark asked.

Perley sat on the steps and pulled out his pipe. "No. Somebody with cold hands is playing the piano up and down my spine. You want to know something? I used to like summer people. I never did like winter people, like the kind we had last December. It never seemed natural to me when folks took time off in the winter and loafed. Summer people, I used to say, are all right. Put their money aside for a nice little holiday, take the kids and maybe the old folks, and go off to the country for a couple of weeks. And the man of the house coming up on Saturdays with a box of candy and his new white shoes. It looked nice. That's what I used to think. I don't know now." It was a long speech, and when he finished he was embarrassed.

Beulah eyed him thoughtfully. "It's the waiting that makes you feel that way," she said. "You know something's going to happen and you don't know what it is. All you can do is wait. You'll feel better tomorrow. And," she added with a leer, "next summer you'll want to take boarders."

She's scared silly, Mark said to himself, but she puts on a good front. "Sure he will," he said. "And he'll hang a sign in his window, like Buster."

Cora Sheffield and Kirby, dressed for riding, came out of the hotel and headed for the lot.

"If I was looking for a crazy person," Perley said, "I'd pick one of them two. Do they want to get their necks broken? This is no weather for riding. If the wind takes a notion, and one of those old elms down the road decides to shed a branch—"

Mark turned to Beulah. "You're wasting time sitting here," he said abruptly. "Talk, talk, talk. I don't want to talk. Go on back to the hotel and hang around the lobby." You can do that, can't you?"

She was startled, but she didn't show it. "I can," she said quietly. "What shall I do besides hang?"

"Anything, but not too thoroughly. Read a magazine, knit. But keep one eye open for the people who go out. Nobody will go far in this weather without a sound—or unsound—reason. Call me on the house phone if anybody does. No matter who, servants, week-enders, anybody who goes through the main gates or down the path to the pool."

"Roberta and Nick—"

"I'll take care of that. And another thing. Check the garage and stable before you go in. Call me if any car is out, or any horse aside from the two we just saw. I'd do it myself, but I can't leave here." There was suppressed fury in his voice.

"Mad because you can't be in two places at once?" she asked flippantly. "I'll check. And if anybody walks through the lobby wearing a hat, I'll follow. That what you want?"

He relaxed. "Yes. Thanks, Beulah. My bark is worse than my bite. But somebody's playing the piano on my spine too, and it feels like Chopin's Funeral March."

"Wait till they get to the middle part," she said. "It's pretty, there." She stood up. "What are you going to do with Joey this afternoon? You can't have her underfoot. You can't have her here. There's too much in the air."

"I know." He looked his distress. "I want her where I can see her, more or less. Where I can reach her in a hurry if I have to. Pansy's out. Too far. Almost everybody's out—up here. I'm even afraid of my own judgment."

"What about me? I can take her."

"To Crestwood? You're crazy. No."

"I mean to the hotel," she said patiently. "Send her over to me when Perley brings her back. I won't take her to my room. We'll play checkers in the lobby in full sight of everybody. And tonight"—Beulah swallowed—"tonight I think I can get a nice girl to take my place. Maid on my floor. Bessy had her in the fourth grade. You—you want Joey out of the way tonight?"

"I do. I simply hadn't got around to arranging it. That's okay then. Perley will leave her with you after Sunday school. She's a cheerful kid. She won't give you any trouble."

"I know she's cheerful. Sometimes I've wondered about it." Beulah had been agreeable too long. "Very cheerful and very calm. Not much heart, if you ask me. Considering that the poor woman was practically her mother—"

He gave her a cold stare. "I'm going inside to refresh what little mind I have left," he said.

She watched him go, and when he was out of sight she turned to Perley. She had never cared for Perley in the old days; his family and hers had been separated by more than the five miles between Crestwood and Bear River. But Perley as a man was at least hardworking and honest. She stepped down to his level with ease.

"Cross as two sticks," she whispered. "What's he got up his sleeve?"

"Truffles." Perley was serious. "Did you ever eat any?"

"Once. They made me sick." She wondered at the grim look he gave her, but she didn't ask why. If Mark was thinking about food, let him. It was a healthy sign.

"Well," she said, "I'm off." She went down the steps and started across the lawn. An ill wind crept around the end of the cottage, hugging the ground; when it reached her, it rose. She finished the trip bent double, her long arms futilely embracing her knees. The wind followed her to the stable door.

She entered with a rush and a moan and collapsed on the oat bin. It was quiet in there and mercifully without weather. The air was sweet with hay, and the only sound was a soft, contented nuzzling. Only two stalls were empty, and that was as it should be.

Miss Rayner's fat bay opened world-weary eyes and looked her over. She did not smell of sugar. The three end stalls were occupied by three dejected hacks. They watched her hopefully, like foundlings on visitors' day, waiting to be chosen. There were no attendants in sight.

They know, she said to herself, they know they won't have many customers today. Up in the loft, sleeping and playing pinochle. "Hey!" she shouted. A trapdoor opened in the ceiling and a red face looked down. "When do you expect Miss Sheffield and Mr. Kirby?"

"One o'clock, Miss."

She was mollified. "All right. I don't want anything." She went outdoors and prudently stuck to the walls on her way to the garage. The wind was slowly increasing. There were no attendants in the garage either, and as far as she knew all the cars were there. On her way out she met a yard boy carrying a pail of water inefficiently.

"Are all the cars in?"

"Yes, Miss." He actually touched his cap. "Did you want to rent one?"

"No. No thanks." Twice she had been called Miss in a nice way. She felt better and walked straighter when she entered the lobby.

At one o'clock Mark sent Perley and Joey over to lunch, with instructions to sit with Beulah. He didn't want food himself and said so, sharply, when Perley pressed him.

"We'll send you something," Joey insisted.

"Get along, both of you," he said. He followed them to the porch and once more he tried hopelessly to change a situation that, for no definite reason, disturbed him. "Be a good kid, Joey," he said, "and reconsider this afternoon. Look at that sky. You'll never get there."

"Yes I will. Mr. Wilcox is a good driver. Aren't you, Mr. Wilcox?"

"It would be a pity," agreed the flattered Wilcox, "if a big man like me couldn't take care of one little girl."

They walked off, hand in hand. Mark returned to his work.

Delaney, Murdoch, Kelso. Kelso, Murdoch, Delaney. Love and hate on the wrong tracks, running through signals, strewing human wreckage where they passed. Delaney. He sat slumped over the page that told the old man's story. Not enough, not enough. What had happened to his daughter? . . . Sutton? He read on.

Joey and Perley returned at two o'clock with identical stories of fried chicken and peach ice cream. He was glad when Joey went in to dress. She was noisy.

Perley, temporarily lulled into a peaceful state by the kind of food and conversation he understood, made an effort to cheer Mark up. "She'd pin a veil on her hair if we'd let her," he said. "She's taking this thing very serious. It seems that nine years old is important because it's next to the tenses. Tenses! You're getting along when you're next to the tenses. I wish I had a girl, too."

Mark's head snapped back. "What?"

"I say I wish I had a girl, too. Most men want boys and sometimes they act mean about it, but not me. I'd like a girl first-rate."

Mark dropped his hand on the open page. "What do you want for Christmas, Perley?"

"It's going without your meals that makes you talk like that," Perley said.

"I'll eat tomorrow. Roberta and Nick get back?"

"Yep. Sat at the table with Miss Sheffield and Mr. Kirby. They looked like they'd had a fight, Sheffield and Kirby."

"He'll call her up some rainy afternoon on beautiful writing paper. What about old Sutton?"

"Didn't come to the dining room. Haskells neither. Miss Pond's getting it all down for you. She's putting it all in a little book like yours. She's sitting by the elevator, and when people go up or come down she looks 'em over from head to foot and puts it in the little book. It don't look good. They all know what she's doing and first thing you know they're going to hide in their rooms. I don't blame them."

"All the better if they do, and don't discourage anything that keeps Beulah busy in one place. Here." He pushed the tin of truffles across the table. "Leave these with the chef when you go out. Tell him I'll see him later. . . . When do you think that storm will break?"

"I make it around five. Maybe before." Perley was suddenly serious. "Does that make any difference?"

"Not to us. Not to you and me. But hurry back from town and come straight in here. I'll want to talk to you. But not now. Do you mind waiting outside now? I'm in the middle of a maze and I think I see the right turn. Do you know what a maze is?"

"Don't tell me," Perley said wearily. He took the tin of truffles and went over to find the chef. When he came back he sat in the swing and thought unhappily of the immediate future. Somebody was playing on his spine again.

Joey joined him a few minutes later. He heard her prattle before she appeared. She was brazenly asking for compliments and getting them. "I would like a girl," he said aloud. "Come on, Joey. We'll beat the rain and get you there in fine shape. Who cares what we look like coming back?"

Mark turned on the lamp. The sullen sky held no light. The curtains flapped at the windows and the air was pungent and unclean. It might have blown from a secret place, closed for a lifetime, now unobstructed and exposed. He turned to the page marked Murdoch and shut his eyes while he thought of Louise Murdoch as she would be today.

There was a light step on the porch. He was ashamed of his involuntary jump, but he crossed the room in one bound. George was reaching for the latch. His face was red and hot and his white jacket was stained. He said, "Could I talk to you a minute, Mr. East?"

Mark held the door open. "Come in." George obeyed, flexing his fingers as if they pained. "What's the trouble?" Mark asked. "Sit down."

George pretended not to hear the last. He knew his place. Although he was sagging with fatigue, he wouldn't sit in the presence of his betters. Not that he wasn't as good as anybody. He was. But you couldn't get around education.

Mark pushed him gently into a chair. "I'm glad you came over. I've been wanting to talk to you. But first, get what's bothering you off your chest."

"It's the old gentleman." The words rushed out. "He's bad again, but this time it's lasting too long. I was up with him all night. I want to call the doctor, but Nick says if I do the old gentleman'll kill me when he gets better. I don't know what to do."

"Who's with him now?"

"One of the maids. She's a nice kid. And I gave him a sedative. I don't like to do that but what else is there?"

Mark didn't ask why Nick wasn't on the job. He took a long breath. "Listen, George. Do you know anything about Miss Cassidy that you're keeping to yourself?"

"No sir! I swear. No sir!" There was no mistaking his look. "I'd of told you if I did. I got respect for the law. My old man was a cop. He got his in a hold-up when we were kids. They buried him with full honors." It was the best recommendation he could give himself and he gave it proudly. "I'd of told you," he repeated. "My old man was a cop."

"Good stuff." Mark hesitated. "Are you willing to forget personal loyalty and answer another one? One that doesn't concern you?"

"Ask it."

"What about Mr. Sutton? Was he ever out of your sight on the night Miss Cassidy was killed?"

The red burned deeply in George's face. "Yes sir," he admitted. "But honest, I don't think it meant a thing." He went on, slowly, dragging the words out. That was the night the old gentleman got away. Went to bed right after dinner like a lamb, and said he was going to read. He was feeling fine, he said, and he told George to go out for some fresh air. And don't hurry back, he said. It was about seven-thirty when George left. He stayed away until nine, talking to the boys in the kitchen, and when he went upstairs the old gentleman was gone.

George didn't tell anybody. He was afraid he'd be blamed. He went hunting alone, and found the old gentleman in the garage. "Don't ask me how he got there," George said. "There I was in the kitchen, facing the door, and I didn't see him pass. He was in a bad way, too. Hiding in a corner and he looked like he'd fallen down. Water and mud all over him. I got him up the back way and put him to bed. He'd dressed himself in his good clothes, too. Well, I wasn't taking no chances, so I put a sleeping powder in his nightcap. And I stood by and watched him go off. Then I went down again to wait for Nick. He said he'd be home early, and I wanted to tell him what happened before the old gentleman got his in. When Nick came back with Miss Rayner, I told him. He didn't blame me, and we went up to give the old feller a look. And there he was—gone again."

"What time?"

"Between half past ten and eleven I guess. I wasn't watching no clocks. You know where we ran him down? Up on the top floor where I sleep. Hiding in a hall closet. Crying fit to break his heart. That's what he's doing today, crying. That's why I'm worried."

"That night—did he ever tell you what was wrong?"

"No sir. He don't think very clear when he's like that. He gets childish. It gives you the kind of willies to watch him. He's like he's seeing things that ain't there."

"And you say he's like that now?"

"Yes sir. He keeps bending over, like, and putting out his hand like he was resting it on a kid's shoulder." George illustrated, with a sober, distressed face and no self-consciousness. "Like he was easing some kid's troubles."

Mark nodded. George straightened up and went on, seriously. "You want to know what I think, Mr. East?"

"I'd like to know. Tell me."

"It's like this. I think when people get very old their childhood comes back to them. It comes back like another person and they don't know it's themselves. They think it's a stranger. The old gent had a hard life when he was young and I think he's seeing his childhood standing in front of him now, crying the way he used to cry. So he puts out his hand because he wants to help. I think it means he's going to die soon. I think this child is himself, and it comes back and walks beside him because it's getting time for them to leave together. . . . Right?"

"Right," Mark said. He gave George a cigarette. "Don't worry about the old gentleman," he said. "I think we can straighten him out. You keep that medicine locked up, don't you?"

"Yes sir. But what about the doctor?"

"We'll wait a bit. If he isn't better tonight we'll get Cummings. . . . George, what about that concert yesterday? Do you know why Roberta suddenly wanted to go?"

"Fed up. Nerves. She's young." He was twenty-four. "They wanted to elope, but I pulled the old Dutch uncle. That stuff's no good, I told 'em. If you got to sneak a thing, it's out."

"What this world needs," Mark said, "is more sons of cops." He gave George another cigarette.

George beamed, and immediately went into a detailed and, to him, engrossing account of the Parmelee ups and downs; the measles time, Ma's leg when the ladder gave way and the kids had to do the wash for two weeks; the old man's first promotion, with steak and French fries. At three-forty-five he looked at his watch. "Got to go," he said. "That old baby of mine could get a notion to wake up and start screaming." He was almost jaunty when he walked out.

Mabel Homesdale stood at the window of her room under the eaves and watched the scuttling clouds. Beneath her stretched five acres of park-like garden, walled in by a tall iron fence. A winding drive, bordered with arching elms, led to the high entrance gate. The gnarled old branches clung to each other and defied the wind. Mabel could hear them even though her window was closed, and they raised gooseflesh on her arms. She thought of the six widely spaced little bungalows at the back of the house, each enclosed in a hedge.

"Terrible weather for such people," she said aloud. "Makes a person feel like giving up. Even healthy people."

She put on a raincoat and went down the back stairs. It was her hour off, she reminded herself, and it was nobody's business if she slept, or did her hair, or took a walk. She moved quietly along the clean, waxed floors, nagged on by the unbroken murmur of coughing that came from behind the lines of closed doors.

Outside, she walked aimlessly down the drive, under the writhing trees, and opened the tall iron gate. She was two miles north of Baldwin, and the nearest house was a mile away. She started down the road. Dark, she said to herself. Funny how it gets dark.

A few yards from the gate she was pleasantly surprised. Someone was coming toward her. She patted her hair and hoped for a soldier, but she was doubtful of her luck. Even in good weather you hardly ever saw anybody; too far out, and most people said the place was unhealthy. Full of germs, they said. Ignorance. She waited, speculatively. The figure drew near. It was Floyd Wilcox.

"Well I'll be!" she cried happily. "A familiar face! What are you doing out here?" He was only a kid, but he could talk.

Floyd glumly announced that he was visiting his grandmother. His mother had made him. She was scared.

"Who wouldn't be!" Mabel shivered all over.

"Not you," Floyd said admiringly. He looked over her shoulder at the big, dark house behind her. The iron gate arched in a semicircle and bore a gilt inscription: "Bide-A-Wee."

Floyd read this with fine sarcasm. "They don't bide so long if you ask me. In one week and out the next, or so I hear." He laughed. "In a pine box."

"Then you heard wrong!" Mabel was indignant. "The Doctor has a fine treatment and he don't lose anybody that comes in time. It's the ones that keep putting it off, and that's their own fault. Whoever told you different, told you wrong!"

Floyd winked. "Is he kind of cracked, the Doc?"

"Certainly not! I never heard such talk! He was educated in Europe and he's got ideas ahead of his time. One of these days you'll see his picture in the paper on account of what he's done! You wait!"

"I'll wait all right. Say, I notice you don't ask George to take his treatments."

"George don't need them. He's a light case. And I don't want to hear any more of that cracked talk, either!"

Floyd shrugged. "Aw Mabel, you can't blame people for talking like that. This is a terrible place."

"It is not! It's wonderful! The Doctor has a new kind of stuff that he puts in veins, and it works like nothing on earth!"

Floyd closed one eye and lowered his voice. "How does it work in number four bungalow?"

Mabel's face flamed. "Who told you about that? The Doctor don't like that talked about! The poor soul is practically dying and would have died in that bughouse if the Doctor hadn't agreed to take the case. Out of pure pity! And it's all legal too! Remember that! And if number four don't get cured it won't be the Doctor's fault. But there's some improvement. I hear the orderlies talking. And I think it's a great work to salvage a human soul. That's what the Doctor calls it." She hesitated. "Still, I don't think he's going to salvage number four. Appetite good, fever down, some lucid moments." She rattled it off. "But we have to be careful."

"Yeah," scoffed Floyd. "Yeah, doctor, yeah."

A low rumble of thunder shook the air. Mabel frowned at the sky. "That's not so good," she said fearfully. "Storms always upset sick people. I ought to go back. What are you going to do?"

"Stay out," Floyd said. "I ain't afraid. I'm sick and tired of my grand-mother's kitchen." He turned and started back toward Baldwin. "See you."

"See you," Mabel repeated. She turned in at the gate and walked briskly up the drive. Halfway to the house she took a cross path that led to the bungalows in the rear.

Joey was basking in public acclaim. She carried more sail in the form of ribbon than any other little girl, and her pennies were brighter than those of the boy called Bubber, the one who had sworn to get Baby Moses. Baby Moses and the sextet of Guardian Angels stood in a neat row on the platform, at Mr. Walters's feet.

Pansy watched Joey with understanding. All through the lesson Joey's eyes had feasted on her choice. In her youth, Pansy herself had battled for just such a picture, only hers had been Daniel in the Lions' Den. It had haunted her dreams, and she had loved it with all her heart. But, she admitted, they did have nicer ones now. Not so fierce and frightening.

Mr. Walters stood on his platform, looking, Pansy thought, more dead than alive: the weather was telling on him, and all that terrible business at his own Covered Dish. He ought to be in bed with a good, nourishing soup. Men who lived alone didn't know how to take care of themselves. When the time for the birthday recognition drew near, she made her way to his side.

"You don't look well," she whispered. "Why don't you leave right after the pictures? I can take charge. I've done it before."

He gave her a grateful look. "Thank you," he said. "I believe I will."

"Slip out the back way," she counseled, "and go straight home. You'll be all the better for a nice lie-down."

She returned to her class, pleased with her foresight. The dim little organist struck a wavering chord on the small organ and Mr. Walters stepped to the front of the platform.

"Josephine Beacham and Bubber Mitchell," he said, "please come forward."

They did, from opposite sides of the room, eying each other warily. Mr. Walters continued. "Many happy returns of the day," he said. He shook their hands and nodded to the goldfish bowl.

One by one the pennies dropped, and fifty voices rose and fell with each one. Nine for Joey and ten for Bubber. Suddenly Bubber saw what his additional penny was going to do for Joey, and he blanched. It was going to give her an extra second, and he wondered if she knew what that meant. She did. By the time his tenth year had rattled to the bottom of the bowl, it was all over. He picked up a Guardian Angel and tried to smile.

Mr. Walters was watching them both, so they turned and walked quietly to their seats. It was a lonesome walk for the Guardian Angel but Baby Moses had his face patted all the way.

Pansy congratulated Joey with a smile. Smart as a whip, she told herself. Fell on that picture like a hawk on a chicken. And you couldn't ask for a better disposition. Good as gold, and never known a mother's love.

Outside, a car crept up the cemetery road and stopped silently. It was the only car there. On bright Sundays the cemetery was crowded with motorists and people on foot, bringing garden flowers to the graves. Today there was no one.

Pansy whispered to the reliable little girl in her class, and the reliable little girl promptly moved into Pansy's chair. Mr. Walters gave the room an admonishing look and quietly departed. Pansy took his place, flushing with importance.

"And now," Pansy said, "we'll sing Joey Beacham's hymn before we have the closing prayer. We sang Bubber's in the beginning, you remember, and we did it very nicely, too. Now we'll have Joey's and we'll do it just as well, won't we? Joey's leaving us soon and we want to give her a real good send-off."

"One, two, three," the organist counted audibly.

The voices rose and Joey's led all the rest. An eavesdropper, hearing the tune and not the words, might think they were singing "Tramp, Tramp, Tramp the Boys Are Marching," but it wasn't that. It was the swell song with the sentiment Mark had so heartily approved. It was also a favorite of Pansy's. She joined in with a will.

> "Je-sus loves the littul chil-drun,
> Loves the childrun of the world;
> Red and yellow, black and white,
> They are preshus in his sight,
> Jesus loves the littul childrun of the world."

They went through two verses.

Unknown to the occupants of that hot and over-crowded room, there was an eavesdropper. A figure stood at the same window where Mark had watched the Sunday before, careful not to stand too close, careful not to be seen. It stood there, smiling. If Pansy had been in her own chair, surrounded by her brood, she would have felt that smile. Something would have drawn her to the window. But Pansy was up at the other end of the room.

Joey's hymn drifted through the same open windows that had released the faint Amen before Miss Cassidy was found.

The smiling figure drew back. There was no hurry. They were going to pray next. Bow their heads and close their eyes and pray. That would be the time.

Pansy, thinking how wonderful it would be if Floyd got the call and studied for the ministry, suddenly found herself singing on alone. The hymn was over and even the children had stopped. She flushed unhappily, and plunged into the closing announcement.

"There are some library books overdue, and we can't have that. There isn't any excuse; you all know better. I want every single book back here next Sunday. Don't forget. And I'd like to remind you that it's going to rain. There's a very bad storm coming up, and you're all to hurry home as fast as you can. Anybody that wants to give somebody a lift will be appreciated." She paused. "And now the Lord's Prayer in unison."

Chairs scraped and knees hit the floor.

"Our Father," began Pansy.

Joey felt someone looking at her. It was like the day Mr. East had come. She turned her head to the window and saw the smiling, beckoning figure. For an instant amazement crossed her face, and then she smiled too. Mr. East had probably needed Mr. Wilcox for his work. That was why Mr. Wilcox hadn't come.

She got up quietly, sent a disdainful look at the bowed head of the reliable little girl, and tiptoed out.

Pansy saw her go. She had one eye open because she liked to look at the small, kneeling figures. Mr. East is outside, she thought vaguely.

"And deliver us from evil," she continued slowly. She loved to say the words and drew them out as long as possible. The children tagged dutifully behind.

The organist struck another chord and they sang the doxology. Once again a straggling Amen floated out across the grass and hung in the trees. But before it had died away a furious clap of thunder rent the air and destroyed all that was left.

Up on the mountain Mark was slouched over the table in the Beacham cottage. When the thunder rolled he raised his head. His watch said four o'clock. He went over to the door and looked out. The sky was livid. He was uneasy, thinking of Perley and Joey on the road.

Perley drove up to the church and looked around. He was a little late; his wardrobe was responsible for that, but he knew Pansy and Joey would be waiting. As he went up the steps he saw a car leaving the far end of the cemetery. It moved out of sight as he watched.

The vestibule was empty and the building silent. In the Sunday school room he found Pansy poring over her library list and frowning. She greeted him with, "Would you drive me out to Mama's or is it too dangerous?"

"Can't take the time," Perley said. "And nobody drives today unless they have to. Floyd's all right if that's what's worrying you. Where's Joey?"

Pansy put a black mark beside a child's name. "Mr. East came for her. Just before we finished. He's always doing that."

"Must have come down to see somebody." Perley was satisfied. "Can you get home all right by yourself, or do you want me to take you?"

"I'll manage. You run along. And do take care, Perley. And call me up when you—when you can. I declare I'm so nervous I could scream."

He patted her plump shoulder. "Nothing to worry about." He started off. "Don't count on any phone calls though. I'll do what I can, but I've got a feeling that when she breaks the lines are going to come down."

He drove up the mountain slowly. The wind tore at the top of his car with ungovernable fury and the trees along the road lashed out as he passed. He listened with misgiving to the twanging wires overhead. If the wires came down they'd all be cut off. It was a bad thing to be cut off.

He drove through the gates, parked the car, and went directly to Beacham's cottage. Mark was poring over a sheet of paper in the living room.

"No trouble?" Mark asked without turning.

"Nope," Perley said. He looked for signs of Joey. Then he remembered. Over in the hotel, playing checkers with Miss Pond. "Road's in poor shape right now," he went on. "And getting worse all the time. Some trees down and it won't surprise me if the wires go too. When the rain comes it's going to be terrible. I feel sorry for the farmers."

"Save your pity for yourself. I want you to listen to what I've lined up."

Perley drew a chair to the table. "Beulah Pond don't like storms any too much," he said. "I've heard rumors that she locks herself in a closet. I was wondering if maybe Joey wouldn't be better off if—"

"She'll be all right where she is. Now—"

Bittner sat in his kitchen window, surveying the road through his binoculars. It was a purely gratuitous gesture. When the storm began he had called the busses home like cattle; they'd been washed the night before at fifty cents a head. Let people use their own cars if they wanted to get killed and filthy.

There was no traffic. The four o'clock branch train had trundled by fifteen minutes before, nearly empty. Two passengers. Bear River boys going up the line to see Baldwin girls. He polished his glasses and frowned.

Ella May, shuffling from icebox to stove to table, was preparing his early supper. He had another at ten.

"You want the cold chicken now and the cold ham later, or the cold ham now and the cold chicken later?"

"Ham. Now."

"Bessy Petty has been over to the Caldwells' for three days now," she droned. "You know what that means. They got brandy. Beulah Pond's going to have her hands full when she gets back. Serve her right, too. What's she doing up the mountain?"

Bittner didn't answer. He had raised his binoculars again and was leaning forward.

"Well?" asked Ella May. "What are you breathing about?"

"Beacham's back," Bittner said. "His car just went by. He's driving like a fool."

"That's what he is." Ella May slapped half a ham on the table. "Come on and eat. You've no call to be watching Beacham. He's got a right to the road, and it's his murder."

Bittner sucked in his breath. "I thought he wasn't coming back until tonight. He must have changed his mind or else he's up to monkey business." He turned the glasses toward Baldwin. "Out of sight now."

He started to wheel himself over to the table. Then, "No!" he said explosively.

"No what?"

"If he came in on the morning train that means he got by me, and nobody does that. And the only other train from New York isn't due for five hours. How did he get here? His car's been at the hotel all the time. How did he get down here in the first place, and why's he going up north again?"

Ella May started to reply.

"Shut up," he said. "I'm thinking."

He turned back to the window and peered at the road. That car. Beacham's car. It went by like a bat out of hell, swinging from side to side. Beacham didn't drive like that. He closed his little eyes and tried to remember something else about the car that didn't look like Beacham. Finally he got it. It was the driver. Beacham always sat up straight, like he owned the world; this one was crouched over the wheel and—he fought down rising panic—this one was the wrong shape. He didn't have any shape at all. He sat like a bundle, a dark, shapeless bundle, huddled over the wheel. . . . Bundle! There'd been a bundle on the seat beside him. A big one. Dark.

He spun his chair around and shot over to the telephone. He was shouting Mark's number before he had the receiver off. "Hurry," he squealed, "hurry!"

Overhead, the elements conspired. A thunderous peal shook the house and lightning ripped the sky. A tree crashed outside the window and took the telephone wires with it. The clouds opened and the rain came down.

Bittner raised the screen and leaned out. He was gripping an old bus horn, the one he used for summoning Ella May. He blew a piercing blast in the direction of the station.

"Amos!" he screamed.

Mark and Perley bent their heads over the paper.

"So much for Delaney," Mark said. "Both Delaney and his daughter hated Cassie. Now file them away in your mind and go on to Murdoch. Louise Murdoch, age thirty-six. Who is she? Is she here?"

Perley swallowed hard. "I don't know what to think," he managed to say.

"You're thinking about the same person I am, but you're not sure. You can't see why she waited all this time. I think we can get around that. Even though Cassie had known her for several years, had seen her almost every day, you must remember that the name wasn't the same and the environment was different. Small details, but worth considering. And in the earlier days when she was in Cassie's charge and known as Louise Murdoch, she had brown hair. Dye that, and see what happens to your mental picture. Her weight, when she was in the hospital, was one hundred and sixty pounds. Take away forty and you have an entirely new person. And what's more, the record says she was an expert dissembler. On her goods days they'd take her up to the roof for exercise, and she'd charm the ordinary convalescents like birds out of a bush. I mean the men, of course. She never talked to the women. . . . Well?"

"It could be."

"It isn't far-fetched. She was never ordinary and never stupid, unless she wanted to be. I think she could change her personality if she needed to. Change that as well as her name."

"She could look older and she could look younger," Perley said thoughtfully. "She could look any way she liked."

"And," Mark went on, "she was only in the hospital six months before her brother took her away. She was only one, in a crowded ward. And a lot of things happened to Cassie between that time and the time she re-met Murdoch, if she did. The old life was far, far behind. She might have said to herself, as we all do sometime, 'That woman reminds me of someone.' No more than that. I mean, no more than that until later, when Murdoch did something that gave the show away." He added, "If it is Murdoch."

Perley was silent. He was sunk in his chair.

Mark went on. "Kelso. You can have a dozen guesses on Kelso, but I'm sure one of them is out."

"Beacham?" Perley said the name with difficulty. "I can't help it, he keeps coming to my mind."

"I know he does. But Cassie had known him for nine years. There's too little time between Kelso's discharge and Cassie's reappearance on the scene as Joey's nurse. . . . Unless she thought he had straightened out. Unless she was sorry for him. She collected shorn lambs." He put his head in his hands. "No, that's wrong. That's out. That's got to be out. I can't fit Roberta in. I don't even know if Kelso was married."

"Stop driving yourself crazy!" Perley's own voice was cracking. "You'll find out tonight. All this talking isn't doing any good. Wait for tonight."

"Tonight may be a flop. They may eat my food, listen to my music, and walk out under their own steam, unblemished. Then I'll have to begin all over again. Or maybe I'll do as Beacham suggests. Turn it over to you and let you hang it on a playful country lad." He picked up the paper again. "Another pleasant feature is that every one of our suspects could be two other people. Peck, for instance, could be Kelso or Murdoch's brother."

"And Delaney could be—"

"Stick to Delaney for the moment. Do you remember what you said just before you and Joey left?"

"I said I'd like a girl. You looked at me kind of funny."

"You also said that most men wanted boys and sometimes they acted mean about it."

"That's the truth, too. They do."

"Apply that to Delaney. Delaney hated his daughter. Could that be why?"

"Sure it could. I've seen it go that way."

"All right. Delaney hated his daughter. Remember that. And Kelso hated his mother. Remember that too. And Louise Murdoch hated all women. Their hatred was a part of their madness. So what have we? We have three people, or rather, we have six—Delaney and daughter, Kelso and mother, Murdoch and brother—six people, three of them hopelessly mad and three of them living in fear of madness. Three of them with definite, separate hates, and all six sharing one hate together. The one hate was Mary Cassidy."

Perley glowered. "You know what we've got to do? We've got to get authority to throw everybody in jail. Everybody we've got the slightest suspicion about. And keep them there until we have time to check their lives from the day they were born. We haven't had enough time. The thing spreads out too far. Down south, out west, all over. That's what we've got to do."

"Wait a minute. There's more coming." Mark spoke slowly. "That common fear of poor Mary Cassidy, that unreasoning hate, was strong enough to bring about her murder. But suppose there was an even stronger motive, a by-product, we'll call it, that outweighed the original. If I'm right, Perley, it's a woman we're looking for."

"Delaney's daughter?"

"I don't know. Maybe Kelso's. Maybe Murdoch herself. We're looking for a girl who should have been a boy. A girl whose mother, or someone, gave her a boy's name, or a version of one. The way Cassie did with Joey. Trying to make amends, trying to give the kid a break. In Joey's case it was successful, but in our case I think it failed. Wouldn't that child, with a bad inheritance to start with, grow up with an ugly scar? Sure she would. And the frenzied love she had for her indifferent father would be so close to hate that you couldn't tell the difference. So—she'd grow into a frightened, bitter, resentful woman, with the knowledge of insanity hanging over her head. Maybe with the knowledge of insanity already perceived. What would that woman do, or think, if she were suddenly faced with Mary Cassidy? If, after years of safe anonymity, she saw recognition slowly come to Mary Cassidy's eyes? We know what she did. She killed her. And what would that woman do when, day after day, she saw Cassie's best job, Joey? Joey, the little girl who made the grade, who wore her boy's clothes proudly and happily. Do you see now why I worry when Joey—"

Over in the corner the telephone shrilled. Mark got up and started across the room. The thunder rolled and the lightning struck.

"That hit!" Perley gasped. "Keep away from the phone." The wind tore at the curtains and the rain swept in. He struggled with the windows. "Keep away from the phone!" he shouted above the roar. "It's dangerous!"

Mark took down the receiver. "Hello," he said. There was no answer. "Hello!" he said again, sharply.

Perley watched anxiously from across the room.

"Dead?" he asked.

"Dead."

Beulah had reached the end of her tether. For the last half hour she had wanted to go up to her room and hide, preferably under the bed, but Perley hadn't brought Joey. She didn't dare leave the lobby again until he did. She had left once, but the switchboard operator had promised to keep an eye on Joey if she came. Perley was late. He was more than late. She told herself he must have stayed in town.

When the storm finally struck she moaned loudly, but there was no one to bring her a reviving drink. Even the clerk had vanished. The operator was the only living soul in sight and she was half dead with fright. When the lightning hit, she'd clapped both hands to her head and screamed.

Beulah went over to her. "Are you all right?"

"I don't know. My ears. I can't hear a thing."

"You can hear me," Beulah said. Her native curiosity compelled her to read the penciled lines on the record sheet. "What's that you've got written down? It says East-Bittner."

"I have to keep a special record for Mr. East. He told me to. There was a call for Mr. East when the lightning struck."

"Were you cut off?"

"I certainly was! Everybody's cut off. Bear River. Crestwood, Baldwin, and heaven knows how many other towns. There'll be no service for hours, you mark my words, and will they call it an act of God? No. They'll call it carelessness, my carelessness." She gave a pleased cackle. "You should have heard Mr. Bittner. So excitable. Life and death, he hollered."

Beulah gave her one terrified look before she ran for the door. She reached the cottage in forty seconds, drenched to the skin, and hurled herself into the living room.

Mark had returned to the table. He was saying, "Frances, Roberta. Check on Haskell."

She screamed, and the two men turned white faces.

"Joey! Where's Joey!"

Mark's voice had no timbre. "Haven't you got her?"

"No!"

Perley rose on unsteady feet. "You came for her," he begged Mark. "Pansy said so! You came and took her before I got there! I thought you brought her home yourself!"

"I haven't left this room."

Beulah heard them with horror. "Bittner," she said thickly, "Bittner was trying to get you when the wires went down. The operator just told me."

They left her standing there. She watched dully as they raced across the lawn, beaten by the rain, pursued by the wind. Then she followed, slowly; she was suddenly too old to run.

Before he reached the garage, Mark knew that Beacham's car would be gone. Beacham was the only man who had sufficient gas.

"Search all the rooms?" gasped Perley.

"Too late. How much gas have you?"

"Enough to get to Bear River, no more."

"We'll have to take a chance." Mark was plunging from car to car, reading gauges. "None here."

Beulah stood in the doorway. "Somebody's coming up the road," she said. "I don't know who it is. He has lights on. He's blinking them. I don't know who it is."

They ignored her. They ran to Perley's car, and in another minute they were through the gates.

She stood where they left her, alone in the driving rain, watching the car as it rocketed down the road. Then she went back to the hotel.

Could it be my fault? she asked herself dully. Have I got to live the rest of my life with that child's eyes looking out of every corner? Why didn't they warn me? Why didn't they give me a name?

The lobby was still deserted when she entered. Even the operator had gone. She sank wearily into a chair. I haven't seen anybody all day, she recalled. Except Roberta and Nick at lunch. Except Cora and Kirby. I haven't even seen them for hours. I haven't seen the Pecks, or Mr. Sutton, or Miss Rayner at all. Or George. Then she remembered that she had left the lobby and gone upstairs for no more than ten minutes. To get her knitting. That dreadful piece of knitting that she carried around because everybody else did. New tears rolled down her seamed face. Why didn't they tell me? she repeated. And then she had another thought. Perhaps they hadn't told her because they didn't know themselves. If they'd known, they'd have been on guard. Even now, driving through the storm on the trail of Beacham's car, they probably didn't know.

She got to her feet and walked steadily up the stairs. On the second floor she began to open doors, systematically, up and down the hall. When she surprised an occupant, she mumbled an apology and moved on to the next. She went into every room, from the first floor to the last, using a hairpin on the doors that were locked. Then she went to the cottages. When she finished, she sat in the Beachams' living room and closed her eyes. She knew the driver of Beacham's car and there was no way to reach Mark. She began to cry again.

Floyd sat under an overhanging rock by the side of the Baldwin road. It was the entrance to a cave he had known all his life. He was dry and safe and happy. The road was awash, trees were down, telephone wires hung like broken, black webs. He fingered the scout knife in his pocket. He wanted to cut a piece of wire for a souvenir; it would look good mounted on cardboard and labeled "The Big Blow of 44." But he was afraid. He didn't understand about wires. They might be alive. He didn't, he told himself, want to die out there in the rain with his face in the mud. He pictured himself lying on his stomach, arms outstretched, his nostrils full of mud and gravel. He held his breath to see what it would be like. It would be terrible.

He heard a new sound above the wind and the rain, and cautiously stuck out his head. A familiar car was coming his way. He watched it, unbelieving.

"Well I'll be!" he said in astonishment. Something stopped him before he could go on. He never could tell his father what it was. He said it was like a hand on his mouth.

The car crept forward, skidded, and went into the ditch. Still he sat there, not moving. He heard himself gasp when the driver crawled out, dragging something wrapped in a blanket. He heard a faint wail and thought his heart would burst. Then he told himself, in one sharp, silent sentence, that he was Perley Wilcox's boy. He crept out of his safe cave on his stomach and traveled forward until he reached a row of sheltering scrub. Then he ran, bent over to make himself smaller than he was. The tall iron gate of Bide-A-Wee was straight ahead.

The car Beulah had seen climbing the hotel road was Bittner's best truck, driven by Amos. When Mark and Perley bore down on him, Amos pulled over and spoke briefly.

"Transfer to this. Leave yours where it is." He pointed to the oil drums in the rear. "Gas. Enough for Canada. Bittner says you're welcome."

Mark and Perley transferred. The truck swung in an arc of flying mud and shot down the mountain. "Bittner tried to get you," Amos said, "but you seem to know what happened. I don't know nothing, so you better tell me."

Mark was silent and Perley tried to explain. His voice was tired and thin, and he repeated himself like a man in a dream.

But Amos understood. "Then Joey Beacham is in that car with somebody that don't like her?" He stepped on the accelerator. It was only a gesture. The truck was already doing eighty.

They swept through Bear River and took the road to Crestwood. Amos spoke again. "Binoculars in that leather case there," he said.

Mark took them wordlessly.

"Sutton?" Perley asked in a low voice.

"No," Mark said. "Roberta and Nick thought so too. That's why they've been acting queer. He hated nurses, because of Nick. No." He searched the road ahead.

"You don't have to worry until we get beyond Crestwood," Amos said. "Bittner saw them there." He hesitated; then, "Bittner says the driver is crazy."

"He's right," Mark said. "But there's something else wrong. There's no train out of Baldwin for hours. Where are they going?"

"Maybe nowhere," Amos said. "There's untouched forests up that way."

"Dark," Perley said under his breath, "dark."

They passed Crestwood, a confused blur of rain, tossing trees and red brick. Bittner's house was lighted from top to bottom. Mark leaned over and pressed down on the horn. A salute to Bittner. He didn't mind giving it.

Another five miles, with the headlights cutting a path and the binoculars raking the road on both sides. The trees were black and repellent. "Slow down a little," Mark begged Amos. "They may have turned off." He knew there was no place to turn. He was looking for a gap in the trees. Amos reduced the speed by ten miles. The rain beat down and the lightning flashed, lending the sodden countryside a false and momentary radiance brighter than noon.

Perley huddled between Mark and Amos. He was afraid to speak another name. So it wasn't Sutton. He'd been sure it was Sutton, and he hadn't felt sorry. But now he was afraid. He remembered the car on the cemetery road. Beacham's. How did it get there? Who slipped out of the hotel under Beulah's watchful eye and took Beacham's car from the unattended garage? How long would it take him to get down to Bear River? Fifteen minutes. It took longer going up. Going up!

He ran over the names of the townspeople on Mark's list. Twenty or twenty-five minutes to drive up in another car, leave it down by the pool, and finish the trip on foot. Get into the garage by the back door, hidden by the trees, take Beacham's car, drive out fast, and that's all there was to it. Stand outside that window and coax young Joey. Somebody she knew and trusted. No, he didn't want to hear the name. He looked at the road ahead and spoke hoarsely.

"Can they get by the border?" he asked. "If they have enough gas, can they get by?"

No one had time to answer. Mark gave a sudden shout. "Stop!"

The brakes screamed. Mark was on the road, running back while the truck still moved forward. The binoculars and headlights had picked out something lying beside the ditch. He found it, and returned. They shot forward again. "What is it?" Perley asked.

Mark showed him a limp square of cardboard. The cattails were no longer green, the water no longer blue, and the lady with the long white veil was entirely gone. Baby Moses, however, could still be recognized in his faded yellow basket.

Perley turned away.

"We're on the right track," Mark said.

Floyd took a familiar route through the grounds. He knew exactly where he was going and what he had to do. Years before, when Bide-A-Wee was the residence of a mill owner, he had played in the gardens. He knew the place from cellar to attic and he knew the old covered walk, curtained with vines and shrubbery, that led from the back of the house to the bungalows. In the old days, the bungalows were guest houses. He plunged ahead, tripping over roots, sinking in the soft wet earth. Once he stopped long enough to look over his shoulder and what he saw made him double his pace. Two people were coming through the gate and starting up the drive

Around the corner of the house he slowed down. He had to. His breath was gone and there was a burning coal in his chest. He clung to the trunk of a tree to keep from falling and ground his teeth in childish despair. He had heard his father and mother talking when they thought he was asleep; he had also heard Mark's censored observations, made at the supper table, and he had accurately filled in the gaps. Miss Cassidy's murderer was coming up the drive with Joey Beacham. Miss Cassidy's murderer was crazy. And number four bungalow was crazy too. Nobody ever really said that, but he knew. Number four was sick and crazy too.

He drew a long, sobbing breath and stumbled down the covered walk, slipping on the wet flags, while the rain drummed on the tin roof overhead and the whipping vines and bushes slapped at his arms and legs. At the end of that dark green tunnel he saw a light.

At the same time, Mabel, snug and dry in the tool shed, was looking back on her recent exploit with pleasure. She had crouched beneath the window of number four until her knees were stiff. What Floyd had said about number four had made her think, and when she thought, she acted. She had wasted most of her time off, but she didn't think of it as a bad waste. More like killing time at the movies, she told herself, only better, because it was real.

Number four had been a scream. Walking up and down like an animal on a rope. Moving a vase of flowers from one table to another and then throwing it on the floor. More like a child than a grown up person. Taking a picture off the wall and smashing it to bits. She hadn't been able to see what kind of a picture it was; looked like a woman from a distance. Standing there in the dry shed, she had to laugh when she thought how number four's room had looked. Glass and water and flowers all over the floor. Spoiling the nice rug. A fine way to act on Sunday, but Matron would fix all that.

She began to feel a little uneasy. Maybe she should have told Matron right away. Told her about the coughing spell too. She shivered a little when she remembered that. Bright red on clean white.

But she hadn't had time to tell anybody anything. The storm had come then, and it was all she could do to get to the shelter of the shed. It was easing up a bit now, not so much thunder and lightning, only the rain coming down like all get out. The hands of her watch told her it was nearly five, although it did look more like nine. She opened the shed door cautiously and gave a little cry of dismay when she saw the dangling telephone lines. George wouldn't be able to give her a ring.

Number four's light was still burning when she ducked into the covered walk.

Floyd saw her coming and fought back an urge to shout her name. He was almost incoherent when he reached her.

"They're coming!" he gasped. "You got to do something!"

She gave him a disgusted look. "Why don't you go back to your grandma's where you belong? If I didn't know you, I'd say you found a bottle."

"Mabel!" He clung to her arm. "Mabel, they're coming up the drive! You got to do something! You got to get help!"

"Help who? This is what I get for fooling around with kids. What are you talking about?"

Between gasps he told her what he had seen. "Number four's in it somewhere! I know! They're going to kill Joey, the two of them! Like Miss Cassidy! Joey's got her hands tied up and there's something over her mouth! Mabel, you got to do something!"

Mabel's eyes were wide with horror. She'd followed the Cassidy case with passionate interest, because of George. And hadn't she been interviewed by Mr. East himself? But why did Floyd keep saying number four? Number four hadn't done anything. Number four had been locked in his room for two years, locked in and doped.

"Crazy," Floyd was saying. "They're both crazy!"

Her shrewd little mind grasped the unrelated pieces and put them together. George had told her a little and she had picked up a few things herself. She was good at picking up things, the wrong things her mother always said. She remembered how number four's orderly had talked after one of number four's spells. He'd quoted number four and she'd laughed, because what he said was terrible. And she remembered that number four sometimes had a visitor, a visitor she'd never seen. She clapped her hand over her open mouth.

Mabel's full but fruitless days had never held more than food and sleep and dubious pleasure, but she knew the answer to what was coming, slowly and irrevocably through the rain.

"God help me," she said under her breath, "what can I do?"

Floyd hung on her arm, his confident thirteen years dissolved in terror. She knew she had to spare him if she could. A kid, that's all he was, a little kid.

"Mabel, Mabel, do something!"

She worked swiftly. "I will, and so will you. You run as fast as you can down the road and holler all the way. Somebody might hear you and come. The telephone's gone."

"I can't leave you alone, Mabel! It ain't safe to leave you alone!" He threw a frantic look over his shoulder. Two figures had entered the covered walk from the far end. In the dark they were no more than shadows. One of them was very small.

"Run," whispered Mabel. "The other way. Don't holler till you get to the gate. I'm going after Matron and the orderlies."

She gave him a push and he stumbled forward, and ran toward the yellow light at the other end. He turned when he reached the bungalows, crossed the gardens, and fled down the drive. He had almost reached the gate when he heard the sound of a roaring motor. He forgot his instructions and screamed. He flung himself against the rain, screaming into the noisy darkness ahead.

Perley heard him first. They had found the abandoned car, and Mark and Perley were running toward the iron gate while Amos followed.

"Floyd!" shouted Perley.

The boy was past speech; they steadied him with their arms while he pointed wordlessly.

When they came in sight of the bungalows they met a stream of white-clad men racing down the covered walk with flashlights. Mabel leaned against the locked door of number four, pounding it with her fists.

"You!" she screamed. "You!"

The uncurtained window finished the half-told story that was locked away in Miss McKenna's files. The madman Delaney, racked with tuberculosis, stood in the center of the room, his hands outstretched. His smiling daughter stood beside him. Those outstretched hands were on Joey Beacham's neck when Mark sent his fist through the glass. Perley's shot cracked out and the door fell. The white clad men closed in. For the last time in her life Delaney's daughter had stood between her father and the world. She was lying at his feet.

There was a knife in almost every pocket, but without discussion and by common consent, it was Floyd who cut Joey free.

"Stretcher," one man ordered. Then he turned to Mark. "Who was she?"

Mark said, "She called herself Rayner."

There was no party that night. The profits to the chef were beyond his wildest dreams. He ate the truffles himself and had nightmares.

After a nap in Matron's room, Joey Beacham went to Baldwin for the second time that night. A young doctor at Bide-A-Wee told her it was the smart thing to do. He had a Viennese accent, but she understood. She laughed when he said: "You go up in a plane and you crash, boom. You go up again, right away, and show people you're tough."

When Beacham's train pulled in at nine o'clock she was on the platform. He took her in his arms.

"Miss me?" he asked.

"Boy!" said Joey. Very tough.

The storm had gone, and over in the west a pale moon struggled through the clouds. Mark looked at Perley. "One crack out of you about a silver lining, and I'll throw you under the wheels."

They didn't return to the Mountain House at once. When Mark talked to Beacham and showed him the truck and the binoculars, they went to Bittner's instead. Bittner was starting in on the ten o'clock cold chicken. He stayed with it.

"Is anybody going to tell me anything?" he asked.

He was told all.

They never would know, Mark said, how Cassie had spotted Miss Rayner. But she had. On one of her lonely drives she may have met her coming away from Bide-A-Wee, crying perhaps, or even elated. Elated because she had safely secreted her greatest treasure. If Cassie had seen that look in Miss Rayner's eyes, it would have been enough to make her wonder. That was the way her mind worked.

She would have watched Miss Rayner after that, and little by little the truth must have revealed itself. The drives they took together had been engineered by Cassie, Mark was sure. She was probing then, not idly, not from curiosity, not for her own sake. "At first I supposed she was thinking of her own safety," he said, "but now I know better. It was Joey she was worried about. She may have seen Miss Rayner watching Joey, and if Miss Rayner was Delaney's daughter. . . . She knew that daughter's history too well. She knew the danger line and how and where the woman would strike if the line broke."

Beacham spoke hopelessly. "Why didn't she tell me?"

"She'd been trained to make her own decisions. She thought she could handle it alone. And I think she wasn't entirely sure until she checked the hospital records. She knew then. And when she came back, I think she went out to Bide-A-Wee and double-checked. I think she saw more than Wilcox and I saw when we looked through the window of number four.

"And I don't think Miss Rayner knew who Cassie was until the day before Cassie went to New York. Cassie wouldn't have gone if she had thought Miss Rayner suspected. It wouldn't have been safe. Then, the day before she left she saw a picture of herself in Spangler's window. She hadn't known it was there. I think it gave her a moment's panic. Spangler says it was a young-looking picture. I can see Cassie standing before that dingy window, staring at the picture screen, seeing herself as she had looked years ago. I'm sure she was frightened then. If Miss Rayner saw that youthful, smiling face she'd know the truth at once. But she couldn't cancel the New York trip. It was too important. So she did the next best thing. She paid Spangler to destroy the picture, and he did, but not soon enough. He had a lot of customers that after-noon and he talked his head off to all of them. He told them about Cassie's visit and showed them the picture. Miss Rayner saw it and the fat was in the fire. I can see Miss Rayner too, holding that little snap-shot in her hand, suddenly recognizing it, fighting back her own panic. Then she knew the motive behind Cassie's attentions, the talks, the drives, the apparently artless questions. And she saw her one happiness crumble into dust. She knew what would happen. They'd find her father and return him to the madhouse."

She must have thought quickly and with deadly accuracy the night of the church supper, Mark went on. And sanely. She wasn't mad then. Not yet. She made a cool and calculating plan to save the one thing she loved. There was no doubt now that she had pushed Nick's arm and retrieved the sixth arrow in the confusion that followed. Or that she had invited Cassie to walk down by the dark well, calmly confessing her identity, perhaps baiting Cassie with a promise to turn her father over to the proper authorities. Then she had killed her and wounded herself, and gone back to the Sunday school to wait.

Her persistent use of full names instead of diminutives, Mark had put down to an old lady's formality. But, he said, he began to wonder after he read the Delaney case history. Delaney's daughter's name was Winifred. Then he decided it was a trivial point, and dropped it. He knew now why Winifred Delaney avoided nicknames. She couldn't trust herself to say Joey.

Another suspicion had come when Joey found the scraps in the incinerator. One of them still smelled faintly of violet toilet water and showed traces of sugar. He remembered how Miss Rayner had wiped her hands on a scrap of cloth the day he untied her horse. Still, he had argued, she might have found it. That fitted in with her passion for thrift. But now he knew it was the challenge of a megalomaniac. She had kept one piece of cloth after she had destroyed the clothes that were a daily, bitter reminder of Cassie's success and one little girl's happiness. That was when the madness began. That was when she planned complete destruction, beginning with Cassie's dog.

Old man Sutton, Mark said, had partly guessed the answer. He may have seen Miss Rayner in the halls the night of Cassie's murder. That was the night he went wandering. He was so close to the end of his own life that he could feel the presence of death in any disguise. He must have seen its reflection in Miss Rayner's eyes. And his love and pity for Nick had made him sensitive to any danger that threatened a child.

"But still I wasn't sure," Mark went on. "Not even when I found an old photograph in her trunk. A baby picture, herself of course, a little girl with her hair combed like a boy's. I was suspicious, but not sure. She took me in completely. Her manner was sound, her conversation normal and in character. She had me fooled. I thought it was going to be—" He stopped. He didn't want Beacham to know his pet villains had been himself, Franny Peck, and the Reverend Mr. Walters. "I thought it was going to be George," he said. He would fix that up with George when he fixed things up for Mabel. Solid silver, Mabel said.

It was nearly midnight when they drove back to the Mountain House, leaving Bittner with a chicken carcass. Amos had gone ahead with the news, but the whole story had to be repeated. Once more gifts were borne across the grass to the Beacham cottage, and this time they stayed there.

"I searched her room after you left," Beulah said. "It was torn to pieces. I found a passport under that picture in the lid of her trunk. Her real name and her age. She was only forty-seven. Only a few years older than Mary Cassidy, and she looked like her grandmother. I didn't know what you knew, but that told me enough."

The next morning Mark and Beulah left the Mountain House and drove down to the bus terminal in Bear River. Follies number three and four were lined up. They boarded number three. They took a seat, looked at each other with a wild surmise, and changed to number four. That child had been there again.

Turn the page for a SNEAK PREVIEW of

A Mark East Mystery
Death of a Doll

HILDA LAWRENCE

CHAPTER ONE

ANGELINE Small stepped out of the elevator at five o'clock and nodded to Kitty Brice behind the switchboard.

"Cold!" she said with a bright grimace. "Have they lighted the fire in the lounge?"

"Yes, Miss Small."

"Good," Miss Small said. But she walked briskly across the square lobby and checked for herself. There was only one girl in the lounge, a night worker in a Western Union office who went off to her job when the other girls came home. Miss Small found this routine confusing. When she went to her own bed at midnight, after coffee and gossip with Monny, she wanted to know that all of her seventy girls were safe and sound in their seventy good, though narrow, cots, sleeping correctly and dreamlessly because they were properly nourished and had no ugly little troubles that they hadn't confessed.

Miss Small switched on more lights, approved the fire and the bowls of fresh chrysanthemums, and spoke to the girl who was huddled in a deep chair with her eyes closed.

"Good evening, Lillian. Or should it be good morning?"

The girl looked up with a long, insolent stare and closed her eyes again.

Time for a little heart-to-heart talk with this one, Miss Small decided. Mustn't have sulks and surliness, such a bad example for the others. Perhaps a tiny note in her mailbox, an invitation to a nice cup of tea in my room. These poor, love-starved babies, I must do all I can.

"Isn't that a new coat, dear?" she asked.

The girl got up and brushed by the outstretched hand. "Excuse me," she said. "I forgot something."

Miss Small watched her cross the lobby with an arrogant stride and enter the elevator. I'll win her over, she promised herself, but I won't say anything to Monny. Poor Monny. She worries so when she knows I've been hurt. . . . She looked at the wrist watch Monny had given her the Christmas before and admired the winking diamonds. Five after five. Monny would be winding up her conference with Mrs. Fister and the meals would be better for about three days. Then they'd have coffee jelly again. I do wish she'd let me talk to Mrs. Fister, she fretted. I know how to handle people.

She returned to the lobby and entered the railed enclosure that was the office. A broad, flat desk faced the street entrance and behind it was the switchboard. A panel of push bells covered the wall behind the board. The bells rang in the rooms at seven in the morning and six in the evening. That was when the dining room opened. They also rang to announce visitors, phone calls, and emergencies. In the five years of its existence Hope House, a Home for Girls, had met and vanquished one emergency—a fire in a wastebasket. At right angles to the desk stood an orderly hive of glass-covered mailboxes, too often empty.

Miss Small glanced at her own box and spoke reprovingly.

"Kitty!"

Kitty gathered herself together and rose in sections. She was a tall, thin girl with poor skin and lips that were faintly blue.

"There's something in my box, Kitty, and you didn't give it to me."

"Headache," Kitty murmured. "I'm sorry, Miss Small, but you went by so fast before, and it's only a note Miss Brady put in."

"Miss Brady? Hand it to me at once, please." Miss Small tried to keep the pleasure out of her voice. Darling olu Monny, she told herself, she's thought of something nice for us to do later on. Maybe the theater, or a really good movie, or a little supper at that new French place. She opened the envelope carelessly under Kitty's curious gaze.

ANGEL [Monny wrote], Fister was frightful, wept all over the place and I'm exhausted. But we've got to keep the old fool happy, so I'm taking her out to tea because—this is what I tell her—because she needs to get out more, and what would we do without her! After that I've got to see Marshall-Gill about the party, she phoned. Angel, you'll have to take over the desk for me until Plummer goes on at eight. There's a new girl coming in, Ruth Miller, I'm afraid I forgot to tell you. Forgive? She's to go in with April Hooper. Explain to her about April, will you? That's something else I forgot, but you'll do it so much better than I would! I'll come to your room at the usual. Yours, M.

Miss Small tucked the note in her blouse and sat at the desk, smiling at the daily report that was fastened to the blotter. Monica Brady's sprawling hand had okayed a suspicion of mice on the second floor, uncovered a flaw in the addition of a plumber's bill, and questioned room 304's explanation of why she had stayed out all night. Under 304's explanation, which was a new one, she found the new girl's registration card. Ruth Miller, age twenty-nine, saleswoman at Blackman's, no family or known relatives. Then came the confidential information in the staff code. Middle class, some refinement, shy, not a mixer, underweight, poor vision and teeth. Probably tonsils. Recommended by M. Smith and M. Smith.

Miss Small frowned. That meant three girls from Blackman's. It wasn't wise to have more than two from the same place. Two could be friends, three could be troublesome.

The front door swung open, admitting a raw, damp wind and a chattering pair who called "Good evening, Miss Small," as they hurried to the elevator. The evening had begun.

From the rear of the lobby a clatter of china and silver began in a low key and steadily rose, the silent switchboard came to life with a series of staccato buzzes, and the front door opened and shut at frequent intervals. In a short time the institutional smell of large-scale cooking and thick, damp clothing had routed the fragrance of burning logs and chrysanthemums. The Hope House girls had lived through another day and were coming home.

At five o'clock Mrs. Nicholas Sutton approached her favorite clerk in Blackman's toilet-goods department on the main floor. The clerk was Ruth Miller. Young Mrs. Sutton, snug and warm in her new birthday sables, slid a shopping list across the counter and made an honest apology.

"I ought to be shot for coming in so late," she said. "You've got all your adding up to do."

Ruth Miller took the list and smiled. In the year she had worked at Blackman's Mrs. Sutton was the only woman customer who had regarded the counter between them as a bridge, not a barrier. In consequence, she gave Mrs. Sutton the same devotion she had once given a star on top of a Christmas tree; they were both remote yet intimate; untouchable but hers.

She read the list rapidly, frowning because she needed glasses and also because she couldn't decide whether or not to tell Mrs. Sutton about her wonderful luck.

They use too much soap at your house," she scolded gently. "You had three dozen two weeks ago. I expect it's the servants, they're all alike, you've got to be firm, Mrs. Sutton."

"I know, I know." Mrs. Sutton slumped into momentary dejection and showed every year of her age, which was twenty. "But have you ever tried being firm with a sixty-year-old woman who wakes you up every morning with a cup of tea because she once kept house for a duke? Hell's bells. Well, charge and send, and I'll put them all on the dole." She smiled at the plain, pleasant girl and wondered for the third or fourth time why she didn't take her away from that counter and put her in the Sutton nursery. She'd be wonderful with baby. "How've you been, Miss Miller? And why aren't you wearing your glasses? That's crazy, you know."

"They're broken," Ruth Miller said. "But I'm getting new ones."

"I should certainly hope so! Crazy to put off things like that. But otherwise you look very chipper."

Ruth Miller's pale cheeks flushed. "I'm just fine," she said. She'd tell Mrs. Sutton why she was fine, too. Some people might think it was silly, but Mrs. Sutton would understand. Mrs. Sutton always surprised you that way. All the money in the world herself but she understood about not having any. "I've got a new place to live," she said breathlessly, and her calm, plain face was almost pretty. "No more subways and furnished rooms with not enough heat and eating any which way! And only six blocks from here, a lovely place, you can't imagine! It's a kind of club, a hotel for girls, with breakfast and dinner, and they even have a room in the basement where you can do your own laundry. It's lovely, and so cheap, and all the hot water you want. I think that's what got me. No hot water is awful."

"No hot water is the devil," Mrs. Sutton agreed. "Are you sure the place is respectable?"

"There's a church group behind it."

"Yah!" Mrs. Sutton jeered. "They're after your soul, you poor thing. Don't give them an inch. How'd you ever find it?"

"Two girls in our stockroom live there, I knew they made less than I do, but they always looked better somehow. You know—nice coats and gloves, and permanents, and all that. So I asked them how they managed and they told me. And then I went over there and talked to the Head, a Miss Monica Brady, and she said she could give me a room with another girl. Eight dollars a week, can you imagine, with the food arid all those privileges! I move in tonight and—" She stopped because

Mrs. Sutton was staring straight ahead and her eyes were as wide as a child's. She turned her own head to investigate, and her heart gave a sickening lurch. On the rear wall, above the elevators, a small red light blinked steadily and evenly. One-two-three, one-two; one-two-three, one-two. The light was little more than a crimson blur, but she could read its silent message too well.

"I know what that's for," Mrs. Sutton said softly. "Old man Blackman is a friend of my father's. But what's the dope? I mean what does the blinkety-blink say?"

Ruth Miller looked down at her hands and saw that they were trembling. She tried to fill in the sales slip, but it was useless. I'm a fool, she told herself; I've got to stop acting like this. She didn't look up when she answered. "One-two-three, one-two means the main aisle, hosiery. . . . It's a woman."

"The idiot," Mrs. Sutton observed cheerfully. "Pulling a thing like that when the store's almost empty. She deserves to be caught. Idiot, she must be crazy. . . . Hey, maybe it's not a professional, maybe it's a kleptomaniac. For Heaven's sake, maybe it's somebody I know! I'm going over!"

Ruth Miller's hands gripped the edge of the counter. "No," she said. "No. Don't do it, don't go. It's not fair, it's awful; don't go, Mrs. Sutton, please."

Mrs. Sutton gave her a quick, surprised look. "Okay," she said carelessly. "You're a nice girl, Miss Miller, and I'm a no-account lug. Well, so long. We're going down to Pinehurst tomorrow, be gone until after Thanksgiving. See you when I get back." She turned up the collar of her sable coat. "Be good," she smiled.

Ruth Miller watched the slim, straight figure as it walked without hesitation to the side-street exit. Mrs. Sutton was avoiding the main aisle where a high voice was raised in tearful expostulation.

It was then five-fifteen. In another fifteen minutes she would begin a new life. She filled Mrs. Sutton's order and sent it down the chute, and tallied her sales-book. When that was done, there were only five minutes left.

Down in the toilet-goods stockroom Moke and Poke, self-styled because they were both named Mary Smith, managed between them to spill a few drops of "Chinese Lily" perfume. They apologized profusely to each other for such carelessness and removed the evidence with fingers that flew swiftly and accurately to ear lobes and neck hollows. It was a crying shame, they said. Five dollars an ounce and ten drops gone. The buyer would have a fit if she knew, and they wouldn't blame her. A little old ten-drop fit. "Chinese Lily." Funny how "Chinese Lily" was the one to spill when "English Rose," twelve dollars an ounce, was standing right next to it. They exchanged long looks and rubbed their elbows in the remains.

"By the way," Moke said, "do you happen to remember by any chance where we happen to be going tonight?"

Poke furrowed her brow. "Are we going anywhere?"

This was repartee of a high and secret order. They leaned against the stock table and shook with silent laughter. They pushed each other about like puppies. They had spoken volumes and said nothing. They were going to dinner with two boys from haberdashery. In Chinatown.

Moke wiped her face with a scented palm. "No kidding, Poke, we did forget something. That Miss Miller's moving in tonight, and we didn't tell her yet that we can't walk home with her."

"Should we have told her?"

"Sure. She may be counting on us. First night and all. And the poor old thing don't know anybody there but us. . . . Whoa! Too late now."

Out in the corridor the closing bell clanged. Upstairs the closing bell was a carillon that dropped sweet notes from vaulted ceiling to marble floor and echoed chastely in crystal chandeliers. But down in the basement it was a gong that screamed against concrete and steel, renewed its strength, and screamed again. Moke and Poke were inured.

"Too late," Moke shrilled above the clamor. "She don't really expect us anyway. Put your money in your shoe, don't ever let a fellow know you got any. Come on." They left the stockroom and elbowed through the crowd that streamed toward the lockers, working busily all the while with pocket mirror and comb.

Ruth walked slowly down the last block. Other people were coming home to shabby brownstone tenements and rooming houses, stopping on the way to buy food at the corner delicatessen, collecting the week's laundry from the Chinaman whose basement window was beaded with steam. She watched them from the secure heights of one who was bound for a warm dinner, a bed with a cretonne cover, and a writing desk of her own. There was a shoe-repair shop in the middle of the block and next to it a dry cleaner's. Very handy, she told herself, especially the cleaner's. For when I get my blue.

The blue was a suit that every woman in New York was trying to wear that fall. It was a bright, electric blue that dulled the eyes and hair of all but the very young, and consequently drew the middle-aged and sallow like a magnet.

Ruth dwelt on the blue. Seventy-five dollars in stores like Blackman's, sixteen-fifty on Fourteenth Street. She had eleven dollars saved up and her week's salary was untouched. She asked herself what she was waiting for. Take out eight for board, she figured rapidly, no carfares, and lunch in the cafeteria is twenty cents. I can do it and maybe a hat to match. And who's to tell me not to? Nobody. This is a new life and I want to look nice. I can do the glasses next month. Who's to tell me the glasses come first? Well, maybe Mrs. Sutton, but—She put Mrs. Sutton out of her mind. I want the blue, I need it. There's nothing like a touch of color after black all day. . . . That Miss Brady said dinner was from six to eight. I'll eat right away and get down to Fourteenth Street. Saturday night, they'll be open late. I'll wear it to the dining room tomorrow. There's nothing like a good first impression, and you never know when you may meet somebody. Some of the girls may have relatives in New York and Sunday's when they'd come to call. And have dinner, maybe. Sunday dinners are always special. . . . She saw herself entering the dining room, alone and poised, sitting at one of the small tables, saying something pleasant to the maid who served her. Wearing the blue.

The house was straight ahead. She went up the steps.

Miss Small raised her head when the door opened. This was a stranger with a suitcase, therefore the new girl. She consulted the card quickly, verifying the name. Miller, Ruth. It was important to get a name right, to make a girl feel as if she were expected and wanted. She stood up.

"Well, Ruth," she said, holding out a hand.

Ruth advanced, blinking in the light of a powerful lamp that a previous social worker had installed for a purpose. It was trained to shine directly in the shifting eyes of board-payers who had spent their money for new clothes and claimed their pockets had been picked again, and in the calm, wide eyes of supplicants for week-end passes to visit what they called married sisters.

Ruth narrowed her eyes and saw a young woman with fair hair and a bright smile. She was disappointed. It wasn't Miss Brady. Miss Brady was dark and thin and her voice was loud and comical. Who was this? Then she remembered. This must be Angel, Miss Angeline Small, the social worker who was Miss Brady's assistant. Moke and Poke had described her. Miss Small does a lot of good, they'd said; she keeps you from making a mistake that'll ruin your whole life for a minute's pleasure.

She smiled at Miss Small when she took her hand. All around her were girls, coming and going, laughing and talking.

Miss Small adjusted the light. "There," she said, "that's better, isn't it?"

It was better, much better. She had almost been blinded by the glare, and now she looked eagerly about her. She could see the other girls clearly.

She saw the dark blue curtains at the dining-room door, the elevator and its uniformed attendant, the telephone switchboard and its operator, the girl with red hair who slouched against the office railing and whistled under her breath. There was a single yellow rose on the desk and an open money box filled with bills and silver. Miss Small had light blue eyes and a rosebud mouth.

"Kitty Brice and Lillian Harris," Miss Small's voice was saying, "this is the new girl, Ruth Miller. She'll be in 706 with April Hooper. Lillian, I'm afraid you'll be late for work, dear. Are you waiting for something?"

The red-haired girl drawled, "Not any more." She removed her felt hat, cuffed it into new angles, and sauntered to the door.

"Seven-o-six," she said over her shoulder, "I'm in 606. Drop down sometime."

Miss Small went on. "Lillian is rather abrupt, but you mustn't mind. And now, my dear, let's talk about you. Do you want your dinner at once or would you rather go to your room first?" It was a stock question and the answer was always the same. Room first. To primp. A faraway look came into Miss Small's eyes. She had made that answer herself three years ago, when she stood where Ruth was standing now, and Monny had smiled across the desk.

A chattering procession passed on its way to the dining room. One girl stopped at the desk and asked for a tray check.

"Who's it for, dear?" Miss Small wanted to know. "Not Minnie May again?"

"Yes, Miss Small. Miss Small, I'd ask you to find me another roommate, I really would, except that I'd have Minnie May on my conscience. I think she needs my influence, I really do, and because of that I'm willing to put up with a lot. But it's hard on me."

"I'll have a little talk with Minnie May later. Didn't I see her just a minute ago?"

"Yes, Miss Small. She came down with me, but she went right up again. She says the whole place smells of last night's fish. She's—well, she's in a state, and it isn't last night's fish, either."

When the girl went away, Miss Small suddenly realized that Ruth Miller hadn't answered her question. She examined her sharply and closely for the first time and was disturbed by what she saw. Why, she's frightened, she told herself. Or is that shyness? No, it's fright. She looks as if she were cornered, or caught, or something dreadful like that. She looks terrified. For a brief moment Miss Small felt the contagion of panic, but she quickly recovered. She rapidly scanned the lobby, but there was nothing unusual that she could see.

The invisible diners chattered behind the blue curtains, as harmless as a cageful of sparrows. Mrs. Fister, the housekeeper, stood by the dining-room door calmly collecting the tray and guest checks. Jewel lounged beside the elevator, waiting for the after-dinner rush. At the switchboard, Kitty's bony hands darted from plug to plug, and her monotonous voice droned on without a break.

Miss Small's eyes met Ruth Miller's for an instant and the girl looked away. She made a quick decision.

"I know what we'll do," she said briskly. "Here's your key, your room is at the rear. Now you run along and look things over, and when you're ready, come down to room 506. That's mine. I have a nice little suite all to myself. We'll have our dinners sent up there, and I'll tell you all about our little rules and so on. Fun? And you'll want to know about your roommate, too. She's just gone in to dinner, but she'll be around later."

"I have to go out," Ruth said. They were the first words she had spoken and they were thick and strangled.

Miss Small nodded agreeably, but she left the office enclosure and followed the shabby figure to the front door. "Some other time then," she said. "But do take your key; slip it in your purse, dear. There, now you're really one of us!" She pretended not to see the shaking, fumbling hands and went on brightly. "And let me have your suitcase. I'll send it up to the room, and you'll find it ready and waiting when you come back."

She carried the suitcase to the desk and shook her head reprovingly when Kitty Brice laughed.

"Didn't want to give it up, did she?" Kitty said. "Hung on like a drowning man. Would you say she peddled diamonds or dope?"

Miss Small smiled wryly. "Another odd one, I'm afraid." She sighed, and returned to her work.

The November night grew older slowly. Outside the cold increased and the street gradually emptied. The front windows of the tenements and rooming houses were thriftily dark; only the lights of Hope House burned through the murky fog.

At ten o'clock the lobby was deserted except for Kitty, nodding at the quiet board, and Miss Ethel Plummer, an elderly spinster who took over the desk at night because it meant free room and meals and didn't interfere with her regular job. Her regular job was piecework which she did at home, fine embroidery executed with sequins, tiny beads, and metallic thread. She sat behind the desk, a shaded light trained on the strip of sea-green gauze that lay across her sheet-covered lap, her steel-rimmed spectacles reinforced with rubber bands to keep them from slipping. Round wooden hoops protected and framed the pearl-and-silver rose that grew under her stubby fingers.

There was one other light, over by the door. The elevator was closed and silent, and the indicator showed it stationary at the seventh floor.

Been up there for the past fifteen minutes, Miss Plummer said to herself. And Jewel doesn't live on seventh, she's calling on somebody. She ought to leave the car down here when she does that, so people can take themselves up without waiting. Having coffee and doughnuts with April, I guess. I couldn't enjoy that myself, sitting there and watching the child fill cups and spoon out sugar. I'll never complain about my life again, I'm really blessed. . . . Thinking about cups made Miss Plummer thirsty.

"Any of that tea left, Kitty?"

"Sure." Kitty crept over with a thermos jug. "You finish it, I've had enough. . . . That's pretty, Miss Plummer. What's it going to be?"

"Front panel of a bride's mother's dress. Big house on Fifth Avenue three weeks from today, if I don't go blind first. Anything happen before I came on?"

Kitty shrugged. "We got a new girl and our social standing remains the same. Kind of cuckoo, but she won't bother me any. This place is getting terrible. Old maids, fresh kids, and people with something the matter with them. If a good-looking girl walked in here, I'd drop dead. So would she, in five minutes."

Miss Plummer snipped a thread. "Now Kitty, you could be pretty yourself if you'd only take a little interest."

"Zilch. I know what I look like." Kitty came closer and lowered her voice. "What's the big idea, Monny taking your sister out to tea? What's Monny got up her well-cut sleeve? Come on; you know. Give."

"I must say you're not very respectful. And it's none of your business, although I don't mind telling you. It's the meals. Miss Brady thinks they could be better."

"If they were better, they'd raise the prices. Let Brady eat out, she can afford it." Kitty hunched her shoulders and peered at the clock. "Nearly ten-thirty, hour and a half to go."

"You've had a long day, dear, and I know you're tired." When she thought of it, Miss Plummer tried to talk like Miss Small. "Poor dear," she added.

"I'm cracking up," Kitty said hopefully. "I'm caving in."

"Then run along, dear, and get a good night's rest. I'll take over the board."

Kitty's gratitude expressed itself in halfhearted objections. "You'll forget to switch it over to Angel's room when you lock up."

Miss Plummer used Miss Small's firm smile. "I wont forget."

"And the new girl went out. She's not in yet. I don't think she knows about self-service when Jewel goes off. Maybe she'll try to walk up. She looks like that kind."

"I'll tell her, dear; I'll take her up myself if she's timid."

Kitty sighed. Thanks. I'll pull bastings for you tomorrow." She crept through the swinging gate and over to the stairs beside the elevator. The elevator's absence made no difference. She lived on the second floor with the maids and minor staff members, and they were asked to walk.

Her room was cold because she had left a window open. She closed it with a slam and sat beside the radiator. There were coffee parties in other rooms, and probably more than coffee in Minnie May's, but she didn't feel like prowling up and down halls and sniffing at closed doors. Tonight she had a pain around her heart and she hated her life. She thought of the years behind her and those ahead. Once she got up and started for the door. She'd go up to April's, she'd say she'd come to get warm. But she didn't go. She stayed where she was, hugging the radiator until even it grew cold.

Miss Small's suite, like Miss Brady's, was not furnished with the regulation maple, but she had done very well with the money she could afford to spend. Miss Brady had antiques from her own New England home, old Persians and heirloom silver, and Miss Small had walked warily in her steps with walnut, hooked rugs, and pewter. The Wallace Nuttings that she bought when she first came had been supplanted by Currier & Ives. Because Miss Brady had laughed at the Nuttings.

Miss Brady wasn't laughing now. She was stretched full length on the low couch, her untidy black head resting on pillows, and Miss Small sat at her feet. Within easy reach was a small table holding a spirit lamp and china. It was the hour for hot chocolate, small cakes, and confidences.

"Light me a cigarette, Angel," Miss Brady said. "Miss me?"

Miss Small complied. "Monny! You know!"

Miss Brady looked pleased. "You've got rings under your eyes. You do too much, you let these kids run you ragged. Look at me. I've been doing this stuff for years, and not a nerve in my body. . . . For God's sake, are you putting marshmallow in your chocolate? Disgusting."

"Sorry." Miss Small spooned the single marshmallow out of her cup and all marshmallows out of her life. "You were so late, Monny. I was afraid you were having more trouble with Fister."

"No. Fister is eating out of my hand. We had rum in the tea and that reminded her of her late husband. So I won on all points. Tapioca, coffee jelly and grape-nuts ice cream are out. Fruit and cheese in. I said I'd pay the difference out of my own pocket."

"Lucky Monny to have her own pocket."

"Stop that. Lucky Monny, period." Miss Brady reached for her chocolate and took a deep swallow. She stretched out again, her long, ugly face relaxed, her eyes smiling. "This is the best part of the day. . . . Marshall-Gill is the one who made me late. Talk, talk, talk, all about nothing. She swore she'd sent the stuff over for the party costumes. Did she?"

"She did. All cut out and sewed, only the masks to do."

"Coo!" Miss Brady said. "She'll be on hand for tea tomorrow, as usual, and sees no reason why we shouldn't do the masks then, Sunday or not. What do you say?"

"Whatever you say, Monny."

Miss Brady's eyes clouded. "What's wrong, Angel? You're miles away, you've got something on your mind. Don't you know you can't hide things from me?"

Miss Small hesitated. Then, "I'm worried," she said simply.

Miss Brady sat up and scowled. "Has some little tramp——"

"No, no, Monny. Everything's all right. I mean, don't look like that! Nothing's happened at all. Only one sick tray, Minnie May, hangover, and only two week-end passes and I know they're legitimate."

"Then what——"

"The new girl, Monny. She came."

Miss Brady was openly puzzled. "Well? What's wrong about that? Isn't she all right? She looked all right to me."

"I don't know, but I have the most awful feeling. As if she were going to—bring us trouble. I'm afraid she's one of the quiet ones that—blow up. You remember that dementia praecox they had at the Primrose Club?"

Miss Brady shuddered. "Out the window, hanging to the ledge by her fingers. That woman down there, Motley, told me it was months before she stopped seeing that girl in her dreams. She had to go to a rest home to get over it. . . . What are you trying to do, scare me to death?"

Miss Small explained. She described the sudden transformation at the desk, the fear that took over eyes and hands, the averted face. "She was natural enough when she came in, exactly as you said on the card. Shy, quite ordinary in a nice, quiet way. Then all at once something happened. She changed, right before my eyes, and it frightened me. Somehow I got the idea that she saw something, or heard something, but I can't imagine what."

"Who was near the desk?"

"I thought of that, too. Just the usual crowd going to the dining room, stopping for mail, nobody that stood out. Wait a minute. Dot came for a tray check for Minnie May."

"Dotty, the girl evangelist! Who else?"

"Jewel at the elevator, Kitty at the board. Kitty noticed it, too; I imagine they all did. It seems ridiculous when I tell it like this. Kitty, Jewel, all of them as drab as Ruth Miller herself. . . . Oh!"

"Got something?"

"Lillian Harris was hanging around. She said something flippant, I forget what it was. Then she went off to her job. The Miller girl went out, too, a few minutes later. . . . She didn't have dinner."

Miss Brady looked thoughtful. "Harris," she said.

Miss Small said quietly, "Lillian doesn't like me."

"I don't know what you mean by that, and I don't see how it fits in here," Miss Brady answered. "Lillian Harris was well recommended, but if she hurts you in any way, out she goes."

Miss Small raised puzzled eyes. "What do you mean when you say she was well recommended? She came here after that rule about references was thrown out."

Miss Brady grinned when Miss Small recalled the rule. They had drafted it themselves and fought for its adoption. They'd argued that a girl's past was her own private business and insisted on her right to live it down if she wanted to. The Board had fought back, prophesied scandal, and lost. From that time on, no one was asked for a reference. The rule was three years old and so successful that Miss Brady sometimes forgot its origin.

"I mean I knew about Harris," Miss Brady explained. "She used to have a friend here, used to visit the friend before she moved in herself." She ran a hand through her hair. "Suddenly I am very, very sick and tired of this job," she said. "There's nothing to it any more, I don't know why I stay. If I had half the sense I was presumably born with, I'd chuck the whole works and take you with me."

"Monny, darling! You're thinking about Europe again!"

"I am, and why not? Don't look at me like that; you know it's been on my mind for weeks. Listen. I get my grandmother's money next month, so why don't we resign? Reasons of health, and that's no lie, you look a wreck; and we'll grab the first boat and stay for a year. Two years, five years, forever. . . . Angel, you look about ten when you smile like that. How old are you anyway? I've never known."

"Thirty-three."

"I'm forty-five and don't tell me I don't look it. . . . Paris, Angel, and Bavaria if they'll let us in, and I'll buy you a little blue hunting jacket and cut your hair in a bang. Look at that clock, after twelve and I meant to go to bed early. Oh well, if you're cheered up it's worth it. Feel better now?"

"Much!"

"That panic about Miller was probably your nerves. You're exhausted and I don't wonder. All these messy brats pouring out their beastly little troubles. Did you tell Miller about April Hooper?"

"Monny! I forgot!"

Miss Brady flushed. "That's too bad," she said. "You knew I hadn't time to do it myself, you knew I was counting on you. It was a very little thing to ask and I should think you'd want to remember—"

"Monny, I'm heartbroken! But honestly, she went away so quickly, she almost ran, and I didn't see her again. Monny, I can't follow a girl

around, I have other things to do, you know that! I'll go up there now,
I'll go at once—"

"Too late." Miss Brady's voice was cool. "I counted on you and you
failed me."

Miss Small said nothing. She winked back sudden tears and turned
away. They sat without speaking.

After a while Miss Brady spoke gruffly. "I'm tired too. Have I time
for another cigarette?"

"Of course." Miss Small offered the box as if Miss Brady were a
stranger.

"I didn't mean anything," Miss Brady said. "Forget it. I'll talk to the
girl myself tomorrow."

"No, I will! I want to!" Miss Small seized the matches and struck
one. They both laughed.

"We mustn't do that again," Miss Brady said.

"No, Monny."

"We nearly quarreled."

"I know. It was my fault."

"No dear, mine."

As things turned out, no one told Ruth Miller anything. She
returned at eleven-thirty with the once-coveted blue in a paper box.
She had forced herself to buy it. It was all she had left of the new life
she had planned.

A few hours before, when she had confidently walked into the
future, she had come face to face with the past. Run, she had said to
herself, run; you still have a chance. But she had been running for years,
from city to city, from job to job, putting time and distance between
herself and a screaming promise, and her route had been a circle. Above
the chatter in the lobby she had heard one voice. In a sea of strange
faces one face was not strange. It's a scheme, she'd said, it's a destiny.
I'm lost.

But she had run again, out into the night, pleading with herself to be
calm. She'd thought of Mrs. Sutton, maybe Mrs. Sutton would take her
in and ask no questions. Maybe she'd listen and advise. But then she'd
remembered that Mrs. Sutton was leaving town. And she'd told herself
that Mrs. Sutton was too young, it wouldn't be fair to frighten her.

She'd begun to cry, standing on a corner and turning slowly and
steadily as if she were surrounded. The fog was thick and the passers-by

were dim and shapeless. She could follow me and I wouldn't know it, she wept; I wouldn't see her. My eyes—

That was when she'd remembered the eye doctor. The only man she knew except Mr. Benz. And his office wasn't far away, an office and apartment combined. She'd talk to him and he'd tell her what to do. He'd been, well—friendly. He'd been, well—interested.

She'd climbed the stairs to his office, but no one had answered her ring. She'd slipped a note under the door, asking him to call her at Hope House. "Leave a message if I'm not there," she'd written, "and tell me where I can reach you. I need some advice. It's important to me." She couldn't tell him how important. She couldn't write a word like death. It would look hysterical.

She'd left the doctor's building and walked to Fourteenth Street, telling herself to buy the blue because he would see her in it. But the scheme took care of that.

Ten minutes after she left the building a cleaning woman swept the note into the hall, down the single flight of stairs, and out into the gutter. Later on the rain washed the words away.

Outside the shopwindow she had looked at the blue and talked to herself again. Talked and argued and planned. Talked about the economy of spending money, argued about the possibility of mistaken identity, planned what she'd say to the doctor when he called. Maybe I made a mistake, she'd said. Lots of people look alike, you're always hearing of cases. There was even a man who looked like the President. And she didn't act queer when she saw me, she acted like she'd never seen me before. So I could be wrong. . . . But she saw her own shaking hands and knew in her heart that there was no mistake.

But I'll go back there tonight, she'd said. I've got to. There's my suitcase and the telephone call. Nothing can happen if I go straight to my room tonight and lock the door. A big houseful of people, I'll be safe for one night. That's all I'll need, one night. He'll call tonight or tomorrow and he'll tell me what to do. Maybe I'll laugh about this in a day or so. I bet I laugh, I bet I do. . . . She'd tried to laugh then but it had sounded wrong.

If I stay in my room, she'd said, I'll be safe. They can put the message under the door. No matter what, I'll keep out of sight until he calls. They have trays, I'll ask my roommate to bring me a tray. I'll tell her I have a headache. If I keep out of sight and don't let her see me again—

Buy the blue, she'd said, buy the blue and then you'll always have it.

Miss Plummer looked up from her embroidery when Ruth came in. "I've been waiting for you," she said kindly.

"Has a telephone call come for me?"

"No dear. You had me worried, staying out so late all by yourself. We lock up at midnight, except in the case of a special pass, and I wondered if you understood. Been buying something pretty?"

"I bought a suit."

"That's nice. My name's Plummer, Ethel Plummer. My sister's the housekeeper here and if you're hungry I think I can get you a little something."

"No thank you, Miss Plummer. I'd rather go to bed."

"You're a sensible girl, I can see that. I've no patience with late hours, although goodness knows I keep them! Your suitcase is in your room, dear, and you can run yourself up in the elevator, that is if you're not timid about machinery."

"I guess I am a little. I don't think I've ever tried to run an elevator."

"Well, never you mind, I used to be afraid myself, but you'll get over it the same as I did. I'll take you up this time and you'll see how easy it is."

On the seventh floor Miss Plummer pointed down a bare, dim hall lined on one side with closed doors. "You see that big door straight ahead? That's the fire door. You go right on through to the other side. There's a short hall back there, with the bath, the telephone, and your own room. It's the only room at that end and it's nice and quiet, almost like a little house set off to itself."

"Miss Plummer?" Her voice broke and she tried again. "Miss Plummer, do outside calls come in on that phone?"

"Oh yes. When that happens we ring a bell in your room." Miss Plummer smiled a good night, and the elevator closed.

Her room was dark. She could hear nothing but she knew someone was there. The unknown roommate, already in bed and asleep. It had to be the roommate, it couldn't be anyone else. She waited in the cool darkness, listening.

A voice spoke, a thin, sweet voice like a child's. "Turn on the light," it said. "There beside the door. It won't bother me."

She found the switch and turned it. In one of the two beds a small girl sat up in a welter of blankets, rubbing her short, fair curls and yawning. Her cheeks were flushed, and she looked like an animated doll.

"Hello," she said. "I had to go back to work after dinner, did you?"

"No, I went shopping." Ruth hesitated. "I'm sorry, but they didn't tell me your name. I'm Ruth Miller."

The small girl laughed. "I knew that. There's not much I miss! I'm April Hooper. That sounds silly, the April part, but my mother was English and she always said there was nothing prettier than an English April. So she called me that. You see, she was always homesick. Are your father and mother dead?"

"Yes." Her suitcase was lying on the other bed and she went over to it.

"Are your grandparents dead, too?"

"Yes." This was an odd conversation. She stared at the little creature smiling and nodding among the blankets.

"So are mine," April ran on. "All of my people are dead. I was born in this block, right on this very spot. They tore down three tenements to make this house, and then my grandmother died and I moved in here. I work around the corner, in the drugstore. Where do you work?"

She prattles like a little kid, Ruth thought. She can't be more than sixteen if she's that. She untied the string on the suit box. "I work at Blackman's."

"Like Moke and Poke. They were born in this neighborhood like me. You'll die laughing, but they have the same name and they're not even related. Mary Smith. But I guess you knew that. That's why they call themselves Moke and Poke. That's cute, isn't it? Have you known them very long? You do know them, don't you?"

"They sent me here." She held up the suit and shook out the folds. She was tired, and April's chatter was too shrill. But she knew she had to be polite. She needed April. April would bring her the trays. "Look, April," she said. She held up the suit.

But April had no eyes for clothing. She rattled on. "Moke and Poke are nice. Some people think they're fresh, but I don't. When the weather's bad and there's ice on the pavement, they call for me. Even when they have dates, they call for me. They take the time. That's nice, isn't it?"

"It surely is." She hung the suit in the closet and closed the door. Chatterbox, she thought wearily. She could have made some comment, she could have said something. I'd have said something in her place.

"I think they're pretty, too," April said. "Their hair is so soft, and they take good care of their skin. It's like velvet. I like to touch their faces and they don't mind. It isn't often that you find a nice person who's pretty too. . . . What do you look like, Ruth?"

Ruth looked aghast at the small figure huddled in the middle of the bed. Why, the child's feeble-minded, she told herself with horror. Why didn't they tell me about her. Feeble-minded. And even Moke and Poke didn't say anything. I can't bear it, I can't, it's too much. She backed away from the clear gaze that was as innocent and candid as the voice.

A cloud came over April's face. "Oh," she said. "I'm sorry, Ruth. That's a shame, that's what it is. Nobody told you about me and I've scared you. But you're not to feel bad about me because I don't mind at all. I'm blind."

Ruth went slowly to the tumbled bed. Her hands automatically smoothed the covers and rearranged the pillow. April's hand found one of hers and held it fast.

"You're not to feel bad, do you hear?" she insisted. "When you're born that way, it doesn't make any difference. But there's one thing you've got to remember, please. You've got to make me turn the lights on. I've got the habit of not doing it because what's the use, but just the same I ought to. That's why I asked for a roommate, to make me remember. It scares the other girls to find me in the dark, like taking a bath and things. So you make me turn the lights on every time, even when you're going out on a date and I'm staying here. . . . I think the room looks nicer that way, too."

"They're on now. . . . Wait." Ruth went to the lamps on the two small desks. "Now everything's on. And you're right, it does look nicer."

She let April talk. April sold cigarettes and magazines at the drugstore. She knew where each kind was. She could ring up sales and make change without a mistake. She was worried about getting old and having to use rouge. She was afraid she'd put on too much.

When the lights were finally out, Ruth lay awake for a long time. She had promised to breakfast with April, in the dining room. There was no help for it. She had no choice. She went back to the first day she had gone to work at Blackman's, to the first time she had talked to Moke and Poke, to all the little things that had fallen into their allotted places in the scheme that led to Hope House. Whose scheme? She covered her face.

ABOUT THE AUTHOR

AMERICAN mystery writer Hilda Lawrence (1906–1976) published her first book, *Blood upon the Snow*, in 1944. Its commercial success inspired two more novels featuring detective Mark East, *A Time to Die* in 1945 and *Death of a Doll* in 1947. Her other books include *The Pavilion* (1948) and a collection of novellas, *Duet of Death* (1949).